the bone yard

JEFFERSON BASS

Quercus

First published in Great Britain in 2011 by

Quercus
55 Baker Street
7th Floor, South Block
London
W1U 8EW

A CIP catalogue record for this book is available
from the British Library.

ISBN 978 1 84916 061 2

10 9 8 7 6 5 4 3 2 1

Typeset by Ellipsis Books Limited, Glasgow

Printed and bound in Great Britain by Clays Ltd, St Ives plc

Praise for Jefferson Bass

'Scientific authenticity is guaranteed. There's a lot of detail about rotting dead bodies and some tense, hard action. If you like Kathy Reichs you'll like Jefferson Bass. Probably more'

The Times

'Brims with terrific forensic detail . . . the real deal'

Kathy Reichs

'Fantastic forensic detail and an engaging hero . . . an authoritative, compelling new voice to the forensic mystery'

Jeff Abbott

'A unique corpse, solid science, quirky humor, and a lovable protagonist . . . Very human, down-to-earth characters'

USA Today

'Jefferson Bass pulls readers right into an engrossing case that combines suspense, humor, and humanity even as it teaches the lessons of science . . . The Sherlock Holmes for bones has arrived'

Katherine Ramsland, author of *The Forensic Science of C.S.I*

'Southern-fried forensics . . . It does taste good going down'

Kirkus Reviews

'Nearly everything known about the science of human decomposition comes from one place – forensic anthropologist William Bass' Body Farm'

CNN

To the White House Boys, and to others – young and old – who have been abused by the people and institutions charged with their safe keeping. May we learn from the mistakes whose painful price you have paid.

PART I

CHAPTER 1

I held the last of the dead man's bones in my left hand. It was his skull, which I cradled upside down in my palm, as comfortably and naturally as an NBA player might hold a basketball. As I searched for a place to hide it, I felt the tip of my index finger absentmindedly tracing the edges of a hole in the right temple. It was a square-cornered opening, about the size of a small postage stamp, and it had been punched by a murder weapon – a weapon I'd tucked into a tangle of honeysuckle vines a few moments before. The honeysuckle was in bloom, and its fragrance was an odd contrast to the underlying odor of death. *Funny thing*, I thought, *how something that smells so good can grow in a place that smells so bad.*

Chattering voices floated up the hillside, growing louder as the people came closer. If I didn't hurry, I'd be caught with the skull in my hand. Still I hesitated, turning the cranium right side up for one last look into the vacant eye orbits. What did I hope to see there – what meaning did I think I might find – in those empty sockets? Maybe nothing. Maybe only the emptiness itself.

As the voices drew nearer, I finally forced myself to act, to choose. I tucked the skull under the edge of a fallen oak tree, piling dead leaves against the trunk as camouflage. Then a worry popped into my head: *Is the pile of leaves too obvious, a giveaway?* But it was too late to second-guess myself; I'd run out of time, and the makeshift hiding place would have to do.

Stepping over the tree, I strolled downhill toward the cluster of people approaching. I feigned nonchalance, resisting the urge to glance back and check for visible bones. A woman at the front of the group – a thirty-something blonde with the energetic, outdoorsy look of a runner or a cyclist – stopped in her tracks and looked at me. Her eyes bored into mine, and I wondered what she saw there. I tried to make my face as blank and unenlightening as the skull's had been.

She shifted her gaze to the wooded slope behind me. Her eyes scanned the forest floor, then settled on the fallen tree. Walking slowly toward it, she leaned down, studied both sides, and then brushed at the leaves I'd piled on the uphill side. 'There's a skull beside this log,' she announced to the group. She said it as coolly as if it were an everyday occurrence, finding a skull in the woods.

'Wow,' said a young red-haired woman in a black jumpsuit. 'Police, one; Brockton, zero. If Dr B decides to turn killer, he'd better steer clear of Florida.'

The redheaded smart aleck was Miranda Lovelady, my graduate assistant. The blonde who'd found the skull so swiftly was Angie St. Claire, a forensic analyst from the

4

Florida state crime lab. Angie, along with the twenty-three other people in the group Miranda had brought up the trail, had spent the past ten weeks as a student at the National Forensic Academy, a joint venture of the University of Tennessee and the Knoxville Police Department. Taught by experts in ballistics, fingerprinting, trace evidence, DNA, anthropology, and other forensic specialties, the NFA training culminated in the two death scenes Miranda and I had staged here at the University of Tennessee's Anthropological Research Facility: the Body Farm.

The Body Farm was perched on a hillside high above the Tennessee River. Here, a mile downstream from the heart of Knoxville, more than a hundred corpses in various states of disrepair were dispersed across the facility's three fenced-in acres. Most of the bodies lay above ground, though some were buried. And in a far corner of the facility, looking like eerie sentinels standing at attention, were three nude men: not standing, actually, but hanging, suspended by the neck from wooden scaffolds. With some misgivings, we had carried out three postmortem lynchings so we could observe the difference in the decomposition rate when bodies decayed off the ground, where they were less accessible to insects. We'd hung the three in the most isolated part of the facility, because important though the experiment was – the research data would help us determine time since death when a hanged body wasn't discovered for weeks

5

or even months – the dangling corpses were a shocking sight. I'd seen them dozens of times by now, yet I still found it unnerving to round the bend in the trail and suddenly encounter the trio. Their necks were stretched a few inches, their faces downcast, their arms and legs angled outward, as if accepting their grim fate with a mixture of resignation and shame. The NFA class included four African-American men, and if I, a privileged white man, felt disturbed by the hanging bodies, I could scarcely imagine the complicated response the black men might feel at the sight of dangling corpses in the woods of Dixie.

Maybe I needn't have worried. Everyone in the class was a seasoned forensic professional, after all; cumulatively, the two dozen students had worked hundreds of death scenes, and some of those had probably included suicide by hanging. The students had competed fiercely to get into the NFA course, and several had told me how thrilled they were to train at the Body Farm – probably the only place on earth, after all, where cinching a noose around a neck was an act of scientific inquiry rather than of suicidal despair or racist hatred or – very rarely – state-administered execution. Here at the Body Farm, as nowhere else on earth, we could replicate death scenes with utter authenticity, even lynchings or mass murders. This particular NFA class – one of two groups that would rotate through the course this year – included crime-scene and crime-lab specialists from as far away as the

6

United Kingdom. They'd spend the morning recovering scattered skeletal remains and other evidence Miranda and I had planted in this part of the woods. After a quick picnic lunch on a strip of grass outside the fence, they'd spend the afternoon locating and excavating a shallow, unmarked grave where Miranda and I had buried three fresh corpses, simulating a gang-style execution by drug traffickers.

She and I had spent the prior afternoon digging the grave and then refilling it once we'd laid the bodies in it. We'd clawed into the clearing's rocky, red-clay dirt with a Bobcat – a pint-sized bulldozer – that a local building contractor had recently donated to the Anthropology Department. The Bobcat was a useful tool; it was also – for me, a guy who'd grown up driving dump trucks at my stepdad's quarry – a fun toy.

Excavating the buried bodies in the afternoon heat was going to be sweaty, smelly work for the NFA class. Already, by midmorning, the temperature was above eighty degrees, and the humidity had topped 90 percent; by late afternoon, East Tennessee would feel like the tropics. Divide the year's 365 days by the number of seasons, and you might think there'd be four seasons of 91.25 days apiece, each season serenely easing its way into the next. Not this year in Knoxville; not on this steamy, smelly day in mid-May.

My own body was doubtless contributing a bit to the scent wafting across the hillside, and not as pleasantly as the honeysuckle was. Like Miranda, I wore an official-looking black jumpsuit, the shoulders trimmed with the skull-adorned patches of the Forensic Anthropology Center. The jumpsuits looked cool, as in stylish, but they were woven of Nomex, a flameproof fiber that, ironically, made them hotter than hell. Despite the heat, Miranda and I had suited up to give the training exercise a more authentic look – and to let the trainees know we took them seriously.

The forensic techs weren't exactly dressed for cool comfort, either. Over their clothes they'd donned white biohazard coveralls made of Tyvek, the slippery, indestructible stuff of FedEx envelopes. Tyvek was featherlight, but I knew from experience that it didn't breathe worth a damn. As the techs knelt, stooped, squatted, and crawled their way up the hillside, setting numbered evidence markers beside the bones and artifacts they found, I could hear, or at least imagined I could hear, the steady patter of droplets on dry leaves: droplets not of rain, but of sweat. If this were an actual crime scene, they'd need to be concerned about contaminating the bones with their own sweaty DNA. I made a mental note to mention that to them once they'd rounded up all the bones. Did the glamorous stars of *CSI* and *Bones* ever shed buckets of perspiration, ever rain monsoons of sweat?

After an hour of searching, the hillside bristled with numbered evidence markers – eighty-seven of them –

flagging the sundry bones, beer bottles, cigarette butts, and gum wrappers Miranda and I had strewn in the woods. The markers resembled the four-inch sandwich-sign numbers restaurants sometimes put on customers' tables to tell the servers which order goes to what table, and I smiled as I imagined a macabre spin on that image: 'Number eighty-seven? Half rack of ribs, easy on the bugs? Enjoy!'

I'd laid all the vertebrae of the spinal column close together, in anatomical order, as they might be found at an actual death scene, so those required only a single marker. Other bones, though, were dispersed more widely, simulating the way dogs or coyotes or raccoons would tend to scatter them over time. My last-minute hiding spot for the skull had actually been a logical place for it. Skulls on a slope tend to tumble or wash downhill once the mandible comes loose; that's exactly what had happened to the skull of former congressional aide Chandra Levy, who'd been murdered in the woods of a Washington, D.C., park in 2001. In the case of my 'victim,' the fallen tree where I'd tucked his skull was lower, I now noticed, than the area where I'd scattered most of the bones. After years of death-scene searches of my own, I'd intuitively picked a natural place for the skull to end up.

The one thing the students hadn't yet found was the murder weapon. I took a sort of perverse pride in that, as I'd been careful to tuck it deep into the honeysuckle.

But lunchtime was coming up fast, and they'd need the whole afternoon to excavate the mass grave. Finally, just as I was about to start offering helpful hints – 'you're cold'; 'getting warmer'; 'really, really hot' – I noticed Angie in scan mode again, her gaze ranging just beyond the ragged circle of evidence markers. Her eyes swept past the honeysuckle thicket, then returned, and she headed toward it, like a dog on a scent. *Getting warmer,* I thought, but I kept quiet as she knelt at the edge of the vines and began parting the leaves carefully. 'Got something here,' she said, and then she laughed. 'Looks like somebody takes his golf game *really* seriously.' With that, she extricated the murder weapon. It was a broken golf club – a putter – and the cross section of the club's head matched the hole in the skull perfectly: a square peg in a square hole.

The flurry of interest in Angie's find was accompanied by a series of groan-inducing golf-club murder jokes – 'fore . . . head!'; 'keep your eye on the skull'; 'I *told* you not to cheat'; and the worst of all, 'say, old chap, mind if I slay through?' The chatter was interrupted by a series of urgent beeps from Angie's direction. 'Oh, crap,' she said, laying the putter on the ground. She peeled off a glove and fished a cell phone from inside her coveralls. Frowning at what she read on the display, she stepped away from the group and answered the call. At first her words were too low to make out, but the tension in her voice was unmistakable, and it was rising. As the tension ratcheted up, the volume did, too. 'Wait. Say that again. Kate *what*? . . . What are you *talking* about? . . . When? . . . How? . . . A *shotgun*? . . . Bullshit. That's not possible. That is just not possible.' Her eyes darted back and forth, tracking something I suspected was hundreds of miles away, at the other end of the call, and she began to pace the hillside. 'Please tell me you're making this up, Ned. Please tell me this is some really, really mean joke you're playing on me. . . . Please tell me you're not telling me this.'

By now everyone in the group was listening, though most were careful not to look directly at Angie. Some people exchanged worried glances; others studied the ground intently, as if the particular twig or bone in front of them held the key to all meaning in the universe. 'Oh, shit. Oh *shit*. Jesus God . . . Have you looked at flights? . . . No, I'll just drive. It'll be just as fast. . . . Okay, I'm leaving now.' She took a few steps down the hillside, returning to where she'd found and flagged the skull. She bent and picked it up, staring into the eye orbits, exactly as I had just before hiding it. 'I have to go by the hotel to grab my stuff . . . I'll be there by midnight. I'll call you from the road.' She was walking toward us now, head down, still talking. 'God *damn* that son of a bitch . . . Look, I have to go.' She snapped the phone shut, shaking her head, a look of bleak dismay on her face as she walked toward Miranda and me. She didn't slow down when she reached us; she simply handed me the skull and kept walking. As she passed, she rubbed her ungloved hand across her dripping face, and I realized she was wiping away tears, not sweat. 'I have to go,' she said again, not looking back. Her voice sounded hollow and haunted. 'I have to go.'

She broke into a jog, ran out the gate of the Body Farm, and was gone.

CHAPTER 2

I'd spent all morning avoiding the task at hand – grading the last student's final exam from Human Origins, the undergraduate course I'd taught this spring – when the intercom in my office beeped. 'Dr B?'

I felt a rush of guilt. I'd been procrastinating for days, and now I'd been caught. 'I know, I know,' I groveled into the speakerphone. 'The grades were due yesterday. The NFA class ran really long. Apparently, Miranda and I buried the bodies better than we meant to. Took the trainees hours to find 'em.'

Peggy Wilhoit, my secretary, was calling from a football field away, literally. The Anthropology Department's administrative offices, including my own spacious and ceremonial office as head of the department, were nestled under Neyland Stadium's south end-zone stands. But my private sanctuary – the small, dingy room where I retreated when I needed to concentrate on a forensic case or a journal article or a stack of overdue exam papers – was tucked beneath the grimy girders of the north end zone. 'I'm finishing the last exam right now,' I fibbed. 'I'll bring you the scores in five minutes.' Across the hundred yards of curving corridor that separated us, I imagined Peggy's bullshit detector flashing and beeping. 'Okay, that was a lie,' I admitted. 'I haven't started grading the last one, but I'll do it now, I promise. So it'll be more like twenty minutes.'

'I'm not calling to nag you about the grades,' she said. 'Although, now that you mention it . . .'

'Forget I mentioned it,' I said. 'Grades? Who said anything about grades? What can I do for you?'

'Someone's on the phone for you. An Angie St. Claire, from the Florida Department of Law Enforcement. She says she was in the NFA class that ended yesterday.'

I was suddenly alert. 'She says right; she was. Put her on.' The phone beeped once when Peggy put me on hold, then beeped again as the call was transferred to me. 'Angie? Hello, it's Bill Brockton. How are you?' There was silence on the other end. 'Angie? Are you there?'

'Yes, sir, I'm here; sorry. I'm fine.' She didn't *sound* fine. She sounded formal, as law enforcement people often do, but she also sounded distracted. No, not distracted; distraught was what she sounded.

'We worried about you when you had to leave so suddenly,' I said. 'I hope everything's okay.'

'Not really, Dr Brockton. That's why I'm calling. I'm sorry to impose, but I . . . I was wondering . . .' Her breath got deep and ragged, and then I heard the sound of sniffling.

'Angie, what's wrong? How can I help you?'

There was another, longer pause; I heard the rustling,

scratching sound of fabric covering the handset and then the muffled noise of a nose being blown vigorously once, twice, three times. 'Dammit, I wasn't going to cry,' she sighed when she came back on the line. 'Oh well.'

'What can I do for you, Angie?'

'It's my sister, Dr Brockton. She . . . um . . . she's dead.' Silence. I waited. 'That call I got yesterday morning – the call that made me leave – it was from my husband, Ned, telling me.'

'I figured you'd gotten some really bad news. I gather it was unexpected. I'm so sorry.' I hesitated, reluctant to pry. Still, she'd called me. 'Was it an accident?'

'No,' she said with sudden vehemence, and then she laughed – a short, bitter bark of a laugh that startled me. 'It was definitely not an accident. That's the one thing we can all agree on.' I resisted the urge to fire off questions. 'She died from a shotgun blast to the head.' The air in my office suddenly turned electric. 'The local coroner says it was suicide. I say it was murder.'

I couldn't resist any longer. 'Tell me about it. Why does the coroner think it was suicide?'

'Because her fingerprints were on the gun. And because her jerk of a husband says it was suicide. He, Don – Don Nicely, how's that for an ironic name? – says she'd been depressed for months, which I believe, and that she'd threatened to kill herself twice before, which I *don't* believe.'

'Why don't you believe it? And why do you think it was murder?'

'Lots of reasons. For one thing, I think – I *hope* – she'd have told me if she felt suicidal. For another, women don't shoot themselves. A woman takes pills or cuts her wrists. She doesn't put a shotgun in her mouth and blow her head off. Only men are stupid enough to do that.'

She had a point there. Sixty percent of men who commit suicide use a gun – I knew this because I'd done a lot of reading about suicide – but only 30 percent of women. And a shotgun? Rare for a woman, I was sure, and difficult. Ernest Hemingway had turned a shotgun on himself – he'd fired both barrels of a twelve-gauge, in fact, a feat that required not just long arms but also quite a lot of desperation and determination and coordination – but Hemingway was a six-footer. I tried to recall Angie's height, but without much success. 'Was your sister tall? Did the coroner measure her arms to see if she could've reached the trigger?'

Angie sighed. 'She was only five three. But it was a short-barreled shotgun. Eighteen inches. She *could* have done it, but she didn't. *He* did.'

The conversation was difficult for me. Clearly Angie was devastated by her sister's death, and I wanted to help her, but I doubted I could corroborate her theory. 'Why do you think her husband killed her?'

'Because he's an asshole. Because he's controlling and manipulative and aggressive. Because he fits the profile of an abusive domestic partner. Because they had a fight the night she died.'

'An argument fight, or a physical fight?'

'Borderline,' she answered. 'They were out at a night-club, and he got mad because she was talking to some other guy. He dragged her out of the bar and shoved her into the truck and laid down a bunch of rubber in the parking lot. There are witnesses to that part. Next morning, he claims, he found her body on the sofa.'

'He didn't hear the shotgun go off in the night?'

'He says he dropped her at the house and went back out. "To think," he says. Yeah, right. And supposedly, when he came home a couple hours later, he walked straight through the living room without seeing the bloody mess on the sofa, and went to bed. Thought she'd gone somewhere, he says. Thought maybe she'd come down to see me. Didn't find her in the living room till he got up a few hours later. So he says. Bullshit, I say.'

'His story sounds weak,' I admitted. 'But the finger-prints on the gun – hard to argue with those, unless you've got some evidence to refute them. Some way to show that he put her hands on the gun.'

'I know,' she said. 'It's driving me crazy that I didn't have a chance to work the scene.'

'Is that because it would have been a conflict of interest for you?'

'It's because she lived a half hour north of Tallahassee, in Georgia. The Cheatham County Sheriff's Office worked the scene, if you could call it "working." The investigator didn't exactly go over things with a fine-tooth comb –

I've talked to him, and trust me, he's no Sherlock Holmes. And the coroner swallowed her husband's story hook, line, and sinker. So they released the scene only a few hours after the 911 call. There are photos, but only a few, and they're not great. I'd've taken dozens, but the guy who worked it took seven. Seven pictures of my sister's death.' She sighed again.

'Was there an autopsy?'

'No. Apparently the coroner took one look at her body and ruled it suicide.'

'Any chance you can persuade him to let a good Florida M.E. take a look?'

'Are you kidding? I've got a better shot at winning the Florida lottery . . . and I don't even buy tickets. You think a Georgia coroner would take a chance on a Tallahassee M.E. coming into his county and revealing him to be an incompetent idiot? Not bloody likely. Besides, it's too late. The body's already at the funeral home. She's being buried tomorrow.'

My mind was racing – a condition I found pleasing, fascinating, and slightly – very, very slightly – worrisome. Before Angie had phoned, I'd felt sluggish and depressed. I was behind schedule in grading the Human Origins exams, not because I'd been stupendously busy, but because I knew that once the grades were posted, I'd be finished until fall, and things would get quiet – unbearably quiet – on campus. I'd told myself that I would use the summer lull to begin writing a journal article recounting an experiment I'd conducted, using sonar to find submerged bodies. But the truth was, I was having difficulty generating any enthusiasm for the task; in fact, so far, all I had to show for hours at the computer keyboard was a blank screen. I'd written a hundred or more opening sentences, but I'd deleted each one after rereading it. In my mind's eye, I saw the summer opening up before me, and frankly, the opening looked a lot like a yawn. I'd probably end up spending most of the summer pretending to write, all the while casting guilty glances at the phone – the damnably silent phone.

Now, though, the phone had rung, bringing me a forensic case, and I felt like a new man: energetic, engaged, and alive with a sense of purpose. I was sorry that the case was the death of Angie's sister. But I was glad that there *was* a case.

'Angie, I have an idea,' I said. 'Do you know any good lawyers in Georgia?'

'No, but I know a lot of bad ones in Florida,' she answered. 'Does that help any?'

'Probably not. Let me call somebody who might be better connected. Maybe he could help us get a court order authorizing a forensic examination.'

One phone call and ten minutes later, I bundled up the exam booklets and dashed the hundred yards to Peggy's office, clutching the bundle against my rib cage like a football. As I crossed the goal line of her doorway,

I imagined a hundred thousand people leaping to their feet and cheering wildly.

Peggy glanced briefly and balefully over the lenses of her reading glasses. 'It's about time,' she said, and turned her attention back to her computer screen. The chorus of congratulatory cheers in my head evaporated, replaced by the solo buzz of a weed trimmer outside the Anthropology Department's grimy windows on the world.

But. *But:* two hours after that, the buzz of the weed trimmer gave way to the song of jet engines, spooling up to take me to Tallahassee.

Later, as the plane descended toward the pines of the Florida panhandle, I looked out the window and saw dozens of plumes of smoke. Florida was on fire.

CHAPTER 3

Angie St. Claire was waiting for me at the security checkpoint when I got off the plane at the Tallahassee airport – an airport that made Knoxville's modest terminal look vast and sleek by comparison. I knew Tallahassee was smaller than Knoxville, but I'd assumed that as Florida's capital, Tallahassee would bustle with air traffic. Apparently I'd assumed wrong.

Angie shook my hand as I emerged, squeezing so hard I nearly winced. 'Wow,' she said, 'when you pull a string, you don't mess around. Who'd you call, the governor?'

'Better.' I grinned. 'I'm friends with a lawyer who's in league with the devil. Well, sort of.'

'Sort of in league with the devil? How does that work?' She started toward the terminal's main exit.

'Actually, I meant that I'm sort of friends with him. But come to think of it, maybe he *is* sort of in league with the devil.' I smiled. 'Seems to be a good partnership, too, judging by his millions. The guy's name is Burt DeVriess – the police call him "Grease" – and he's a slick, smart attorney. He's flayed me alive on the witness stand a few times, but lately we've worked together on a couple of things.' I didn't mention that one of the 'things' was a case in which I'd been framed for a murder, and that Burt had saved my hide; that, I figured, was a story for another, distant day, perhaps – or perhaps not. 'I called Grease right after I talked to you. He got in touch with a colleague in Atlanta whose law partner or wife or sister – hell, in Georgia, she could be his partner *and* his wife *and* his sister – anyhow, *some*body who has connections in that neck of Georgia. So there should be a couple of pieces of paperwork waiting for us at the Cheatham County courthouse. One's an injunction to delay your sister's burial by twenty-four hours. The other's a court order authorizing us to examine the body in the mean-time.' The glass door slid open, and we stepped out into sunshine and steam.

As we crossed the parking lot, I caught the smell of smoke in the air. 'From the plane, it looked like half your state's burning.'

'It is.' She made a face. 'Most of the panhandle is owned by timber and paper companies. They've got huge tracts of gangly cultivated pines – slash pines, I think – planted in rows like crops. They burn the underbrush every spring so nothing competes with the trees for water and nutrients. It's destroying the natural ecosystem. The longleaf pine, the slow-growing native species, is headed for extinction, and so are a lot of the plants and animals that used to live in the longleaf pine forests. Don't get me started.' She clicked her remote key, and a blue Chevy Blazer a few rows back beeped at us. I was expecting an

FDLE vehicle, but judging by the QUESTION AUTHORITY bumper sticker, this was Angie's own car. Suddenly she stopped. 'Dr Brockton, I can't tell you how much I appreciate what you're doing for me.'

I smiled. 'You don't have time to tell me – not till we're in the car, anyhow. The courthouse closes in an hour, and we're, what, fifty-nine minutes away?'

'You've obviously never ridden with me.'

Thirty minutes later, we crossed the state line, and ten minutes after that, the Blazer skidded to a stop in front of the Cheatham County courthouse in downtown Mocksville. The papers were waiting for us at the office of the court clerk, who handed them over to Angie only after she'd carefully examined our identification and our faces. 'Shame,' the woman said, reminding me that we were in a small town where everyone knew everyone else's business – and generally had strong opinions about it. 'She was your sister, wasn't she?' Angie nodded. 'It just don't seem right.'

Angie nodded. 'Thank you,' she said, managing a small smile.

The woman drew herself up and stared at Angie across the counter. 'What I mean is, it don't seem right messing with her now. Seems like she ought to have a quiet, decent burial, so she can rest in peace, instead of being poked and prodded at by people like you.'

Angie's head snapped back as if she'd been slapped.

Then her eyes got fierce, and I thought for a moment she was going to vault the counter and punch the woman. Instead, she spun and strode out of the courthouse, her heels clacking like gunshots on the black-and-white checkerboard of the marble hallway.

By the time I caught up with her, she was already in the car, slamming the door. I got into the passenger seat just as she clutched the steering wheel and began to weep – deep, racking sobs that made the car tremble like some frightened animal with wheels instead of legs.

'People . . . like . . . *you*,' she gasped. 'How dare she? People like me are the only ones who give a damn about what really happened to Kate.' She took a few heaving breaths, then the crying shifted from angry to mournful. 'People like me didn't do enough to save her.' She leaned her head on the steering wheel. I squeezed her shoulder awkwardly, just once, and then we sat in silence for a few moments before heading to the funeral home.

Morningside Funeral Home occupied a small, tidy brick building on the edge of Mocksville, alongside a memorial garden adorned with brass urns and plastic flowers. The receptionist – *Lily*, said her name tag – seemed flustered by our arrival, but she got a lot more flustered when Angie explained who we were and why we were there. She bloomed a splotchy crimson and looked from Angie's face to mine, and back to Angie's again. Angie finished by saying, 'So could we see the body now, please?'

The flustered woman stood up from her desk. 'You need to speak with Mr Montgomery,' she said. She held up both hands, as if warding off evil, and backed through a doorway into an inner office. The door closed behind her, and I heard voices speaking in hushed, urgent tones.

Eventually the door reopened, and a tall, pale man with a wispy gray comb-over emerged. His upper body didn't move or sway in any way that corresponded to his footsteps; it simply glided forward, as if he were on casters. 'Hello, I'm Samuel Montgomery,' he said. The name seemed to ooze out of his mouth in a way that made my ears feel greasy. He held out a hand for me to shake, so I took it. It was as cool and flaccid as the hand of a dead man after rigor mortis has come and gone. Angie also shook his hand, and I saw the surprise and distaste flit across her face as she did. 'What can I do for you?'

Angie repeated the explanation she'd given to the receptionist, then handed him the twenty-four-hour injunction and the court order authorizing us to examine the body. He studied the documents somberly. Gravely, even. Finally he looked up, handing the pages back to Angie. 'I'm sorry to say that we have, ah, a bit of a problem, Ms. St. Claire.'

Angie took a long, slow breath. 'What sort of problem?'

'I received a phone call earlier today from Mr Nicely – the, ah, husband of the deceased – saying he wished to make a slight change in the arrangements. He asked that we proceed quite, ah, expeditiously.' He looked down, brushed a few flakes of dandruff from the lapel of his pinstripe suit, then looked up again, but not quite all the way up, so his eyes stopped just short of meeting Angie's and my own. 'I've just returned from the cemetery. The, ah, deceased – Mrs Nicely – was buried an hour ago.'

Angie and her husband – Ned, an ornithologist for a Tallahassee environmental education center – dropped me at a hotel in downtown Tallahassee. Our new plan, which I hoped Burt DeVriess's colleague could help with, was to obtain an exhumation order allowing Kate Nicely's body to be dug up and examined. I wasn't terribly optimistic about the chances – it's one thing to delay a burial, but another, bigger deal to dig up a corpse. But between Grease's high-wattage connections and Angie's law enforcement credentials, it might work.

I'd suggested staying at the Hampton Inn, a chain I'd always found clean, comfortable, and affordable. Instead, they booked me at the Hotel Duval, a stylish and recently renovated hotel whose lobby was an Art Deco study in green glass, black granite floors, and – overhead – thousands of luminous soap bubbles. The bubbles, I realized upon closer inspection, weren't actually soap; they were spheres of thin blown glass, suspended from the ceiling on spider-thin threads of clear nylon. The illusion was remarkably convincing.

After I'd rubbernecked sufficiently, I ambled to the front desk, where the clerk greeted me with an obliging smile and began checking me in. 'Do you have a room preference, Mr Brockton?'

'Nonsmoking, please.'

'Of course. And do you have a color preference?'

'Excuse me?'

'A color preference. Our rooms feature six different color themes. We have refreshing blues, uplifting yellows, energizing citrus, exhilarating reds, peaceful neutrals, and serene greens. What are you in the mood for?'

What *was* I in the mood for? A juicy hamburger and a hot shower were the only things I was truly in the mood for. I felt overwhelmed by the pressure to choose. 'I'm so used to boring beige,' I told her. 'So the rooms are all basically the same? Only the wallpaper's different?'

'Oh, it's not just the wallpaper,' she chirped. 'The entire color palette is coordinated – the walls, the art, the bedding, the flowers.'

I asked her to repeat the colors. 'Okay,' I said, 'since I'm in Florida, I'll try energizing citrus.'

'Good choice.' She smiled approvingly, her fingers clattering across the keyboard energetically. Then her smile faded. 'Oh, I'm so sorry; we don't have anything available tonight in citrus.'

I shrugged. 'Okay, how about green? What was it – serene green? If I can't have energy, I'll take serenity.'

Again her fingers clattered; again she looked disappointed. 'Oh, dear, I'm afraid there's nothing in our serene greens, either.'

'So, what is there?'

She did a search. 'I can put you in peaceful neutrals.'

'I'm feeling ambivalent about the neutrals,' I joked. Her brow furrowed; either she didn't get the joke or she thought it was lame. 'Peaceful neutrals will be just fine,' I assured her. She brightened and made me a key card.

Peaceful neutrals, I learned when I opened the door, were variations on a theme of boring beige.

Angie and Ned had offered to take me to dinner, but I'd declined; Angie was upset – she'd lost her sister, she suspected her brother-in-law of murder, and now she and her family had been denied even the chance to bury Kate. The last thing Angie needed to spend her evening doing was making small talk with me. I was getting hungry, though, so I called the front desk to ask about nearby restaurants. The Duval, it turned out, had both a steakhouse restaurant and a rooftop bar. The sun was going down and the temperature was dropping by the time I settled peacefully and neutrally into the room, so I decided to take in the view from on high and hope that the rooftop bar's menu included variations on a theme of burger. The bar was on the eighth floor – not exactly the Empire State Building, but then again, Tallahassee wasn't exactly New York, so maybe eight stories high was high enough.

In Tallahassee, eight stories proved to be plenty. The Duval inhabited a slight rise, and the rooftop terrace offered a pleasant view of downtown Tallahassee, the stately old and ugly new capitol buildings, the campus of Florida State University, and the lush, woodsy neighborhoods to the city's west and north. It couldn't compete with the vistas from Knoxville's highest buildings, which offered sweeping panoramas of the Tennessee River, Neyland Stadium, and the Great Smoky Mountains. But the Duval bar offered other scenery, I soon noticed, as a series of strikingly beautiful waitresses paraded past: lovely, leggy young women, possibly FSU students, though they might well have been models. They wore stretchy black dresses that fitted so snugly, it appeared each dress had been custom-knitted onto a waitress at the beginning of her shift. A textiles engineer and an anatomist must have collaborated on the design; the high hemlines managed to show every available inch of leg, but nothing more, even when the women bent over to deliver drinks or food. I tried not to stare at these remarkable fusions of form and function, but I didn't entirely succeed.

And even though the desk clerk hadn't been able to put me in a citrus room, I felt energized.

It must have been the cheeseburger my waitress had brought me – thick and juicy, topped with crisp, smoky bacon – that restored my flagging energy.

*

The bedside phone rang early the next morning. It was 7:18, according to the clock on the nightstand; normally I'd have been up for a couple of hours by this time, but despite the peaceful neutrals adorning my room, I'd had trouble falling asleep. I'd channel-surfed until midnight, then gotten caught up in a PBS documentary about the 'lost boys of Sudan,' the many thousands of boys whose families were killed and whose lives were destroyed by a genocidal civil war in Darfur. As I watched, I tried to imagine my young grandsons, Walker and Tyler, in similar circumstances. What if my son and his wife were hacked to death by machetes in front of their sons? What if the boys were taken captive and forced to fight – forced, at ages eight and ten, mind you, to murder other children's families – in the service of the very men who'd killed their own parents?

In bleary-eyed hindsight, it hadn't been wise to watch such a disturbing show so late at night. But I wasn't sorry I'd seen it. It was easy, all too easy, to ignore the inhumane treatment inflicted on millions of vulnerable people around the world. The United States and the United Nations had stood by while nearly a million people were massacred in Rwanda, and had dragged their feet while tens of thousands were raped and murdered in the Balkans. After watching the Sudan documentary, I still didn't know what to *do*, but I decided I wanted to do *something* to make a difference, however small, for people who didn't have the rights and freedoms I'd enjoyed all my life. During the night, as I'd tossed and turned, I'd resolved to donate regularly to Human Rights Watch.

Now, still groggy from troubled sleep and violent dreams, I took a while to answer the phone. It was Angie; no surprise there, since she and her husband were the only people who knew where I was staying. 'Good morning,' she said. 'How are you?'

'Uh, great,' I mumbled.

'You don't sound great. You sound comatose.'

'No, I'm fine,' I insisted. 'That's just the serenity talking. Any news?'

'Only that there's no news.' She sighed. 'My lawyer says he might not hear anything till late in the day. Maybe your devilish buddy Grease will get faster results. Meanwhile, I was calling to see if you might want to take a look around the crime lab while we're waiting. Scope out the competition, long as you're here.' She hesitated. 'Oh, and if you'd be game to look at something that's just come in – a skull that a guy's dog dragged in from the woods . . .'

In fifteen minutes I was showered and shaved and dressed, waiting for Angie down in the lobby, beneath the fragile, illusory canopy of glowing glass bubbles.

The Florida Department of Law Enforcement occupied three square buildings, three stories apiece, a couple of miles east of downtown Tallahassee. Actually, although it looked like three buildings, it was technically only one building, composed of three identical squares, joined – just barely – at diagonally opposite corners of the middle square. I'd Googled 'FDLE' while I was waiting in the Duval's lobby for Angie to pick me up, and one of the hits took me to a satellite photo. Zooming in on the complex from low orbit, I'd gotten the feeling I was gazing down on three diagonal tic-tac-toe squares, each of them measuring two hundred feet across. In the middle of each square, the satellite photo showed a large garden courtyard, whose grass and trees looked inviting even from hundreds of miles overhead.

Angie turned off a winding, tree-lined street into a parking lot that fronted the complex. Even though I'd seen the satellite photo, I was unprepared for how big it looked at ground level. FDLE had nearly two thousand employees, and the headquarters complex looked large enough to hold most of them. 'This is quite a place you've got here. I'm envious.'

'Envious? Isn't your ivory tower fancier than this?'

I snorted. 'Obviously you didn't visit the Anthropology Department when you were in Knoxville.' She shook her head. 'We're housed in the bowels of the football stadium, underneath the stands.' She looked at me skeptically, as if she thought I was pulling her leg. 'I'm serious. They bricked in the space under the stands. In the 1940s and '50s, Stadium Hall was the football players' dormitory. When it got too run-down for the jocks, UT built a new athletic dorm and put nonathletes in the stadium. When it got too dilapidated for the regular students, the university gave it to the anthropologists. But hey, I'm not bitter.'

'I'll never complain again.'

She swooped past the main entrance – a glassy lobby in the center building – and bore right, to the southeastern corner of the complex, in the direction of a sign that read EVIDENCE. Unlike the glassy main entrance, the evidence-intake door was inconspicuous, tucked in the corner of the southeastern square. Even with the help of the sign, I'd have had trouble locating this entrance.

Angie signed me in and handed me a visitor badge, then unlocked a steel door that led to a glass-walled hallway, flanked on one side by the garden courtyard and on the other by a series of specialized labs: DNA. Firearms. Toxicology. Chemistry. Latent Prints. Photography. Documents. Computer Forensics. The chemistry lab had large windows along the hallway – 'the aquarium,' Angie called it, and the chemist swimming behind the glass looked mildly annoyed by my presence. Then he saw I was with Angie, and his frown gave way to a smile and a nod.

The crime lab occupied the entire second floor of the square. Halfway around, at the corner where the laboratory square joined the complex's central square – administration and agents' offices, according to Angie – was the facility's main entrance, which opened into an area that was half lobby, half museum. The walls were lined with plaques and displays, including several glass cabinets highlighting the case of serial killer Ted Bundy, who was caught and eventually executed after a 1978 rampage in Tallahassee. In addition to photos of Bundy and the Florida State University sorority where he killed two young women and seriously injured two others, the display cases included plaster casts of Bundy's teeth, which helped convict him of the FSU murders: during his assault on one of the victims, he bit her left buttock, and the distinctive bite mark was used as evidence at his trial. 'Maybe it's just because I know what he did,' I remarked to Angie, 'but even his teeth look sinister. Almost vampirelike.'

'I totally see that,' she agreed. 'I guess it's good he didn't have braces as a kid. Might've been harder to get a conviction.'

The display was a sobering reminder of the high stakes involved in forensic investigations. If Bundy had been caught and convicted after his first murder, dozens of young women – more than thirty by Bundy's own admission, and as many as one hundred according to some estimates – would have escaped terrible fates. 'Okay,' I said, 'let's hope the skull you want me to look at isn't the work of a serial killer.'

'Amen to that,' she agreed grimly. 'Speaking of the skull . . .' She led me along one more stretch of hall, which closed the square and brought us back to where we'd begun, at the southeastern corner of the complex. 'Hang on just a second.' She signed herself into the evidence room and emerged, moments later, holding a jawless skull in gloved hands. 'I told the medical examiner you were going to be here, and he sent this over. I think he was glad to hand it off to a bone guy.' She nodded at a steel door just across from the evidence room. 'You mind getting that for me?' I opened it, and she led me into a simply furnished room that was a combination office and lab; a computer workstation occupied the interior wall, a countertop lined the windowed wall, and a large table filled the center. The room was well lit and was even better cooled; the windows were dewy with condensation from the chill.

'Wow, no danger of getting heatstroke in here.'

'The lab is always cold. Other parts of the place are always too hot. Go figure.' She shrugged. 'The thermostat's in another building, downtown. Miles away.' She checked her watch. 'The case agent assigned to this should have been here by now. Stu – Stuart Vickery. Great agent, but bad with a watch. If he offers to take you to the airport this evening, say no – you'll miss your flight for sure. But we can go ahead and get started, and catch him up when he gets here.' She set the skull on the table, resting it on a beanbag cushion to protect and stabilize it. She pointed to a big box of blue gloves on the counter. 'You want gloves?'

I did want gloves. The skull had been given a cursory

cleaning by time and, presumably, the M.E.'s office, but it remained slightly greasy, and despite the rapid whoosh of the cooling system, the aroma of decomposition was already noticeable.

I took a pair of gloves from the box and tugged them on. 'I wear gloves a lot more often than I used to. Back in my younger days, I didn't glove up if I was handling clean, dry bones. Now I've gotten a lot more careful. A couple months ago I had a case where a woman died from a contaminated bone transplant. She got toxic shock syndrome from a bacterium called *Clostridium sordellii*. It's pretty common in soil, and generally harmless, but it got into her body and started multiplying like crazy. By the time they realized how sick she was, she was a goner.'

'They tried antibiotics?'

'Yeah, something powerful – like, the H-bomb of antibiotics. The antibiotics killed the bacteria, but by then the bacteria had produced lethal levels of toxins. Nasty stuff. A bad way to die.' I shuddered at the memory. 'Hell, it's made me kinda skittish about working in the yard. Get a cut or a scrape, a germ like that gets in, and if the conditions are just right – or just wrong – you're done for.'

'Life's iffy,' she said drily. 'It's a wonder any of us make it out alive.' She was trying to joke – she was trying desperately to hang on to work and routines and normal ways of living life – but it came out sounding bitter. She must have heard the bitterness, because she apologized.

'No need,' I assured her. 'Sorry I got gloomy on you. Let's see what we can figure out about this particular mortal.' I started by leaning over and simply looking. The skull wasn't complete; the mandible was missing, so the upper teeth rested directly on the beanbag, creating the effect of a big, almost comical overbite. After a moment I picked it up from the cushion and turned it upside down, studying the teeth and the roof of the mouth.

'First of all, can you tell if this person's been dead for more than seventy-five years? If so, the skull goes to the state archaeologist.'

'I'd say less. For one thing, it's in pretty good shape – not a lot of erosion or crumbling – which suggests that it's not too old.' I gave a sniff. 'So does the fact that there's still a little tissue on it.' I held it toward her so she could sniff it, and she made a face. 'But that's not all. See that filling? Twentieth century, for sure; hard to be a lot more precise than that, unless we do a radioisotope study to find out if the person died before or after the cold war heated up.'

'What do you mean?'

'People born after the bomb – after all those H-bomb tests spread fallout all over the planet – have higher levels of carbon-14, a radioactive isotope, in their teeth and bones. It's called bomb-spike carbon.'

'*That's* scary.'

I agreed. After a closer look at the top of the cranial vault, I handed the skull back to Angie. 'How about you tell me what you can figure out about this person.'

She flushed. 'Gee, I don't know. I mean, you're the expert.'

'Best way to become an expert is to learn. Best way to learn is by testing your knowledge.' I gave her an encouraging smile. 'Come on; I can't exactly flunk you if you get a thing or two wrong.'

'Okay.' She drew a deep breath. 'It looks small, so I'll go out on a limb and say it's a woman. The nasal opening is narrow, so that would make her a white woman.' She turned it upside down. 'No wisdom teeth, so maybe she's still a teenager. But then again, my wisdom teeth still haven't come in, and I'm thirty-four, so I know not to put much weight on that.' She flipped it again, studying the dark zigzag seams where the plates of the cranial vault knitted together. 'The skull sutures are prominent, so she can't be very old.' She rotated the skull slowly, scrutinizing it from all angles. 'No bullet wound that I can see. Looks like the dog crunched on both cheekbones before his owner took it away from him.' She gave the skull a final inspection, then shrugged. 'That's it. That's all I've got.' She handed it back to me. 'So, how'd I do? Pass or fail?'

I smiled. 'Pretty well. You're right about the race. White. And the age – it's a young person. You get points for noticing that the third molars hadn't erupted, and more points for realizing that the skull sutures haven't started to fill in yet. Those don't fully fuse and start obliterating until the thirties and forties.'

'Okay, so what'd I lose points for? Did I get the sex wrong?'

'Maybe. So yes.'

'Huh?'

'It might be female, might be male. Can't tell – it's too young.'

She frowned. 'You're saying it's a dead kid?' I nodded. 'Crap. Tell me what I should have looked for, to know it was a big kid rather than a little woman.'

'Well, it's not just the size, but the proportion. Ever seen a baby's skull?' She nodded. 'So you probably remember, the cranial vault looks huge compared to the rest of the face, almost like it's been inflated like a balloon.' She nodded again. 'This cranial vault isn't that disproportionate, but it's still large for the facial structure, relatively speaking.' She peered at the skull again, then at my head, and then, in a mirror on the wall, at her own. 'Another thing.' I pointed at the supraorbital ridge, the shelf above the eyes. 'If this were an adult woman, the edge of this ridge would be sharp. Here, take off a glove and feel the difference between mine and yours.' She hesitated. 'Go ahead.' She peeled off her right glove and pressed the tips of her fingers to her eyebrows, then to mine.

'Yours feel like a Neanderthal's.'

'Well, back in the days of cavemen, guys who could shrug off a whack in the head were more likely to survive and reproduce than guys who had skulls like eggshells,' I explained. 'In females, thickheadedness wasn't as crucial to survival as prettiness was. Women's skulls evolved to be more delicate, with thinner brows and smaller muscle markings – "gracile" is the nerdy anthropologist's word for it. Looks kinda like "graceful" but rhymes with "hassle," which is what women's lives are filled with.' She smiled. 'Want me to tell you more about the age?'

'Sure. How much can you narrow it down, and how do you do that?'

I cradled the skull in the palm of my left hand. 'Let me show you something in the upper jaw, the maxilla.' A prominent line ran along its midline, starting just behind the incisors. I traced the line with my right pinky finger. 'See this seam?' She nodded. 'This is the inter-maxillary suture.' Running crosswise were two others. 'This one, just behind the front teeth, is the incisive suture, and back here at the molars is the palatomaxillary suture.' She nodded again. 'So, in the same way the cranial sutures fuse and fade over time – obliterate – so do the maxillary sutures. My maxillary sutures are fused solid by now, like they've been welded shut. Yours probably are, too. How would you describe these?'

She bent down and took a close look. 'It looks like the roof of the mouth is cracked.'

'It looks cracked,' I agreed, 'but it's not; it just hasn't

finished growing together. That tells us we're looking at a subadult. A teenager, maybe even preteen. That's consistent with the smaller size of the skull, too. Be a big help if we can find the rest of the bones.'

'From your lips to God's ear,' said Angie. 'We did a grid search across a pretty big area around the cabin. A quarter mile in every direction. That's almost forty acres. Nothing so far.'

Just then the door opened and a fiftysomething man walked in, nodding at Angie. His clothes were rumpled, his white shirt bore a coffee stain, and he held an unlit cigar clamped between his teeth. If he'd been wearing an old raincoat, I'd have taken him for Columbo, the bumblingly brilliant television detective from the 1970s. He took out the cigar, shifted it to his left hand, and held out his right. 'Sorry I'm late,' he said. 'Slow line at Starbucks. Stu Vickery. Good to meet you. Angie came back from Tennessee raving about the Body Farm.' He shook my hand, then shifted the cigar from his left hand to his right before clamping it back between his teeth. I wondered how many times in his life he'd repeated that sequence of movements: remove cigar with right hand, shift cigar to left hand, do something with right hand, shift cigar back from left hand, put cigar back into mouth. I wondered, too, how long an unlit cigar would last before it got totally soggy and crumbled in his mouth.

'Angie and I were just taking a look at the skull,' I

said. 'Angie, you want to tell him what we know so far about the sex, race, and age?'

'Me?'

'You. It's a pop quiz, to see if you were paying attention.' She took the skull from my hand and drew a deep breath, then succinctly recapped everything I'd said about the cranial sutures, the muscle markings, the maxillary sutures, and the ambiguous gender. 'Good job,' I commended. 'You made a hundred.' She smiled slightly and flushed a faint shade of pink.

Vickery removed the cigar, studying the damp, bitten end as if it might contain some guidance. 'So we've got a Johnny or a Janie Doe, teenager or less. What more can you tell from the skull? Any idea how this kid died?'

'We were just about to get to that,' I said. I took the skull back from Angie and pointed to the left cheek. 'You can see that the zygomatic arch, which connects the cheekbone to the temporal bone, has been gnawed off. There are fresh chew marks at both ends of the arch.' Angie and Vickery both leaned in to peer at the damage. 'Now look at the right cheek. What do you see?'

'The arch is missing there, too,' said Vickery. 'But it doesn't look like Fido's to blame for that.'

'Exactly,' I said. 'The right zygomatic arch wasn't chewed. It was snapped.'

'And it's darker than the chew marks,' Angie observed.

'And what do you suppose that means?'

'It happened a while back?' I nodded but kept quiet,

to encourage her to finish the thought. 'At the time of death?'

'Yes. Probably. More or less,' I said. 'It's stained the same color as the rest of the skull. That means the bone was already broken when the soft tissue began decomposing. But see how the edges of this break are a little less jagged than the edges of the other zygomatic arch, the one the dog snapped? It's possible that this break was already beginning to heal before the kid died.'

Vickery frowned, causing his cigar to twitch in his mouth. 'What does that tell you about the timing of the injury? Can you be any more specific?'

'Not much more specific,' I answered. 'Antemortem or perimortem – before death, or right around the time of death.'

Vickery nibbled on his cigar. 'Couldn't it have happened sometime afterward? Like, when the body was buried or dumped out of a car or whatever?'

'Never say never,' I answered. 'But I'm pretty sure this fracture occurred days or even weeks before death. And I'm pretty sure the other fracture was the fatal one.'

Angie and Vickery both looked down at the skull, then up at me. Angie spoke first. 'What other fracture?'

'This one,' I said, tracing a thin line that angled up the skull from just above the left ear, up through the temporal bone and into the parietal, which formed the top of the cranial vault. I'd rubbed a thumbnail over the line; the break in the surface was so subtle I could barely feel it, but it was there, and it showed no signs of healing, so I knew that it had occurred at or near the time of death.

Vickery spoke through cigar-clamping teeth. 'So it's likely, or at least possible, that this kid was murdered?' I nodded. 'May I?'

'Sure.' Before I had a chance to add 'but you might want gloves,' he took the skull from me and raised it close to his face, his eyes ranging up and down the fine, dark crack. He rotated it, scrutinizing the crack from all angles; he tried peering through the eye orbits to see the inner surface of the cranial vault, but the openings were too small.

He handed the skull back to me, and took his cigar out of his mouth. 'Eww,' said Angie. Vickery gave her a puzzled look, then followed her gaze down to the cigar he now held between contaminated fingers.

'Eww,' he echoed. 'I hate it when I do that.' He tossed the cigar into a trash can, then washed his hands with sanitizer from a pump dispenser mounted on the wall beside the door. 'No offense, Doc,' he began, pointing at the fracture, 'but this doesn't look all that bad to me. I mean, it's not like the skull's bashed in. You certain this would be enough to kill him?'

I shrugged. 'Certain, no; confident, yes. A defense lawyer could probably hire another anthropologist or a pathologist to disagree in court. But on the inside of the skull, right about here' – with my pinky, I traced a line

44

that crossed the fracture at its midpoint – 'runs the middle meningeal artery. The fracture could have ruptured that artery, causing a cerebral hemorrhage. Obviously *something* killed this kid, and my money's on this fracture.'

Vickery fished a tan leather case from an inside coat pocket and extracted a fresh cigar. 'Okay, I'll buy it. For now. Until we find bullet-riddled bones or a knife in the ribs.' He unwrapped the cigar, tossed the cellophane in the trash, and began gnawing on the end of the replacement.

'Mind if I ask you something, Agent Vickery?'

'I do if you call me "Agent Vickery." I don't if you call me "Stu."'

'Okay, Stu. Do you ever light 'em? The cigars?'

'Never. And it's not just because every place has banned smoking. Truth is, I hate the smell of cigar smoke. But I like the smell of cured tobacco. Like the flavor, too, in small doses.' He gave the cigar an appreciative chomp. 'But chewing tobacco – doing dip – that is one *nasty* habit.'

'You'll get no argument from me about that,' I said, thinking back to my close Copenhagen encounter of the nausea-inducing kind. I chose not to point out that Stu had a thin line of brownish drool trickling from the corner of his mouth.

It's possible he noticed me looking at it, or maybe he simply felt a tickle on his chin; in any event, he took a handkerchief from his pocket and dabbed. 'So,' he said to Angie, 'did you ask him yet?'

Angie turned red. Silence hung like a soap bubble in the air, so I popped it. 'Ask me what?'

'Um . . .' She hesitated. 'Ask if you'd consult with us on this case.'

'Which case? *This* case?' I raised the skull into the center of the triangular space defined by the three of us. Angie nodded. 'Do you mean in a bigger way? More than a take-a-quick-look sort of way?' She nodded again. 'Don't you have forensic anthropologists in Florida who can help you with this?'

She looked sheepish. 'We're a little shorthanded right now.'

'What about Tony Falsetti,' I said, 'over in Gainesville? Doesn't he do a lot of work for FDLE?' Tony, who was a Knoxville native and a fine forensic anthropologist, had been hired some years ago to teach at the University of Florida. My impression was that his lab at UF worked with Florida investigators in the same way my own lab consulted with the Tennessee Bureau of Investigation and other agencies.

'He's gone,' she said. 'To Yugoslavia, or what used to be Yugoslavia. I sent him an e-mail, and he wrote me back from Sarajevo. He's working on a huge project to identify people killed in the Balkan civil war. They're searching for his replacement, but they haven't filled the position yet.'

I named another former student, now teaching in Tampa, at the University of South Florida. 'Did you try her? I think she consults on forensic cases.'

'She's in Africa all month,' said Angie. 'Teaching Nigerian medical students about skeletal trauma.'

'Nigeria? Well, good for her. Sounds like I need to keep better tabs on our graduates, though. Maybe I should put tracking collars on them.'

'Ha,' said Vickery. 'While you're at it, could you put shock collars on a few of my colleagues?'

I laughed, and Angie laughed, too, which did my heart good. 'So,' she said, 'any chance we could beg, borrow, or steal an hour or so more of your expertise before I put you on your flight back to Knoxville?'

I pulled out my pocket calendar and took a look. I'd blocked out the next two weeks to write a journal article – an account of an experiment in which we'd tested the ability of side-scan sonar to image a body we'd submerged in the Tennessee River – but my heart wasn't in the project.

'Tell you what,' I said. 'I'll make you a better offer. If you can sign this skull over to me for a few days, I'll take it back to Tennessee, finish cleaning it, and write a forensic report on it. Then I'll see if I can get you a facial reconstruction. There's a forensic artist who works in the bone lab, and she does great work. If Joanna can put a face on this skull for us, somebody might recognize it.' I paused. 'And if you can find me a cheaper place to stay, I'll come back for a week and help you look into your sister's death.'

Angie, not Stu, nearly caused me to miss my flight back to Knoxville. The reason was not that she was bad with a watch; the reason was that she took us on a three-hour detour to Associated Services.

Associated Services – was there ever a vaguer name? – cleaned up messes. If your house got flooded by a broken pipe or a monsoon – as hundreds of homes did in 2008, when Tropical Storm Fay dumped twenty inches of water on Tallahassee – Associated Services would pump out the water, remove the sodden carpet, replace the soggy, moldy drywall. If you bought a run-down house that was jammed with junk and filth, they'd shovel it out and scrub and disinfect it for you. And if your sister's brains got spattered all over her living-room sofa and carpet and subflooring, the strong-stomached employees of Associated Services would don their biohazard suits and their respirators, clean up the bloody mess, and dispose of it safely.

Joe Walsh, whose father had started Associated Services thirty-five years before, met Angie and me at the company's warehouselike facility near the campus of Florida State University. The building – brick and corrugated metal – had offices in the front half, a warehouse in the back. At one end of the building was a large gravel parking lot, surrounded by a chain-link fence topped with concertina wire. Five company vans were parked in the lot, as was a pair of black enclosed trailers emblazoned with two-foot-high biohazard warning emblems.

Walsh emerged from the front door and led us into a simply furnished office, motioning us onto a sofa. 'I'd offer you coffee, but it's from this morning, so I wouldn't be doing you a favor by letting you drink it.'

He'd sounded hesitant, even suspicious, when Angie had called him – she'd phoned as she was driving me back to the Duval to check out – but as she'd talked about her sister's death, and about why she and I hoped to sift through the shattered, spattered debris the company had removed from Kate's living room, he'd lowered his guard, at least enough to agree to meet with us.

'I Googled you after I got off the phone,' he said to me. 'I'd heard of the Body Farm, but I didn't really know much about it. That's interesting work you do there.' I thanked him; then there was a brief, awkward pause before he went on. 'I'm sorry if I seemed rude on the phone,' he said. 'You get all sorts of calls in a business like this, you know? I had a guy call me once, asking questions about what we'd do to clean up a scene where somebody'd died this way or that way, and it sounded like he was planning ahead, you know? Trying to make some choices on the front end. I told him the first thing we'd do is make sure law enforcement had investigated thoroughly and released the scene. He hung up pretty quick then. So next thing I did, I called the sheriff's office and gave them his number off my caller ID and suggested they check him out.'

'It wasn't by any chance a Georgia number,' asked Angie, 'sometime in the past couple weeks?'

'No, ma'am,' he said sympathetically. 'That call came from Sopchoppy, and it was two, three years ago.'

'Too bad,' she said. 'Be great if your caller ID could point an incriminating finger at my scumbag brother-in-law.'

He shrugged apologetically. 'Wish I could help you there, but I can't.'

'But you *can* help us by letting us look through the debris you took out of my sister's house.'

He winced and sighed. 'Here's the thing, Ms. St. Claire. I'm more than happy to cooperate with law enforcement. If FDLE wants to examine this material, all you need to do is bring me a court order, and I'll be glad for you to take it over to the crime lab and go through it with a fine-tooth comb. But I can't let you go through it here. It's a biohazard, and I can't take a chance on the liability.'

'Angie and I work with biohazardous materials all the time,' I pointed out.

'But not on my property, you don't,' he said. 'If you got sick and sued, it could ruin me. My family, too.'

'No offense,' I said, 'but it seems to me that even the dumbest lawyer in Tallahassee could create reasonable doubt in a jury's mind about the source of any nasty bugs Angie and I might happen to come down with.'

Walsh smiled, but he shook his head. 'Maybe so, but I don't have enough time or money to take that chance.'

'How about this,' I suggested. 'How about if Angie and I sign liability releases, in blood, promising not to hold you or your company liable for anything that might happen?'

'It's not just that,' he said. 'If we go opening up biohazard bags, our neighbors – businesses and residents right around here – are going to smell it and get upset. I can't afford to risk the ill will.'

'I understand your concern,' I said. 'The Body Farm is only a few hundred yards downhill from a condominium development in Knoxville – fancy condos up on a bluff over the river – and on hot summer days when the air is just sitting still, our neighbors sometimes aren't too happy.' I gestured out the window behind me. 'But look out there. You really think anybody's going to catch a whiff of anything right now?'

He looked; a storm was blowing up, and across Madison Street trees were swaying in the wind – a wind that would have whisked away the odor from a hundred corpses, let alone from some bloody cushions and carpeting.

Ten minutes later, he swiveled in his chair and took two hastily drafted liability releases from a computer printer on a table behind him. Angie and I glanced at what we were promising not to hold the company liable for: illness or injury, emotional trauma, even old age and eventual death, or so it seemed. We scrawled our signatures, and Walsh unlocked the chain-link gate so we could pull into the back lot alongside the biohazard storage trailers.

I'd somehow imagined that the cleanup crew had hauled away the sofa and flooring materials intact, more or less, except for the damage from the gun blast. When I saw what we'd be sifting through – how thoroughly everything had been disassembled – my heart sank. The frame of the sleeper sofa had been stripped down to the bare metal of the folding mechanism, and all the porous materials – the heavy batting of the cushions and the mattress, the blood-soaked carpeting, the rubber carpet pad, and the waferboard subflooring – had been cut apart and sealed into plastic biohazard bags inside cardboard boxes measuring two feet square. Before we could search the scene, we'd have to reconstruct it.

On our way over, Angie and I had made a quick stop at Home Depot to procure the makings of a bare-bones crime-scene kit, since she wasn't allowed to use FDLE resources for an outside case. We'd bought Tyvek painter's coveralls; rubber gloves; dust masks; curved needle-nose pliers; wooden dowel rods; tape measures and yardsticks; quarter-inch wire screening; a staple gun; and a large plastic tarp. After suiting up, Angie and I spread the tarp on the concrete floor of the warehouse, then began opening boxes and reassembling the scene, like some bloody, three-dimensional jigsaw puzzle. We started with the four pieces of waferboard that had been cut and pried from the floor joists. Pieced back together, the chunks of subflooring formed a roughly thirty-inch square, with a bloody six-inch hole at its center, and with assorted drips and runs at irregular intervals around it. Next we unpacked the padding and carpet and put those in position; they, too, had been cut, rather than folded, to fit into the boxes. Then we set the sofa frame in place, using a wooden dowel to center the holes one atop the other. Next, unfolding the bed's metal frame, we pieced the cut mattress back together and refolded it, and finally wedged the sections of cushions into position. Once everything was in place and we'd rechecked and adjusted the alignment of the holes, Angie took dozens of photos with her camera – wide, medium, and tight shots – from every conceivable angle, with and without the scale provided by the yard-sticks and tape measures. Finally satisfied that she'd documented the assemblage thoroughly, she allowed me to begin searching it – which meant disassembling the scene we'd just spent an hour painstakingly reassembling.

The couch was a sobering testament to the destructive force of a twelve-gauge at close range. The shot had blown a ragged hole through the seat cushion, up near one arm of the sofa. The hole was about three inches in diameter at the top of the cushion, where Kate's head had lain; it was twice that diameter at the bottom of the cushion, as the force of the blast – not just from the slug itself, but also from the column of air forced out of the barrel ahead of the accelerating slug, as well as the hot gases from the exploding gunpowder behind the slug, pushing it – had widened in the shape of a cone. By the time it tore through the mattress and out the underside of the sofa, the shock wave had grown to a foot in diameter, though much of its force was then dispersed and absorbed by the carpet and padding.

While Angie took more photographs, I used a flashlight and the forcepslike pliers – whose long, slender jaws I covered with the fingers from a rubber glove, to avoid damaging bone fragments or lead – to pick through the ragged walls of the blasted tunnel. The cushion and mattress were covered with a reddish-brown spray of blood, mixed with bits of tissue and short strands of hair; embedded here and there within the walls of the tunnel were shards of bone – plenty of them, but none large enough to be readily identifiable. 'Not much to go on here,' I remarked, 'except for the angle of the shot itself.' Angie lowered the camera and looked with her eyes rather than the lens. 'If it were me,' I went on, thinking out loud, 'I'd've sat on the sofa and leaned over, bracing the butt of the gun on the floor. That would've put spatter all over the walls and the ceiling.'

'I know,' she agreed grimly. 'Everywhere.'

'But if,' I went on, 'for some reason I decided to lie

down instead, I think I'd probably prop my head up on the arm of the sofa. But see how vertical the hole is?' She nodded. 'That means her head was lying flat on the sofa, and the gun was straight up and down. That's a lot of weight to hold at an odd angle. Seems strange. Wrong.'

She nodded grimly. 'Everything about it seems strange and wrong.'

But apart from the nagging sense that the angle of the shot was unusual, what did we have, really? Nothing, I was forced to admit as we reboxed the sofa cushions and sections of mattress, refolded the bed frame, and set the sofa aside so we could pack the ravaged layers of flooring once again. With the sofa removed, the circle of blue tarp showed through the hole in the carpet and pad and waferboard. The plastic was bright and clean, cheerful and mocking. I stared at it in frustration, and then with curiosity and the glimmer of an idea. 'So your sister's house,' I said, looking at the splintered edges of the subflooring, 'it must not have been on a concrete slab.'

'No. Crawl space.'

I turned to Joe. 'Did y'all by any chance do any cleaning under the house?'

'Sure,' he said. 'If you leave contaminated dirt in the crawl space, it smells like somebody died under there. Makes the whole house stink, and that just traumatizes the family all over again.' Suddenly he smacked himself in the forehead. 'Duh, I'm sorry – I got so interested in watching you work, I forgot to bring you the dirt. There's two boxes of it in the other trailer; I'll bring 'em right over.'

I asked him to bring me a clean, empty box, too, and I stretched the wire screen across the top of this one, then folded the edges of the screen over the edges of the box and stapled them to hold the screen taut. As Angie slowly dumped dirt onto it, I jiggled the box and brushed the dirt across and through the mesh, sifting the soil, prospecting for nuggets of bone. There was nothing in the first box except screws, nails, bottle caps, and old fragments of broken bottles. I was nearly through screening the second box of dirt when two small objects danced into view on the shimmying mesh. The first, about an inch long and half an inch in diameter, was the lead slug from a shotgun shell. I was glad we'd found it, because if we hadn't, I'd worry that we'd failed to search thoroughly, but I wasn't sure the slug would shed all that much light on things: there was no question that Kate had been shot, nor any question about what gun had fired the shot; the only question was who had pulled the trigger, and I knew the slug couldn't answer *that* for us.

The second object was a piece of bone about the size and shape of a pencil eraser. 'Now, *that's* interesting,' I said to Angie.

'What is it?'

I plucked it from the dirt with my gloved fingers. 'It's the dens epistrophei.'

'Um . . . refresh my memory?'

'The dens epistrophei is a little peg of bone that sticks up from the top of the second cervical vertebra, the vertebra called the axis. This peg fits into a notch on the atlas, the first cervical vertebra, to form a pivot point.' I rotated my head to the right, to the left. 'When I do that, my atlas is pivoting on the axis, rotating around the dens epistrophei.'

'And what does finding it tell us?'

'I think it tells us more about the angle of the gun. Hang on a second.' I sifted the last of the dirt, and sure enough, I found a second shard, one whose concave surface nested perfectly with the convex curve of the dens. 'This is the back of the atlas. It's not as hard as the dens epistrophei, but it was shielded by it.' I showed Angie and Joe how the pieces fit together. 'Normally a shotgun suicide blows off the parietal and occipital bones – the top and the back of the head,' I explained. 'I've never seen one where the neck got blasted, too.' I squinted at the bones. 'Hard to say for sure, but it looks like there might be a wipe of lead on the dens. See that dark streak?'

Walsh leaned in to take a look and asked, 'And would that tell you something important?'

'Maybe,' I answered. 'It would tell us that the neck was destroyed by the projectile itself, not by the shock wave around it. It helps you figure out the angle of the gun, and whether the angle is consistent with a self-inflicted wound. If we were doing this at the Regional Forensic Center in Knoxville, I'd X-ray these bone fragments to see if that streak really is lead. But anyhow, I suppose we should turn this over to the Georgia Bureau of Investigation as is, and let them do the test for lead.'

'Maybe. If they're willing.' Angie sighed. 'Thing is, the evidentiary chain is all shot to hell already. I mean, you know and I know that nobody's messed with this stuff since it got hauled away from the scene. But legally, in terms of admissible evidence, that wouldn't count for jack.'

'We sealed those boxes right there at the house,' Walsh protested, 'and they've been locked in the trailer ever since.'

'But in court,' she pointed out, 'that wouldn't carry any real weight, would it?' I shrugged, but she had a valid point. 'For instance, what would your devilish lawyer pal – Grease? – what would he do about this, if he were defending Kate's husband?'

'He'd rip you and me and Joe here to shreds,' I conceded. 'In fact, by the time he was done, he'd probably have the jury believing that the three of *us* had killed your sister, so we could frame your saintly brother-in-law.' I hesitated before asking the question that had suddenly reared its ugly, demoralizing head. 'But if what we're doing isn't going to be admissible anyhow, why are we doing it?'

'Well, at the risk of contradicting myself, I think that even if it's not admissible, it might be persuasive,' she argued. 'Might persuade the judge to sign an exhumation order. Might persuade the GBI to investigate, and maybe *they'd* find evidence that *would* be admissible. So that's one reason we're doing it. The other reason is, I need to know what happened to Kate. If I'm wrong in thinking Don killed her, I need to let go of that idea and face the fact that she shot herself. But if I'm right – and I'm pretty sure I'm right – I want to know for damn sure.'

'It might never be possible to know for damn sure,' I pointed out.

'Maybe not. But I'm not ready to give up on that possibility yet. Not ready to give up on Kate yet.'

I admired her loyalty and bravery. 'Me neither. Let's see if this is enough to get us an exhumation order, and maybe a nibble of interest from the GBI. Now let's get out of these bunny suits and get me to the airport.'

CHAPTER 4

'Holy *shit.*' The Tallahassee airport security screener looked like he'd seen a ghost when my bag went through the X-ray machine. I'd tried to warn him – 'You're going to see a human skull in that bag,' I'd said – but instead of taking in my meaning, he'd simply looked annoyed and told me to please step through the metal detector. By the time I stepped through, he was frantically summoning his supervisor. The pair huddled briefly over the screen, then the supervisor radioed for *his* boss. While awaiting the arrival of higher authority, he motioned me forward with his left hand – and laid his right hand on his weapon.

'Sir, we'll need to open your bag,' he said. I was amused by the contrast between his mundane words and his panicky tone, but I figured it would be unwise to laugh at a man who had one hand on a gun.

'Be my guest,' I said, in what I hoped was a soothing, I'm-not-a-serial-killer voice. 'I'm a forensic anthropologist – a bone detective – and I'm a consultant to the Tennessee Bureau of Investigation and the Florida Department of Law Enforcement. That skull is from an FDLE case I'm working on.' I paused to see if the wind had shifted any; he still looked suspicious, but no longer openly hostile.

'There's a TBI badge and an FDLE evidence receipt in the side pocket of my bag. I'm taking the skull up to Tennessee to get some help identifying it.' At the rate this was going, though, I wasn't feeling confident about making my flight and getting to Knoxville, at least not on the flight that was scheduled to leave in forty minutes.

The supervisor eyed me with continuing suspicion, but his hand moved away from his gun. 'I'll still need to open the bag.'

'Of course. The skull is old and fragile, so if you unwrap it, please be really careful. You might want gloves, too.' They looked back and forth from the bag to my face. Behind him, I noticed another uniformed TSA official hustling toward us. It didn't take a lot of brainpower to deduce that this guy was in charge. 'I think your boss is here,' I said, nodding toward the fast-approaching newcomer. The two supervisors conferred briefly in hushed voices, then the higher-level manager gestured toward my bag. His underling tugged the zipper hesitantly, as if the bag might contain a live snake, and gingerly removed the cardboard box from inside and raised the lid. Within the box, the skull was swaddled in a layer of bubble wrap and surrounded by foam packing peanuts. They leaned down and peered in, shooing peanuts aside with gloved fingers. 'It's very fragile,' I pleaded. 'Please be careful. If it gets broken, it'll be harder to identify the victim and catch the killer.'

My words finally seemed to sink in. The boss looked

up. 'You say you've got some sort of documentation about this?'

'I've got an evidence receipt from FDLE, the Florida Department of Law Enforcement. I've also got my consultant's badge from the Tennessee Bureau of Investigation.' He pondered this, then unzipped the side pocket I was pointing toward. He fished out the papers and the leather wallet that held my TBI shield.

'So you're Dr William Brockton, PhD?' It was clear, from the incisive questioning, why this one was in charge.

'I am. I teach anthropology at the University of Tennessee. When I'm not causing trouble for the TSA.'

The joke seemed to cut some of the tension. 'Tennessee,' mused the midlevel guy. 'What kind of football team is Tennessee gonna have this year?'

'Probably pretty good. But probably not as good as Florida's.'

'Probably not,' agreed the big boss. He gave me a smile that combined smugness, superiority, and pity. And in the pitying part of that smile, I saw that after enduring a few more barbs about football, the loser unlucky enough to live in Tennessee would make his flight after all.

The rusty venetian blinds in the windows of the bone lab were shut – at least, as shut as their fraying cords and tattered tapes allowed them to be – but the morning sun still poured through gaps where slats had been broken or bent during the past forty years. On hot mornings,

63

even early in May, the stadium's steel girders and masonry foundations worked together like an immense solar oven, collecting the sun's heat and radiating it through the south-facing wall of windows in the bone lab. During pleasant months of the year, the bank of tables lining those windows offered plenty of daylight for studying bones, but during summer and winter, the extremes of heat and cold along the expanse of glass tended to drive students as far away from the windows as possible.

Miranda Lovelady was putting bones – the bones of the golf-club victim, I noticed – in a long cardboard box as I entered the lab. The box was three feet in length, with a one-foot-square cross section. We had thousands of such boxes stacked on shelves beneath the stands of the stadium. Each box contained the bones of a human skeleton, cleaned and neatly arranged. Several thousand of the skeletons were eighteenth- and nineteenth-century Native American skeletons from the Great Plains, which I'd excavated decades before, early in my career. Another thousand were modern skeletons from bodies donated to the Body Farm over the past twenty years. And a few hundred contained the broken, burned, shot, or stabbed skeletal remains of murder victims.

A small, separate compartment at one end of each box held the skull – in the case of the box Miranda was repacking, the putter-punched skull – while the main compartment housed all other bones (and, in this box, the broken putter). The long bones of the legs and arms lay parallel, the ribs spooned up together, and the vertebrae clumped, strung together on cord like bony beads on a warrior's necklace. As the door closed behind me, Miranda looked up and asked, 'How was your weekend?' Then she looked down at the box in my hand and added, 'Whatcha got?'

'Fine,' I answered. 'And a skull from Florida.'

'Florida? Who sent you a skull from Florida?'

'Nobody. I went and got it.' Her eyebrows shot up in an interrogatory manner. 'I made a quick trip to Tallahassee. Got there Thursday. Came back Friday night. Spent the weekend cleaning this.'

'Do tell.'

'Angie St. Claire – the forensic tech from the state crime lab – called Friday and asked me to help look into her sister's death. That's why Angie left here so suddenly on Wednesday.' Miranda nodded and opened her mouth to speak, but I didn't give her a chance. 'Anyhow, while I was down there for that, a sheriff's deputy brought in this kid's skull from one of the rural counties outside Tallahassee. I thought I'd ask Joanna to do a reconstruction.'

Miranda clearly wanted to ask more, but I excused myself to talk to Joanna, and Miranda left with the bone box, presumably to reshelve it in the collection room.

Joanna Hughes was working at a small table – 'her' table – on the opposite side of the room. Joanna's table was unlike any other in the lab. Most of them were covered with trays of bones or skeletal fragments: bits of skull on one, for instance; gnawed ribs on another; a jumble of vertebrae on a third. Joanna's table, by contrast, held beautiful human heads or, more precisely, beautiful clay sculptures of heads. Joanna was an artist who restored faces to the skulls of the unknown dead.

As I crossed the lab, Joanna leaned back from her current project, frowned, and then grabbed the nose and twisted it completely off the face.

'Ouch,' I said. 'That's gotta hurt.'

Joanna turned and smiled, waving at me with the wad of clay she'd just amputated. 'He was getting too nosy for his own good,' she cracked.

Unlike the handful of other people in the lab, Joanna wasn't a student; she had an undergraduate degree in forensic art – a degree program she'd created herself, through persistent and articulate pleas to the Art and Anthropology departments. She'd taken courses in anatomy, anthropology, and art, with one goal in mind: to restore faces to the dead. Somehow she'd known, even as a child, that this was the work she felt called to do. Joanna's reconstructions were a last-ditch effort to identify someone once all other avenues had been exhausted. If her combination of art and skill allowed her to re-create the face of someone who'd gone missing or been killed years before, there was a chance – a slim chance, but better than none at all – that someone might see a picture of her work, in a newspaper or on television, and call the police to say, 'Hey, I know who that was.' So far, she'd done twelve reconstructions, and five of those had led to identifications. In some fields that success rate would seem dismally low, but in the real world of cold-case investigations, it was remarkably high. She was batting over .400, and the work was a lot more meaningful than swatting a ball over a center-field fence. The woman was good. Very, very good.

I wished the department could put Joanna on salary, because her work was important and her skills were rare. The sad reality, though, was that we just didn't have the money. So she worked for peanuts, charging law enforcement agencies a pittance for the time it took to do their reconstructions. Tight as law enforcement budgets were, I suspected that Joanna occasionally did reconstructions for free, if the investigator – or the skull itself – told her a particularly moving tale.

Joanna had made a believer out of me two years earlier. I'd been contacted by a family whose matriarch had gone missing twenty-five years before. The woman had disappeared one fall, and when a female skeleton was found the following spring, it seemed logical for investigators to think that the skeleton was hers. The medical examiner had concluded that the bones were indeed hers, and she'd been buried in the family plot. The identification wasn't conclusive, though, because the case happened before the advent of DNA testing. So, a quarter of a century later – after the O. J. Simpson trial and the show

CSI had made DNA a household word – the family had asked to have the bones exhumed and DNA samples taken. After examining the bones – which showed me nothing that contradicted the medical examiner's identification – I pulled a couple teeth and cut two cross sections of bone, which the family planned to send to a DNA lab, along with cheek swabs from one of the woman's daughters and one of her granddaughters. After taking the samples, I put the bones back in the coffin and – within hours after it was unearthed – it was reburied. Several months later, startling news arrived: the DNA lab said that the skeletal woman in the coffin was not, in fact, the woman the M.E. and the headstone proclaimed her to be. The daughters and granddaughters of the missing woman were not, the lab reported, genetically related to the woman buried in the family cemetery. The district attorney reopened the case of the missing woman, as well as a second case: the case of the mysterious, unidentified woman in the coffin.

That's when Joanna had entered the picture. We exhumed the coffin a second time, and this time I brought the mystery woman's skull back to UT. Joanna studied its shape, then spent two weeks sculpting the face she thought had once resided on the skull. When I walked into the lab and saw her finished handiwork, I was stunned. Guided by nothing more than the shape of the skull and the information that it was a middle-aged white female, Joanna had sculpted a face that bore an astonishing resemblance to one of the missing woman's daughters. Could the resemblance really be purely coincidental? Or was it possible the DNA lab had erred? Eventually – many months and many complications later – we learned that the DNA lab had botched the analysis . . . and that the M.E. and the headstone had been right all along. If not for Joanna's remarkable reconstruction, though, the investigation would surely have continued down the wrong path, and we'd never have learned the truth.

So now, as I unwrapped the skull that had caused such a furor at the Tallahassee airport, I handed it to Joanna with a powerful mixture of hope and pessimism. 'It's Caucasian,' I said, 'somewhere around age twelve, plus or minus a year or two. Beyond that, I can't give you much to go on. Might be male, might be female.'

She took the skull from me and cradled it in both hands, turning it this way and that to inspect it from multiple angles. 'Where'd it come from?'

'Florida. Somewhere in the woods. A dog brought it home.'

'And the sex is a complete coin toss? You're not leaning one way or the other?'

I shook my head. 'I wish I were. Can you split the difference? Do an androgynous face?'

'Sure, why not? Kids *are* androgynous, till they're not. Main difference is how they wear their hair. If I make it vague, a relative should be able to fill in the gender blank.'

She looked at the skull again. 'I've never done a reconstruction on a skull that was missing the mandible. Any suggestions?'

I thought for a moment. 'Well, you could just take an educated guess and freehand it, based on what you know about anatomy. But it might be easier if you could borrow a mandible from somebody of the same race and age.' I searched my mental memory banks. 'Seems like we have a couple of skeletons in the collection that might be in the right zone. Miranda can search the database by age; I'd try ages ten to thirteen, see what pops up, and use whichever one fits best. Just don't forget where you got it, and be sure you put it back in the box, once we've taken plenty of photos and you're ready to take the clay back off.'

'Okay. I'll try to get started on it this afternoon. Assuming I can get this guy's nose fixed this morning.'

'Great. Any idea when you might be done?'

'Pushy, pushy. Well, usually it takes me two weeks, but I don't have two weeks this time.'

'Because I'm so pushy?'

'No, because I'm nine months pregnant, in case you hadn't noticed, and my due date is in six days.'

'Oh,' I said, embarrassed. 'I knew that.' That was mostly true; I *did* know she was pregnant, of course – she was as big as a barge, and she waddled when she walked – but I'd lost track of how far along she was. 'You look terrific. I hope the birth goes really well.'

'Ha. What you mean is, you hope the baby doesn't come till after I've finished this reconstruction for you.'

I laughed. 'That, too.'

As I was dashing up the flight of steps from the bone lab to the departmental office, I bumped into Miranda on her way back from the collection room. 'So tell me more,' she said. 'How was Florida?'

'Interesting. Frustrating. I'm actually going back.'

She blinked. 'Going back? When?'

'Now.'

'*Now?*'

'Well, soon. As soon as I do a little research, and as soon as Joanna finishes the reconstruction.'

'How come?'

'Well, for one thing, I promised to do a report on the skull.'

She frowned and eyed me suspiciously. 'So, let me see if I understand this right. You have to go back to Florida to write about a skull that's here in the bone lab?'

It sounded absurd when she put it that way. 'Well, they're looking for the rest of the bones now, and I'd like to be there when they're found. Besides, I told Angie St. Claire I'd help her look into her sister's death. Burt De Vriess has an attorney friend in Georgia who's helping us get an exhumation order, so I can look at the body. The local coroner says it was suicide, but Angie feels pretty sure the husband did it.'

'So Angie's freelancing, and you're freelancing with her?'

'I guess you could say that.'

'Are you doing anything else with Angie?'

'How do you mean?'

'Are you falling in love with her?'

'In love? With Angie? Heavens no.' Miranda looked startled by the force with which I said it. 'Not that there's anything wrong with Angie. She's great. I *like* Angie – she's smart, she's good at her job, and she's fighting an uphill battle to find out if her sister was murdered. I'd like to help her, that's all.' Miranda still looked skeptical – and I realized she had reason to doubt my candor. It hadn't been long, after all, since I'd kept her totally in the dark about my role in an undercover FBI sting, one aimed at shutting down an unscrupulous tissue bank. Miranda had believed I was selling corpses from the Body Farm to the tissue bank, and by the time the truth came out, her faith in me had been shattered. Viewed in the light of that recent history, her current skepticism was understandable. 'Okay, there is one other thing,' I said. Her eyes narrowed, and she drew back, on guard now. 'The other thing is, it's . . . too *quiet* around here at the moment. UT's on break, my son and his family have gone to the beach, and unless somebody finds a dismembered body or a mass grave in the next hour or so, I'll go stir-crazy. I'm going back to Florida because there's something to *do* there. Something besides writing this damn sonar article I've been avoiding for months.'

Her expression softened, and she let out a big breath.

'Okay, I can believe that. But what if all hell breaks loose up here while you're down there?'

'If you need to work a death scene while I'm gone, call Hugh Berryman or Rick Snow.' Hugh and Rick were former students of mine who were now board-certified as forensic anthropologists. 'I called them during my layover in Atlanta. They've offered to cover for me the next couple weeks.'

Miranda nodded. 'Okay. But if you end up moving to Florida before I finish my PhD, I am going to be *so pissed* at you.'

I smiled. 'Then you'd better start writing that dissertation. And I'd better get going on the experiment I need to do for Angie.' I started up the stairs, but Miranda grabbed me by the arm.

'What experiment?'

I was caught. 'You're not going to like it.'

'If you tell me I'm not going to like it, that means I'm going to *hate* it.' She'd put on her interrogator face, her inquisitor face. '*What* experiment?'

'Thing is,' I began, trying to ease into it, 'Angie's sister's death was ruled a suicide. But suicide by shotgun is rare, especially among women. Angie and I sifted through everything the cleanup crew took out of the house, and in the dirt from the crawl space, I found the dens epistrophei and a piece of the axis. Which makes me think there's something funny about the angle of the shotgun.'

Miranda's eyes narrowed. 'Oh, no. You wouldn't. Dr B, tell me you wouldn't.'

'We're trying to get an exhumation order to dig up the body. The stronger we can make the case, the more likely a judge is to let us do it.'

'You mean you plan to take one of our bodies and just blow the head off?'

'Not exactly.'

'Then what *do* you mean?'

'I mean not exactly one.' Her eyes narrowed to slits.

'Christ. How many?'

'At least two.' She groaned. 'Actually, three. To do it right, I need three.' She groaned again, louder.

'Jesus, you're going to destroy three donated bodies – wreck three specimens that were supposed to go into the teaching collection – on the off chance that some Georgia cracker of a judge will be swayed by that?'

'Why not?'

'Why not? Why *not*? Because these bodies have been donated to us, *entrusted* to us. We're supposed to study them, learn from them, treat them with respect. We're not supposed to abuse and mutilate them.'

'There are no restrictions on how we use donated bodies,' I said. 'You know the language of the donation form by heart. Legally, we're entitled to do whatever we want to them.'

'I'm not talking about what we can do *legally*,' she countered. 'I'm talking about what we can do *ethically. Morally*.'

'Why is shooting them worse than letting bugs and raccoons and buzzards feed on them?'

'Because that's the cycle of *nature*,' she protested. 'Because that's what *happens* to bodies.'

'So does this,' I pointed out. 'Not as often, but sometimes. Don't we have a right, even a responsibility, to study *this* cycle, the cycle of violence? To understand more about how it affects bodies?' She made a face of distaste and shook her head slowly. 'Am I remembering wrong, Miranda? Weren't you the research assistant who helped me put two bodies in cars and set them on fire a couple of years ago? And at this very moment,' I reminded her, 'don't we have three bodies dangling from nooses?' She scowled, annoyed that I was boxing her in. I decided to stop bludgeoning her and appeal to her sense of justice, which ran strong and deep. 'Look, I know it's disturbing. But remember the experiment I did for Burt DeVriess in that murder case a couple years ago? I stabbed a body, trying to re-create the path of what a medical examiner called the fatal wound. But I couldn't do it; it was physically impossible to make a knife zigzag around the spine and the rib cage the way the M.E. said it had. Remember that?' She nodded. 'If I hadn't taken a knife to that donated body, Grease's client – an innocent man – would've been convicted of murder.' Her scowl eased slightly, and her shoulders – which had cinched up toward her ears – dropped back to horizontal. 'You've got a younger sister, Miranda. What's her name? Cordelia?'

'Not fair,' she said, but she didn't sound like she really meant it. 'Ophelia.'

'What if Ophelia's partner murdered her, and was getting away with it? Wouldn't you want to do everything possible to bring the truth to light? Wouldn't you want other people to do that, too?'

She sighed. 'We've got two bodies in the cooler at the morgue – they came in over the weekend – and another on the way down from Oncology this morning, probably still warm. Do you want to use those, or use the three we buried for the NFA class last week?'

'Any of the fresh ones women?'

'One. The cancer patient. Forty-two. Ovarian cancer.'

I winced. 'I hate to put her through anything more.'

'She won't feel it. And she's a better stand-in for Angie's sister than some eighty-year-old guy would be.'

'You're right. Okay, let's use her and whichever others are youngest and slightest.'

'Okay, I'll let the morgue know we're coming.' She started past me down the stairs.

'Oh, and Miranda?' She stopped, on the same stair where I was standing. 'Thanks.'

She smiled slightly. 'I live to serve. Anything else?'

'Well, long as you're asking, have you got a twelve-gauge?'

She reared back and punched me in the shoulder, hard. Almost as hard as I deserved.

76

CHAPTER 5

The woman's body jerked, her arms and legs flopping, as the shotgun blast slammed her head backward and the slug punched through the base of her skull, through the sofa, and into the earth below. Her limbs twitched in brief aftershocks, then grew still. Even through the protective earplugs, the roar of the gun was almost deafening, and it took a few moments before the dull rush in my ears subsided and was replaced by the normal background sounds of the Body Farm: the rotor blades of a Lifestar helicopter making its final approach along the Tennessee River to UT Medical Center; a police siren wailing out on Alcoa Highway, a half mile beyond the hospital; the chittering of an indignant squirrel overhead and the metallic thuds of a jackhammer chipping away at an unwanted piece of concrete somewhere across the river; the whir of the autofocus mechanism on the camera with which Miranda was photographing every aspect of the violent experiment and its effects.

'I've been in police work for a lot of years, and I never shot anybody before,' said Art. 'Now I've shot three, in the space of twenty minutes. I sure hope this isn't the start of a trend.' Art Bohanan – a longtime colleague and friend, and a senior criminalist with the Knoxville Police Department – stepped back from the blasted body and wiped the bloody barrel of the shotgun with a rag. The rag was already smeared with blood and tissue from the prior two shots, into the prior two bodies. His white Tyvek biohazard suit looked like something a slaughterhouse worker had worn for a double shift on the killing floor. Art surveyed the blood spatter on the suit. 'And the sheriff's office down in Georgia didn't find a mess of bloody clothes in the husband's laundry hamper? Wasn't there a husband-shaped clean spot on the floor or the wall, where his body blocked the spatter?'

I shrugged. 'The photos didn't show much. He didn't call it in until eight or ten hours after it happened. He had plenty of time to get rid of his clothes and do some cleaning. I don't know about the spatter pattern; maybe he wiped some things down with bleach; hell, maybe he used a sheet or a shower curtain or something to contain the spatter. I figure we'll never know, since the scene was worked so poorly and cleaned up right away. I'm just hoping we learn something useful by wrecking three perfectly good skeletons.'

Miranda and I had laid our three research subjects side by side on a trio of secondhand sofas, procured from Goodwill for twenty bucks apiece and positioned atop waferboard and pads of dirt I'd bulldozed into place with the Bobcat, our miniature bulldozer. The pad of dirt was a foot deep; I'd put big road signs – SCHOOL CROSSING,

SLOW CHILDREN AT PLAY, and DEER CROSSING, with the image of the deer already riddled with bullet holes – under the dirt as a secondary backstop. Judging by the test shot Art had fired through one end of a sofa, just before we placed the bodies, the dirt itself was thick enough to stop the slug and collect all the debris. But it couldn't hurt – it could never hurt, I figured, although I'd forgotten this lesson in my life from time to time – to have contingencies and backups and backstops.

The first shot Art had fired, into the body of a small sixty-two-year-old white male, had been angled the way I'd expect in a shotgun suicide: the trigger down around waist level, the barrel pressed against the underside of the chin, rather than in the mouth. That shot, as I'd expected, had taken off the top of the cranium and some of the occipital, but had left the cervical spine unscathed. His second shot, into a medium-sized, twenty-eight-year-old black male, had been fired into the mouth, angled closer to straight on, though still slightly upward. That shot had blown off the back of the head and the base of the skull; the concussion had also fractured the first two vertebrae, but it had not destroyed them.

Art had fired the third shot into the mouth of the female cancer victim straight on, at a ninety-degree angle to the body. This shot, I saw with grim satisfaction, had obliterated the occipital and shattered the top of the spinal column, sending fragments of vertebrae splintering into the dirt. As I sifted the soil from beneath the mangled corpse, I found myself growing surprisingly nervous. What if I'd misinterpreted the bone trauma? What if I'd told Art the wrong trajectory? What if I'd ruined three perfectly good skeletal specimens for nothing?

Then, as I sifted the dirt from beneath the woman's body, I saw bone fragments – familiar-looking fragments – shimmy into view as I shook the coarse wire screen. 'Bingo,' said Miranda, zooming in with the lens as I paused to look closer. 'There's the dens epistrophei, and that looks like the back of the atlas. Good geometry, Dr B.' *Whir, click. Whir, click click click.* 'Good shooting, Art.'

'Not exactly sporting,' said Art ruefully, 'but if it persuades GBI to open a case, maybe it's done some good.'

Looking at the three ravaged bodies, I hoped he was right about that. I also hoped that the shattered skulls and spine might shed light on other, similar cases. I felt a debt, an obligation, to these three donors, and I realized I could repay the debt by sharing what I'd learned in forensic lectures and scientific articles. 'Thank you, thank you, thank you,' I said silently to each of the bodies. And again, aloud this time, to Art and Miranda: 'Thank you.'

Joanna finished the facial reconstruction on Thursday afternoon – only four days after she'd started, which was a speed record for her. She was urged on by occasional contractions, which, luckily, turned out to be false labor.

She wasn't thrilled with the reconstruction, but then again, being a perfectionist, Joanna was almost *never* thrilled with her reconstructions. She'd had to make some compromises, for the sake of the sexual ambiguity. As a result, the youthful face she'd sculpted could have been either a long-haired boy's or a short-haired girl's; it could also, without much of a stretch, have belonged to a mannequin in the children's section of Target. In the absence of well-defined male or female characteristics, the face had an unavoidable, unsatisfying blankness. Still, if a photograph of the reconstruction were seen by the right person – by someone who'd once known this child – that person's memory might well fill in the blankness, and perhaps more easily than if Joanna had done a more detailed face. The goal in reconstructing a face wasn't to nail the victim's likeness with magical pinpoint accuracy; the goal was to hint, to suggest: to get close enough to the mark to prompt someone, somewhere, to call and say, 'That looks like so-and-so, who went missing years ago . . .'

But the vagueness made me uneasy, as vagueness generally did, in any arena in my life.

The clay-covered skull stared up at me from a hatbox in the passenger floorboard of my truck. I was taking a chance, carrying it that way; I probably should have put the lid on and tucked the box securely behind the driver's seat, but – vague and unsatisfying though the face was – I wanted to be able to glance at it from time to time during the eight-hour drive to Tallahassee. Maybe, just maybe, something in the face would trigger some insight that had been swimming unseen beneath the surface of my mind for the past few days.

The blank face in the box wasn't the only ambiguity accompanying me on the drive south. Several months before, I'd made love to a librarian who'd been helping me research the history of Oak Ridge, Tennessee – the birthplace of the atomic bomb, and the location of the recent murder of an atomic scientist. Just days after sleeping with the librarian – Isabella – I'd been stunned to learn that it was she who'd killed the scientist, in a bizarre act of vengeance for the suffering that the bombing of Nagasaki, Japan, had caused her family. Some weeks after that, as the FBI tried to follow Isabella's trail, I'd been even more stunned to learn that she might be pregnant. I'd received a cryptic message from her that seemed to confirm her pregnancy: from San Francisco, she'd mailed me an origami bird – a paper crane, symbol of peace – that contained, within its folds, a much smaller crane. Two months had passed since I'd received the origami message: two months in which I'd twisted in the wind, wondering where Isabella might be; wondering if she were indeed pregnant with my child; wondering whether she'd be caught; half hoping she would be; half hoping she wouldn't. A psychologist I'd consulted, as I'd sorted through my conflicting feelings, had summed up my dilemma. 'You're at a crossroads,' he'd said, 'a place of not-knowing. And you need to pitch your tent there for a while.'

So even as I steered my GMC pickup south on I-75 toward Atlanta and Tallahassee, I was pitched in my karmic tent, camped at an intersection from which fog-shrouded roads diverged toward unseen, unknowable futures. I was not an especially happy camper.

CHAPTER 6

Angie met me the next morning at the FDLE evidence-intake door. 'Welcome back. How was your drive?'

'Not bad. Atlanta was slow, but that gave me a chance to check out the skyline. I came through right at dusk, when the buildings were starting to light up. Looks like the architects there are running a "Fanciest Roof" contest – spires and arches and flying buttresses everywhere up there, glowing like Christmas.'

Vickery greeted me with a nod that included a slight additional wag of the cigar. Then he removed the cigar and used it to point at the box under my arm. 'I see you brought along a friend. Glad you had some company.'

'Not much of a conversationalist,' I joked, then got serious. 'So. A missing kid; maybe a murdered kid. How do you plan to get the pictures out to the public?' As soon as Joanna had finished the reconstruction, I'd e-mailed a batch of photographs of it, along with a draft of my forensic report on the skull. But Joanna's work would pay off only if it were seen by someone who recognized the child's face.

'We've posted the pictures and a summary of your report on CJNet,' she said. I must have looked blank, because she added, 'Criminal Justice Network. Our state-wide intelligence Web site for law enforcement.' I nodded. 'Our public information officer already sent a press release to all the news outlets in the state,' Angie went on. 'Here's one for you.' She handed me a printed copy. Underneath the FDLE logo was a headline, contact information, and three thumbnail-size images of the reconstruction. I skimmed the copy.

FDLE SEEKS TO IDENTIFY CHILD'S SKULL FOUND IN APALACHEE COUNTY

On May 17, a citizen contacted the Apalachee County Sheriff's Office (ACSO) to report finding a skull on his property. After responding to the scene and determining that the skull appeared to be human, an ACSO deputy contacted the Apalachee County Medical Examiner, who in turn contacted the Florida Department of Law Enforcement (FDLE) for forensic assistance.

A forensic examination at the central FDLE crime laboratory in Tallahassee confirmed that the skull was of human origin, and that the individual had been deceased for a substantial period of time – months or years, perhaps even many years. Further examination by a forensic anthropologist indicated that the skull was that of a white juvenile, approximately ten to twelve years of age, of unknown gender. A fracture in the skull indicates that the child died from blunt-force trauma to the left side of the head. FDLE and ACSO are investigating the case as a homicide.

Anyone with information on this case, including the identity of a missing boy or girl approximately ten to twelve years of age, is encouraged to call FDLE or the Apalachee County Sheriff's Office.

The press release ended with contact phone numbers and e-mail addresses for FDLE and the sheriff's office. Attached were three additional pages bearing eight-by-ten enlargements of frontal, profile, and half-profile photos of the reconstruction. 'Looks good,' I said. 'Any decent leads yet?'

'It's a little early yet.' Vickery shrugged. 'We've had a few calls, including one from a guy who says that *he's* the missing child.'

I laughed. 'Did he say how he manages without his skull?'

'No,' Vickery deadpanned, 'but I'm guessing the lack of a skull makes it a lot easier to go through life with his head up his ass.'

Any additional jokes were cut off by the whoop of a police siren, which turned out to be Vickery's cell phone ringing. He scanned the number on the display and raised his eyebrows. 'Vickery speaking' he said. 'You must have radar or ESP, Deputy. I'm in the lab right now with the forensic anthropologist, who just brought the skull back with the clay facial reconstruction . . . What? Slow down, I can't understand you . . . Hold on, I'm gonna put you on speaker.' He flipped open the phone. 'You still there?'

'I'm here,' came an agitated male voice. The sound was distorted – loud but muffled, the way it might sound if the deputy was shouting into the phone. 'I'm out here at the Pettis place. The damn dog's done it again.'

'Done what?'

'Brought in another one.'

'Another bone? Well, that's a start,' said Vickery. 'Now, if he'll just bring us another couple hundred – is that about right, Doc? Aren't there two-hundred-something bones in the body?' I nodded. 'If he'll just bring us another couple hundred, we can put this kid back together.'

'Not another bone,' yelled the deputy. 'Another kid. A different kid.'

'Deputy, this is Dr Bill Brockton,' I interrupted. 'I'm the forensic anthropologist. What makes you think it's somebody different?'

'Because unless that first kid had two heads, it *has* to be somebody different. Pettis's dog just dragged in another skull.'

CHAPTER 7

Highway 90 shimmered and melted in the afternoon heat. Just ahead, it was a straight, flat ribbon of asphalt that became a straight, rippling river in the middle distance, then seemed to flow directly into the sky as it neared the western horizon. I half expected the pavement to evaporate beneath our wheels, molten and miragey as it appeared, but somehow the margins between asphalt and liquid, between liquid and sky, skittered ahead of us at a steady sixty-five miles an hour, the same speed the Chevy Suburban was traveling.

Angie, Vickery, and I were in the crime lab's Suburban, headed from Tallahassee to the boondocks of Apalachee County, an hour west and a world away from the hum of the state capital and the forensic labs of FDLE. The deputy who'd called in the skull had arranged to rendezvous with us in McNary, the county seat of Apalachee County, and caravan with us to the property where the dog, the owner, and a second skull awaited us.

Eventually a small town shimmered into view, as if it were being conjured out of the waves of heat; as if the buildings and cars and even people took a few minutes to coalesce. McNary, Florida – population 'nary too many,' according to Vickery – solidified into a sleepy, pretty little town, its central square occupied by a century-old, cupola-capped courthouse that was surrounded by live oaks and flowering azaleas. The streets bordering the courthouse square were fronted by an array of small, local businesses: a three-chair barbershop, still sporting a spinning pole of spiraling red and blue stripes; the Stitch 'N Sew, whose display window proclaimed CHURCH HATS SOLD HERE and offered beribboned, bespangled evidence to back up the claim; Miss Lillian's Diner, where a sandwich-board sign on the sidewalk listed the day's specials as meat loaf, mac and cheese, green beans, and four varieties of pie; the Casa de Adoración, a storefront Hispanic church whose members Vickery described as 'a cross between Catholics and snake handlers'; two bail bonding companies, AAA Bail and Free As A Bird Bonds; a pawnshop offering DIAMONDS, GUNS, AND PAWN; and a hardware store whose sidewalk frontage abounded with lawn mowers, wheelbarrows, racks of gardening tools, and a handful of olive-drab hunting blinds perched on fifteen-foot stilts. As we passed the hunting blinds, I looked up, half expecting to see rifle barrels aimed at our passing vehicle.

A few blocks west of the courthouse, we passed a huge column of gray nylon fabric, a cylinder a hundred feet tall and thirty feet in diameter, glowing in the sun and rippling in the breeze. I pointed it out to Vickery. 'What on earth?'

'Dunno. Looks like one of those weird artworks by that foreign guy – what's his name? Crystal? Cristoff? The dude that wraps buildings and islands and small countries in fabric?'

'Christo,' said Angie. 'But I don't think this is art.'

'Looks like art to me,' said Vickery. 'Prettier than a lot of paintings I've seen.'

'Didn't say it wasn't pretty,' she said crossly. 'But I think if we peeked behind that curtain, we'd find a water tower and a crew of guys with sandblasters or paint sprayers.'

On the outskirts of McNary – which were no more than a quarter mile from the inskirts of McNary – Angie pulled into a McDonald's. An Apalachee County sheriff's cruiser idled in the grass beneath the shade of a maple tree at the back corner of the parking lot. As she eased the Suburban to a stop at the edge of the pavement, a lanky deputy emerged from the cruiser, wiping his fingers with the tatters of a napkin. The three of us climbed out – it felt like stepping into a blast furnace – and swapped greasy, salty handshakes with the deputy, Will Sutton. 'Sorry,' he said, 'I should've gotten more napkins. Y'all want something to eat? Last chance for a while.' We declined, and in another minute we were headed westward again into the liquid shimmer of Highway 90.

Turning left off 90, we took a state highway south for a few miles, then turned west onto a county road for a few more. Then, at a sagging wooden gate that looked permanently open, we eased onto a small dirt road. The road, barely more than a pair of sandy tracks, wound through stands of pines and moss-draped live oaks; every now and then, small branches and beards of Spanish moss slapped and slid across the windshield. Where the ground was dry and the sand was loose, the Suburban spun and slewed in the slight curves; occasionally, we dropped into water-filled depressions that were axle-deep, flinging great sheets of sandy water high and wide, cascading over the already-spattered vegetation encroaching on the road. The Suburban seemed to need its four-wheel-drive and high ground clearance, yet fifty yards ahead of us, Deputy Sutton's Ford sedan managed just fine, aside from a thick layer of mud and sand accumulating as it rooted through the wallows.

A mile back in the woods, the deputy's cruiser turned out of the tracks and parked in a small clearing beneath towering pines. We pulled in beside him, and I noticed a tiny, tin-roofed cottage tucked at one edge of the clearing. The clapboard siding was painted forest green, and the structure looked like it had escaped from a gang of state park cabins fifty years before and had holed up in this remote hideout ever since. A battered Ford Escort station wagon sat rusting in the yard, its wheels up to the hubs in weeds.

Our arrival was heralded by the baying of a gangly

black-and-white hound that bounded off the front porch and galloped toward us. As the Suburban stopped he reared up, putting his paws on Angie's windowsill and thrusting a snuffling muzzle through the open window. 'Nice doggie,' Angie said, her tone somewhere between sarcasm and hope. She held a tentative hand toward him, close enough to sniff but not close enough to bite. After a quick whiff, the dog gave the hand a sloppy lick with a long, deceptively swift tongue. 'Nice.' She grimaced, reaching for a container of wipes in the console.

'At least he's friendly.' I got out, and the dog loped around to my side of the car to check me out. After sniffing me briefly, he shifted his attention to the right front tire, which he marked with a liberal sprinkling of pee. 'Well mannered, too.' Sutton got out of the cruiser, and the dog gave him a perfunctory sniff and marked one of his tires, too, though with only a few token drops. Clearly he'd sized up the group and found the FDLE contingent to be the alpha dogs.

The screen door of the cottage groaned open on a rusty spring. 'Don't mind Jasper,' called a stringy man who bore a vague resemblance to his dog. 'He never did meet a stranger.' The screen whacked shut as the man descended the two porch steps and shambled toward us. He wore loose, faded jeans, cinched above bony hips with a belt of cracked black leather. On both thighs the denim was worn through to the layer of horizontal white threads; between gaps in the threads of one leg I glimpsed a scrawny thigh that was nearly as white – and nearly as thin – as the threads themselves. The man's T-shirt looked as if it had been used for years as a painter's drop cloth; I couldn't tell if it was white under all the layers of color, or dark with numerous smears of white amid the other colors. *Is a zebra white with black stripes*, I found myself trying to remember, *or black with white stripes?*

Angie stretched out a hand for him to shake. 'Good to see you again, Mr Pettis. How you doing today?'

'Gettin' by, Miss Angie,' he said, shaking his head doubtfully. 'Battery on my damn car's gone dead, and I need to patch a couple holes in my damn roof, but I can't complain.'

'There's always something, isn't there,' said Angie, who had a much bigger cause to complain, but who refrained. 'You remember Special Agent Vickery and Officer Sutton,' she told him, and Pettis nodded. 'And this is Dr Brockton. He's a forensic anthropologist – a bone detective – who's helping us out on this case.'

'Bone detective,' he mused. 'Like that gal on television? That one they call Bones?'

'Like her,' I said. 'Except she's got fancier equipment than I've got.'

'Fancier looks, too.' He grinned.

I laughed. 'Yeah, and she's probably a lot smarter than I am. I just do the best I can with what I've got to work with.'

'That's all a man can do,' he said agreeably. 'You want to see Jasper's latest find?' I nodded. 'It's up here with the rest of the stuff he's dragged in.' He led us up the steps and onto the screened-in porch. The screen was rusted, with several dog-sized rips in it; I suspected it did as good a job of keeping mosquitoes out as it did of keeping Jasper in. A wooden shelf, shoulder-high, ran nearly the width of the porch, mounted to the side of the house with triangular wooden braces. Perched on the shelf were a half-dozen skulls: three deer, an alligator, a cow, and a human, which – like the first one – lacked a mandible.

'That's quite a collection,' I said. 'I've seen anthropology departments with smaller collections than Jasper's building here.' I donned a pair of gloves from my back pocket and lifted the human skull from the shelf. The light on the covered porch was dim, so I headed back into the daylight. Even in the dimness, though, I could tell that this skull had a grim story to recount.

The other four people gathered around as I studied the skull, turning it slowly to inspect it from all angles. Pettis leaned in close as I flipped it to inspect the mouth. 'So what-all can you tell from this?'

'Quite a bit,' I said. 'None of it very cheerful. Let's start with the teeth, since we're looking at them right now.' Two of them, the central incisors, had been snapped off at the gum line. 'These were probably broken by a blow of some sort,' I said. 'Maybe he just tripped and fell on the sidewalk, but more likely, somebody knocked them out. Maybe with a baseball bat or a piece of pipe. If we can find the lower jaw, I'll bet the central incisors are missing from it, too.' I studied the remaining teeth. 'One of his twelve-year molars is gone, and the jawbone's already starting to resorb, to fill the empty socket. Four of the other teeth have unfilled cavities.' I pointed with my pinky to one of the six-year molars. 'This cavity goes deep enough to reach the root. That had to be painful. So this was a poor boy; he probably never even went to the dentist.'

'So it is a male,' said Angie. 'I thought so; this skull's a good bit bigger than the other.'

'He's bigger, several years older,' I said. 'Still a subadult, though.' I pointed to the roof of the mouth. 'Remember how open the sutures in the palate looked in the other skull? These are nearly fused, but not quite. So this boy – young man, really – could be sixteen, seventeen. Judging by how that socket's already filling in, he probably lost that missing molar not too long after he got it. I'd say he started out poor, and things went downhill from there.'

Vickery used his cigar to point to a jagged gap behind the left ear opening, at the base of the temporal bone. 'Looks like a fair-sized chunk of bone is missing.'

I nodded. 'The left mastoid process – the heavy piece that's almost like a corner of the skull – has been knocked clean off. That's a pretty stout piece of bone, so something hit him hard. Again, maybe something like a baseball bat. A two-by-four. A rifle butt.'

There was a sober pause while they took this in.

'What about time since death?' asked Angie. 'Was this kid killed around the same time as the other?'

'Hard to say.' I shrugged. 'There's a little bit of tissue on this one, too, so they could be from the same time period. But the range of uncertainty's big. They might've died the same day; they might have died years apart.'

'But we know we have two adolescents,' Vickery mused, 'at least one of them male, maybe both of them male.' I nodded. 'Both killed by blunt-force trauma, both found in the same general area. So we're probably looking for a serial killer?' Angie drew a long, grim breath.

'Hmm,' I said doubtfully.

Angie's eyes swiveled up to mine. 'Hmm? What do you mean, "hmm"?'

'Well,' I hedged, 'on the one hand, we've got two young victims, who were found near one another.'

'On the other hand?' asked Vickery.

'I don't know a lot about serial killers,' I began, 'but don't they often choose similar-looking victims? Take Ted Bundy, for instance. Didn't he target women who looked like his ex-girlfriend?'

'Bundy said the cops had made too much of that,' Vickery answered, 'but then again, Bundy was a monster and a liar, so how much stock can you put in what he said? I actually thought all his victims did resemble one another.' He studied me. 'Are you saying these two kids didn't look similar? How can you tell?'

All eyes were on me. 'Well, "similar" is in the eye of the beholder, right? But if you asked me to pick out two similar-looking boys from a crowd, I probably wouldn't pick a young white boy and an older black boy.'

'This one's black?' Pettis was the one who asked. 'How can you tell that?'

'Couple ways,' I said. 'First, look at the teeth again.' I turned the skull upside down again. 'See how bumpy the tops of these teeth are?' I pointed to the numerous, irregular cusps of the molars. 'We call teeth like that "crenulated," and they're a distinctive feature of Negroid skulls. If you run your tongue over the surfaces of your molars, you'll find that they're smoother than that.' I paused to give them a chance to do the experiment, and through the flesh of their cheeks, I saw their tongues probing their teeth.

I turned the skull, cupping the damaged back of the head in my left palm, pointing the broken incisors skyward. 'The jaw structure here is classically Negroid. See how the jaw juts forward? It'd be easier to see if the incisors weren't broken, but the teeth angle also. And the lower jaw, if we had it, would jut forward, too. It's called "prognathism." Our white faces are flatter –

the shape's called "orthognathous" – and the jaws don't slant forward like this. There's an easy test you can do with a pencil. Or a cigar. Stu, can you demonstrate for us? Take your cigar and hold it straight up and down, and lay it across your mouth and chin.' He did. 'See how it touches the teeth, the chin, and the base of the nose?' Heads nodded. 'If Stu were black, it wouldn't lay flat like that. It would angle out from the nose, or from the chin, because of the way the teeth and jaws slope. Another thing' – I felt myself warming to my mini-lecture – 'is the nasal opening. See how wide it is? And see these grooves in the bone underneath it? They're called nasal gutters. They help funnel air into the nostrils. Caucasians don't have nasal guttering; we've got a nasal sill that limits how fast air can flow. That's because Caucasians evolved in colder climates, breathing colder air. In Africa, on the other hand—'

Suddenly Stu smacked his forehead with his left hand, causing all of us to jump. 'Son of a *bitch*,' he exclaimed. 'I can't believe I didn't think of this before.'

'Think of what?' asked Angie.

'We've got two dead boys, right?'

'We know this one's a boy,' I said. 'Hard to be sure about the first one.'

'There used to be a boys' school – a reform school – somewhere in this neck of the woods. A long time ago. Maybe not in Apalachee County, though. Over in Miccosukee County? Or maybe Bremerton.' He looked at the deputy. 'Any idea how far we are from the county lines?'

'Probably not more'n a couple miles from either one,' said Sutton. 'We're kind of in a corner here.' He pointed to the northwest. 'Moccasin Creek's the boundary with Miccosukee. Bremerton's close, too; due west, maybe. But I never heard of a reform school anywhere around here.'

'Hell, it probably closed ten years before you were born,' Vickery told him. 'Burned down sometime in the sixties or seventies, I forget when. Terrible fire. A bunch of the boys died. They never rebuilt the school. Just sent the survivors to other places.' He looked at the skull again. 'Doc, any chance these two kids died in the fire?'

I studied it again. 'Maybe. Smoke inhalation, possibly, but there's no way to tell that without soft tissue, and the soft tissue's long gone. But these skulls both had fractures.'

Vickery frowned. 'But don't skulls fracture in a fire?'

'Yes and no,' I said. 'Not like this. When a body burns, the skull breaks into small pieces, about the size of a quarter.'

'How about if a wall or a roof collapsed,' he persisted, 'and hit the kids on the head?'

'It's possible,' I acknowledged. 'But if the bodies weren't burned beyond recognition, seems like they'd have been sent home to be buried.'

'If they *had* homes,' Angie observed.

'Good point,' I conceded. 'Probably be worth finding out more about the fire – pictures, news accounts, official reports. Be interesting to take a look at the site, too.'

'I'd be up for that,' seconded Angie. 'Any idea who owns the property now?'

'No,' Vickery said, 'but it shouldn't be hard to find out. If it's still owned by the state or the county, we might not even need a search warrant.'

Pettis cleared his throat. 'Not to cause trouble, but does that mean you-all needed a warrant to search my property?'

Vickery laughed. 'We'd be in trouble at this point if we did, huh? But nah, we're like vampires – if you invite us in, you're stuck with us. If you don't invite us in, we have to stay out.'

'Well,' interjected the deputy, 'unless there's an active crime scene. For instance, if a human skull turns up, we can do at least an initial search even if you don't want to cooperate.'

Pettis frowned. 'But I called you. If I didn't want to cooperate, why would I call you?' I smiled; the man had a point.

'And we sure do appreciate your cooperation,' Angie threw in quickly.

Pettis's frown turned into a smile. 'Well hell, I'm glad to help. Seems like the right thing to do. Couple kids dead; be good to figure out who they were and how they died. Besides, truth is, me and Jasper kinda like the excitement. It's pretty quiet out here most of the time. Ain't it, Jasper? Huh, Jasper? Jasper, what do you say?' The dog, hearing his name three times in quick succession – the pitch rising each time – capered and spun, and gave a yodeling version of a bark.

'Speaking of Jasper,' I said, 'did you happen to see what direction he came from when he brought either skull home?'

'Nope. Wish I had. Like I told Miss Angie here, way it happened was, I was sleeping in the bed. It was right about daybreak.'

'Excuse me,' I interrupted, 'was that the first time, or this time?'

'It was both times. Jasper, he's kind of a night owl. Likes to roam around while I'm asleep. So there I am, sleeping like a baby, and Jasper jumps up in the bed with me. He mostly just does that if there's a thunderstorm, 'cause he's scared of thunder. But sometimes he does it if he's real pleased with himself. So anyhow, there I am, dreaming about something or other, and I feel Jasper curl up beside me, and he's slurping and gnawing on something that keeps bumping me in the leg. First time it happened, I 'bout jumped out of my skin when I saw what it was. Second time, I just said, "dammit, dog" – 'scuse my language, ma'am – "you have got to quit doing this."'

*

Where should we begin? What were we searching for, and how hard should we search? Did the two skulls come from the grounds of the school? If so, were they victims of the fire that destroyed the place in the 1960s? Or was there another, darker story?

Those and a hundred other questions spun through my mind as the black Suburban hummed northwest toward Bremerton County, taking Angie, Vickery, and me toward what had once been the North Florida Boys' Reformatory.

U.S. 90 almost, but not quite, managed to dodge Bremerton County altogether. As it was, the highway cut through such a small corner of it that even as I passed a faded sign announcing BREMERTON COUNTY, I glimpsed another, a hundred yards ahead, reading MICCO-SUKEE COUNTY. Midway between the two signs, a two-lane county highway intersected 90, and Angie slowed the Suburban.

'Turn left,' Vickery instructed.

Angie made the turn. A mile down the empty road, she glanced at Vickery. 'You're sure that was it?'

'Pretty sure. Unless our Bremerton County agent is having some fun with us. I asked him how to get to the old reform school from Highway 90 in Apalachee County. He had no idea – he's only been assigned here about six months – but he checked with the sheriff's dispatcher, and she said to turn right there where we just turned.'

'Wait.' Angie took her foot off the gas. 'We were supposed to turn *right* there?'

'No. *Left* there. Right *there*. *Exactly* there.'

I laughed. 'Are you two secretly married?'

'Good God, no,' exclaimed Angie.

'Hey,' Vickery squawked, 'you don't have to sound so horrified. Some women have actually liked the idea of being married to me. You know. Briefly.'

Angie chortled. 'Stu's left a string of broken hearts and wealthy divorce lawyers in his wake.'

'Only three,' he said. 'So far. But I'm starting to look for future ex-wife number four.'

A few miles farther, we came up behind a sheriff's cruiser, its blue lights flashing, tucked on the shoulder behind a black Ford pickup. 'That's Stevenson in the F-150,' said Vickery. 'I'll tell him we're here.' He sent a quick text from his cell phone, and the truck began easing forward. The cruiser whipped around it, then turned right. The truck followed, and Angie fell in behind them. The pavement was cracked and buckled, knee-high with weeds in places. Fifty yards off the highway, a rusted chain was stretched across the road between rusted steel posts. We stopped, and a big-bellied deputy got out and inspected the chain and the padlock. He leaned back into his car and took out the radio microphone; after a brief exchange, he got off the radio and popped the trunk of the cruiser. Leaning in, he rummaged around, emerging with a bolt cutter whose handles were as long as my arm. He spread them wide and nibbled at the lock with the jaws; the chain clanked to the weedy pavement.

A half mile farther in the pavement ended in a loop, and we eased to a stop in front of four tall, widely spaced columns of Virginia creeper. At the tops of the four tangles of vines, I glimpsed a few crumbling courses of chimney bricks and – perched on one of these – a glossy crow, who cawed indignantly and flapped to a nearby pine tree as the five humans emerged from the vehicles.

Vickery introduced Angie and me to Stevenson, the young FDLE agent; Stevenson, in turn, introduced the Bremerton County deputy, Officer Raiford, who studied me as if I were an unusual zoological specimen. 'Tennessee,' said Raiford, after he'd completed his examination. 'Well, how in the world'd you end up out here in Bremerton County? Musta pissed somebody off pretty bad.' He laughed at his joke, then turned his head and shot a stream of brown tobacco juice a few feet to his right. 'Y'all's football program's been having some troubles the last few years.'

'Tell me about it,' I said, fervently hoping he wouldn't.

Luckily, Stevenson intervened. 'I printed out some aerials and a topo map of the site. If you want, we can spread 'em out on the hood of the car.'

'Trunk'd be cooler,' pointed out Vickery. Stevenson nodded and laid a folder of printouts on the back of the cruiser. The topmost image was a satellite photo off Google, zoomed in close enough to show the entry road and the turnaround loop where we were parked. The four vine-clad chimneys were reduced to pairs of small specks in the photo, but they cast long, parallel shadows across the dirt and scrubby grass.

Next were two aerials taken in the 1960s, according to Stevenson. One aerial showed a small but tidy complex of a half-dozen buildings in a large, mostly open lawn. I recognized the four chimneys, which were divided between two main buildings: a dormitory, which held beds for a hundred boys, and a multipurpose building, which Stevenson said housed the classrooms, dining hall, kitchen, and administrative offices. The four remaining buildings, he said, were an infirmary, a chapel, and two equipment sheds.

Underneath this first aerial was a second aerial showing three buildings crammed into a small clearing in the woods. 'What're those?' asked Vickery.

'Ah, those,' said Stevenson. 'Very interesting. Those were the colored buildings, for the Negro boys. This was a segregated institution. The Florida legislature required the facilities to be a quarter mile apart.'

'Wow,' Angie said sarcastically, 'so much progress in the century since the Civil War. Sad thing is, there are still folks around here who miss those days.'

Stevenson pulled out additional pictures of the segregated facilities – the phrase *black-and-white photo* took on an added shade of meaning – and spread them on the trunk. The two main buildings and the chapel for the white boys were simple but appeared well constructed, neat, and carefully maintained. Their many-paned windows were large and occupied much of the walls; the interiors would have been flooded with light, and I imagined the windows offering the boys pleasant views of oaks, pines, and magnolias. The buildings for the black boys, by contrast, looked flimsy, unkempt, and virtually without windows – rickety barns, essentially, for human animals.

'Jesus' – Angie marveled – 'widely separate and *hugely* unequal. Even the cages had a double standard.'

'Yeah, the colored buildings were an afterthought,' Stevenson commented, unnecessarily. 'The main part was originally built as a CCC camp – Civilian Conservation Corps – in the 1930s. During World War II, it housed conscientious objectors – mostly Quakers who didn't believe in war. They dug ditches and paved roads and fought forest fires; some of them worked in the state mental hospital over in Chattahoochee. Some served as guinea pigs for medical experiments – *that's* a weird parallel with the Nazis, huh? After the war, when the conscientious objectors left, that's when it became the North Florida Boys' Reformatory.'

'So it was a reform school from the mid-1940s,' I said, 'until when?'

'Burned to the ground in August of 1967,' he said.

Looking at his youthful face, I suspected that the fire had occurred at least a decade before either he or the sheriff's deputy was born. 'Terrible fire. Undetermined cause. Nine boys died, and one of the guards.'

'Good heavens,' said Angie. 'Nine boys died? That's nearly ten percent. Must've been a really fast-spreading fire.'

'Apparently,' Stevenson answered. 'Not surprising – look at those old buildings. Firetraps. Late August, the days hot as hell, the wooden siding and cedar shakes like tinder waiting for a match. When I buy firewood, I pay extra for fatwood lighter that looks a lot like those shakes. Lightning strikes, a guard drops a cigarette butt in the pine straw, whatever, and *whoomph*. Anyhow, after the fire, the rest of the boys were transferred to other correctional facilities.'

'Was everybody accounted for,' I asked, 'or were some missing and presumed dead?'

'Don't know,' he said. 'We've got some people doing research on the history of the place. Looking for records, first-person accounts. If we're lucky, we might find a sixty-year-old who was doing time there and lived to tell the tale.'

As we walked the site, I noticed rectangular depressions in the ground – low spots where I could see traces of foundations, barely discernible amid the bushes and vines that had been swallowing them for the past four decades.

I wasn't convinced that searching the ruins would tell us much – I'd not noticed signs of recent disturbance here, at least not yet – but the site was complex, and I didn't want to rush to pull the plug.

I was poking around the ruins of the dormitory when I heard the call of nature, so I headed for the nearest line of trees. As I neared the tree line, I stepped on an old flagstone, a two-foot-square island of flat sandstone in a sea of weeds. The stone wobbled slightly beneath me as my weight shifted. I took my next step, then stopped and turned back to the flagstone. I put an exploratory foot on it and bore down gently. It did not move. I put my full weight on it and leaned forward, and when I did, it rocked again, barely perceptibly.

I trampled the weeds along one side of the stone and knelt. Using the triangular tip of my trowel, I dug two small handholds beneath the edge, then wiggled my fingers into the dirt and lifted. The stone was heavier than I'd expected – it was a couple of inches thick, and must have weighed a hundred pounds or more – so I was unable to budge it from my kneeling position. Getting to my feet, I bent down, then reminded myself, *Lift with your legs, not your back.* Crouching, I did my best imitation of an Olympic weight lifter, grunting with the strain. The stone came up slowly at first, but the higher it tipped, the less effort it required. By the time I had it on edge, I could balance it with one hand.

I could also see, within the hole that had been covered

by the flagstone, a large metal can – a paint can, perhaps? – its top thinned and perforated by years of rust, transformed into metallic lacework. I called Angie over and showed her my find. She photographed the can, its hiding place, the flagstone covering, and the surroundings. Then she carefully eased the can out of the ground and set it atop the stone. As she did, water sluiced through the perforations in the lid. She tried peering inside, but it was too dark and murky to make out anything. She eyed my trowel. 'You think you could get that lid off without maiming yourself?'

'I'll try.' I slid the tip through the biggest of the perforations in the lid, wiggling it gently to widen the opening. Once it was several inches in, I pried gently upward. The trowel tore the crumbling metal easily, and it took only a minute to sever the lid completely.

'The forensic can opener,' Angie cracked. 'First time I've seen one of those in action.'

Using the blade like a spatula, I lifted the lid – a small, rusty pancake – until it cleared the rim. Inside the can, barely visible above the murky water, was the edge of a small, soggy book.

Angie plucked it from its watery grave. It was a hardcover black book, bearing no title or label. It appeared to be a journal or ledger book, but its pages were stuck tight, so its meaning remained as effectively concealed, at least for now, as it had been in its hiding place. Angie carefully bundled it in a double layer of Ziploc bags and labeled a seal on the outer bag with a black Sharpie. 'I'd like to get this to the lab pretty quick,' she said. 'Maybe air-dry it overnight so it doesn't start to mold. If our documents examiner's still there by the time we get back, I'll hand it straight off to her.'

'You're the boss,' I said. 'And my ride back to civilization. Whenever you want to go, just say the word.'

Five minutes later we were on the road to Tallahassee, with a camera full of photos of ruins and one lone piece of evidence. *Potential* evidence. For all we knew, the book's pages – its fused, soggy pages – were as blank as the empty eye orbits of a skull.

CHAPTER 8

I spent a few hours the next morning catching up, by phone, with Knoxville. First I made sure that Miranda wasn't fighting any serious brushfires – 'No, things are pretty quiet here,' she assured me. 'No forensic cases, just a couple of donated bodies that can stay in the cooler till you get back. Between the boys' skulls and Angie's sister's case, sounds like you've cornered the market on all the interesting action. I'm envious.'

I laughed. 'Come on down; we'll put you to work. The pay's great. Even better than the slave wages UT pays you.'

'So that means I'd actually have to fork over money to come work my butt off?'

'Just about. The pay stinks. So does the work. But hey, the hours are long, the air's like a steam bath, and the mosquitoes hunt in packs.'

'Who could resist?'

Next I spent a while on the phone with my son, Jeff, making sure that my grandsons had not, through some series of unfortunate events, been shipped off to a perilous reform school during my absence. 'Gosh, Dad, thanks for the vote of parental confidence,' said Jeff.

'Hey, no offense,' I said. 'This case down here just reminds me how fortunate we are, and how vulnerable kids can be. Give 'em a big hug from Grandpa Bill.'

I met Angie at the crime lab at eleven. I was picking her up for an early lunch, at a place she described as 'one of Tallahassee's national treasures.' She wouldn't tell me what delights the menu held, but she'd sounded so sure I'd like it that I'd skipped my free breakfast in anticipation.

First, though, she signed me into the lab and led me down the hall past the photo lab, to a door marked DOCUMENTS SECTION. She rapped briefly on the door, then led me in without waiting for an answer.

Inside, a gray-haired, bespectacled woman sat hunched over a table, peering through the magnifying lens of a desk lamp. It was exactly the type of lamp and magnifier I had on the desk in my office under the stadium for examining bones. I half expected to see some bone fragment in the circle of light, but the woman was peering – and frowning mightily – at the muddy book I'd fished from the ground the prior afternoon. 'Hey, Flo,' said Angie. 'This is Dr Brockton, the forensic anthropologist who found the book. Dr Brockton, this is Florence Winters, our documents examiner.'

'Nice to meet you, Florence,' I said. Her frown twitched. 'You don't look too happy. Is the book not telling you anything helpful?'

'Call me Flo,' she said, without glancing up. 'Unfortunately, I'm afraid it's telling me I've made a mistake. I put it under an exhaust hood overnight to dry out, and now the pages are fused together. So instead of a book, what we've got is a brick. A brick of old, brittle paper.' To prove her point, she tugged gingerly at the covers, which refused to part.

On the table beside the lamp was a tray of tools. Two of them resembled miniature kayak paddles made of stainless steel. They sported thin, flat blades at each end, joined by a slender round shaft. One of them was smaller than the other – its blades were about an inch long, and the shaft connecting them measured perhaps six inches in length; I vaguely remembered using something similar in chemistry lab, thirty years before, to scoop bits of powder onto a balance-beam scale. The tray also held an ordinary-looking butcher knife and an implement that appeared to be an oversize letter opener made of white plastic. 'I've tried prying the pages apart with the microspatula, the regular spatula, the knife, and the Teflon spatula,' said Flo. 'The metal spatula blades are so small they just tend to break the paper apart. The Teflon spatula's too blunt; if I forced that in, it'd turn some of the pages to mush.'

Angie pointed to the butcher knife. 'What about that? Can't you slide that in and give it a twist?'

'That's what I was hoping,' Flo said, 'but the pages aren't actually flat – see how they ripple? – and the paper's really fragile. I tried going in at that corner, but instead of separating the pages, the knife was slicing through them.'

I leaned down and studied the corner and saw a small, straight incision cutting through the crinkled layers. 'So there's no way to open it up without destroying it? It might be the Rosetta stone, or might just be a bunch of blank pages, but we'll never know which?'

Flo smiled slightly. 'Never say never. Just before you got here, I was talking with a documents conservator at the National Archives, in Washington. She's been working on a similar problem – some waterlogged codebooks from World War Two.'

'Codebooks?' I'd not spent a lot of time pondering the work of the National Archives; I knew they had a bomb-proof vault that contained an original copy of the Declaration of Independence, but aside from that, I suppose that if I imagined anything about the archives, it would be warehouses filled with boring bureaucratic file cabinets. This secret-code project, though, cast a new, moodier, and sexier light on the Archives. 'Whose codebooks?'

'The U.S. Navy's.'

I was puzzled. 'But doesn't the U.S. Navy already know its own codes from World War Two?'

'Probably,' she answered, 'but all they could tell from the book's cover was that it contained classified information. So they needed to see what was on the pages to know what sort of classified information, and whether they could declassify it.'

I'd always had an interest in World War II history, so even though it was a complete digression, I stayed with it. 'And where'd they find this soggy codebook?'

'Originally it was on a navy destroyer, the USS Peary, sunk by the Japanese in a surprise attack.'

'The Peary was at Pearl Harbor?'

'No, Australia. Two months after Pearl Harbor, the Japanese attacked U.S. and British ships in Darwin. It's sometimes called "the Australian Pearl Harbor" – they actually dropped more bombs on Darwin than they did on Hawaii – but the attack wasn't so crippling. This destroyer, the Peary, was one of eight ships they sank.'

'Fascinating though the history and cryptology lesson is,' Angie began.

'Cryptography,' I corrected.

'Cryptography. Right. Whatever. How does the Seventh Fleet's secret code for "soggy pages" help us with this?'

'I was just getting to that,' said Flo, sounding peeved. I wondered if she was peeved at Angie for interrupting, or peeved at me for digressing. She might also, I realized, have been peeved at me for finding such a problematic project for her. 'She – Lisa, the woman at the National Archives – suggested a couple of things to try. First thing, which might or might not work, is to soak the book in methanol, then dry it out again.'

'Hmm,' Angie commented. 'I'm not sure "might or might not work" inspires a huge amount of confidence.

That's the best the National Archives can offer? Aren't they the brain trust for this sort of thing?'

'They are. But every project's different,' Flo countered. 'At least, that's what she said. The methanol might make the pages a little stiffer. And that might make them easier to pop apart with a knife or a spatula.'

'But it might not,' I said.

'It might not,' she confirmed. 'If not, we go to Plan C.'

'I'm afraid to ask,' said Angie. 'What's Plan C?'

'Wet the book again.'

'At the risk of sounding dumb,' I asked, 'isn't Plan C the same as Plan A?'

'Actually, *this* was Plan A,' Flo observed, rapping a knuckle on the dry book of fused pages.

'But he's got a point,' said Angie. 'What do we gain by going back to where we were?'

'We get another chance. Like Thomas Edison, when he was trying out different materials for lightbulb filaments.'

Angie looked doubtful. 'Didn't it take him, like, a hundred tries?'

'More like a thousand,' Flo said.

'A thousand?' Angie's face fell. 'You think it's worth it? I'm not sure the results are going to be all that illuminating.'

I smiled at the bad pun – there were few things I liked better than bad puns, except worse puns – but Flo looked peeved again. 'Never know unless we try.'

'Maybe not even then,' Angie replied.

'Maybe not even then,' Flo agreed. 'But somebody went to some trouble to hide this. If I can, I'd like to find out why.'

Peevish or not, I decided, Flo was good people. 'Angie and I are about to grab some lunch,' I said on the spur of the moment. 'You want to go? Stu – Agent Vickery – is meeting us there. Bringing a criminologist friend, too. Why don't you join us? Angie says the place is really special.'

'Can't,' she said. 'Got two forgeries to work on after this. Thanks, though. Where you going?'

'Shell's,' said Angie, smiling, then raising a shushing, 'top secret' finger to her lips.

'Ah, *Shell's*,' said Flo. 'That *is* someplace special.'

CHAPTER 9

What I held in my hand was halfway between bone and flower: cold and hard as stone, but scalloped, sinuous, and lustrous. It was beautiful, in a rough-hewn way, but at the moment my fear was trumping my aesthetic appreciation.

Angie and I were lunching at the Shell Oyster Bar – better known to the locals as 'Shell's' – and it was indeed special, in its own sort of way. Shell's was a ramshackle little café on Tallahassee's south side, just across the proverbial tracks. The parking lot was small, which was just as well, since the restaurant itself could seat only about thirty people. I glanced around the interior. The linoleum on the floor and the beige paneling on the walls looked forty years old, and half a dozen of the acoustic ceiling tiles were stained and sagging from roof leaks. 'You picked this place for the ambience, right?'

'I picked this place because it's the real deal. Great oysters, reasonable prices, and no fancy airs.' She was right about the lack of airs: the customers who jammed the place were eating directly off cafeteria trays, drinking beer straight from the can, and wielding flimsy plastic forks. I didn't actually mind the ambience, despite my sniping comment. What I minded was the oysters. I felt moderate concern about the eleven raw ones glistening on the plate the waitress had set on the table between Angie and me, and I felt high anxiety about the twelfth oyster, the runt of the litter, which I had slowly lifted toward my mouth as Angie watched.

'I don't know about this,' I said.

'Oh, come on. You spend half your time up to your elbows in bodies and gack, and you're scared to eat an oyster?' She looked simultaneously amused and appalled.

'The difference is, I don't put the gack in my mouth,' I pointed out. 'I ate a raw oyster once a long time ago, and all I can say is, I haven't felt moved to eat another one. Chewy and slimy, that's what I remember – like a cross between gristle and a loogey.'

'Eww, that's disgusting.' She grimaced. 'Clearly that was not an Apalachicola Bay oyster you had. Probably some inferior product from the Chesapeake or the Pacific Northwest.' She spooned a dollop of horseradish from a tiny paper cup onto the largest of the oysters, squeezed a lemon wedge over it, and then plucked the shell from the plastic tray and waved it in my direction. 'Look, this is a thing of beauty.' The oyster quivered moistly beneath the fluorescent lights. Angie raised the shell to her lips and tipped it up, slurping slightly as the oyster slid into her mouth. She chewed a few times and then swallowed. 'Yum.' She beamed. 'You better move fast, or you'll lose your chance. There's only ten more on the plate.'

'And this is it? This is all we're having for lunch? A dozen raw oysters?'

'Maybe not.' She shrugged. 'We might need two dozen. I'm kinda hungry.'

As Angie reached for another oyster, I noticed a thin, faint line on the side of her index finger. 'How'd you get that scar? Mind my asking?'

She looked puzzled until she saw where I was looking; then, in the space of a few seconds, her face shifted through half a dozen expressions: amusement, wistfulness, sorrow, anger, confusion, peace. 'I nearly chopped off my finger when I was ten,' she said. 'My sister Kate – she was seven at the time – was trying to cut down a tree. She was flailing away at it with a hatchet, but not really doing much beyond bruising the bark. So I took the hatchet from her and said, "Here, let me show you how to do it." I put one hand on the tree, for balance, I guess, and reared back and took a whack. Lucky for me I just caught the edge of my finger with the blade. An inch higher, and my coworkers would be calling me "Stumpy." As it was, I got off with just a few stitches.' She traced the scar with her other index finger, smiling slightly. 'God, I haven't thought about that in years. "Here, let me show you how to do it." Famous last words, huh?' She shook her head. 'We were so close when we were kids. I was so protective of her. How the hell did I let her down so badly? How'd I let her get in so far over her head?' She jabbed at her eyes with the flimsy paper napkin. 'Dammit.' She set the empty shell down on the tray.

I set mine down, too. 'I'm sorry, Angie.' Mortified by my clumsiness, I stared down at the oysters pooled in their brine. 'I didn't mean to remind you of it all over again.'

She shook her head. 'It's okay. How were you supposed to know? Besides, I don't want people tiptoeing around, walking on eggshells for fear they'll say something – who knows *what* – that might remind me of Kate. I'd *hate* that.' She fingered the scar again. 'This is my reminder of an adventure, a story we shared. It's a souvenir I'll carry on my skin for the rest of my life. Like a tattoo, carved by a hatchet. How cool is that? But it gets invisible to me, and I forget it's there. So thanks for reminding me. I'm glad you asked.'

'Me, too, then.' I looked up at her, no longer mortified. 'I won't tiptoe.' An unexpected wave of memory and emotion washed over me suddenly – a rogue wave that hit me almost hard enough to capsize me – and I turned away.

'What? I thought you promised not to tiptoe.'

'I did. I won't.' I turned back toward her. 'I know what it's like when people tiptoe around you. Makes you feel invisible but also hugely conspicuous at the same time.' She waited. 'My father killed himself when I was three.'

Her eyes widened, and she nodded once, very slowly. 'Do you want to tell me about it?'

I shrugged. 'I don't actually know much about it. He'd invested heavily in the commodities market – soybean futures or pork bellies or something; I don't know what. Not just his own money, but a lot of money for other people, too – friends who wanted in on what was starting to look like a sure thing. And then the price went into free fall and he lost everything. He went into his office and shot himself.' I shrugged. 'That's about all I know. We never talked about it. That was the one unspoken rule at my house growing up: don't talk about it; tiptoe around it. '

'Did your mother remarry?'

'She did. Actually, she married my dad's brother, my uncle Charlie.' I smiled. 'Charlie was a fine man. Treated me like a son. I thought of him as my dad; I *called* him Dad. Although . . .' I hesitated again. 'The older I get, the more I miss my father; the more I wonder what kind of relationship I could have had with him. It makes me feel a little disloyal to Charlie, but I miss my father.'

'Nothing disloyal about that,' she said. 'There's room in a heart for a lot of people. I've got another sister, Genevieve – the oldest – who's still alive. Would I have more love to give Genevieve if I didn't still feel love for Kate? I don't think it works that way. I think it works the other way around – I think I've got a bigger heart for Gen because of Kate. And I bet you've got a bigger heart for Charlie because it's growing to take in more of your father. Loss can make you smaller, or it can make you bigger.

Just depends on what you do after it.' She dabbed at her eyes, then looked at the ruins of her napkin and laughed. 'God, they really do need better napkins at this place.'

I lifted my paper cup of iced tea. 'Here's to getting bigger, not smaller.'

She reached for her cup, but didn't lift it. 'You mean that?' There was a mischievous gleam in her eye.

'I do.'

'Let's see about that.' Letting go of the cup, she lifted another oyster from the tray and held it toward me. 'To getting bigger, not smaller.'

'Uh-oh,' I said. 'There's no graceful way out of this for me, is there?'

'The best way out is all the way in.' She grinned.

I studied the remaining oysters. My inclination was to reach again for the smallest. Instead, I forced myself to take a big one. I spooned on a dab of horseradish and squeezed a lemon wedge over it, as I'd seen Angie do, and then – for good measure – sprinkled a dollop of cocktail sauce on top. I lifted it by the edges, careful not to slosh the brine. 'To bigger, not smaller,' I said, clicking my oyster shell against hers. I brought the shell to my lips, feeling the roughness of its outside against my lower lip and the pearly smoothness of the inner shell against my top lip. The shell was cold from the bed of crushed ice in the platter. As I tipped the shell slowly, the brine – salty, lemony, and tangy – trickled into my mouth.

'Don't think about it,' Angie coached from across the

table. 'Just do it.' I tipped the shell higher, and the oyster slithered into my mouth. 'Chew three times, then swallow.' The memory of my one prior oyster tasting came rushing back, and I nearly gagged, but then I bit down, and my distaste and fear were swept away by a wave of flavor and texture that somehow seemed to embody the ocean itself: salty, clean, and – to my amazement – light and slightly crisp. How could an oyster – a mollusk, for heaven's sake – be light and crisp and clean?

I laid the shell down slowly. 'So,' she said, 'what do you think?'

'I think maybe you're right,' I said. 'I think we might need two dozen.'

We were just polishing off the first dozen when Angie's phone rang. 'Hi, Stu. Yeah, we're still here. Y'all come on. But you better hurry. I'm not sure how well stocked Shell's is, and our friend here has decided he likes oysters.'

Vickery brought with him a patrician-looking man who could have been either a well-used sixty or a youthful seventy. He wore silver hair, black suspenders, a red bow tie, and alert, sparkling eyes. He extended a hand as Vickery made a no-nonsense introduction. 'Dr Bill Brockton; Dr Albert Goldman.' I wiped the oyster brine from my hand and shook. 'Dr Goldman teaches law and criminology at FSU's Center for the Advancement of Human Rights,' Vickery told me, although Angie had already briefed me on his credentials while we were waiting, 'and one of his specialties is juvenile justice. If anybody can give you the skinny on reform schools in the 1950s and '60s, it's Al.'

Goldman shook my hand, then eyed the last two oysters on our plate hungrily. 'I hope you told them to save a few dozen of those for me.'

'I can't promise it,' I said. 'You've been welcome to my share up to now, but we might be competing from here on out.'

He grinned. 'I've been a regular here for thirty years. I might have a slight edge if the supply runs short.'

Goldman and Vickery squeezed into chairs alongside Angie and me at the cramped table. Goldman craned his head in search of our waitress, but she was busy with another table at the moment. 'Stu's been guest-lecturing in my criminology classes for the last, what, ten years or so?'

'Hmm. I'd say more like thirteen,' Vickery mused. 'Divorce number one. I remember because I got served with the papers as I was getting into my car to head over to your class for the first time.' He half smiled to himself. 'I was feeling all sorry for myself, then I got to campus and there were all these gorgeous students – way too young for me, but still, seeing them reminded me that there might be life after divorce.' He laughed. 'But that's not what we're here to talk about.'

I smiled. 'It might be more entertaining, though.' I looked at the FSU professor. 'I'm a physical anthropologist, Dr Goldman, so I don't have as much perspective on institutions like prisons and reforms schools as a cultural anthropologist might. I'm trying to wrap my mind about the notion that these two kids – one of them only ten or twelve – might have been killed while they were in protective custody. Is that really a possibility?'

He raised his eyebrows. 'Protective custody? Protective of whom? Whatever gave you the idea that a reform school is in *any* way protective of kids? Reform school is all about protecting the rest of us *from* kids.'

I felt embarrassed, like a student who's given a dumb answer in class. 'Well, I probably misused the term, but if you're trying to reform kids, don't you – the state, I mean, or society – don't you have a responsibility to keep them safe while they're in custody?'

'Oh, naive one,' he said kindly. 'Let me remove a few of the scales from your innocent eyes.' He handed me a photocopy of a newspaper story, which I saw had been printed in a Miami paper in 1961. 'Go ahead, read it,' he encouraged. 'But it might make you lose your lunch.'

BOYS FLOGGED FOR BAD GRADES
Students Beaten Bloody at North Florida Boys' Reformatory

This is not a story for the faint of heart or the weak of stomach.

This is a story about troubled boys, hard men, and the brutal extremes to which 'spare the rod, spoil the child' can be taken in the name of discipline.

Twenty miles outside the north Florida hamlet of McNary sits a cluster of white wooden buildings that has the spare appearance of a small army outpost. The structures were built in the 1930s as a Civilian Conservation Corps work camp, but since 1946 they have housed the North Florida Boys' Reformatory. The institution's bland and hopeful name belies the violence that is one of its regular routines.

Every Saturday morning boys are lined up and taken into a shed beside the school's dining hall. Two by two the boys walk in, but often they must be dragged out, because they cannot walk. Their buttocks and thighs have been reduced to raw, bloody pulp by what can only be described as floggings.

School officials say the punishments meted out to boys are strict but fair. 'We have to maintain discipline,' said the school's superintendent, Marvin Hatfield. 'We have to be firm. Remember, these are not choir boys we're working with. These are boys with a history of getting into trouble. We only punish a boy if he gives us a good reason, and we try not to go overboard.'

But boys and men who have endured or witnessed the punishments paint a different picture, one in which children as young as 11 years of age are beaten savagely with a heavy strap. This reporter spoke with four former students who had spent time at the school within the past five years. None of the four was willing to have his name printed, for fear of reprisals. One young man reported receiving 100 lashes with the strap as a punishment for fighting. The other three said they had received anywhere from 20 to 40 lashes for infractions such as smoking, cursing, or simply making bad grades. 'I made a C in math,' said one, 'and I got 40 licks for that.'

Pressed about the practice of administering beatings for bad grades, Superintendent Hatfield explained and defended the policy. 'We expect boys to apply themselves to their studies and make good grades. If they don't, they receive demerits. If they get too many demerits, they stay here longer. So if a boy is eager to finish up his time and go home, he can volunteer to take a paddling instead of demerits.'

One former school employee offered this description of what Supt. Hatfield calls a paddling. 'They take the boys into the shed two at a time,' said the man, who – like the boys interviewed for this story – was unwilling for his name to be printed. 'There's two guards and two boys. There's a wooden bench and an iron bed in the shed. One boy sits on the bench and waits his turn while the other one is taken to the bed. They make him lie facedown on the mattress and grab hold of the bar at the head of the bed. If he doesn't lie still and quiet the whole time, they start all over again.'

The strap used to administer the beatings is designed to inflict serious pain, according to the man. 'The strap is five feet long and four inches wide, with a wooden handle at one end. It looks like the leather strop that a barber uses to sharpen a straight razor, but it's thicker and heavier than that. It's two layers of leather with a thin layer of metal sewn in between the layers.

'Swinging the strap is a well-honed skill,' he added. 'The guard takes a big windup, like a baseball pitcher or a tennis player. He swings his arm up over his head and then brings it down. The end of the strap whips across the ceiling and down the wall before it hits the boy. You can tell the boy hears it coming, because he'll stiffen up and try to brace for it when he hears it hit the ceiling. There are strap marks all over the ceiling and all down the wall.'

The young man who said he'd received 100 lashes for fighting said it was the worst pain he could imagine. 'I thought I would die,' he said. 'I wished I would die. They had to carry me to the infirmary. I couldn't walk for a week, and I had scabs for a month. I still have the scars. I guess I always will.'

Critics of corporal punishment have repeatedly called for a ban on the practice at the school, but those calls have gone unheeded for years.

And so, year after year, the floggings continue.

'There's blood all over that shed,' said the former school employee. 'There's blood on the floor, blood on the walls, blood on the ceiling. There's blood on people's hands.'

I looked up, and Goldman raised his eyebrows in a question. I handed the article back to him. 'Terrible,' I said. 'Like something out of the Inquisition. Or antebellum slavery.'

'Or Abu Ghraib,' he said. 'Or Gitmo.'

I didn't want to argue the politics. 'But these were kids. Wasn't it illegal?'

'Funny how that worked,' he said. 'Beatings aren't allowed – and weren't allowed back then – in adult prisons. But corporal punishment *was* permissible for juveniles. The rule was – the trick was – it had to be the sort of punishment a "loving parent" would give.'

I tried to reconcile the contradictions, but they were like magnets whose poles couldn't be forced together. 'A loving parent? Beating a twelve-year-old boy a hundred times with a five-foot strap?' I imagined children who were only slightly older than my own grandsons – ages eight and ten – being beaten until they couldn't walk. Goldman was right: the idea nearly made me sick. 'It was torture. How did they keep getting away with it?'

He shrugged. 'Nobody really gave a damn about those kids. Some were orphans, some had parents that were glad to have the state take the kids off their hands for a while, or forever.' He made a face of distaste. 'You know the best way to create career criminals?' He didn't give me much time to consider the question before he supplied the answer himself. 'Bring them into the juvenile justice system to "reform" them.'

'Oh, surely that's too cynical a view,' I argued. 'If they've come to the attention of the juvenile justice system, they're already in trouble, aren't they? It doesn't seem fair to call the system itself part of the problem.'

'*Part* of the problem? The system might be the *whole* problem. America's criminal justice system is like a self-replicating computer virus. There are more than *two million people* behind bars in this country. We have the highest rate of incarceration of any nation on earth.' I'd heard that before, so it wasn't a total surprise, but what Goldman went on to say was a different perspective than I'd heard before. 'By their mid-thirties, one-third of black male high school graduates have spent time behind bars; more than *sixty percent* of black high school dropouts have. You know when that trend began?' I shook my head; I didn't. 'In the 1960s, right around the time the civil rights movement started making headway.' Put in that context, the statistics seemed especially troubling. 'And most of it starts with kids. Train up a child in the way he should go, the proverb says, and when he is old, he will not depart from it.' I'd never heard that repeated with such irony. 'The one thing our juvenile justice system excels at is creating career criminals. That's the biggest predictor for becoming a career criminal: being incarcerated as a juvenile. And the cost of incarcerating juveniles is *huge*, not just for food and guards and barbed wire, but for all those adult prisons we have to build to house them once they're grown-up criminals. We could save a couple of million bucks for every career criminal we *didn't* create, if we'd stop creating them.'

'What about counseling and drug treatment and other

services that kids get once they're part of the system? Don't those make a difference?'

'Interesting question.' He caught the eye of the waitress and beckoned, and she nodded in an I'll-be-right-there sort of way. 'There was a really ambitious and well-funded project in Massachusetts back in the 1930s and '40s – the Cambridge-Somerville Youth Study, it was called. It was designed to identify kids who were at high risk of becoming criminals, and to provide them with all sorts of educational and medical and social services to steer them toward solid, productive lives.' I searched my memory banks for any scrap of knowledge I might have about it, and I came up dry. 'Kids and parents and social-worker types *loved* it,' he went on. 'It became the gold standard, the holy grail, for juvenile services. Kids who completed the program were tracked and interviewed, and years later, they were still saying glowing things about it. Things like, "That program saved my life," and "Without that program, I'd have ended up in prison." Impressive, huh?'

'Sounds great,' I said.

'But here's the kicker. So here's this legendary model program, right? But another twenty years down the road, when the kids were now middle-aged, some new researchers did a follow-up study, and guess what? The kids who'd gotten all that great help actually turned out worse than similar kids who *didn't* get the help. The Cambridge-Somerville kids were more likely to have committed serious crimes, or turned alcoholic, or gone crazy, or died, compared to the control group – a group of other high-risk kids who'd gotten *nothing*. Leaving kids the hell alone turned out to be better for them than this gold-plated program, which actually proved harmful.'

'So you're saying the answer is to do nothing? The best way to keep them from drifting into crime is to look the other way?'

He shrugged. 'You know the biggest single factor that steers boys away from crime? Getting a girlfriend.'

Angie gave a brief laugh. 'So instead of sending them to juvie, we should sign them up for Match.com?'

He smiled. 'Maybe. Delinquency is something kids outgrow – unless we confirm them as "delinquents" and lock them up with other, older delinquents, who teach them worse things; who teach them to be better, badder criminals.'

What he was saying had a certain logic to it, but it seemed to dodge the bigger question of social responsibility. 'But what's the chicken, and what's the egg? How do you separate cause from effect? I mean, kids don't just get randomly snatched up and sent to lockup for no reason. A kid has to do something to get pulled into the system in the first place, right? Steal a car, rob a store, vandalize a school, or *something*?'

'Something,' he conceded. 'But that "something" can be as simple as being defiant at home. Or playing hooky a few times. Or living with a single mother who gets arrested, so the kid gets sent to a foster home, where maybe he gets abused and starts doing drugs and it all goes to hell from there. Tiny, tiny things can start kids spiraling down the rabbit hole, especially if all the kid has done is pick the wrong parents or the wrong color skin or the wrong socioeconomic class.'

I couldn't argue with that. I'd lived long enough to recognize that random luck – good luck and bad luck – could play a big role in shaping a kid's life; after all, what if my grandsons had been born in black skin instead of white skin? Had been born in Darfur or Rwanda instead of in Tennessee? But I wanted an answer, a solution, so I pressed him. 'So what would you do if *you* ran the circus? Just open the cages and let out all the animals?' I'd intended for the second question to be a witty riff on the old cliché, but it came out harsh and judgmental. 'Sorry. I didn't really mean that the way it sounded.' At least, I *hoped* I didn't. He waved off the apology, though I thought I saw a flicker of disappointment in his eyes. 'But seriously, what would you do?'

'I'd light a single candle, and I'd keep cursing the darkness. I'd try to bring evildoers to justice, especially the evildoers who hide behind uniforms.' He took a breath, gearing up. 'I'd redistribute wealth. I'd do away with poverty and disease. I'd close the prisons, and spend all those billions of dollars on schools and health care and jobs instead.' The waitress appeared at our table, and he beamed at her. 'And I'd love a dozen oysters, with extra horseradish and lemon.' She scurried toward the kitchen with the order. 'Sorry to get on my soapbox, but I'm appalled by how much money and how much human potential we squander locking people up. What if society renounced the right to use violence against kids – what if we just said, "We don't do that"?'

'It's a complicated problem,' I acknowledged. 'And except for the oysters, those things you're talking about aren't quick fixes. They'd require fundamental changes in our whole society.'

'God, I sure hope so.'

I nodded at the newspaper article he'd brought me. 'May I keep this?'

'Of course.'

I folded the page and tucked it into my pocket. 'At least this school isn't still in business. Let's hope that sort of brutality is a thing of the past.'

He gave me an ironic smile. 'Martin Lee Anderson.'

'Excuse me?'

'Martin Lee Anderson. Look him up. You won't have any trouble finding him.'

Thirty minutes after I'd happily polished off seven Apalachicola Bay oysters, I settled myself in front of a computer at the Leon County Public Library, in downtown Tallahassee, and typed 'Martin Lee Anderson' into the Google search bar. In a fraction of a second – thirteen one-hundredths of a second, the screen informed me – the search engine found 7,600,000 hits. I clicked on the first one, a Wikipedia entry ominously titled 'Martin Anderson death controversy,' and began to read: 'Martin Lee Anderson (c. January 15, 1991–January 6, 2006) was a 14-year-old from Florida who died while incarcerated at a boot-camp-style youth detention center, the Bay County Boot Camp, located in Panama City, Florida, and operated by the Bay County Sheriff's Office. Anderson collapsed while performing required physical training at the camp. While running track, he stopped and complained of fatigue. The guards coerced him to continue his run, but then he collapsed and died.'

It sounded like a sad accident, but hardly the same sort of abuse as the reform school beatings detailed by the article Goldman had brought me. Over the years, I'd read many stories of teenage athletes – usually high school football players – who died of heatstroke or heart failure during hot summer practices.

But the more I read about Anderson's death, the less it seemed to be simply a sad accident. A YouTube video, taken from a surveillance camera, had recorded how the guards 'coerced' Anderson. The image was grainy, and the view was often obscured by the cluster of guards, but the clip seemed to show the black boy being knocked to the ground, dragged around, and subjected to punches and choke holds by a group of seven guards. During most of the 'coercion' – which continued for half an hour – a nurse stood by and watched; eventually, she knelt down and used a stethoscope to listen for a heartbeat, and after she did, two guards jogged away to summon emergency medics. But by then it was too late.

What I saw on the video was disturbing, but what I read was even more disturbing. The local medical examiner initially ruled that Martin Anderson's death was an accident caused by sickle-cell trait, a blood disorder in African Americans that sometimes distorts red blood cells, limiting their capacity to carry oxygen. But the boy's family and the NAACP challenged the M.E.'s findings and demanded a further investigation. The U.S. Department of Justice launched an investigation, the original medical examiner was fired, and the boy's body was exhumed for a second autopsy by a different M.E. The investigation revealed that Anderson's mouth had been covered by guards while ammonia capsules were held beneath his nostrils. The second M.E. reached a far different conclusion from the first one. With his mouth clamped shut and ammonia fumes repeatedly forced up his nose, Martin Lee Anderson, age fourteen, died of suffocation.

The end of the video clip showed the boy's limp body being hoisted onto a gurney and wheeled away – barely two hours after he'd gotten off the bus for his first day of boot camp.

The more things change, I thought, *the more things stay the same*. No wonder Goldman had given me that sad, ironic smile when I'd said that brutality to kids was a thing of the past.

CHAPTER 10

We'd arranged for Kate Nicely's body to be brought into the embalming room of Morningside Funeral home, figuring it would be equipped with an exhaust fan to remove odors and a floor drain to remove fluids. Thanks to Burton 'Grease' DeVriess and his two degrees of separation from a Georgia judge, the coffin had been freshly exhumed, though I knew that *fresh* would not be a word likely to describe the corpse sealed inside.

When Angie and I arrived, we presented ourselves once again to the receptionist, Lily – whose name, I realized, was perfect for a woman who made her living from the dead. As before, Lily looked flustered by our arrival, or possibly by our mere existence; again, she fled swiftly into the inner sanctum of her boss's office to announce us. Once more, the lugubrious Samuel Montgomery emerged, and I asked if everything was ready for us.

'We have a slight, ah, problem,' Montgomery breathed, causing me to have a powerful sense of déjà vu, a sensation that only intensified when Angie asked what *sort* of problem we had. 'Well . . .' He hesitated. 'I don't know if you were aware of this, but we were not able to embalm the, ah, deceased.'

'My sister, you mean,' said Angie sharply. 'You weren't able to embalm my sister. Because her head was blown off?' Montgomery drew back. 'Or because her husband hustled her into the ground so fast?'

'Both the, ah, nature of her injuries and the timing of the arrangements made embalming impossible,' he said. 'As a result, we're unable to bring the body inside. The, ah, odor is quite strong.' From the look of distress on his face, he might almost have been experiencing the odor at this very moment. He looked from Angie, whose face was a stony mask, to me. 'Surely you can understand? When people come here to pay their last respects, they don't want . . .' He trailed off.

Angie finished the sentence for him. 'They don't want it to smell like somebody's *died*?'

Montgomery sighed. 'Well, yes, if you insist. The entire *building* would smell.'

I could understand Angie's edginess, but I could also appreciate his dilemma. 'So what do you suggest?'

'We have a maintenance building for the cemetery,' he said. 'A garage and shop area. It's not fancy, but there's electrical power. Fluorescent lights. Water. No air-conditioning,' he added apologetically, 'but fans, which would help keep the air moving through.'

'That's fine with me,' I said. 'Angie?'

She started to say something, then bit it back and simply nodded.

*

142

The bad news was, Morningside's maintenance shop was a corrugated metal building that soaked up the midday sun, creaking and popping as it expanded in the heat. The good news was, the ceiling was high, and the thick concrete slab under our feet still retained a trace of the spring's coolness. The better news was, the building had a garage door in the front and another directly opposite it, in back, and the fans Montgomery had mentioned – a pair of industrial-sized blowers with blade assemblies that might have come off a small aircraft – transformed the funeral home's shop into a cross between a landscaper's shed and a NASA wind tunnel. Montgomery had placed the coffin on a wooden workbench, which was about waist-high. As he unscrewed the lid and tilted it off, I caught a strong whiff of decomposition, but the smell swirled away swiftly, sucked out of the building and mixing with the scent of the longleaf pines and honeysuckle vines and road-killed deer and armadillos of south Georgia and north Florida.

The coffin was a bottom-of-the-line model, made of cloth-covered particleboard. It had not been sealed in a watertight burial vault, so the fabric was caked with mud and the particleboard was already becoming waterlogged. My work had trained me not to sentimentalize death or the trappings of funerals, but I couldn't help thinking how little this woman must have mattered to her husband, so swiftly and so cheaply had he put her in the ground.

We'd been joined by a Cheatham County deputy – a hangdog-looking fellow named Chumley – and a grizzled death investigator named Maddox from the Georgia Bureau of Investigation. A former police detective who'd retired after thirty years of interrogating homicide suspects, Maddox had recently embarked on a new career of observing victims' autopsies. Assigned to the medical examiner at the GBI's central-region lab in Dry Branch, Georgia – a small town just east of Macon – Maddox had driven south three hours to join us, and he wasn't happy about it. 'Hell,' he said, 'this would've been only thirty minutes from the southwestern lab, in Moultrie.'

I asked the obvious question. 'Then why didn't Moultrie send somebody?'

'Nobody in Moultrie to send anymore,' he grumbled. 'We closed that lab last spring. Budget cuts. The main lab and the other regional labs are swamped, and there's a big backlog of evidence from local law enforcement agencies. Penny wise, pound foolish, if you ask me. But nobody did.' He smiled ruefully. 'Including you. Sorry to spout off.'

'It's okay,' I said, turning my attention to Kate's body.

Her face was beginning to droop, but it was largely intact. Her front teeth were snapped, as I'd expected, from the abrupt kick of the shotgun barrel, but the skin of her face was unbroken. The undertaker who'd arranged the body in the casket – Montgomery himself, he confirmed when I asked – had propped the head in an

144

approximation of a normal resting position. To do that, he'd used a small cylindrical pillow to fill the space formerly occupied by the base of the skull and the back of the neck. That pillow, like the bigger, rectangular one beneath it, was damp with blood and body fluids. I leaned down and turned the head gently to one side with my gloved hands. It flopped easily; the base of the skull and much of the cervical spine had been blasted away, and what remained of the head was attached to the body only by the soft tissue of the throat.

The only sounds were the groans of the building and the whoosh of the fans, but I was acutely conscious of Angie beside me, as motionless but as tense as a bear trap primed to snap with bone-crushing force. I stepped aside to give her a moment. I'd expected her to be overwhelmed with grief, but instead she seemed to draw strength from the sight of her sister's body. It seemed as if she grew taller and stronger, somehow; her eyes glittered with anger, and her mouth twitched with what I'd have sworn was a grim smile. 'I'd thought it'd be hard to see Kate's body,' she said, 'but this isn't my sister anymore. This is just evidence now.'

After a moment she nodded, and then she, Montgomery, Maddox, and I lifted the body out of the casket – Chumley begged off helping, citing a bad back – and shifted it onto a metal gurney. Next I retrieved the soggy pillows and repositioned them beneath the head and neck.

Angie had brought a camera, and she began taking

photos – wide shots, medium shots, close-ups, dozens of them – documenting the damage done by the blast. Carefully I tilted and rotated the head, then rolled the body onto its stomach so Angie could capture the wound from all angles. I'd found streaks of lead on a few of the bone fragments I'd recovered from the cleanup company's biohazard boxes, but the exposed edges of the bones of the skull and neck – portions of the third cervical vertebra and the top of the fourth vertebra – showed no signs of lead. That didn't surprise me; I knew from other gunshot deaths I'd worked that the shotgun slug itself would punch straight through, but the force of the air pressure and burning gases would create a wider cone of destruction. After Angie had thoroughly photographed the wound from every possible distance and direction, I placed the body faceup again, replicating how she'd lain on her sofa the night she died. Maddox kept quiet, but he watched closely; Chumley, meanwhile, had excused himself to 'check in with the dispatcher'; evidently checking in was a detailed procedure, because the deputy never reappeared.

We had brought with us a wooden dowel, three feet long by an inch in diameter, as a stand-in for the shotgun. Angie had suggested bringing an actual gun, but I managed to dissuade her, on the grounds that it would be physically harder to handle than the dowel. I'd stopped short of adding 'emotionally harder, too'; that, I felt sure, went without saying. I threaded the dowel through the jaws and out the back of the head, positioning the end – the 'muzzle' of the dowel, so to speak – on the pillow directly at the center of the circle of missing flesh and shattered bone. Assuming the slug and explosive gases had emerged from the gun barrel in a symmetrical pattern, centering the end of the dowel would show us the angle of the gun when it was fired.

I checked and rechecked the position, and turned to Angie, who was taking more photos. 'Does that look centered to you?' She lowered the camera, crouched to study the dowel's position on the pillow, and adjusted the angle by a fraction of a degree. Then she frowned and put it back exactly where I'd had it.

During the past twenty years, I'd examined three shotgun suicides. In all three cases, the barrel had been angled upward, at roughly a forty-five-degree angle, with the butt of the stock down around waist level. But unless I'd badly misjudged the geometry, in this case the gun had intersected Kate's body at a ninety-degree angle, and the shot had been fired from straight on: an unnatural and awkward angle.

Suddenly one of the death-scene photos – the ones taken by the sheriff's deputy the day Kate had died – sprang unbidden to my mind. I turned to Angie. 'You brought in the folder you've been keeping on your sister, didn't you?'

She nodded at the end of the workbench. 'Got it right here. Why?'

'Let's take another look at the photos the deputy took.' She set down the camera, opened the file, and slowly flipped through the handful of pictures. I looked over her left shoulder; Maddox looked over her right. 'That one,' I said, when she reached the next-to-last photo. It was a close-up of the business end of the shotgun. I laid the dowel on the gurney and peered at the picture, wishing I had a magnifying glass. 'There,' I said, pointing a purple-gloved pinky at a small metal peg jutting up from the gun barrel. 'What's that?'

'That? That's the gun sight.'

'No, I mean what's that *on* the gun sight?' Snagged on the peg was what appeared to be a shred of pink lint. But it wasn't lint; it was human tissue. That in itself wasn't surprising, since the blast had spattered a lot of blood and tissue. Still, something about the way it hung from the sight nagged at me; it appeared not so much spattered as torn. I took a final squint at the photo, then turned and inspected Kate's mouth. On the inner surface of the left cheek I found it: a horizontal laceration about half an inch long, extending to the corner of the mouth. It was exactly the sort of laceration the sight might make as the gun barrel kicked. I showed the laceration to Angie, then gave Maddox a chance to look. 'Anything about this strike you as odd?'

Angie bit her lip to concentrate, and her eyes darted back and forth from the photo to the corpse as she tried to work it out. I'm sure she would have, given another minute, but I couldn't wait. 'You'd think the gun sight might gouge the roof of her mouth, or knock an extra chip from one of her top teeth, or maybe gash her upper lip, right?' She nodded, frowning. 'But the *corner* of her mouth?' I picked up the dowel and reinserted it. 'That means the gun was twisted in her mouth, like so.' I rotated the dowel a quarter turn counterclockwise. 'Which would have made it even harder to hold at that angle. You see what that means? It means that the gun wasn't fired by the person lying *on* the sofa.'

'It means,' she said as Maddox reached for his phone, 'that the gun was fired by a person standing *beside* the sofa.'

An hour later, Kate Nicely was sealed once more in her cheap coffin. Maddox had arranged for her to be taken, in the back of a Morningside hearse, to Dry Branch, Georgia.

Me, I would be headed for Washington, D.C., early the next morning. While Kate was headed for the GBI lab, I was bound for the Smithsonian Institution, and I was taking with me the second skull, that of the African-American boy whose left mastoid process had been shattered.

CHAPTER 11

The computer mouse scrolled down a list of files, and a click later, the screen filled with the life-sized likeness of a skull: the likeness of the second skull Winston Pettis's dog had dragged home from the Florida woods. Joseph Mullins, a forensic-imaging specialist, wiggled his mouse, and the skull's intricate image rotated on the screen as if spinning in space. I'd seen many CT scans of skulls in the past few years, but I never ceased to marvel at their detail.

I had hoped to coax another swift facial reconstruction out of Joanna Hughes before she started her maternity leave, but Joanna's baby had other ideas: the day after she finished the androgynous face I'd taken back to Tallahassee, she'd gone into labor, and had given birth to a beautiful daughter. So instead of sending the second skull to Knoxville, I'd brought it instead to Alexandria, Virginia, home of the National Center for Missing and Exploited Children. My presence here at Mullins's elbow wasn't necessary; in fact, it was probably a time-wasting distraction for him. For me, though, it was a fascinating and eye-opening experience. I'd spent fifty thousand frequent-flier miles for my plane ticket from

Tallahassee to Washington, D.C. – a foolish waste of miles, by any rational measure. But by my reckoning, time was short, the miles had been gathering dust anyhow, and the chance to watch Mullins work was well worth the hasty trip.

I'd started the morning, bright and early, by renewing my acquaintance with the TSA screeners at the Tallahassee airport. I knew to ask for the supervisor by name as soon as I approached the checkpoint, and, perhaps not surprisingly, he remembered me from my prior trip. I'd tried to get a laugh from him by asking, 'Do you want to search my carrion bag?' – I all but dug my elbow into his ribs as I said 'carrion' – but he obviously didn't catch the pun.

From Tallahassee I'd flown – through Atlanta, of course – to D.C.'s National Airport. I'd spent a pleasant, productive lunchtime with Ed Ulrich, a former student of mine, who was now a physical anthropologist at the Smithsonian Institution. Borrowing from the Smithsonian's vast collection of skulls, Ed had found a mandible that articulated nicely with the cranial vault of the black Florida teenager. Once we'd cobbled the pieces together, one of the Smithsonian's radiology technicians had run the skull through the museum's CT scanner. After that, Ed had steered me here, to the high-tech office of Joe Mullins.

Mullins, like Joanna Hughes, was skilled at re-creating human faces on bare skulls, guided by the architecture of the bone itself and by my insights about the boy's age, race, and sex. Over the years, the National Center for Missing and Exploited Children – whose initials, NCMEC, were pronounced 'NICK-meck' – had gained renown for its 'age progressions' of missing children's photos. Starting with the last or best photos of a missing child, NCMEC's age-progression artists created images showing how that child might look two years later, and four years later, and so on, up to early adulthood. Their results spoke for themselves: their age-progression photos had made it possible for people to recognize and identify hundreds of missing children, sometimes many years after they'd disappeared.

But facial reconstruction was a newer and smaller niche at NCMEC, and Mullins was the only artist on staff who filled it. His method was a fascinating combination of old-school artistry and gee-whiz technology. He had a degree in fine art, but his workstation was straight out of *Star Trek*. To the right of his monitor stood a gizmo that looked like a small robotic arm – an arm with two elbows instead of just one, and a penlike stylus on the end where a hand ought to go. My assistant, Miranda, frequently used a similar-looking device, a 3-D digitizing probe, in the UT bone lab. Miranda used it to take measurements of skulls: all she had to do was touch the tip of the probe to prominent points, or landmarks, on the skull – the bridge of the nose, the tip of the chin, the cheekbones, the brow ridge, the crown of the head, and so on – and the digitizing probe would capture the spatial coordinates. Once she'd touched all the landmarks, the skull's key dimensions would be recorded in our forensic data bank, which contained measurements from thousands of other skeletons. If the skull was an unknown – a John or Jane Doe, rather than a Body Farm donor whose identity was already known to us – our ForDisc software could then tell us the likely race and the sex of the unknown skull by comparing it to measurements from known skulls. ForDisc gave us a computerized way of doing, in a matter of minutes, what it had taken me decades to learn to do. I still made my own judgments, and I tended to make them faster than Miranda could digitize the measurements and run the software. ForDisc was a useful backup, though . . . and once, when the software and I had disagreed about the race of an unknown skull (I'd said 'white' and ForDisc had said 'black'), I'd been wrong and ForDisc had been right.

But NCMEC's digital arm had a very different use than ours did. As I watched, Mullins gripped the stylus and used it to move the computer's cursor – a tiny icon shaped like the stylus – to a drop-down menu on one side of the screen. There, he latched onto a small cylindrical shape representing a tissue-depth marker and dragged it over to the CT image of the skull, then stuck it onto the bridge of the nose. He swiftly repeated the process with more markers, which he attached to other landmarks along the midline of the skull: the top of the head, the center of the forehead, the brow ridge, the end of the nasal bone, the tip of the chin, and the indentation between the base of the nose and the top teeth. He moved the stylus swiftly and fluidly, with no wasted movements, but I found myself wondering how he knew exactly when to click the button that seemed to transfer the markers from the stylus to the skull. 'Do you just hover over the right spot? How do you let go of the marker and get it to stick to the skull?'

'I'm just pressing it on,' he said. 'I feel it when I bump up against the bone.' He saw me puzzling to take this in. 'Here, try it.' He rolled his chair to the side and allowed me to take his place at the computer and grip the stylus. I moved it tentatively back and forth, up and down, in and out, and then in a series of spirals. It moved freely, almost weightlessly, in all directions, with virtually no friction, as the tiny icon flitted and spiraled across the computer screen, floating around and above the image of the skull.

'That's cool,' I said, 'but I still don't quite get how you transfer the depth markers onto the skull.'

'Move it in closer, all the way onto the skull.'

'But how will I know when I'm there?'

He smiled. 'You'll know.' I centered the stylus over the forehead and eased it forward, as the icon on the screen mimicked the movement. 'Just shove it,' he urged. 'Don't worry; you can't hurt it.' I pushed the stylus forward; the arm swung freely . . . and then stopped as abruptly and firmly as if it had hit a wall. I pulled it back toward me, then moved it forward again. Again it jolted to a stop when the small icon bumped the forehead. Intrigued, I slid it downward, feeling both friction and undulations as it moved over the contours of the forehead and the brow ridge. Suddenly, as I dragged the stylus across the lower edge of the brow ridge, the arm slid forward and the stylus icon plunged into the right eye orbit. As I watched, astonished, it careened through the opening at the back of the orbit – the opening through which the optic nerve had once connected with the brain – and disappeared from view. I tried pulling it back out, but it resisted my efforts.

'Help,' I squawked. 'What have I done?'

Mullins laughed. 'You're trapped inside the cranial vault now. You can come out where you went in, or out the nasal opening, or even out the foramen magnum at the base of the skull, where the spinal cord comes out. I'm guessing you know all the emergency exits from a skull.'

I moved the invisible stylus in various directions, but didn't manage to free it from the cavity where I'd trapped it. As I struggled to free it, I found myself growing nervous, verging on panic. What if I'd broken the system, trapped the stylus in some permanent, irretrievable way? Finally it occurred to me to close my eyes and move the stylus by feel, exploring the inner contours of the cranial vault. In my mind's eye, I replaced the stylus with a tiny version of myself – a miniature spelunker within the cavern of a cranium – sliding my hands around the rough-surfaced perimeter, reaching overhead to feel the top of the vault, bending down to probe the gaping pit of the foramen magnum that opened at my tiny feet. My brief panic gave way to delight. The contours fascinated me; as I retraced the right side of the cranial vault, I felt the zigzag seam of the cranial suture where the frontal bone joined the parietal, then, just behind that, the grooves where the middle meningeal artery had once run, bringing blood to the brain. If this had been the first skull Pettis's dog had found, I might have been able to feel the subtle fracture line that intersected the groove. But this was the second, more damaged skull, so I felt my way to the left side of the parietal bone, where the mastoid process had been broken off by a powerful blow. Sure enough, the stylus snagged on the ragged edges of the break, and I winced as I imagined a slow-motion version of the bone's shattering.

'This skull was brought home by a dog,' I told Mullins. 'We're still looking for the rest of the bones.'

He nodded. 'One of the first reconstructions I did was a case like that,' he said. 'A dog in Vermont found a skull somewhere in the woods. The sheriff's office looked and looked, but they couldn't find anything else. Finally they put a tracking collar on the dog, hoping he'd go back for more.'

'And did he?'

'Nope. They never found anything more than the skull.

But we got an identification from the reconstruction. Turns out it was a severely retarded boy who'd been killed by his dad. People thought the boy had been put in an institution somewhere, but he'd been murdered and dumped in the woods instead.'

'It's possible that this boy, our boy here, was institutionalized and then murdered,' I said. 'A reform school. A mighty grim one, by all accounts.' I continued feeling my way around the interior of the cranial vault. 'This is amazing.' I'd spent thirty years examining skulls – usually their exteriors, though sometimes their interiors as well – but never before had I explored one in this way, as if I were a spelunker in a cave. The experience was mesmerizing and moving: an intensely intimate encounter with the skull of this unknown young man. Finally, after what must have been several minutes, I realized I was holding up progress on the reconstruction. I imagined the location of the foramen magnum and then imagined myself as a cliff diver, diving down into a small pool of deep water, swimming downward and out to the side. I opened my eyes just as the stylus reappeared on the left side of the skull, hovering roughly where the ear had once been.

'Amazing,' I said again. 'I could spend hours doing that.'

'It's addictive,' he agreed. 'Like a video game, only real.'

'Ever see that sci-fi movie *Fantastic Voyage*?'

'Sure, I have it on DVD.' He grinned. 'A submarine full of scientists gets shrunk down to the size of a molecule and injected into a guy's bloodstream.'

'Right. What is it they need to do? Blast a brain tumor with a laser beam?'

'Close; a blood clot,' he corrected, 'in the brain of a Russian defector. Cool movie. The wonders and perils of the human body. Wouldn't that be cool, if we could actually take that trip?' I liked this kid.

Reluctantly I scooted my chair aside and turned the computer back over to him. 'Okay, it's all yours. How long will it take you to do the reconstruction?'

'Depends. A week, best case. Two weeks, if you hang around and help.' He laughed.

'Never fear,' I said. 'I've got to get back to Tallahassee. But if you can pretend I'm not here right now, I'd love to look over your shoulder for a few minutes while you work on this.'

'Be my guest. I'll get the rest of these depth markers on pretty quickly, then start sculpting the muscles of the face.'

In a matter of minutes – or so it seemed, though maybe it was longer and I just lost track of time – the skull bristled with rodlike depth markers projecting from its landmarks. Thin-skinned areas, such as the forehead, nasal bridge, and chin, sported nubby little markers, less than an eighth of an inch thick; in the fleshier regions of the cheeks and lower jaw, the markers jutted out nearly an inch. Ten markers were positioned along the skull's midline, and another eleven were arrayed on each side. Mullins rotated the skull to make sure he'd not omitted any, slowly at first, then faster, like a gruesome version of a spinning top.

After a few moments the skull slowed and stopped, facing forward. Then, using the stylus in click-and-drag mode again, Mullins began grabbing strands of virtual clay from the left side of the screen and pressing them onto the skull's right cheek. As more and more strands angled downward from the cheekbone toward the corners of the mouth, I realized that they represented bundles of muscle fibers. 'So you sculpt every muscle, one by one? You can't just put on a layer of clay and contour it to the thickness of the depth markers?'

He shook his head. 'Nope. Well, you can – I've tried that, and yeah, it's a lot faster – but it doesn't look right. You just can't fake the contours of the face. You've got to lay the foundation of muscles underneath the skin. No easy shortcuts.'

Fiber by fiber, as I stood and watched, Mullins continued sculpting in virtual clay. Finally I eased away silently so as not to distract him again. The muscle he was creating as I left was the zygomaticus: the muscle that had once tugged this murdered black boy's mouth into a smile.

It had been a long, long time since he'd used that muscle.

CHAPTER 12

The high-powered, high-tech worlds of the Smithsonian Institution and the National Center for Missing and Exploited Children seemed far away as Angie and I bumped and slewed down the dirt road to Winston Pettis's north Florida cabin for the third time. I hoped this time would prove to be a charm. I'd retrieved my truck from the Tallahassee airport at ten the night before – had it really been only fifteen hours since I'd boarded the flight to D.C.? – and had staggered into bed at the Hampton Inn, which I'd persuaded Angie was more comfortable (and more affordable) than the posh Duval. She'd fetched me at midmorning and – after a quick errand at a sporting-goods store – we'd headed to Pettis's neck of the Florida woods.

As we rolled west again on the long, straight stretches of Highway 90, Angie handed me photocopied pages, covered with an uneven, barely legible scrawl. I felt a rush of adrenaline. 'Is this what I think it is?'

She nodded.

The soggy book had not, she told me, responded well to the methanol soak the documents examiner had tried. After Flo had soaked it in the alcohol and redried it, it had become an even more brittle brick of fused paper. So she'd begun a laborious deconstruction process, one that would require reinforcing and then peeling off the sheets of paper one at a time.

After carefully teasing off the fiberboard cover, she'd pasted a sheet of Japanese tissue onto the first page in the book – a blank one – by brushing a thin layer of wheat-starch paste onto the tissue. The tissue itself was as thin and transparent as gossamer, yet it was remarkably strong, according to Flo. It was handmade in Japan from the inner bark of the *kozo*, or paper mulberry, whose fibers were pounded with boards to break them into individual strands. Pasted to a weak, pulpy page of the diary, the Japanese tissue provided a near-invisible web of reinforcement, allowing her to peel off a sheet without tearing it. Thus it was, page by page, a few painstaking sheets a day – paste, dry, peel; paste, dry, peel – that Flo hoped to crack whatever secrets were coded within the buried book.

As I read the words scrawled on the pages, I felt my heart begin to pound.

I cant write much. If they catch me at it Ill get a whipping for sure.

I found this notebook behind the nurses desk when I was sweeping up. It had fell between the desk and the wall and it look like it had been there a long time because there was spiderwebs and dead bugs on it. so I think she forgot about it a long time ago and will not miss it. there was a pencil stub in her trash can. and this Prince Albert tobacco can in the dump. I don't know why somebody would throw away this can. It has a picture of Prince Albert in a fancy coat and hat, and the lid fits tight, just like on a paint can, but there's a little metal key like a bottle opener that slides clear around the top of the can so you can pry the lid open whenever you want to. The can still smells good when I open it. Theres a few bits of tobacco down in the bottom. I thought about cleaning them out when I first found the can but I'm glad I didn't because I like the way it smells.

Papaw use to smoke Prince Albert and his cloths and his car always smelled like this. One time when I was little I asked him could I take a puff on his pipe. He laughed at me and said lord no, boy, youd be sick as a dog. I didnt believe him so I kept asking and asking until finely he let me. The smoke made me cough and get dizzy and then I threw up. Papaw laughed when I was coughing but when I threw up he felt bad for me. then my ma heard me and came outside. she got mad at me for smoking and got mad at Papaw for him letting me smoke. A 7 year old child should not be smoking she said, and a old man with no teeth should know better than to let him. you both need a good thrashing to beat some sense into you. Papaw said go right ahead but she had better start with him first, and he reckoned even if he was a old man with no teeth, he bet he could still turn her over his knee like he used to when she was just a little shit-tail. she looked even madder when he told her that, but she never whipped me then. she waited till the next day, when he was gone, and then she whipped me twice as hard.

I can smoke without coughing now. Even cigarets, but I dont smoke much. For one thing its hard to get cigarets here, you have to steal them from one of the guards or staff, and if you get caught stealing it might be the last thing you ever do. Stealing or trying to run away, those are the surest ways to wind up in the bone yard. Thats what Jared Mcwhorter told me, and hes been here almost a year. So he should know. Besides I dont even like the taste of the smoke. its just something to do.

We got a new boy yesterday, Buck. He is from over at Perry, which is east of Tallahassee, he said. He got caught throwing rocks through some church windows, which is worse than what I done, which was only playing hookie. But it still dont seem worth sending him to this place for. so he mustve got in trouble before. or maybe hes a orphan and they didn't want him at the orphanage no more. I will find out when I can. but I have to be careful about talking to him. You can get the shit beat out of you for talking. Talking dont get you in as much trouble as smoking, and for sure not as much as stealing or running. But talking is not worth a beating.

there is nigger boys here, but not in our building.
they are in some other buildings just down the road. I
wonder if they get treated as bad as what we do.

I have to stop now or Ill be in trouble for taking me
so long to take the trash to the dump. Writing is not
worth a beating. But I will write again when I can.

'Amazing,' I said. 'Scary. What do you suppose he means by "bone yard"?'

'Whatever he means, I'm sure it's not good.' Angie shook her head. 'Poor kid.'

'Kids,' I said. 'Plural. He's just the one who's writing it down.'

We turned off the highway for the blacktop county road, then turned down the dirt lane to Pettis's cabin.

Jasper bayed and bounded out to greet us, rearing up and resting his paws on the sill of Angie's open window. Winston Pettis shambled down the steps and leaned his elbows on my window. 'Howdy, Doc; Miss Angie,' he drawled through the opening. 'What brings you out this way today? Jasper call y'all to say he'd found anything new?'

'Not exactly,' Angie began as we got out and Jasper inspected her more thoroughly and personally, 'but we're hoping maybe he will soon. We sure would like to find where those skulls came from.'

'Well, I know Jasper'd be glad to tell you where he found it, if he could. I wish he could talk.'

'That'd make our job a lot easier,' she agreed. 'But since he can't tell us, we're wondering if he might be able to show us.'

'Show you?' Pettis looked puzzled. 'I reckon he'd be glad to, but how you gonna get him to do it?'

She smiled. 'That's where we'd like to ask a favor of you, Mr Pettis. Would you be willing for us to put a tracking collar on him, see where he goes for a few days? Maybe he'll bring back another bone, and we can back-track. See where he got it.' She'd latched onto the idea when I mentioned the Vermont case that Joe Mullins had told me about. Vickery had endorsed giving the technology a try, given that there seemed to be nothing to lose. So while Vickery had headed off to interview local old-timers about the North Florida Boys' Reformatory, Angie and I had returned to Pettis's cabin in hope of conducting a field study of canine carrion foraging.

Pettis rubbed the back of his neck, then rubbed the stubble on his chin. 'You're not talking about one of them shock collars, are you? I wouldn't feel right about putting a shock collar on Jasper.'

'No, sir,' Angie assured him. 'I'm talking about a GPS tracking collar. Hunters use 'em to keep track of where their bird dogs or coonhounds are. I've got one right here in the truck, if you'd like to see it.' Without waiting for an answer, she returned to the truck and grabbed the collar and receiver from the backseat. The collar itself was a black nylon band, about an inch wide, with the word *Garmin* in white letters on one side. A black plastic housing, about twice the thickness of a shotgun shell, was attached to the lower part of the collar, and a six-inch flexible black antenna stuck up from the top. Pettis eyed the rig doubtfully. 'See, there's a GPS receiver in the collar,' Angie explained. 'It pinpoints the dog's position by comparing signals from a network of satellites up in the sky.' She paused, giving him a chance to ask questions, but he didn't. 'There's also a transmitter in the collar that sends us a signal every few seconds, telling us where he is,' she went on. She showed Pettis the handheld receiver, which was about twice the size of my cell phone. 'This display screen shows us where he is.' She held out the screen for his inspection. 'The black triangle in the middle of the map is the location of this receiver. See that little picture of the dog, beside it? That shows us he's right here.'

Pettis looked at her dubiously. 'I know he's right here, Miss Angie. I'm lookin' at him. And I know that receiver's right here. I'm lookin' at it, too.'

Angie laughed good-naturedly. 'Okay, this isn't a very good demonstration. You willing for us to put it on Jasper, so you can get a better idea how it works?' Pettis frowned. 'It'll just take a minute,' she cajoled.

'And you're sure it won't hurt him?'

'It won't hurt him a bit. I promise.'

'Well. All right, then. If he's willing. Jasper, you willing to try that thing on?'

Angie handed the collar to Pettis. 'Jasper, set on down,' he said. The dog sat, and Pettis strapped it on, frowning and shaking his head. 'I sure wouldn't want to wear it,' he said. 'Jasper, you sure about this?' The dog cocked his head, and Pettis laughed. 'Well, if you don't care, I reckon I shouldn't care.'

Angie said, 'So, does he like to chase sticks?'

'Who, Jasper?' Pettis guffawed. 'Jasper likes to take naps. You want to track him takin' a nap?'

She smiled. 'You particular about what he eats?'

'Well, I don't much like it when he brings skulls into the bed,' Pettis said. 'Besides that, I don't much care. He's a dog, you know?'

Angie opened the back door of the truck again and leaned in. When she emerged, she had a hamburger patty in her hand, which we'd procured at McDonald's on our way. 'Hey, Jasper,' she cooed, waving the burger near him. The dog's head snapped around and his nostrils flared. 'Want a treat?' She made another quick pass with the burger near his nose, too quick for him to make a grab. 'Want it? Huh, Jasper, you want it?' She waved the burger back and forth as she said it. The dog's eyes were locked on the burger like a fighter plane's targeting radar, and his head swiveled in perfect sync with the movement of the patty. 'You ready, Jasper?' She cocked her arm back. 'Go get it, Jasper!' With that, she flung the burger across the clearing and into the brush. The dog tore after it. 'See,' she said, pointing to the screen.

She'd zoomed it in as close as it would go. The small dog icon, which had been superimposed on the triangle, suddenly flashed to a new position, halfway across the screen. As Jasper snuffled his way through the bushes, the icon moved every five seconds. Then, after a brief pause that was punctuated by loud smacking noises in the underbrush, the icon made its way back to the triangle, arriving shortly after Jasper did.

'Okay,' Pettis conceded, 'looks like it works, close up, anyhow. How far away can that thing see him?'

'Seven miles, says the company that makes it,' said Angie. 'That's if the terrain's flat and there's nothing in the way between the collar and the receiver.' She scanned the flat terrain around the cabin. 'We might need to find a piece of higher ground to get better line-of-sight reception. Anyplace nearby that's higher up?'

'Hell, yeah,' he said. 'How about a hunnerd fifty feet higher up? There's a old fire tower right over yonder.' He pointed. 'I'd check the stairs and the floorboards pretty careful before I trusted it, but it looks to be in pretty fair shape, at least from the ground.'

Angie cocked her head, much as the dog had done a few minutes before. 'So you're willing for us to track Jasper for a few days, see where he goes, see if he brings another bone back from one of those places?'

'Sure, why not,' he said. 'On one condition.'

'What condition?'

'If he shows you where the rest of them bones are,

you've got to give him another hamburger. Sound reasonable?'

'You drive a hard bargain, Mr Pettis.' Angie laughed, and they shook hands. 'We'll get somebody out here to check the tower later today. Oh, we'll need to change the battery in the collar every couple days. Is that okay?'

Pettis scratched his stubble again. 'That might require some additional compensation,' he said. Angie looked worried. 'Better make it a cheeseburger.'

'You and Jasper drive a hard bargain, Mr Pettis. But you've got me over a barrel. A cheeseburger it is.'

He grinned. 'Pleasure doing business with you, Miss Angie.'

Breakfast anytime, promised the marquee of the Waffle Iron, a glass-fronted cinder-block diner on the main street of Sinking Springs, the tiny county seat of Bremerton County. The sign appeared to date from the 1950s or early '60s; the diner's name was outlined in script by glowing tubes of neon, and so was the profile of a cartoonish chef, who wore a puffy white hat and served up a golden neon waffle. Underneath the sign's offer of breakfast were two alternatives: *Lunch Specials* and *Fried Cat*. It was only when I did a double take that I noticed the word *Fish* tucked on a separate line underneath. The fried cat must have been pretty tasty, because the parking lot was packed fender to fender with pickups and SUVs.

After our errand at Pettis's, Angie and I had returned to explore the ruins of the school further while Vickery mined the courthouse records for information about the reform school, or old-timers who might still remember it. We rendezvoused with him shortly after dark in the Waffle Iron's parking lot.

Every head in the diner swiveled in our direction when we entered, sizing us up frankly and reminding us clearly that we were outsiders. Angie and I ignored the stares; Vickery took the opposite tack, nodding and waving amiably at various patrons, as though they'd greeted him in a friendly way. We ran this visual gauntlet to a back corner of the diner, where a booth had just opened up. As we slid onto the plastic benches, Angie and Vickery with their backs to the wall, the clatter of silverware and chatter of conversation gradually resumed.

The waitress who came to take our order was young, slightly plump, and pretty. I saw her taking the measure of the three of us – glancing at our ring fingers, considering whether Angie was married to either Vickery or me. She must have decided Vickery was fair game, because when she asked for his order, she flashed him a dimpled smile that was orders of magnitude brighter than the token one she'd given me. She held the pen a few inches above the order pad and tilted her head slightly to one side, raptly waiting his decision. 'And what would you like, sir?'

Vickery slowly removed the cigar from the corner of

his mouth. 'I'm open to suggestions,' he said. 'What would you say is the tastiest thing on the menu?'

The waitress reddened slightly, but her smile broadened. 'I'd say it depends on what you're in the mood for.'

I saw Angie's eyes roll in disgust. She turned to Vickery and laid a hand on his arm. 'Do tell us, *darling*, what you're in the mood for.'

Vickery glared at her. 'I'm not sure, *sweetheart*,' he said, 'but weren't you planning on having a little humble pie for dessert?' Angie laughed, and the waitress – undone by the exchange – dialed down her demeanor from flirtatious to businesslike. Angie ordered the chicken-salad plate, Vickery got fried eggs and bacon, and I decided to try the fried cat.

As the waitress scurried away to put in our order, Vickery nibbled his cigar briefly, then took it out and frowned at it. The tip was crumbling, and flecks of soggy tobacco clung to his lips and tongue. He laid the cigar across the ashtray, pulled a few napkins from the black-and-chrome dispenser, and swabbed his mouth. 'So tell me, Doc,' he said, 'what put the "forensic" in anthropology for you? How come you're hanging out with cops instead of fossil hunters or museum donors?'

'One thing led to another,' I said. 'Early in my career – while I was still working on my PhD dissertation – I spent summers in South Dakota, excavating old Indian graves for the Smithsonian. It was pretty quiet out there; big ranches, not many people. Not much excitement for the police, either. DUIs, mostly; occasionally a burglary or barroom fight or some cattle rustling. So we got a fair number of visits from the sheriff's deputies and the state police. They'd come by almost every day – just to make sure we were okay, they said, but mostly they were bored, and we were the most reliable entertainment around. So whenever they'd come by, we'd show them what we were excavating that day, or bring out something interesting we'd found a day or two before – scalping marks, bashed-in skulls, whatever.'

'So instead of the bookmobile,' Angie cracked, 'y'all were the bonemobile.'

'I guess we were.' I laughed. 'One of the skeletons became kinda famous, and we had cops coming to see him from half the state. It was an adult male in his forties – no spring chicken, by Plains Indian standards. He had an arrowhead embedded deep in his right femur, about halfway between his hip and his knee. Right about where his thigh would've been gripping the ribs of a horse, riding bareback.'

'Cool,' said Vickery. 'You think he bled to death? Or died of infection?'

'Neither.' I grinned. 'That was what was so interesting about it. The bone had healed and smoothed around the arrowhead – remodeled, we call it – which meant that he'd lived for years after being shot with the arrow. It was so deep they couldn't get it out, so they just cut off the arrow, and he carried the point around in his leg for years. Probably hurt like hell for a long time, maybe for the rest of his life. Then, five or ten or twenty years later, he got clubbed to death – back of his skull was completely crushed – maybe because he couldn't run fast enough when some Sioux came after him with a battle-ax.'

'Wow,' said Angie. 'That's a great show-and-tell exhibit. Beats the pants off our plaster casts of Ted Bundy's teeth. I'd sure come out and take a look, if I were a South Dakota deputy. It's like the History Channel meets *CSI*.'

'Exactly,' I said. 'Listening to the bones, hearing the story they can tell, even if the story's two centuries old. Anyhow, one day, a South Dakota state trooper who'd seen the arrowhead skeleton came back out to the site. This was back before cell phones were everywhere, mind you, and there was no way to get ahold of us except to come out there in person. We were way off the grid.' Vickery nodded. 'So this state trooper comes out. Corporal Gustafson, I think his name was. No, wait; that's almost it, but not quite. Gunterson. Yeah, Gunterson.' I gave my head a shake. 'Funny how I can dredge up that guy's name after thirty years, but can't remember where I left my pocketknife this morning. Anyhow, Gunterson asks if I'd be willing to take a look at a skeleton that a cattle rancher'd just found.'

'What kind of skeleton? Old or new? Indian or white or what?'

'That's exactly what the trooper wanted to know. I said I'd be glad to take a look.'

'And?'

'Exposed bones in a dry wash. Not Indian.'

'How'd you know?'

'Indians have shovel-shaped incisors – their front teeth are scooped out on the back side. So do Asians. Caucasian incisors are pretty much flat across the back.'

Angie rubbed her teeth, then asked, 'Old bones, or new?'

'Old enough to be bare and sun-bleached. New enough to have an amalgam filling, though that could have been anytime in the twentieth century. She – it was a woman in her twenties – had only two cavities, so she was probably born sometime after the 1950s.'

'How do you figure that?'

'That's when America's cities and towns started adding fluoride to their drinking water.'

'A dastardly commie plot,' teased Vickery.

'Indeed,' I said. 'Those Communists wanted our kids to have strong teeth. So this woman was all set for the commie takeover, dentally speaking. Although it's possible that she grew up earlier, before fluoridation, in an area where the groundwater's naturally high in minerals.'

'Interesting,' he mused. 'You can tell all that just from the teeth?'

'You can tell a lot more than that just from the teeth,' I said. 'You can also tell that she had good dental care as a kid, because the one filling she had was in a second molar – a "twelve-year molar." But then something happened, her life changed for the worse. She had a big unfilled cavity in one of her third molars – her wisdom teeth – which means that she wasn't going to the dentist anymore. Maybe she'd run away from home; maybe she was on her own and not making enough money to afford dental care. I've seen this a lot over the years, and often far worse, in murdered prostitutes – they leave home, lose touch with their families, fall on hard times, can't afford a dentist. So their teeth start to go. Which makes them less attractive, and makes it even harder for them to earn money. Vicious downward spiral.'

Angie picked at the chicken salad with her fork. 'So this dead woman in South Dakota – she was a hooker?'

'Don't know,' I said. 'Unfortunately, she was never identified. Maybe a hooker, maybe a hitchhiker; maybe both. The body was dumped in a draw near Interstate 90, not far from an exit. I'm guessing a trucker picked her up, had sex with her, then killed her and dumped her body hundreds of miles from where she'd gotten into the truck.'

'And how do you know she was killed?'

'Because her hyoid bone – the U-shaped bone in the throat – had been crushed. Means she was strangled.'

Vickery nodded. 'I'll buy it,' he said. 'It all fits together. Too bad. Young women without money are very vulnerable. Not many options, and plenty of people ready to prey on them.' He inspected his cigar again, frowned at it, and laid it on his plate, alongside his knife and fork and one uneaten bite of mashed potatoes. 'So *that* was the case that got you going on modern forensics?'

'I guess it was,' I said. 'After that, word got around South Dakota that I was willing to look at modern bones and bodies. At the end of the summer, when I went back to the University of Kansas, a KBI agent called me up. Turned out that he was the brother of a South Dakota sheriff I'd helped. Pretty soon I was looking at bones from all over Kansas. And by the time I moved to Tennessee, the TBI and the Tennessee state medical examiner knew about me, and asked me to consult on cases.' I sopped up the last of my coleslaw sauce with the last bit of hush puppy. 'So. Like I said, one thing led to another. South Dakota led me to north Florida. And raw oysters. And fried cat.'

I left the Waffle Iron full and happy. The diner's food was good, and I'd enjoyed reminiscing about my summer excavations in South Dakota. We'd parked the Suburban in the back corner of the parking lot, which had largely emptied out by now. As we neared the vehicle, I noticed a folded paper underneath the left windshield wiper – a sale circular or political flyer, I figured. 'Uh-oh,' I joked over my shoulder to Angie and Vickery. 'Looks like we've gotten a parking ticket. These Sinking Springs folks sure keep an eye out for foreigners.' I plucked the paper from beneath the wiper blade and unfolded it. It was not a circular or flyer; it was a hand-lettered note on plain white paper. It read, 'Find the Bone Yard.'

I stared at the note; it was the second time I'd read the words *bone yard* today, but this note, I felt certain, had been written half a century after the diary entry. I shifted my fingers to a corner of the paper and showed the message to Angie and Vickery. Angie whistled softly. 'I guess I shouldn't have handled this,' I said. 'Sorry. I might have just contaminated some evidence.'

Vickery shrugged, then took out a clean handkerchief and carefully wrapped the note in it, then handed it to Angie. 'Hell, everything's evidence of *something*, Doc,' he said. 'This whole world's one big crime scene. The trick's figuring out what to send to the lab. And where to stop stringing the tape.'

As Angie and I followed Vickery's taillights back to Tallahassee, I phoned my son, who was at Myrtle Beach with his wife and two boys. 'Hi, Dad,' said Jeff when he answered. 'How are you? What's up?'

'I'm fine. Still in Florida. I just wanted to talk to Walker and Tyler.'

'So, what am I, chopped liver?'

'No, of course not.' I laughed. 'I just wanted to talk to the boys. Just wanted to tell them . . .' Tell them what? Tell them how lucky they were? Tell them not to become orphans, not to be abused, not to get sent to reform school, not to get murdered and dumped somewhere in the woods?

Yes. Those things, and more.

Jeff put the speakerphone on and handed the phone to the boys.

'Grandpa Bill,' said Walker. 'I caught a fish today.'

'I went *body surfing*,' Tyler shouted.

'Wonderful, boys,' I said. But what I meant was 'what wonderful boys.'

CHAPTER 13

My shovel scraped across a chunk of timber a few inches beneath the ground, near one of the chimneys. The timber was black and crumbling; as I leaned down to inspect it more closely, I saw that it was rotted but also charred. It was embedded in earth that was undisturbed – that is, as I dug deeper, I saw that there were no other artifacts beneath it – so I guessed that the wood had been a floor joist rather than a ceiling joist or rafter.

Angie and I had returned to the ruins of the reform school; Vickery had spun off to start interviewing people about the school's grim life and fiery end.

I wondered if Angie and I might find charred bones amid the ruins – Stevenson's initial research hadn't ruled out the possibility that one or more bodies hadn't been recovered after the fire – but it was a big job: the ruins were a whole *bunch* of haystacks, and whatever skeletal needles lay hidden in them might well have crumbled to rust or to dust by now.

I'd spent the morning skimming vegetation and the top layer of burned material from the center of the dormitory area. My clothes were soggy and grimy and my back was grumbling, so I was relieved when Vickery's

Jeep pulled up and emitted a brief chirp of the siren. He rolled down the window and waved Angie and me over.

'What's up?' she asked.

'Let's take a ride,' he said.

'In air-conditioned comfort? Sure thing. Where we going?'

'To see some reform school alumni.'

I looked down at my sweat-soaked clothes and took a quick sniff under one arm. The news from there wasn't good. 'I'm pretty rank. Maybe I should stay here.'

'Nah, jump in, Doc. I don't think any of these folks will object.'

The air was cranked all the way up, and the blast of cold on my wet skin gave me goose bumps. Glancing at the console between the front seats, I noticed a hand-drawn map. It appeared to be a drawing of the school site; the buildings had been crudely outlined, and a dotted line led northward from the site to a sketch of what appeared to be a tree, with an X beside it. Vickery studied the map briefly, then put the Jeep into gear and continued around the drive. Just beyond the remnants of the buildings, he slowed to a crawl, then cut the wheel to the left and jounced us off the road. As the vehicle swayed and lurched along, I realized we were following what was left of a dirt road, although high weeds and small bushes swished and screeched against the under-side of the vehicle, and occasionally we had to swerve around trees that had grown up in the roadbed. Scattered amid the oaks and pines were magnolias, their dark, glossy leaves dotted with cupped white blossoms. Rolling down the window, I drank in their sweet, heady perfume.

After perhaps a quarter mile, the track meandered up a slight rise and around an immense live oak. The trunk was a good eight feet thick, and the lower branches – some of them nearly two feet in diameter – curved down to rest on the ground before turning skyward. The effect was of a small grove of trees, rather than one single tree. The branches themselves were thickly carpeted with ferns, as if the forest floor were actually a living thing consisting of many layers and levels . . . which it *was*, I realized. 'Amazing,' I said, 'the way the ferns are colonizing the trees.'

'Those are resurrection ferns,' Angie replied, and I thought, *live oaks, dead boys, resurrection ferns.*

As we rounded the far side of the tree, Vickery slowed the Jeep, and Angie gasped, 'Oh my God.'

Just ahead, in a patch of ground between two huge branches of the live oak, stood three rows of knee-high crosses – four crosses in two of the rows, three in the other; eleven crosses in all.

Vickery eased the Jeep to a stop alongside the nearest row of crosses. 'Welcome to the Bone Yard,' he announced.

PART II

CHAPTER 14

We walked in silence toward the eleven crosses, mysterious and haunting in the grotto formed by the live-oak canopy. The crosses appeared to be made of galvanized metal pipe, two or three inches in diameter. On the tops of the horizontal pieces, the metal was a dull, mottled gray; underneath, it was black with mildew. Someone had gone to considerable effort to construct the crosses – their uprights and horizontal pieces had been neatly miter-cut and welded together – but neither the crosses nor the ground bore any sort of plaque or inscription, any indication of whose bones might lie within these graves, or how long they'd lain there.

'This is amazing,' Angie whispered. 'How'd you find out this was here?'

'I tracked down the former superintendent, Marvin Hatfield.'

She looked as surprised as I felt. 'Hatfield? The guy quoted in that old newspaper story about the beatings?'

'Yep. Good old spare-the-rod, spoil-the-child Hatfield.'

'I'm surprised he's still alive.'

'So is he, probably. He's ninety years old, in a wheelchair and on oxygen, but his mind's still fairly sharp.

He lives in a nursing home in Dothan, Alabama, about an hour from here. Did you know he became commissioner of the Department of Corrections a couple years after the fire?'

'Why, no,' she said, 'but it makes perfect sense, doesn't it? "Hey, Hatfield, I see that your school burned down and killed a bunch of kids. Great work! I'd like you to take over our prisons and do an equally fine job with them?" You suppose that's how the phone call went?'

Vickery shrugged. 'Could be. We're looking into whether somebody pulled a string with the governor to get him the promotion. Don't know if we'll be able to find one, though, this many years after the fact. Anyhow, I told Hatfield about the skulls, asked if he thought they might have come from the grounds of the school. He closed his eyes and thought about that for a while – that, or checked out for a little nap; hard to be sure. Then he said they might have come from the ruins, since they never found a couple of the bodies after the fire. When I told him what the Doc said, that there didn't seem to be any signs that they'd been burned, he said, "Well, then, they might have come from the cemetery." Being the world-class interrogator that I am, I said, "What cemetery?" According to Hatfield, boys occasionally died at the school – nine in the fire, of course, but also from illnesses and other accidents, too. Most boys who died at the school were sent home to their families to be buried, but if they didn't have relatives who claimed them, they'd be buried on the grounds.'

It made sense, now that he said it, though it hadn't occurred to me as a possibility before. Perhaps it *should* have; after all, unclaimed bodies accounted for a third of the corpses that ended up at the Body Farm. For some reason, though – naïveté or idealism or some combination of the two – I'd assumed that dead children were different from dead derelicts; I'd assumed there'd always be someone who wanted to claim them, bury them, mourn them. And my experience had borne out that assumption: the thousand skeletons in our collection included virtually no children, so maybe it wasn't surprising that I was unprepared for the sight of a graveyard for reform school orphans.

A butterfly, luminous yellow, fluttered above a cross. 'Did Hatfield refer to the cemetery as the Bone Yard?'

'Not exactly. He never used the term, so finally I did. I asked if the cemetery was what the boys used to call the Bone Yard.'

'You *are* a world-class interrogator,' Angie observed drily. 'What'd he say?'

'He looked startled – said he hadn't heard those words in forty years – but then he said yes, he *had* heard it referred to by that name. When I asked if he could tell me where it was, he drew me that little map. Pretty good memory for a ninety-year-old.'

I walked down one row of crosses and back up another.

'Was his memory good enough that he could tell you who's buried here? And what killed them?'

He pulled out a notepad and consulted it. 'Three were boys who died in the fire in 1967. Six of the nine fire victims were sent home for burial by their families, but three of them were orphans who'd been in foster care before they got sent to reform school. The guard who died in the fire was also buried here. Two boys who died of the flu in the winter of 1958, which was a couple years before he took over. One boy who drowned on a class canoe trip. Another who fell off a tractor that was mowing the grass; he got run over by the bush hog.' I gave an involuntary shudder. 'He didn't remember any of the other circumstances – said most boys buried in the cemetery died before he took over, and he couldn't recall what the records said about the rest of them.'

Angie frowned. 'And did he tell you where to find these helpful records?'

'They were kept on-site, at the school. So they burned up in the fire. That was before the wonders of central-ized record keeping.'

'Very handy,' she observed. 'What about the guard? What was his name? Why'd they bury him there?'

'Also no family, according to Hatfield. Said the boys were his only family. He died trying to save their lives. Hatfield couldn't remember the man's name.'

'What about the trauma?' I asked. 'Did you tell him both the skulls we found had been fractured?'

'He said he didn't know anything about that. He took a hit or two of oxygen, then circled back to the one that fell off the tractor; asked if that might be one of them.'

'It's possible,' I conceded. 'If the housing of the mowing attachment hit the head just right, it could have knocked the mastoid process loose. But what about the first skull, the one with the hairline fracture in the temporal bone?'

Vickery shrugged. 'He said he was sorry he couldn't be more helpful, but most of the deaths happened before he took over.'

I wasn't ready to let go. 'What about the beatings? Did you ask about those?'

'I did. I showed him a copy of the newspaper story. He got mad, turned red in the face; I actually thought he might stroke out on me. Said that story was a pack of lies – inaccurate, irresponsible, and cowardly – and he'd sure like to see how some goddamned bleeding-heart reporter would keep order among a bunch of juvenile delinquents without swinging a paddle every now and then. Then he started wheezing and said he was really tired and he didn't know anything else that might help us, and could he please take his nap now?'

Angie blew out an exasperated breath. 'That's it? "I don't care if some boys were murdered – it's nap time"? Christ almighty.'

'Look, I'll go back and talk to him again once I have more questions, but he was clearly done. I didn't see anything to be gained by interrogating him to death.' I couldn't help but laugh. 'On the way out, I did ask him who else might know about the cemetery or the deaths. He shook his head. "Young man, I have no idea," he said. "That was a lifetime ago. Those boys were already lost by the time they got to us. Why on earth would anybody know or care after all this time?" I hate to say it, but I'm afraid he might be right.'

'I care,' said Angie.

Vickery nodded slightly in agreement, or at least acknowledgment. He looked at me. 'So, Doc, can we figure out who's buried here? Does each of these crosses mark a grave? And do these crosses mark *all* the graves? Or might there be more?'

'All good questions.'

'I suppose,' Angie said grudgingly, 'we could dust off the old reliable root finder.'

I smiled at the name, though I had no clue what it meant. 'Root finder?'

'That's what the crime-scene folks fondly call their ground-penetrating radar,' Vickery explained. 'What is it you told me GPR really stands for, Angie? Great Pictures of Roots?'

'Ah,' I said, the light dawning. I'd seen ground-penetrating radar in action before, and I had to admit, I'd been whelmed: far from overwhelmed, but not totally underwhelmed, either. In theory, GPR made perfect forensic sense: radio-frequency pulses, directed into the ground, would be bounced back with different intensities by materials of different density. Dense materials – undisturbed soil, for instance, or metal pipelines, or rocks, or roots – would send back stronger signals than looser materials, such as a human body, or the disturbed dirt of a recently dug grave. In my admittedly limited experience, interpreting the on-screen images required a fifty-fifty mixture of high-tech aptitude and psychic power. One of my graduate students had done a research project in which she used an advanced prototype GPR system to image bodies buried under slabs of concrete – a realistic simulation of a murder in which, let's say, a man kills his wife, buries her in the backyard, and then pours a new patio to conceal her grave. My student's project had shown me two things: first, that someone skilled at reading the cloudlike images on the GPR's display might have a pretty good shot at determining whether or not a particular patio was hiding a body (or at least a body-sized area of disturbed soil); and second, that I was *not* that skilled someone, since to me, most of the subterranean images looked like the rainstorms on the Weather Channel's radar.

'Well, if you don't want to use the root finder, we could try divining,' I suggested.

Vickery looked puzzled. 'Divining? What, like praying?'

'No. Divining, like dowsing. Like water-witching.'

He snorted. 'The business with the forked stick?'

'As my assistant Miranda would say, the forked stick is *so* last century,' I said. 'The state of the art these days is coat hanger, man. You take apart one of those coat hangers from the dry cleaners. You know, the kind that has the round cardboard tube for your pants to drape over?' He stared at me, so I hurried on with my explanation. 'You cut the cardboard tube in half, then cut two pieces of the wire and bend them into L's. Stick one end of each L in each piece of the cardboard tube, and use the tubes for handles, to let the wires swivel freely.' I struck a stance like a Wild West gunslinger, my hands mimicking a pair of revolvers. 'Then you walk the search area with the exposed wires level, parallel to the ground.' I headed slowly toward one of the crosses. 'When you come to a body, or a grave, the wires cross.' I pivoted my fingers toward one another. 'Or sometimes swivel sideways.' I wiggled my fingers back and forth.

Vickery removed his cigar and studied me closely, apparently trying to decide whether I was pulling his leg or had gone truly mad.

'Ah, the forensic coat hanger,' said Angie. She mimicked my gunslinger stance. 'Stranger, you'd best be gone by sundown,' she drawled à la John Wayne, 'or I'll fill ya fulla starch.'

Vickery hooted, and even I was forced to smile, despite feeling some embarrassment. 'Hey, scoff all you want, but my colleague Art Bohanan swears by it.' Vickery rolled his eyes. 'Art says he mapped a bunch of graves in an old family cemetery this way.'

'No slam on Art,' Angie said, 'but I've read some journal

articles about divining for graves. A few years ago, there was an archaeologist in Iowa who did a big literature search and a bunch of interviews and some simple experiments. From his research, at least, he concluded that it's totally ineffective. He says the wires move when you slow down, or bend over, or your posture shifts because you've stepped down into a low spot. Basically, it's like a Ouija board – it works because you *make* it work, subconsciously.'

I shrugged. 'Well, I know a research scientist who's also a believer. His theory is that as a body decays, it turns into a big biochemical battery, giving off electrical currents that the wires pick up.' I pointed my divining-rod revolvers at Angie. 'Say, little lady, ya wanna go back to grad school and get yourself a PhD? Divining would make a dandy little dissertation.'

She held up both hands. 'I surrender. I wish Art were here right now. I'd be happy to put him to the test. We could check his accuracy by bringing in the forensic backhoe.'

'See, *now* you're talking some useful technology,' said Vickery, and I smiled. Unlike *forensic coat hanger*, the term *forensic backhoe* was actually used in all seriousness, or at least in *some* seriousness, by police and anthropologists. A forensic backhoe was identical to a basement-digging backhoe or a ditch-digging backhoe; the fancied-up terminology simply acknowledged that a backhoe could be used, by a skilled operator and an experienced scientist, to excavate with surprising precision. I'd used forensic backhoes many times in my career, just as I'd used forensic shovels, forensic trowels, forensic paintbrushes, and even forensic saucepans on forensic kitchen stoves. Stoves I'd ended up replacing, not once but twice, when the bones I was cleaning boiled over, forever contaminating the unreachable nooks and crannies of the forensic burners. 'But, fascinating though this discussion of technology is,' he added, 'I do feel duty bound to bring us back to the questions at hand. How do we identify who's buried here? And how do we figure out which of their skulls that damn dog brought home?'

'I'm not sure those two questions are actually related,' I said slowly, the realization coming clear only as I said it. I pointed to the lush ferns surrounding the eleven rusting crosses. 'Unless there's something I'm not seeing, nothing – and nobody – has been dug out of this cemetery in years. Not by that dog or by anybody else.'

Vickery's face fell, and the wind went right out of his sails. He'd been so proud of his find, and it was a remarkable one. But as we took a critical, appraising look at the markers – I couldn't help thinking of the old hymn 'When I Survey the Wondrous Cross' – it became more and more clear that this was not the source of Jasper's finds.

Before taking Angie and me to the cemetery, Vickery had called to alert his boss, the FDLE special agent in charge of a batch of counties in the Florida panhandle.

Now he phoned headquarters again with an update, and though I didn't hear the details of the call – Vickery headed down the overgrown road on foot as he began to talk – I could hear notes of disappointment in his voice.

Angie, meanwhile, was already documenting the grave-yard. She started by taking photographs of the cemetery as a whole, then of each row of crosses, and then of the individual markers. Then she enlisted my assistance, which consisted mainly of holding the end of a fifty-foot tape measure as she sketched the site and noted the locations of the crosses. After she'd finished the sketch, she reeled in the tape, which slithered and twitched its way through the ferns like a yellow ribbon snake.

'Just for kicks,' she said, snapping the crank into the case of the reel, 'why don't we probe one of these, see if these crosses really do seem to be marking graves, or if they're just decorative accents.'

'We have probes in the Suburban? Why didn't you say so sooner?'

'What, and miss that great seminar on the forensic coat hanger?'

She retrieved two probes and a fistful of survey flags from the back of the vehicle and handed one of the probes to me. It was a stainless-steel rod, four feet long and about the thickness of my index finger, with a one-foot handle across the top that formed a tall, skinny T. 'Pick a grave, any grave,' she said. I pointed to the cross closest to us, which was at one corner of the cluster of markers. 'Which side of the cross do you suppose the grave would be on?' I shrugged; without a plaque or marker – and with such dense ferns underfoot – it was impossible to tell.

'How about we probe both directions? That way, no matter which way the grave is dug, we'll find it. If it's there to find.'

Starting a foot above and below the cross, we pushed the probes into the ground. Mine went in easily, halfway up to the handle, before hitting tightly packed soil; Angie's, on the other hand, hit hard clay half a foot down. Working our way farther from the cross – and to either side of our starting points – we probed repeatedly. Again and again mine passed through loose, disturbed earth, and I marked each of these holes with a survey flag; again and again Angie's probe hit hardpan just below the topsoil. Finally, after I'd lengthened and widened my grid considerably, I began hitting hard dirt, too, which told me that I'd reached the margins of the disturbed area, and was now encountering undisturbed soil. I stepped back so Angie could photograph what I'd flagged. The ten flags defined an oval-shaped area of loose, disturbed soil, about two feet wide by six feet long: just about the size hole you'd dig to bury a teenage boy.

Angie was adding notes to her sketch when Vickery returned at a jog. He was sweating and breathing hard.

He took in the flags, and his eyebrows shot up. 'Looks like you two have been busy.'

'You were gone awhile, so we found something to do,' said Angie. 'Quacks like a grave to me, even if it isn't where the dog's been digging. What's up?'

'This cemetery is gonna stir up a shit storm,' he said. 'Even if the skulls didn't come from here. The commissioner – the big boss, the head of FDLE,' he explained for my benefit, 'has a call in to the governor. I'm afraid we're about to have a lot more people looking over our shoulders.'

'Maybe that's the best thing that could happen,' I offered. 'Seems like the boys at this school fell through the cracks all those years ago. Maybe now people will finally pay some attention.'

'Maybe,' conceded Vickery. 'But I wouldn't bet my pension on it.'

CHAPTER 15

The Twilight Motor Court was well named; I suspected the sun had set on its glory days – if indeed there had ever *been* glory days – decades ago. The motel consisted of seven cinder-block bungalows, which might have been new and clean in the 1950s, but which now ranged from seedy to crumbling. The two that sat farthest from the road were roofless and windowless. Mine, number three, seemed intact, but the ridgeline of the roof sagged, the paint on the trim was peeling, and the bottom of the door sported a wooden fringe where the outer layer of veneer was peeling and splintering. An ancient air conditioner in the side wall rasped and clattered, its wobbly fan grazing the cooling vanes at random intervals.

Given the complexity created by the revelation of the cemetery – given the shit storm that was brewing, as Vickery put it – he and Angie had decided we should stay nearby, eliminating the two-hour round-trip to and from Tallahassee. The nearest place to stay – the only place to stay that was within a half hour of the school site – was the Twilight.

As I wriggled the reluctant key into the lock, the knob

rattled in my hand. I twisted gingerly, half expecting it to come off. It didn't, but once the door scraped open, I almost wished it had. The room was dank and musty, a few degrees cooler than the outdoors but even more humid, and my eyes and nose began to itch at once from the onslaught of mold spores. The floor was upholstered with shag carpet – an unfortunate 'update' from the 1970s, I guessed – that was pea green with reddish-brown stains . . . or maybe reddish-brown with pea-green stains. The sagging double bed was topped with a polyester bedspread of similar vintage, color, and contamination, and I shuddered to think what biological stains might fluoresce under the glow of an alternate light source. Suddenly I felt nostalgic for the Hotel Duval, with its peaceful neutrals, its glowing ceiling bubbles, and its luminous waitresses.

A seething, spattering sound emanated from the bathroom. I found the light switch and flipped it; a dim, bare bulb in the ceiling revealed a hissing faucet in the porcelain sink and a dribbling shower in a cracked fiberglass bathtub, another 'update' added twenty or thirty years before. Both fixtures were streaked and stained with rust, as was the toilet. I leaned down and twisted the knobs on the bathtub. The shower's dribble doubled in volume, but lacked the pressure required to form an actual spray.

My cell phone rang, causing me to jump. The number was Angie's.

'Hey there,' I answered. 'Welcome to the Bates Motel. Watch out for the guy with the butcher knife.'

'One difference between this and *Psycho*,' she said. 'The bathroom in *Psycho* actually had a shower curtain.'

'You can have my shower curtain. I sure don't need it. Have you checked the water pressure?'

There was a pause, and I heard gurgling in the background. 'I see what you mean. This'll make it hard to rinse off the soap.'

'You've got soap? You must have the deluxe suite,' I joked, peering at my soap dish, which was empty except for the layer of mildew. 'You FDLE fat cats sure know how to travel in style.'

'Hey,' she squawked, 'the way the BP spill screwed our tourism revenues, we're lucky we're not sleeping under a bridge. FDLE's budget had already been cut to the bone in 2008 and 2009. Now we're amputating whole sections. Won't be long before we start selling brownies to buy rape kits. Or sending out e-mails to all our friends and relatives: "Please sponsor my next crime-scene search! I need to raise five thousand dollars in pledges before the corpse gets cold!"' I laughed, but her point was serious.

'It's worrisome,' I agreed. 'Forensic technology – just like medical technology – gets more sophisticated all the time, but that means it gets more expensive, too. Which homicides get the VIP treatment, and which ones do we cut corners on?'

'Black men don't generally get the VIP treatment.' She

paused. 'Neither do battered women,' she added softly.

'I'm sorry, Angie,' I said. 'I wish there were more we could do.'

'Me, too.' She sighed. 'Anyhow. So, astonishingly, there's not a four-star restaurant here at the lavish Twilight Motor Court. Shall we go back to the Waffle Iron?'

'Fine with me; I like the Waffle Iron. But let me get cleaned up first.'

'Yeah, good luck with *that*,' she said. 'Just come knock on my door whenever you're ready. I'm in number four, the palatial place next door. You'll recognize it by the duct tape holding the window together. I just talked to Stu, and he's ready, so once you're clean and shiny, we'll saddle up and go.'

I headed for the shower, but the combination of anemic water pressure, rust stains, mildew, dirt, and dead bugs was too much for me. I did find an ancient bar of soap in the rusted medicine cabinet, so I managed to get tolerably clean taking a sink bath.

Ten minutes after we'd talked, I knocked on Angie's door. The brass number was missing, but beneath the outermost layer of peeling green paint was a four-shaped remnant of peeling red paint. Angie hadn't been kidding about the duct tape: a missing windowpane had been replaced with cardboard, which was held in place with brittle, curling duct tape.

'Come in,' she called. She was sitting cross-legged on her bed – the same scary-looking bedspread I had, though her stain pattern appeared slightly different, like variations in a modern artist's series of paintings on a theme of scuzzy bedspreads. Lying open on the bed in front of her was a wallet-sized album of photos. The dozen or so pictures were snapshots of a life: Kate as a baby, swaddled in the arms of a nervous and proud four-year-old sister; Kate riding a pony at her sixth birthday party, a cone-shaped party hat rubber-banded to her head; Kate pitching for her high school softball team; Kate graduating from nursing school; Kate in a wedding gown, flanked on one side by Angie, her matron of honor, and on the other by a groom who'd been scissored from the photo; Kate and Angie standing with a wizened old woman with dyed red hair, too much rouge on her cheeks, and eyes that looked like an ancient version of Angie's.

The most poignant images in the set were four black-and-white photos of the two sisters, as grown-ups, playing dress-up in antique clothing. They wore high-collared Victorian gowns, sequined flapper dresses, fitted hobble skirts, silly poodle skirts. In each picture, their hairdos harmonized with the clothes; so did their expressions, which ranged from prim to saucy to sophisticated. 'These are great,' I said. 'Tell me about them.'

Angie smiled. 'Ah. That was a great weekend. Kate and I took a road trip to see my grandmother, up in Akron, Ohio, on her ninety-fifth birthday. Her mind was still sharp, but her health was starting to fail, and we figured it might be our last chance to celebrate her birthday with her. Anyhow, at some point Saturday morning, Kate said something about needing a new pair of jeans, and Grandma made one of those typical geezer comments about how much better clothes used to be, back in the day. So we were humoring her, but also teasing her – "Right, Grandma, these kids today don't know beans about how to dress" – and she said, "You girls should look through those trunks of clothes up in the attic." So we did, and it was amazing. She was right – the clothes *were* a lot cooler back in the day. She had stuff she'd worn in the twenties and thirties and forties; she had stuff *her* mother had worn back at the turn of the century, and stuff *our* mother had worn in the fifties. We spent all afternoon Saturday trying on clothes and fixing our hair, while my cousin took pictures and Grandma told us stories about the Roaring Twenties and the Great Depression and World War Two.' She shook her head with a wistful smile. 'Funny thing about your grandparents. They're already old, or at least you *think* they're old, by the time you know them. So you never picture them as little kids, or wild teenagers, or scared young parents, or anything except old folks.' She took back the photos and looked at the picture of the old woman. 'Grandma became a real, three-dimensional *person* to me that day, you know?'

I nodded. 'Is your grandmother still alive?'

'No. She had a stroke two months later. I'm so glad we took that trip.' She flipped through the series of dress-up photos. 'That was the last trip Kate and I took together. Two months later, she met Don Nicely. And now she's fading into monochrome memories of the good old days.'

There was a knock on the door. 'Let's eat,' growled Vickery. 'I'm starving.'

Angie folded the picture wallet closed and tucked it in her purse. After she did, I noticed, her thumb rubbed circles around the hatchet scar on her index finger – a way of hanging on to a more tangible memory, I guessed – and I doubted that she even realized she was doing it. I remembered a line from a Shakespeare play, spoken to Hamlet by the ghost of his murdered father – 'Remember me. Remember me. Remember me.' I felt certain Angie would remember Kate always; I prayed that she would not be haunted by her sister's ghost forever.

Our second meal at the Waffle Iron was more somber than our first. Angie seemed to have turned inward. Then Vickery handed us more pages from the diary Flo was deconstructing, which didn't seem likely to lift our spirits.

I'd thought I was hungry, but as I began to read, I lost all appetite.

Jared is dead, and Buck might be dying.
We were in the dining hall last night. Dinner was
pinto beans and cornbread. I was sitting across from

Buck. Jared McWhorter was sitting on one side of him. While Cockroach was saying grace, Jared reached over and grabbed Bucks piece of cornbread off of his plate. Hes taken food from me before, and from lots of other boys. Hes one of the biggest, roughest boys so he always gets away with it.

But last night Buck got mad and grabbed ahold of Jareds wrist with both hands and started trying to get his cornbread back. Jareds stronger than Buck, but Buck wouldnt let go. Give it back, give it back, he was saying. His teeth were clenched tight together, so he sounded like an animal growling Give it back you bastard. I tried to shush him up, but he was to mad to listen. Give it back, give it back. He was growling louder. Cockroach said a quick Amen and started looking around to see who was making noise during the blessing.

Jared had reached under the table with his other hand and started pinching Buck to make him let go. He must have pinched him real hard because Bucks eyes closed and he made a kind of a squealing yell through his teeth, but he never let go. Then he bent down and bit Jareds hand.

Jared let out a big yell and jumped up. Buck was still holding on to him with his hands and his teeth, so when Jared jumped up he pulled Buck with him. The bench caught the back of their legs and made them both fall over backwards onto the floor. Cockroach blew his whistle one short time then three long times, loud, to call the other guards, but Buck and Jared just kept on fighting. Jared was yelling and punching Buck in the face, or trying to, but he was having trouble getting any good licks in because Bucks face was mostly covered by his own arms and Jareds arm. So then Jared put his other hand on Bucks throat and started to choke him.

Thats when Cockroach got there and started trying to pull them apart. He wasnt having much luck with his one hand, so he started kicking. He kicked Buck in the back and the ribs three or four times, and that was enough to make Buck let go and curl up into a ball. Buck hollered at the first kick, then grunted at the second kick and then he just whimpered like a dog thats been hit by a car and is dying. Cockroach kicked Jared three or four times too, in the belly and in the nuts. The last two kicks were hard enough to lift him mostly up off the floor and send him skidding. Jared puked out some bloody looking vomit and just lay there on his side making a gurgling sound.

Four other guards came busting into the dining hall then. They looked at Cockroach, who was standing over Jared, looking down with his face all twisted up and purple and his nostrils open wide like a horses. One of the guards, Mr Delaney, squatted down and looked at Jared, then looked up at Cockroach. Hes in bad shape, said Mr Delaney. I don't think he's breathing right. We best get him to the infirmary. Goddammit said

Cockroach. Alright get him out of here. Mr Delaney and Mr Whitlock reached under Jareds arms and raised him up off the floor, face down, and dragged him out the door. His knees and feet were dragging the floor, and I heard his shoes thump down the wooden steps and scrape across the dirt and roots in the yard. The third guard, Mr Tillman, was squatted down looking at Buck, who was groaning and whimpering. I reckon we should take him to the infirmary too, said Mr Tillman, but Cockroach said no. He aint hurt, said Cockroach, hes just pretending. Come on and help me bring him down to the shed. Mr Tillman looked at Cockroach and said are you sure about that? and Cockroach said goddam right Im sure. Come on. So he and Mr Tillman grabbed Buck under the armpits and hauled him up and started carrying him toward the door. Buck started crying and saying please dont, please dont. Shut up, boy, said Cockroach. Buck got his feet halfway under him. I dont think he was trying to walk, I think he was trying to stand up and plant his feet and stay in the dining room. but he was to weak. They ended up dragging him out the same way theyd dragged out Jared, except Buck was crying and pleading and trying to get his legs under him.

The fourth guard, Mr Ewbanks, stayed behind with us while we ate. Nobody talked or even looked at anybody else, we just kept our heads down low over our plates. I ate about three bites and then I felt I was about to get sick, so I quit eating and just stirred my food around with my spoon. After a few minutes Mr Ewbanks had us clear the table and march back to our dormitory.

It took me a long time to go to sleep. I dreamed Cockroach was making Buck bite his own arm and chew it and swallow it.

The next morning Bucks bed and Jareds bed were both empty still. At assembly Cockroach told us that because of the fight in the dining hall, we were confined to the dorm for the morning. He said Jared had been taken to the doctor in Quincy to get stitches for the bite in his arm and Buck was in the infirmary.

I will not tolerate fighting, Cockroach said. The next boys I catch fighting will be severely punished. Do you understand? Yes sir, we all said. Severely punished, he said again. Do you understand? Yes sir, we shouted.

That afternoon during work time, I went to sweep and empty the trash in the infirmary. There was four beds in the infirmary. Two of the beds had clean white sheets on them. One of them had been stripped, but there was blood at the head and in the middle, and brown and yellow stains in the middle, too. The nurse, Mrs Wilcox, was sitting beside the fourth bed and she bent over Buck. He was lying on his stomach, with no cloths on, and she was using tweezers to pick at his bottom and his back and his legs. Bucks bottom was all black, with bits of bloody fuzz sticking up from it. I knew, from what Id heard about other whippings, that the bits of fuzz were bits of his shorts that had been shredded and pounded into his skin by the strap.

The strap was one of the first things I heard about when I came. It was like two long barbers strops sewn together, with a piece of metal between them to make it stiffer and heavier. One boy said they used to use a big wooden paddle for the beatings, but they switched to the strap because you can beat a boy longer and harder with a strap than what you can with a board.

Cockroach is the worst. I think its account of he lost his left hand. Theres different stories about how he lost it. Some say it got run over by a plow. Others say no, it was a sawmill blade what got it. Others say a gator ate it, but I dont believe that one. Whatever caused him to lose it, he aint never got over it, and hes been taking it out on boys ever since. Especially when hes swinging that strap. Punishing us for having two good hands, I reckon.

Bucks legs were black down to his knees, and so was his back, up nearly to his shoulders. His breath was fast and shallow, and whenever the tweezers touched him he would twitch and whimper, but real quiet, like he was too weak to do it loud. I said Buck, are you okay? It was a stupid thing to say, but it was all I could think of. You mind your own business, said Mrs Wilcox. Hes going to be all right. Its what he gets for starting a fight. He never started it, I said. She looked up at me then with a sharp look. Not another word from you, she said, or itll be your hind end looking like this tomorrow. Get the trash and then come back and get that mattress. Its ruined. You need to haul it to the dump, too.

I dont think I can carry it by myself, I said.

She pointed out the window at Cockroach, who was smoking in the yard. You want me to call him back and tell him you didnt do like I asked?

I thought about what he might do if she told him that. No mam, I said, I can do it. You dont need to call him. Ill be back for it as soon as I empty the trash.

Wash out that can real good after you empty it, she said.

The trash can was full of wet, smelly rags. When I dumped it, they slithered out and plopped on the ground, and slimy reddish brown liquid dribbled out of the bottom of the can. I couldnt help it, I bent over and puked right on top of the whole mess.

There was a water hose behind the infirmary, so I rinsed out the trash can and washed out my mouth and took a drink. I noticed stuff from the trash can spattered on my shoes, so I rinsed those, too, while I let the trash can drain. Then I took it back inside and went to get the mattress.

Mrs Wilcox wasnt in the room, so I leaned down real quick and whispered to Buck, can you hear me? His eyes opened and he whispered yes. How bad are you

213

hurt? Real bad, he said. I cant walk. I dont know if I
can ever walk again. I squeezed his hand. Im sorry
Buck. Ill pray for you.

Hes dead, Skeeter, said Buck. Jareds dead. They
wrapped him up in a sheet and dragged him out of
here by the feet. His head was dragging like a sack of
rocks. I heard them say they were taking him to the
bone yard.

Mrs Wilcox was coming, so I let go of Bucks hand
and grabbed the mattress real quick. I dragged it
across the floor and out the door. When the corner
bumped down the steps, I thought about Jareds head
bumping that same way.

I pushed away my plate of catfish, which had grown
cold as I'd read. I'd eaten only a few bites, and I noticed
that Stu and Angie hadn't done any better with their
dinners than I'd done with mine. 'Jesus,' Angie commented
as she laid down the pages. 'Welcome to hell.'

Vickery took out a fresh cigar, which he unwrapped
slowly. Instead of chomping it, he rotated it between his
fingers, studying first one end and then the other, as if
the cigar might provide some answer to the age-old
question of evil. 'Hell,' he said, 'would be too good a
place for the guys who did this.'

CHAPTER 16

'Well, there's good news and bad news,' Vickery said when he got out of his Jeep at the cemetery the next day.

Angie kept her eyes on the probe she was shoving into the ground at the foot of one of the pipe crosses. 'What's the bad news?'

'The bad news is, the governor doesn't want us to disturb the graveyard.'

Now she looked up. 'What the hell? I was hoping we could finish probing today, maybe get the forensic backhoe out here tomorrow. Why doesn't he want us to dig it up?'

'He told the commissioner there's no indication that anyone buried in these graves was the victim of a crime. Unless we find compelling evidence that links these graves to crimes, he says, it would be a desecration to disturb the cemetery.'

'Desecration? To find the truth? Give me a break.' She studied his face. 'Do you think maybe he's covering up something?'

'I doubt it.' He shrugged. 'This looks like a bees' nest, and I can see how the governor would rather we didn't whack it with a stick and stir up the bees. If we start pulling bodies from the ground, lawyers are gonna be lining up to sue the state for millions. Besides, forensically, it'd be tough to identify the remains, wouldn't it, Doc?'

'Probably,' I conceded. 'Unless they're in good coffins and watertight vaults, they'll be down to bare bone. You might be able to get mitochondrial DNA out of the bones or teeth, but how much would that tell you? Mitochondrial DNA doesn't give you a unique identification – it just tells you whether two individuals share a common female ancestor. Besides, who would you compare these boys' DNA *to*?'

Angie looked inclined to argue with me, but Vickery didn't give her the chance. 'Look, the doc agrees that neither of the skulls came from here, so finding where the skulls *did* come from needs to be our top priority.'

'Well, I say let's give the bees' nest a good whack,' she said. 'That seems like our job. I'm amazed it hasn't gotten into the press yet. Disappointed, too.' She looked from the probe to the other crosses. 'Maybe we'll find something as we map it,' she said. 'More graves than we've got markers. I don't know. Hell, maybe a probe will snag on a murder weapon.'

Vickery shook his head. 'The commissioner says to leave it alone. Says respect for the sanctity of a cemetery takes precedence. Photographs. That's it, for the time being. We have to pull the plug, even on the probing.'

'Unbelievable,' she groaned.

'I've got people looking through the state archives and old newspaper stories,' he said. 'I'm hoping Hatfield was wrong about all the records being lost in the fire. Maybe we'll turn up something that lets us make a stronger case.' Angie shook her head angrily, and I wondered if some of that anger stemmed from her frustration about her sister, whose death had similarly fallen through the investigative cracks. 'Don't you want to hear the good news?' Angie looked skeptical. 'Remember,' he said, 'the cemetery's not where the real action is.' He gave a canary-eating smile. 'Our pal Deputy Sutton just phoned me. He got a call from Winston Pettis this morning. The dog's brought home another bone.'

I felt my own face break into a smile. 'Good boy, Jasper! Another skull?'

He shook his head. 'Not this time. Sounds like a leg bone, maybe a femur. Long, with a big, round knob on one end.'

'Could be a femur,' I agreed, 'but it could also be a humerus, an upper arm bone. And it might be animal. Horse, cow, deer. Maybe even panther or black bear; you have those down here, right?'

'A hundred years ago, yeah. Not in my lifetime.'

'You should spend more time in the crime lab,' Angie said. 'I've had deputies bring me bear bones two or three times and swear they were human.'

'Actually, the bones of a bear's paw look a lot like human foot bones,' I conceded.

'Yeah, well, I've also had deputies bring me goat bones and swear they were human.'

The idea that the bone might be animal seemed to take some of the wind out of Vickery's sails, so I tried to steer the conversation back to a more encouraging course. 'Well, Jasper seems to have a taste for humans,' I said, 'and he appears to have found the mother lode.' A realization hit me. 'Hey. If it *is* human, and if the GPS collar worked, then he's just shown us where he found it, right?'

Vickery smiled around his cigar, his sails billowing. 'Shall we go pay another visit to the Pettis mansion?'

CHAPTER 17

As we pulled into the clearing beside the secluded cabin, Vickery leading the way in his Jeep, I imagined the scene that had transpired in the predawn hours: the dog leaping onto the mattress in the darkness, circling a couple times as if to trample down grass, and then curling up proudly beside his owner with a ripe femur. I smiled as I pictured it.

On our prior two visits, Jasper had bounded out to greet us; I was surprised that he wasn't racing to see us this time. I was disappointed, too, I noticed. 'I guess Jasper's gotten bored with us,' I sighed.

Angie gave the horn two quick toots as she stopped the Suburban – a friendly way to announce our arrival – and we all got out and headed up the rickety steps to the front porch. Vickery rapped on the screen door. 'Mr Pettis?' he called out. 'Hello?' He waited a few beats, then opened the screen and crossed the porch. Angie and I followed, and I detoured to inspect the shelf that held Jasper's bone collection, hoping to see the latest addition. Again I was disappointed.

Knocking on the cabin's only door, which led into the kitchen, Vickery called out again. 'Mr Pettis, are you here?' No answer. He knocked again, hard; the two large panes of glass in the top half of the door, which were held in place by only a few remnants of brittle putty, rattled and threatened to tumble to the porch. 'Mr Pettis?' Vickery put his face to the glass, cupping his hands around his eyes to cut the glare. He shifted his face to the other pane of glass for a better angle. 'Oh Christ,' he muttered, then, 'Get down, both of you.' He unholstered his gun and clicked off the safety.

'Stu,' said Angie in a low voice, 'what is it?'

'Get down,' he repeated. 'You, too, Doc. Get down and stay down.' Angie dropped to a crouch, and I followed suit. 'I think something bad has happened here.' He stepped slightly to the side of the door. With his left hand, he took a handkerchief from his hip pocket and draped it carefully over the doorknob, then gave a slight turn and pushed the door open with the barrel of the pistol. 'Mr Pettis?' By now, huddled at the far end of the porch with Angie, I felt fairly certain Pettis wasn't going to answer.

Vickery leaned forward just long enough for a quick look through the open door, then leaned swiftly back again. After a moment he risked a second look, this one not so brief, and then eased through the door, leading with the weapon. 'Christ,' he said again, loudly. '*Damn* it. *Fuckin'* hell.'

'Stu?'

'Pettis is dead. God *dammit*. The dog, too.'

'Oh, *shit*,' said Angie. 'Can you tell what happened?'

'Hang on. Let me clear the place.' Inside, I could hear the agent's breathing, deep and fast, with occasional shufflings of his feet as he moved through the small dwelling, which had only one main room – a combination living room, bedroom, and galley kitchen – and a tiny bathroom, as I remembered it. Finally he reappeared in the doorway, drenched in sweat, his chest still heaving. He holstered his gun, mopped his head with the handkerchief he'd used to open the door, and shook his head grimly. 'Shot. Must've been right after he called the sheriff's office. Blood's coagulated, starting to dry. Bunch of flies have already found their way in.'

'Shot? Both of them?' Angie got to her feet. 'Who on earth would shoot those two? And why?'

'Don't know who,' said Vickery. 'Got an idea why, though.'

'Why?'

'The collar's gone.'

My head began to buzz, and I sat down on the porch. 'The GPS collar? You think he and the dog were killed because of the tracking collar?'

'That's my theory, until something better comes along,' he answered. 'I'd say we can rule out a drive-by shooting, since we're out in the middle of damn nowhere.'

'Probably robbery, too,' added Angie, 'if all that's missing is the collar. That collar wasn't cheap, but it's sure not worth shooting somebody over.'

'Not,' Vickery added, 'unless you're afraid of where the track might lead.'

Dead, the simple man and the friendly dog. It wasn't supposed to happen like this. I'd worked on a lot of forensic cases over the past couple of decades. I was good at them, and I liked my role. I came in long after the crime, helped recover bones, sometimes identified a murder victim or figured out the manner of death or the time since death. Then, sitting in my quiet sanctuary beneath Neyland Stadium, I wrote my report. My hands – safe inside my latex gloves and my sheltered office – stayed nice and clean. Always. Always before, anyhow.

Now Winston Pettis and his dog were dead, and they'd apparently been killed because of the GPS tracking collar. The collar I'd suggested putting on the dog.

Sitting at the far end of the screened-in porch, I bent my head into the corner and threw up.

Angie shepherded me outside to keep me from compromising the crime scene any further than I already had. Before leading me across the sandy yard to the Suburban, she stooped and checked the ground closely, looking for footprints that were not ours; looking for footprints we hadn't unknowingly obliterated on our way in. *This world is one big crime scene.* As we made our way slowly across the scrubby grass and weeds, she shook her head in frustration. Then, as we reached the vehicle, she brightened. She pointed to a faint track in a bare patch of dirt behind the Suburban. 'Looks like we might have a tire impression,' she said. She crouched beside it. 'Not the clearest one I ever saw, but maybe better than nothing.'

Vickery's first call was to the Apalachee County Sheriff's Office. The dispatcher patched him through to the sheriff, whom Vickery briefed on what we'd found. 'Do you want your folks to handle this? Your deputy, Sutton, is on his way over here already . . . Right, to get the latest bone the Pettis dog brought back . . . No, sir, we haven't found that bone. And the tracking collar we'd put on the dog is gone, too . . . Yeah, that is a shame . . . Do you want us to just secure the scene till Sutton gets here?' He nibbled on his cigar as he listened. 'Actually, Sheriff, we've got a good crime-scene analyst here; a bone expert, too – the forensic anthropologist that looked at those two skulls.' He seemed to take satisfaction in something the sheriff said. 'Okay, do y'all want to call the M.E.? And the funeral home? It usually takes a while for the hearse to show up . . . Okay, will do. . . . You know we aren't trying to step on your toes here, but we'll be glad to go ahead and start working it. You sure that's what you want?' He motioned 'go' to Angie, who nodded and seemed to shift gears almost instantly, into crime-scene mode – the same intense mode I'd seen when she and I had reconstructed the sofa on which her sister had died, and then again when we'd examined Kate's body. 'All right, Sheriff, we'll get started. See you soon.'

Vickery's next call was to his boss, the special agent in charge of FDLE's Tallahassee region, to bring him up to speed on the murder and the sheriff's request for forensic assistance. At the same time Angie phoned her boss, the supervisor of the crime lab. As she talked, she took a roll of crime-scene tape from the back of the Suburban and stretched it between two pines at the end of the turnoff from the dirt road into the yard. 'I haven't been inside yet,' she was saying as she came back. 'Vickery went in looking for the guy, found him and the dog.' She crouched beside the tire track she'd shown me. 'Looks like we have at least one tire impression. I didn't see any shoe impressions, but I'll take a closer look. . . . *Is* there somebody who could assist? . . . Great, send Rodriguez. Thanks.'

Angie started by photographing the cabin itself, then took pictures of the faint tire track from various angles and distances. Next she added a position marker – '1' – and a ruler for scale and took another series of photos of the impression. Then, drawing from bins in the back of the Suburban, she filled the pockets on her cargo pants with more evidence markers, gloves, and paper-bootie shoe covers before heading inside to begin photographing the death scene. During the next ten minutes, I glimpsed occasional flashes of light through the porch screen and the kitchen door, as if a small thunderstorm were occurring inside the cabin. 'Okay, Stu,' she called, 'I've got the basic photos, and I've done a quick search. I'm not seeing shell casings so far, and there's not a lot of blood spatter to speak of.'

'Got a guess about the bullet caliber?'

'Medium,' she said. 'Maybe .38.'

'Could be,' he mused. 'Or maybe a .45.'

'Looks to me like he was standing by the bed when he was shot, or maybe sitting on it, and he fell backward. Lots of blood pooled in the mattress under him, and more on the floor by the dog. But I'm not sure there's a lot to work with in terms of spatter or trajectory.'

'Yeah, that's sorta what I thought,' he said. 'Ready for me to come in?'

'Sure, come on. Just don't touch the kitchen doorknob. Maybe we'll get lucky there. You haven't touched the inside knob, have you?'

'Nope. Okay, I'll come poke around, see if it looks like somebody else has gone through his stuff; see if we can find his next of kin.'

While Angie and Stu worked the interior, I tried to console a disbelieving and distraught Deputy Sutton, who arrived moments after they went inside. 'I just talked to him a few hours ago.' Sutton shook his head. 'He was joking and laughing. So proud of that dog. Couldn't wait to show us what Jasper'd gone and found this time.' The young officer appeared close to tears. 'I had to work an accident. If I'd come right when he called me, this wouldn't have happened.'

'I know how you feel,' I said. 'I'm the one that suggested

we put the tracking collar on the dog.' A question popped into my head. 'If somebody killed him to get the tracking collar,' I asked, 'how do you reckon they *knew* about it?'

'Hell, this is Apalachee County,' he said without hesitation. 'Everybody knows everybody's business here.' Angie had said basically the same thing about Cheatham County, Georgia, I remembered – and for that matter, the same was true of rural Tennessee. Suddenly he looked even more stricken than before, if such a thing were possible. 'Oh, Lord,' he said. 'I was talking about it with one of the other deputies the day y'all put it on.'

'Talking where? At the courthouse? At a coffee shop?'

He flushed. 'Talking on the radio. Anybody with a police scanner could've heard it.' He now looked more in need of consolation than ever, but I could think of nothing consoling to say about the irresponsibility of broadcasting, quite literally, information about how Pettis was cooperating with an FDLE investigation.

Over the next hour, the dirt lane leading to the cabin became clogged with law enforcement vehicles, which parked in a line outside the crime-scene tape Angie had stretched between the pines on either side of the turnoff from the dirt road into the cabin's yard. The first to arrive was another Apalachee County sheriff's cruiser, driven by the sheriff himself, a wiry sixtysomething-year-old with a face of leather and a white handlebar mustache. On his heels came the county's medical examiner, a general surgeon named Bradford, who seemed content to defer to FDLE as soon as he'd pronounced Pettis dead of a gunshot wound to the chest. Then came an unmarked Ford sedan driven by Stevenson, the FDLE agent who'd brought us photos of the reform school the day we'd first visited the site. Vickery sent Stevenson to seek information from Pettis's 'neighbors' – the nearest of whom was two or three miles away – and the few hardscrabble businesses along the county road.

The FDLE crime-scene truck lumbered into view, a boxy black vehicle that looked like a cross between an ambulance on steroids and a Winnebago on Weight Watchers. Driving it was Rodriguez, the forensic tech Angie's boss had promised to send. Compact and muscular, Rodriguez had a shaved head, olive brown and glossy in the dappled light beneath the pines. Along with Rodriguez was a second tech, a young woman with long blond hair – Whitney, though I couldn't tell if that was her first name or her last – whose arrival was a pleasant surprise to Angie.

Rodriguez set to work on the tire track behind the Suburban. Pouring water into a large Ziploc plastic bag that contained powder, he kneaded the bag until the mixture inside was the consistency of pancake batter – a thick liquid that I recognized as dental casting stone: the same stuff, I realized, that FDLE had used to cast Ted Bundy's teeth. Watching him from ten feet away, I said, 'Those aren't the Suburban's tracks, are they?'

Rodriguez didn't look up. 'Not unless the Suburban's wearing a worn-out set of off-road tires,' he answered. 'With a big chunk out of one of the tread lugs.' I smiled; clearly he knew what he was doing, and if he ever ran across that same tread on a vehicle, I felt sure he'd be able to show a jury that it matched. The tire-tread impression might not be quite as chilling – or as damning – as the cast of Ted Bundy's teeth had been, but it might, just possibly, serve as a small evidentiary nail in the coffin of whoever had killed Pettis and Jasper.

As Rodriguez was lifting the hardened cast from the ground, a silver Lexus SUV arrived, looking badly out of place despite the blue lights flashing through its grille. The driver looked out of place, too – a hawkish, forty-something guy with a thirty-dollar haircut and a crisp Brooks Brothers shirt, cinched with a yellow silk tie. Heads turned; the crime-scene techs and even several of the agents stared with a mixture of curiosity and disdain at his fanciness, but Vickery smiled slightly. 'The shit storm just escalated,' he said. He headed for the Lexus, shook hands with the new arrival, and after conferring briefly, brought him over to me. 'Clay Riordan, chief deputy state attorney,' the man said.

'Bill Brockton. Pleased to meet you.'

'Agent Vickery speaks highly of you.'

'That's kind of him.'

'Let me see if I've understood Agent Vickery correctly, Dr Brockton. He says you don't think the two skulls that the victim's dog brought home came from the burial ground at the North Florida Boys' Reformatory.'

'No, I don't think they did. I know this is Florida, and things grow fast down here, but the vegetation at that cemetery looked like it hadn't been disturbed in years. I just don't see any way the dog got those skulls from that burial ground.'

'So where *did* he get them?'

I shrugged, and Vickery said, 'That's what we were hoping to learn from the GPS collar we put on the dog.' Riordan nodded, then excused himself to take a look inside.

Another unmarked car appeared, but this one didn't stop at the house; instead, it continued farther down Pettis's dead-end road. Thirty minutes later the car returned and stopped, and a pale young man with short, dark hair and wire-rim glasses got out. He held out a hand to me. 'You must be Dr Brockton, the anthropologist.' I nodded. 'I'm Nathaniel James – Nat – from the Forensic Computing Section. Nice to meet you.'

'You, too, Nat. I'm a little surprised to see you out here. I wouldn't have pegged Mr Pettis as particularly wired.'

'No, he wasn't what I'd call wired,' said Nat. 'But *we* are. I just retrieved the GPS receiver and the flash drive I set up in the fire tower. We don't have the collar that was on the dog, but I'm pretty sure we do have the data it transmitted.'

If he was right, would that mean we'd find the source of the bones? And would it mean that Pettis and the dog had not died in vain?

Darkness had fallen by the time we left the cabin and headed back toward the lavish comforts of the Twilight Motor Court and the Waffle Iron diner. Angie and Whitney had bagged Pettis's body, and it was loaded onto a panel-truck van from a local funeral home, which would transport it to the small hospital where Dr Bradford would autopsy the body. After much arguing and a series of phone calls, the dog's body had been added to the van, for delivery to a McNary animal hospital. I had hoped that Jasper would be buried beside Pettis, but I suspected that he'd be unceremoniously dumped in a ditch somewhere beside Highway 90.

The forensic techs had finished their work in the house, but Vickery had asked the sheriff's office not to release the scene until after we'd seen what Nat James was able to learn from the GPS data captured by the receiver and stored on the flash drive. Deputy Sutton's penance – for he continued to feel guilty about failing to prevent Pettis's death, and possibly even contributing to it – was to keep vigil at the property until we returned the next day.

As Angie and I bumped along the dirt road back to the highway, her phone rang. She glanced at the display. 'Oh my God,' she said, 'it's Maddox, from the GBI.' She flipped open the phone. 'Mr Maddox, it's good to hear from you. Did you get my messages? . . . I understand. It's been busy down this way, too . . . So how's the investigation going? . . . Well, have y'all questioned Don? . . . Okay, that's a good start. Have you *charged* him?' Angie was silent, and as far as I could tell, Maddox was silent, too. Finally she said, 'Mr Maddox? Did I lose you?' She took her foot off the gas, and the Suburban slowed to an idle. 'I don't understand, Mr Maddox.' She put the transmission in park, and the Suburban lurched and slithered to a stop. 'You mean not *yet*, right? You mean you aren't charging him *yet*. But you *will*, won't you?' Panic and despair were rising in her voice, and as they did, I felt sorrow welling up in me. 'But *why*? Why *not*? He *killed* her, Mr Maddox. That man put a shotgun in my sister's mouth and blew her *head* off. You *know* that. You saw her body. You saw the trajectory. You saw that she didn't do that to herself, Mr Maddox.' Pleading now. 'But you saw it. You saw it, you saw it, you *saw* it.' She was choking on the words now; they came out as a guttural, ragged whisper that I suspected was not even audible at the other end of the line. 'You saw it.' I heard a beep as she disconnected the call and let the phone fall beside her. She turned and stared at me, hollow-eyed in the dim light from the instrument panel. 'He says he doesn't think they'll charge him. So far they don't have enough evidence to make a case. They're sending Kate's body back to be reburied.'

I stared at her, feeling helpless. 'I'm sorry, Angie. So very sorry.' I struggled to find some words of comfort. 'Maybe it's not over yet. Maybe they'll reconsider. Maybe we can come up with something else.'

'What else? There *is* nothing else. It's done.' She shook her head. 'She's like one of those dead boys whose graves we just saw. Nobody gives a damn.'

'*You* give a damn,' I reminded her.

'A lot of good that's done her. I've let her down. And it's killing me.'

'Don't let it. Don't give up – on her or on yourself. *That* would be letting her down.'

She drew a deep, shuddering breath, put the Suburban in gear, and drove us to the Twilight in sad silence. Vickery's car was parked outside his bungalow, and a light showed through the threadbare curtains. 'I don't feel like going to dinner,' Angie said. 'You and Stu go on without me.' I started to protest, but she waved me off. 'Really. I'm exhausted,' she said as we got out. 'I'd be lousy company, and I can't eat. I just want to sleep.'

'You sure you'll be okay?' She nodded. 'I'm sorry,' I said again, acutely conscious of the inadequacy of the words. 'Sleep well. I'll see you in the morning.' She headed for her door, and lifted a weary hand by way of a good-night.

I showered as quickly as the anemic water pressure would allow, then headed for Vickery's bungalow. Angie's light was still on, so I decided to check on her before collecting Vickery. I tapped lightly on her door. She didn't answer, and I realized that her air conditioner was even noisier than mine, so I knocked again, harder this time. The door was unlatched, apparently; it swung open from the force of the knock, and as it did, my blood froze.

Angie St. Claire was lying on her bed. In her mouth was the muzzle of a shotgun.

CHAPTER 18

'Angie, *don't*,' I shouted from the doorway.

She jerked convulsively, wild-eyed, and the shotgun fell from her hands and tumbled to the floor. Instinctively I ducked and covered my head with my arms, but there was no blast from the gun. The only blast was a piercing shriek from Angie.

'Son of a *bitch*,' she yelled, scrambling to a sitting position against the headboard as I dove for the gun. 'You scared the living *shit* out of me.' She pounded the mattress a few times with her fist. 'Thank *God* that thing's not loaded. You'd be picking my brains off the floor for sure.' She took a deep breath and whooshed it out, then took in another and let it out more slowly. 'Wow,' she said, and then she looked at me and laughed – actually *laughed*. I was still kneeling on the floor, clutching the gun and staring at her, as confused as I'd ever been in my life. 'Bless your heart, how *awful*,' she said. 'You must have thought I was about to pull the trigger.'

'Well, yeah. *Weren't* you?'

'No. I'm not suicidal. I'm just . . . *obsessed*, I guess. Still trying to figure this thing out. Still trying to understand how in the world my sister ended up with a Mossberg twelve-gauge in her mouth.'

'I thought we already figured that part out.' I got to my feet, my heart still pounding, and took a few deep breaths of my own. 'Learn anything new?'

'Yeah,' she said. 'Always make sure the door's locked when you're doing something questionable in a low-rent motel.'

I tried to smile, but it felt more like a grimace. I laid the gun on the bed, after making sure the safety was on.

Suddenly I heard a door banging somewhere nearby, then heard Vickery yelling, 'Angie? Are you okay? *Angie?*'

'Oh, shit,' she said in a low voice. She tucked the gun into the gap between the bed and the wall. 'Keep this between us, would you? I don't want Stu to think I'm cracking up.' She held my eyes for an instant, and I nodded. Then she tucked her feet beneath her and sprang into a standing position on the mattress.

Vickery appeared in the doorway, breathing hard, on high alert, his pistol in his hand. He looked at Angie, standing on the bed, then at me, then at Angie again. 'I heard a scream. What's wrong?'

'Nothing,' she said. 'Sorry to scare you. It was just a mouse.' He stared at her, his eyes still wide, his nostrils flaring, his breath rasping loudly enough to be heard over the air conditioner. 'A *mouse*? You're kidding me, right?' He turned to me and rolled his eyes. 'Doc, is she pulling my leg?'

I shrugged. 'I didn't see the mouse. But I sure heard the scream.'

Angie stepped off the bed and sat on the edge of the mattress. 'I was lying down, resting for a minute before dinner. I felt something crawling up the leg of my pants, and I freaked out. Sorry, guys.'

Vickery shook his head. 'Jesus, Angie. And everybody thinks you're tough as nails.' He holstered his gun. 'What's it worth if I keep my mouth shut about this?'

'Stu, are you blackmailing me?'

'I sure am.'

'Uh . . .' Clearly she was struggling to switch gears. 'Well, could I buy your silence with the meat-and-three special at the Waffle Iron?'

'I was thinking more like a lifetime supply of cigars,' he answered. 'But I'm a reasonable man. Throw in a piece of apple pie, and the mouse incident stays in the vault.'

'Shake on it,' said Angie, 'and let's go eat. Dr Brockton, will you be my witness?'

'Sure, I'll be your witness,' I agreed.

But a witness to what? I wondered all through dinner – the dinner Angie had earlier said she didn't want. There was a reason I wondered. As we'd left Angie's room to head to the diner, I'd glanced back at her bed, and my eyes had caught sight of a small box sitting on the lower shelf of the nightstand. I wouldn't have staked my life on it, but in the instant before she switched off the lamp, I thought I'd glimpsed the image of a shotgun shell printed on the side of the box.

I continued to wonder about Angie after we returned to the Twilight, and then my wondering shifted gears, became more personal and more painful. I wondered about my father, and the moments just before he pulled the trigger and shot himself. If someone – anyone: my mother, a client, even my own three-year-old toddling self – had come into his office and found him with the gun to his head, might he have explained away the scene, put away the gun, and set about cleaning up the financial mess he'd accidentally made?

I would never know, of course. And therefore I would forever wonder. 'Remember me, remember me, remember me.' The ghost whispering those words was not Angie's sister nor Hamlet's father this time, but my own.

CHAPTER 19

The next morning Angie, Stu, and I returned to Pettis's place. We were met there by ten crew-cut-sporting students who'd been bused over from the Pat Thomas Law Enforcement Academy, a training facility located in the nearby town of Quincy.

We were also met by Nat James, from the Computer Forensics Section. 'Do you want the last track,' he asked Angie, 'or do you want the *dog's* last track?'

'Aren't those the same?'

'Nope,' he said. 'There's a slow, loopy track in the middle of the night. And then there's a straight, fast track yesterday morning, about an hour after Pettis called Deputy Sutton. That one heads away from the cabin and out the dirt road to the highway, moving about twenty miles an hour. Then, at the highway, it turns north and accelerates to seventy-five miles an hour.'

'It's the killer,' breathed Angie. 'The collar is tracking the killer as he drives away.'

'Where does it go?' demanded Vickery.

'It ends.'

'You mean he stops?'

'No. I mean he gets out of range. The collar's still moving fast, then the receiver loses the signal.'

'Crap,' said Angie.

'Leave it on,' said Vickery. 'Maybe he'll come back.'

Nat nodded. 'I thought of that. I'm rigging a satellite link, so if the receiver picks up the collar's signal again, it'll relay the new track to my computer right away.'

Angie carried a handheld GPS into which Nat James had loaded Jasper's track, so the route we took would be superimposed on the map of Jasper's. Slung over one shoulder was her crime-scene camera, and tucked into the belt of her cargo pants was a bundle of orange survey flags. In addition, she'd enlisted students to carry two shovels, two trowels, a couple of baggies of gloves, more survey flags, a partial roll of crime-scene tape, and paper evidence bags.

Stu carried his cigar. I carried a half-dozen detailed topo maps, which Nat James had brought us. The computer whiz was right: FDLE, or at least his piece of it, was highly wired. The day that Pettis had agreed to putting the GPS collar on the dog, Nat had come out to put the finishing steps on the tracking technology. He'd connected the receiver – the small display on which a hunter could see his dog's position – to a flash drive, which captured the location coordinates that the collar transmitted. He'd reset the tracking interval from five seconds to thirty, to stretch the battery's life. Then he'd concealed the pair of devices high in the nearby fire tower, as Pettis had suggested, for maximum range.

Most of the dog's coordinates clustered around and inside the cabin. The one notable and intriguing exception was the long, looping ramble that the dog had taken during his final night.

The top page of the printout I carried was an overview of the area, including a bright red 'you are here' dot marking the location of the cabin. From it, a squiggly red line meandered to the northeast before looping back. The other five pages each showed enlarged views of segments of the route Jasper had covered before returning with the bone. According to the tracking data, Jasper had covered seven miles during his final outing. As the crow flew, though, he'd remained within a three-mile radius of home.

Vickery had suggested that we retrace the dog's footsteps exactly, but Angie disagreed. 'I doubt that the dog did a lot of wandering with a big bone in his mouth,' she reasoned. 'He obviously wasn't looking for a place to bury it, since he brought it back, right? See how the last part of the track looks fairly straight? It's like he was hurrying home with his new treasure.'

'I think I see what you're saying,' I said. 'You think we should follow the track in reverse.' She nodded, and Vickery agreed, so we lined up at the edge of the clearing side by side, Angie at the center, flanked by Vickery and me, with five trainees on either side. Angie had us spread out, arms stretched wide, until our fingertips were barely touching. 'That's your spacing,' she said. 'Try to maintain it. I'll set the pace. We'll stop and re-form the line whenever it gets too ragged, but try to keep it fairly even.' On her signal we began moving forward in unison, more or less, scanning the ground for bones, signs of recent digging, or anything else out of the ordinary.

The first mile or so took us through pine stands that were relatively free of undergrowth, and we made good time. Jasper had also made good time on this stretch, his home stretch: the red thread of the GPS track was marked on the map with a string of small dots, showing his location at thirty-second intervals. Judging by the spacing of the dots and the scale printed on the map, the dog had covered the final mile in just ten minutes. It took us twenty-five minutes, partly because there were occasional stops to examine holes in the ground – the burrows of various animals, according to Vickery, including one that he swore, with a straight face, had to be a python's hole – and partly because Angie had to call several halts to straighten and tighten the ragtag line.

A half hour after we'd started the search, we halted once more. This time it wasn't to inspect an animal burrow or to re-form ranks; this time it was to figure out how, and whether, to cross a coffee-colored stream that lay in our path. Angie, who'd zoomed her GPS all the way in to pinpoint where Jasper had crossed, pointed to a narrow, muddy notch in the bank. 'Dog tracks,' she said, and I saw that she was right. 'That was a damn good collar.' I squinted at the map, which showed a narrow blue squiggle corresponding to the brown water before us. The fine print that bordered the squiggle sent a chill down my spine: the stream was named Moccasin Creek, and I was reasonably certain the name wasn't a reference to footwear.

Moccasin Creek moved sluggishly between high, eroded banks bordered by overhanging branches. Lurking amid the leaves, camouflaged by the foliage, were countless snakes, I felt sure, draped liked venomous garlands, just waiting to drop upon us as we waded, neck-deep, in the murky waters. My nightmarish reverie was interrupted by Vickery. 'Mind if I take a look at that map?' I handed it over, and he studied it briefly. He stepped closer to the bank and peered upstream and downstream, then huddled with Angie and me. 'We could have big problems if we cross this creek,' he said quietly.

'I'm glad I'm not the only one who's nervous about snakes,' I said.

'Huh?' Vickery looked puzzled. He reexamined the map, then shook his head. 'Actually, Doc, I'm more worried about humans than reptiles.' Now it was my turn to look puzzled. 'We're in Apalachee County right now,' he went on. 'But over there? The other bank? That's Miccosukee County.'

'Oh, good grief,' Angie groaned. 'So what?'

I was inclined to take Angie's view. 'No offense,' I

ventured, 'but FDLE has jurisdiction statewide, right? You can go into any county in Florida.'

'Theoretically, yeah,' said Vickery. 'But like I told Pettis the other day, we have to be invited by the locals – in this case, the Miccosukee County Sheriff's Office. And Miccosukee County Sheriff Darryl Judson is not an inviting kind of guy. He's old as dirt, hard as nails, and mean as a stepped-on cottonmouth.'

'Oh, come *on*,' Angie said. 'Really, Stu? You're actually worried about crossing a little bitty corner of Miccosukee County?'

'Hey, I've been around a long time, but I need to hang on a little longer to get my pension,' Vickery shot back. 'Three years longer, to be precise. I've heard stories about Sheriff Judson. He's got friends in high places – his father was a state senator or some such, back in the day – and he's got dirt on other folks in high places, too. I never heard of anybody who won a pissing match with Sheriff Judson.'

'Can't we claim innocence by way of ignorance? That we were walking in the woods and we didn't know what county we were in? Circle back and ask for forgiveness instead of permission?'

He shook his head. 'If Judson made a big stink and the brass took a close look at your GPS or the maps Nat printed out for us, they'd see the county line. Then they'd have to decide if we were lying or just stupid. That would make it even worse.'

'Stu, we're working a homicide,' she argued, 'and we have got reason to believe that it's linked to a prior homicide – more than one, in fact – that was committed in Miccosukee County.'

'The fact that a dog might – emphasis on *might* – have dug up these age-old skulls in Miccosukee County,' he retorted, 'is not going to carry a whole hell of a lot of weight with a territorial sheriff whose private kingdom has just been invaded.'

'Think about the guy who killed Pettis,' she challenged. 'Maybe he already knows where the skulls came from, maybe not. But he's got the collar, and he's got a head start on us, right?' Vickery nodded grudgingly. 'If he's looking, and he gets there ahead of us, he might wreck the scene. Can we afford to take a chance on that?'

'You're not the one whose neck is on the line,' he retorted. 'I'm the case agent. If anybody gets hung on the cross by Sheriff Judson or one of his Tallahassee cronies, it'll be me.'

'Call Riordan,' said Angie. 'If he tells us to keep going, it's on him, not you, right?'

Vickery frowned. 'Shit.'

'Come on, Stu, grow a backbone,' she snapped. 'Are you really just gonna mark time for the next three years? Is that who you want to be?' Vickery reddened; he snatched his cigar from his mouth and rolled it angrily between his thumb and fingers. 'That poor son of a bitch back there died trying to help us,' she pressed. 'Don't we owe him at least a good *try*?' Vickery's jaw clenched and unclenched. As he continued rolling the cigar, I noticed the pressure of his grip increased. Shreds of tobacco sifted through his fingers as he slowly crushed the cigar to bits.

'Goddammit,' he muttered. 'You're right.'

Angie smiled. 'Good man. You want to call Riordan anyhow? Just to cover your ass?'

'Not particularly, but I guess I have to.' He pulled the phone from his belt and dialed the prosecutor. 'So,' Vickery began after a few throat-clearing preliminaries, 'we think we're closing in on the bones . . . I hope so, too. But we have a slight wrinkle, and I figured you'd want a heads-up . . . Well, unfortunately, the damn dog didn't pay too much attention to county lines and jurisdictions when he went sniffing around, if you catch my drift . . . What I mean is, we've tracked the dog as far as the Apalachee County line. If we want to keep tracking him the rest of the way to his hunting ground, we've got to cross into Miccosukee County . . . Yes, sir, I'm sure about that. I'm looking at his paw prints right now where he came across the creek from Miccosukee. Exactly, that's Sheriff Judson's county . . . I know, I know – Judson does put the "dick" in "jurisdiction," doesn't he?' Vickery forced a laugh. 'Well, we just didn't know – the GPS track from the collar didn't show us the county lines . . . Yes, sir, you're right, you're absolutely right. We *should've* taken a closer look. But we didn't. So here we are, out here in the middle of nowhere. Out here in the middle of a search that we think might lead to something . . . With all due respect, sir, I disagree. I believe we ought to keep going . . . No, sir, I *don't* want to start a shooting war with the sheriff. But I also don't want to let a hot trail go cold . . . No, sir, I *don't* think it can wait till tomorrow . . . Look, whoever killed Pettis took the collar off the dog. You're aware of that, right? . . . *No*, sir; no, *sir*, I am *not* condescending to you, I'm just making sure you're aware that the collar's gone . . . So the killer might be able to download the same data we've got, cover the same ground we're covering.' Angie had made this same argument to Stu; now, she shook her head doubtfully and appeared about to interrupt him, but Stu held up a hand to shush her. 'No, sir, I don't know that to be a fact, but I just don't think we can afford to take that chance, can we? What I *do* know is that if we spend twenty-four hours kissing the sheriff's ass, our chances of finding whatever's out here in the woods get worse, not better . . . I understand that this puts you in a tough spot, and I wish the dog had stayed in his own damn county, but he didn't. If you tell us not to go on, we won't, but I hope you won't do that . . . All right, thank you, sir. . . . You'll call the sheriff? Okay, I appreciate that . . . Yes, sir, I'll be sure to keep you posted . . . I guarantee it – you'll be the first to know if we find anything . . . Sorry to put you on the hot seat. Thank you, sir. Talk to you soon.' I had never heard so many 'sirs' in such swift succession, but they seemed to have helped. Vickery hung up, blew out a long breath, and shook his head. 'Well, *that* was fun.' He turned to the group and put on a smile. 'Okay, people, let's find a way to cross Moccasin *fuckin'* Creek that won't get us drowned or snakebit.'

The steep, narrow notch where Jasper had crossed the stream looked risky, so Angie asked for volunteers to seek out an easier place to cross. She recruited two to jog upstream and another two downstream. 'Turn around in ten minutes,' she instructed, 'whether you've found a good crossing or not. We don't have time for a big detour.' While they explored, we studied the detailed maps Nat had printed out for us. On the other side of the creek, the dog's track was practically a beeline for half a mile or so, then it reached a spot where he seemed to loiter and explore. 'That, I'm hoping, is where we might find something,' she said.

Her phone rang – an incongruous, startling sound, deep in the woods as we were. 'Hi, Nat. What's up? . . . Really? No kidding? . . . Hang on a second. Let me put you on speaker, so Stu can hear, too.' She flipped open the phone and pressed a button. 'Nat, you still there?'

'I am,' came the computer analyst's voice.

'Okay, back up and start over, if you don't mind.'

'I'm getting data from the tracking collar again. Remember, I left the receiver in the fire tower and rigged it to a satellite link? So if I got a signal from the collar again, it would send the new data to my computer?'

'I remember. Go on,' Vickery prompted.

'A minute or two ago, I started seeing the collar again. Looks like it's on a county road, about four miles south of Pettis's place. Moving away fast – sixty, seventy miles an hour. It'll be out of range again in a second.'

'Call Operations,' Vickery ordered. 'Tell 'em we need everybody who's anywhere near that road. Stevenson might be the nearest, but I don't know where he is.'

'Hang on, hang on, it's slowing down!' James's voice was loud, distorted. 'It's stopping! It's stopped! Wait. Oh, crap, it's gone. We've lost it again.'

'Out of range?' asked Vickery. 'How'd it go out of range, if it was stopped?'

'Oh, wow. The place where it stopped? It's a bridge over a river. . . . Let's see . . . the Miccosukee River. I betcha the collar's drifting down to the bottom of the river right now.'

'Shit,' cursed Vickery. 'Call Operations. Give 'em the location. See if we can seal off that road. Get 'em to pull in the local cavalry, too. Which county?'

'Uh . . . Bremerton on one side of the river, Miccosukee on the other.'

'Shit. Same jurisdictional mess we're in out here in the woods. Okay. Tell Operations we need help from both counties. We need to question anybody who's on that road, anybody who might've been.'

*

249

As Vickery was winding up the conversation with Nat James, the pair of recruits who'd jogged downstream returned with good news. A large tree had fallen across the stream only a few hundred yards away, they reported; the trunk was two feet in diameter, with branches that could be held for balance most of the way across.

Angie tied a strip of crime-scene tape to a tree trunk beside the muddy notch in the bank, to make sure we could pick up the trail again directly across from where we stood. Five minutes later, when the other pair of trainees returned from their search in the opposite direction, we headed downstream to the fallen tree. It was indeed a fine makeshift bridge, I thought.

Stu didn't think so. He sized up the trunk nervously. 'I thought it would be fatter.'

'Jesus, Stu,' said Angie, 'it's as wide as a sidewalk.'

'But not as flat. And a lot higher up.'

'Tell you what,' she offered. 'You can watch everyone else go across and see how they do. Then, if you're still nervous, you don't have to do it.'

He considered this only briefly. 'Nah, that's okay. It's like jumping off the high dive the first day of swimming season. The longer you think about it, the scarier it gets. Might as well get it over with.' With that, he plucked the cigar from his mouth and hoisted himself onto the trunk, making the move with surprising agility for a sixty-year-old with a bit of a belly. He walked quickly, on the balls of his feet, extending both arms for balance, making small circles in the air with the cigar to compensate for his occasional wobbles. When he reached the opposite bank, he pivoted on the trunk. 'Okay, quit stalling, you yellow-bellied, lily-livered cowards,' he called. 'We're burning daylight here.'

Angie was the last to cross. Before hopping off the trunk, she tied a long streamer of tape as high in a branch as she could reach so we could find our bridge more easily in the dark, if need be. We walked quickly up the Miccosukee bank of the stream until the yellow tape, the paw prints, and the GPS confirmed that we were back on the dog's trail. 'Okay,' Angie told the group, 'from here, we've got about another half mile or so where he was moving pretty straight and fairly fast. So line up, spread out, and let's go.'

Our progress was slower on this side of the creek; at some point the land here had been cleared, and what had grown back, in place of pines and live oaks, was a field of briars. Game trails, including the one the dog had followed, formed low, narrow tunnels through the stickers, but without crawling on all fours, we were forced to pick our way through, and our progress was punctuated by a chorus of curses and yelps.

There were supplemental curses from Vickery when he learned that Stevenson, two other agents, and four county deputies had failed to apprehend any vehicles within miles of the bridge across the Miccosukee River, and a network of side roads made it impossible to seal the area. Vickery looked close to flinging his phone into the briars; he settled instead for snapping his cigar in two and then hurling it away.

Thirty sweaty, scratchy minutes after we'd entered the briar patch, the stickers thinned out, giving way once more to live oaks, pines, and waist-high ferns. Angie called a halt and scrutinized the GPS screen. 'Okay, we're getting close to an area where the dog hung out and wandered around awhile,' she said, 'so look sharp.'

We'd barely started forward again when she held up a closed fist – the 'stop' signal – and pointed. Ten yards ahead, directly in her path, was a low heap of dead ferns and freshly scattered dirt. Angie crept forward, motioning for me to join her. I moved slowly, inspecting the ground carefully before each step. Angie reached the spot before I did; when I joined her, she was staring down into a shallow hollow, roughly a foot in diameter and a foot deep. Paw prints and claw marks edged its rim. Within the hole, I saw shreds of black plastic sheeting. And jutting from the tattered plastic and the clumped dirt, I glimpsed the ends of three ribs.

CHAPTER 20

Angie unslung her camera, removed a bundle of survey flags from her belt, and began flagging and photographing the grave. She started with wide-angle shots, showing the grave amid the wooded setting, then she worked her way closer, taking medium shots of the disturbed earth. Gradually she moved in for close-ups of the hole and the exposed bones within it.

Vickery phoned the prosecutor. 'Mr Riordan, we've just found a shallow grave. It's been recently disturbed . . . Yes, sir, unfortunately, we *are* in Miccosukee County . . . Well, we haven't excavated it yet, but several bones are exposed, and Dr Brockton feels pretty confident they're human . . .' I was surprised to hear him laugh. 'Well, I *guess* we could dig it up and move it across the creek into Apalachee. But then we'd have to kill all these trainees so we don't leave any witnesses.' He laughed again, which I hoped was a sign that on the other end of the call, the prosecutor was making his peace with the jurisdictional briar patch into which we'd strayed.

As Vickery talked and Angie photographed, I began to explore the surrounding ground. Angie had waved the recruits back, to keep them from trampling the scene, but she'd asked me to take a look around. She didn't have to ask twice.

We were in another grove of massive live oaks – immense, sprawling trees that must have been hundreds of years old. At their bases, they were wider than my arms could span; ten to fifteen feet above the ground, their trunks branched into six or eight or ten or twelve secondary trunks, each one twice as big around as I was. The limbs that spread from these secondary trunks were blanketed with resurrection ferns – named, Angie had told me, for the way they shriveled up and 'died' during dry spells, then came back to life at the return of rain. Over the decades, some of the trees had lost large portions to disease or storms, and some of the trunks were splitting and half rotted. Yet there was remarkable life and beauty in the ancient trees, even the ones that were starting to die. Overhead, their branches laced together into a canopy that was as high, as wide, and as beautiful as the nave of a Gothic cathedral. Beards of Spanish moss, some of them twenty feet long, hung from the limbs and swayed gently in the late-afternoon breeze. The leaves and ferns and moss caught most of the sun; what light sifted through, to the lush carpet of ferns on the ground, was filtered by the foliage to a soft, silvery green.

And in the sifted, silvery-green light, beneath the resurrection ferns, I saw a second grave, also freshly disturbed, about thirty feet beyond the first.

A stone's throw from the second grave, I saw a third. This – *this* – had to be the Bone Yard.

After his conversation with the prosecutor, Vickers phoned FDLE's operations center to call in the crime-scene cavalry – and to confer on the best way to get them to our location. As it turned out, we were only a mile north of the ruins of the North Florida Boys' Reformatory, although the school lay in yet another county. 'Interesting,' Vickery observed, 'that the school itself, and the official cemetery, are in Bremerton County, but these graves are hidden up in this little corner of Miccosukee County. Coincidence? I don't think so.'

Once Vickery had grasped our proximity to the school, he sent the academy trainees skirting the edge of the grove of oaks. At the far end, one of them found the remnants of an overgrown dirt road – a track that headed in the direction of the school. The dispatcher in the operations center would send reinforcements to the school; meanwhile, Vickery would send two of the recruits to lead them the rest of the way to us.

Ninety minutes after Angie had spotted the first grave – and thirty minutes before we were likely to run out of daylight – we heard the low whine of an all-wheel-drive SUV laboring through the woods, its progress punctuated by the screechings of underbrush and tree branches scraping the belly and the sides of the vehicle.

The vehicle was not, it turned out, the vanguard of

the FDLE cavalry. A big off-road pickup – a Chevy Avalanche, wearing markings of the Miccosukee County Sheriff's Office – muscled along the overgrown road. It stopped at the crime-scene tape that had been stretched across the mouth of the road to keep vehicles out, and then the engine revved. The Avalanche rumbled forward, pulled the tape taut, and snapped it. The vehicle jounced toward us and slammed to a halt, narrowly missing one of the graves. A grizzled, bowlegged man got out of the cab; his legs and arms were thin with age – I'd have pegged him as a seventy-year-old, at least – but he had a stringy strength about him, like beef jerky. Despite the thinness of his limbs, he had a substantial beer belly hanging over his belt, a sizable wad of tobacco in his cheek, and a major-league scowl on his face. His gaze swept the scene, taking in and rapidly dismissing the crew-cut trainees, pausing and sharpening on the flags marking the three graves, and then settling fiercely on Stu, Angie, and me. 'Which one of you's Vickery?'

'That's me, Sheriff. Stu Vickery.' The agent stepped forward and offered his hand. The sheriff turned aside – but only slightly – and spat tobacco juice. 'Sorry for the surprise. We were surprised, too.'

'Surprised? A *surprise*? Is that what you call it when you bring a search party into my county without so much as a by-your-leave? Is this what FDLE calls a surprise party? Because I'll tell you, Vickery, I do not take kindly to surprises. Not in my county.'

Vickery flushed. 'I understand, Sheriff. It was a tough call. We were on a crime-scene search, and the trail led straight across the creek. Led to these three graves. I wish they were on the other side, in Apalachee County, but they're not. So here we are.'

'And here is where you can get the hell out of right now.'

'Right now? How?'

'I don't give a good goddamn, Agent Vickery. Not my problem. You found your way in here easy as pie. You can find your way right back out again. You're good at following a trail, looks like. Ought to be a lot easier to follow it back out, now that it's been beaten down by you and your posse.'

'You've got three shallow graves here, Sheriff. How do you aim to handle them? What kind of forensic resources have you got in Miccosukee County for excavating multiple graves?'

'A kind that's none of your damned business, pissant. Now, you can turn around and walk out of here, or I can call in my deputies and we can haul you down to the Miccosukee County Jail. But I don't think you'd like it there, because I got some prisoners right now that have serious anger-management issues. They don't like authority figures, and I figure they'd go ape-shit over a bunch of snotty-nosed FDLE folks.'

The standoff was interrupted by the brief whoop of a siren. A silver SUV paused at the broken strip of crime-scene tape, eased forward, and then backed up beyond the margin of broken tape and parked. The door opened and Riordan, the prosecutor, strode through the ferns in his fancy, city-slicker clothes, managing to look both out of place and yet somehow right at home. By the time he reached us, a ragged caravan of vehicles had begun arriving and parking behind the silver Lexus. First came the crime lab's black Suburban, driven by Whitney, one of the crime-scene techs I'd met at the Pettis place. The Suburban was followed by a Miccosukee County Sheriff's cruiser, driven by a deputy who chose to remain in the car, the engine running. Eventually FDLE's crime-scene truck lumbered into view, announced by a new round of scraping and snapping as it bulled a wider, higher swath through the branches than the smaller vehicles had cleared.

Last to arrive was a pickup towing a generator and light tower, the sort of high-intensity work lights used by highway crews at night. As the number of people, vehicles, and pieces of equipment multiplied, the nature of the scene changed. We'd arrived to a scene of lush natural sights, sounds, and smells: shades of leafy green, mossy gray, and crumbling brown; a chorus of woodpeckers, insects, and chirping frogs; the scent of honeysuckle, magnolia blossoms, pine needles, and decaying leaves. Now all those were being trumped by the fluorescent colors of crime-scene paraphernalia;, the rumble of vehicles and generators; and the acrid fumes of gasoline, diesel, and sweat.

The prosecutor huddled with Sheriff Judson and Stu. I heard raised voices – actually, only one raised voice, which was the sheriff's. He paused in his tirade long enough for Stu to give some low answer that I couldn't make out; occasionally I caught a few sentences in Stu's voice and, eventually, a long, conciliatory-sounding summation by the prosecutor. Finally I heard my own name; I strained to hear what was being said about me, but a silence followed the words *Dr Brockton*. After a moment, my name was repeated – louder this time – and I realized with a guilty start that Stu wasn't talking *about* me; he was talking *to* me.

'Sorry, I was daydreaming,' I answered.

'Could you come confer with us for a minute?'

'Sure.' I jogged over, and Stu introduced me to the sheriff.

Riordan nodded a hello. 'We appreciate your helping us out,' he said. 'I gather this is more than you'd bargained for when you offered to take a quick look at that first skull for FDLE.'

'A little more,' I admitted. 'But it's an interesting case, and I'm glad I can help.'

The prosecutor cleared his throat. 'Sheriff Judson was wondering how long it might take us to excavate these graves. He has limited manpower, and he'll need to assign a deputy to the scene while we're here. Agent Vickery here says you're the expert.' He nodded at Stu, as if I might be unsure who Agent Vickery was. Stu returned the nod, as if confirming that he had indeed said that. 'The sheriff's hoping maybe we can be through by midnight. What do you think?'

'Unfortunately,' I said, 'I think it's a bad idea to excavate graves and search an area this big in the dark. The lights on that tower are bright, but they won't begin to illuminate this whole area. Besides, even with bright lights, we're bound to miss things we'd see in the daylight.' I added, 'With all due respect, the people in these graves are already dead. They can't get any deader by morning.'

Vickery smiled. The sheriff worked his jaw muscles, and the veins in his neck bulged, but before he could explode, the prosecutor asked smoothly, 'And if we start the search in the morning, how long would you estimate it might take to recover the bones from the graves?'

I'd already been giving this matter some thought, since the clock was ticking on my two-week window of availability. 'Well, that all depends,' I hedged.

The sheriff spat another string of brown juice into the ferns. 'Depends on what?'

'Depends on how many more graves there are.'

The sheriff's rheumy eyes bored into me. 'The hell you say.'

I held his look. 'We know there are three. At *least* three. Who's to say we won't find four, or fourteen, or even forty?'

'Bull *shit*.'

I shrugged. So far, two line searches of the grove by

the recruits had failed to disclose any more open graves, but I didn't want to rule out the possibility of additional, undisturbed ones.

'There might be more, there might not. But we won't know until we look.'

'Look where-all? You plan to turn my whole damn county into a crime scene?' When he said it, I couldn't help wondering if maybe the whole county might *be* a crime scene, and I remembered Vickery's words – 'this whole *world's* one big crime scene' – but I kept those thoughts to myself.

The prosecutor spoke up. 'Sheriff, I don't think anybody's suggesting we go overboard. But Dr Brockton has a point. If we know of three graves in this specific area, we need to make sure there are *only* three. And to do that, we have to take a closer look.'

The sheriff spat again. 'You go digging around on some damn fishing expedition here, there's gonna be newspaper and TV reporters crawling all over the place.'

'If we *don't* go digging around,' said Riordan, 'there'll be even more reporters crawling around, doing stories about cover-ups in Miccosukee County.' He said it calmly, as if he were stating an obvious, neutral fact, but I thought I detected a hint of a threat in the prosecutor's words. I wasn't the only one who detected it; Vickery and Angie both carefully avoided making eye contact with anyone, and the tendons in the sheriff's neck tightened, stretching his wattle into webs of splotchy flesh.

'Tomorrow,' growled the sheriff.

'Great. We'll start tomorrow,' agreed Riordan.

'You'll finish tomorrow.'

'What do you mean?'

'I mean do whatever the hell you have to do, but get it done tomorrow. I want your fancy asses out of my county twenty-four hours from now.'

'We'll do our best,' said Riordan. I was impressed with how coolly and levelly he managed to say it.

'I said tomorrow,' repeated the sheriff.

'And I said we'll do our best.'

The sheriff spun on his heel and stalked away. He conferred briefly with his deputy, then slammed the door of his truck, and with impressive force, I thought, for a man his age. As he fishtailed away, his wheels – which boasted the glossy sidewalls and deep tread of new tires – flung shreds of ferns and dirt into one of the open graves.

Angie knelt and studied the ferns beside the spot where Judson had been standing, then – using a glove she fished from her pocket – she carefully plucked and bagged the end of a fern. The leaves were damp and slimy with what I realized was a mixture of tobacco juice and spit. Angie had just collected a DNA sample from Sheriff Darryl Judson.

'That went well,' said Riordan. He motioned Angie over, without seeming to grasp what she'd just done, then looked around our small huddle. 'Okay, how do we make that happen?'

Stu and Angie looked at each other, then at him. Stu said, 'Make what happen?'

'Clear this scene in twenty-four hours.'

'You're kidding,' said Angie. 'Right?'

'Wrong. We need to recover these three sets of remains and do whatever additional searching we need to do by the end of the day tomorrow. Unless we find something else by then – and by "something else" I mean more graves – we need to pack up and roll out of here at sundown.'

'Sir, no offense,' Angie persisted, 'but how the hell are we supposed to search an area this big in that amount of time?'

'Swiftly and efficiently, I suppose.' He gave her a tight smile. 'You've got technology for this, right? Didn't FDLE spend a lot of taxpayer dollars on a ground-penetrating radar system? Isn't this exactly what that technology's designed for?' Angie opened her mouth, and I expected to hear the words *root finder*, but Riordan held up a cautionary hand, so she kept quiet and he went on. 'Like the sheriff said, do whatever the hell you have to do, but get it done tomorrow. Good night. And good luck.' With that, he, too, left, though his departure was not as showy as the sheriff's. It reminded me of an old saying, an insult I'd first heard as a kid: don't go away mad; just go away. He just went away.

Stu looked from me to Angie. 'So. What next?' Angie shook her head glumly; Stu frowned and chewed his cigar.

'I have an idea,' I said.

A flurry of phone calls, explanations, and pleadings ensued over the next three hours. What we needed was hard to find, and when we needed it was almost instantly. The whirlwind of calls and arrangements occurred against a backdrop of logistical and vehicular chaos, because the ten trainees who'd helped with the search needed transportation back to the law enforcement academy in Quincy, and Stu's vehicle needed to be ferried to the new scene from Pettis's cabin. Eventually all the logistical and vehicular loose ends were tied up beneath the buggy glare of the work lights, but by the time we left the scene, it was going on eleven o'clock. Two junior FDLE agents remained behind, camped out in the cab of the crime-scene truck, sharing night-shift guard duty with Sheriff Judson's unsociable deputy.

Following a dozen sets of tire tracks, Stu's Jeep and Angie's Suburban lurched and scraped down the unfamiliar dirt road. A half mile down, we found ourselves passing the makeshift cemetery of pipe crosses. It made macabre sense, I supposed, that the clandestine graves would be located in the same general area as the marked graves, but hidden farther – geographically farther and morally farther – from what had passed for civilization at the school. As our headlights illuminated them, the crosses cast long shadows that reeled and skittered as we jounced and angled past.

From the cemetery we easily made our way back to the burned-out ruins of the reform school, and then the blacktop road and the county highway. On our way back to the Twilight, we dashed into a lonely-looking Circle K to snag a late 'dinner' – the Waffle Iron was long since closed, and even the convenience store was about to shut down when we showed up. In the gritty passenger seat of the Suburban, I dined on a bruised banana, a pack of stale peanut-butter crackers, and a pint of chocolate milk as we headed for the proverbial barn – the pestilential barn – that was the Twilight Motor Court. It was midnight by the time we turned off the blacktop and into the sandy parking lot. Ten minutes after midnight, I got out from under the dribbling shower, folded down the biohazard-laden bedspread, and crawled between the dingy sheets of the lumpy bed.

Tired as I was, I expected to close my eyes and find myself spiraling swiftly into sleep.

Instead, I found myself spiraling deep into memory, spinning thirty years back in time and fifteen hundred miles away. I found myself in South Dakota, seeking the long-lost graves of dead Indians.

CHAPTER 21

Vickery had asked me how I'd gotten into forensic cases, and the answer had been 'South Dakota.' South Dakota was also where I'd first thought that if I wanted to move the earth – or at least a few long layers of it – a diesel engine and a wide steel blade might pinch-hit for a lever and a place to stand.

The engine and the blade were on an earthmoving machine – an aging LeTourneau 'Tournapull' – and as it coughed and rumbled forward on the prairie, it carried my hopes and my potential ruin with it. A fraction of an inch at a time, the Tournapull's angled blade eased down into the South Dakota soil and shaved off a layer, the way a carpenter's plane shaves a sliver of pine off a plank. In this case, though, the sliver was eighty feet long, ten feet wide, and two hundred years deep.

I'd spent the prior year – the summer after earning my master's degree in anthropology – leading a crew of students at this same archaeological site, an Arikara Indian village whose timber-and-sod huts had once housed hundreds of people. Inhabited between the early 1700s and the early 1800s, the village was now on the verge of being inundated by the rising waters of a new reservoir. Anything we hoped to learn about the village and its inhabitants would have to be learned fast – unless we wanted to call in scuba divers. The previous summer, the water level had been twenty feet below the site's lowest areas; now waves were lapping at the very margins of the village.

We'd worked feverishly the prior season. Gridding the entire site into hundreds of five-foot squares, marked by stakes and string, we'd dug down by hand, inch by inch, through dozens of test squares. Over the course of the summer we'd managed to find and excavate thirteen graves – great progress, by most measures, but maddeningly slow in the face of the rising waters. It hadn't been easy to convince the Smithsonian – the expedition's sponsor – to let me trade my trowel for a road grader this season; they worried about the damage that heavy equipment could inflict on fragile old bones. I argued that even though the technique was experimental and seemingly risky, there was much to gain and virtually nothing to lose by bringing in earthmoving equipment. Saying no posed zero risk of damaging bones, but it also offered zero hope of recovering more than a relative handful of skeletons. In the end, I won an important but provisional victory: I could cut one eighty-foot trench with the grader, and if the technique proved successful at finding graves without damaging bones, I could forge ahead full speed.

But despite my confident arguments in Washington,

D.C., I'd felt anxiety carving into me as the steel blade sliced into the soil. I was counting on the wind that swept across the Great Plains, unrelentingly but also consistently. Year after year, decade after decade, the wind carried powdery alluvial soil – the infamous dust of the dust bowl – across the Plains, sifting it down amid the grass stalks at the steady rate of one inch every ten years. So sixteen or eighteen inches down – in theory, at least – the Tournapull would uncover what had been the surface layer back to the early 1800s, when the village had been abandoned, fire-building and pot-breaking had moved elsewhere, and grave digging had ceased. We'd see the ground the Arikara had worked with hoes fashioned from bison scapulae. We'd find, I hoped, the circular graves they'd scooped out to bury warriors who'd fallen in battle, women who'd died in childbirth, children who'd succumbed to smallpox, the invisible new enemy unleashed by the whites.

The eighty-foot test cut lay alongside a row of squares we'd excavated a year before – squares that had contained many of the thirteen graves we'd found. I was gambling that this area was part of a larger burial ground, and that somewhere in the next eighty feet, the blade would intersect and reveal more graves.

As the machine crawled along, I checked the cut's depth repeatedly with a wooden stake I'd cut to length. To play it safe, the machine would make multiple passes, each one shaving off another two inches of topsoil. The soil was grayish brown, almost as fine as flour or cocoa powder. As the blade bit deeper and deeper into the earth, the walls of the trench began to resemble a cutaway drawing from a soil-science textbook. Below the mat of roots, the soil was darker and denser, sprinkled with round pebbles and the occasional larger rock – the size of a fist or a grapefruit – that had once been a mighty boulder, before its encounter with the glacier. Whenever I saw one of the larger rocks, I worried that it might be a skull, that the grader just cut through a grave and a destroyed a skeleton. My relief upon seeing that no, it was just a rock, was mixed with disappointment: no, it was just a rock.

Pass by pass – two inches, four, six, eight, ten, twelve – my anxiety deepened along with the cut. Perhaps my bold experiment was a failure. Perhaps I'd laid out a swath that contained no graves at all . . . or perhaps graves galore dotted the ground on either side of my trench, their skeletal inhabitants grinning at my foolishness in picking exactly the wrong path. Or perhaps there were indeed graves in the grader's path, but the blade somehow masked them in its passage.

Midway along the ninth pass of the eighty-foot cut, just as I started to despair, my eye caught a subtle difference in the surface of the exposed dirt. *There*: eighteen inches down, was a faint, familiar circle in the soil, three feet across, slightly darker in color and almost imperceptibly looser in texture than its surroundings – like a powdery version of a fresh asphalt patch plugging a big highway pothole. Could I be imagining it? I knelt to examine it, my heart racing. At the nearer edge of the rim – the edge first crossed by the steel blade – the soil within the circle had separated slightly from the soil outside the circle. The curved, quarter-inch gap marked a line where looser, disturbed dirt had been pulled away from the denser, undisturbed soil surrounding it. On the far side of the circle's rim, the blade had shoved a corresponding handful of the loose dirt outside the margin of the circle, where it had tumbled onto the packed dirt in a miniature avalanche.

As I leaned closer, my eye caught a flash of color amid the drab soil. Taking my trowel from the back pocket of my pants, I flicked away crumbs of soil with the tool's triangular tip, revealing a tiny sphere of cobalt blue, pierced by a cylindrical hole. The blade had uncovered a blue glass bead, the sort used as currency by the Indians and early white traders. The bead told me beyond a doubt that this circular disturbance in the prairie soil was the grave of an Arikara Indian, containing bones and a few possessions and trade goods for the afterlife.

Over the rumble and growl of the diesel engine, I heard a shout and looked up. Doug, one of the ten under-graduate students on my summer crew, was standing in the cut ten feet beyond me, pointing at the ground and waving his straw hat in excitement. I stood for a better look. By now the grader was nearing the end of the swath we'd marked with flags. Between where I stood and where the machine was slowing to an idle, the other nine summer students were dancing, pointing, and dropping to their knees in the dirt, clustering around another half-dozen faint circles, another half-dozen graves.

I raised my trowel high above my head and cut loose with what I imagined to be the battle cry of a triumphant Arikara warrior. The students stared at me, then, one by one and two by two, they joined in.

Unlike whites, the Arikara tended to bury their dead in a folded position, either sitting up or lying on one side, tightly tucked in a fetal position. The reason was simple: two hundred years ago, the Indians had only the simplest of tools. To dig graves, they used crude hoes, which they made by lashing a buffalo scapula to a stick or to a buffalo femur. These Bone Age tools were wielded by women, for burying the dead was considered women's work. Try burrowing down through prairie sod with a buffalo bone and you, too, would surely settle for a compact, shallow grave, just as the Arikara squaw who'd dug this grave had doubtless done.

Pulling rank, I claimed the first grave as my own private dig and began troweling into the soil. A few inches down, I came to a layer of crumbling wood, the remnants of the sticks and brush that had been put here two centuries before to deter scavenging by coyotes and rodents. Carefully I teased the wood fragments apart, setting them on a wire screen that would be used to sift everything that came from the ground.

The dirt was soft and the work went quickly – 'summertime, and the diggin' is easy,' I heard myself singing – and before long I felt the tip of the trowel contact something hard. Probing gently for the object's boundaries, I found that it was large and round, and a few minutes later, I was looking at the top of a cranial vault, stained a dull grayish brown from two centuries in the prairie soil. I used the trowel to lift powdery triangles of soil from around the skull, and then switched to an artist's brush to dust the skull itself.

The skull was that of a young adult male, large and robust, with a heavy brow ridge and prominent muscle markings. The left side of the skull had been crushed. By what, I wondered: a horse's hoof? a cavalry soldier's rifle butt? a Sioux war club? Reaching down, I touched the skull gently, tracing the edges of the gaping hole, brushing the intact bone surrounding it. As my fingers grazed the forehead, they encountered an unexpected roughness in what should have been smooth bone. Brushing away more dirt, I leaned down to inspect the forehead. In a crude arc from one side to the other, the forehead bore the jagged, ragged cut marks of a hasty scalping. A foe, probably a Sioux warrior, had sliced through the front of the scalp and then given the hair a hard yank, peeling the hair and skin backward, off the top of the head, and all the way down to the back of the neck. If the Sioux brave had survived the battle, he would have displayed the scalp triumphantly, boasting of his prowess, when it came time to count coup and tally the number of Arikara they'd killed.

In my mind's eye, I pictured the triumphant Sioux warrior, and then, in my imagination, I *became* the triumphant Sioux warrior. And at that moment – when the boundary between past and present, between South Dakota and north Florida, between reality and magic, turned shimmery and elusive and impossible to pin down – sleep finally caught up with me.

Or so I assume, because the next thing I knew, my cell phone was warbling to tell me that it was 5:30 A.M., and the rattling, musty air conditioner was reminding me emphatically that I was in bungalow number three at the Twilight Motor Court. And the Twilight was neither dream nor vision.

CHAPTER 22

Day was breaking – oozing up out of the steamy ground of the panhandle, more like it – as we approached the turnoff to the reform school. The eastern sky was turning a watery gray, and by that hint of light, I saw the hulking yellow shape beside the highway. 'Looks like maybe somebody up there likes us,' I said. Pulling ahead of the gear-laden trailer, we led the way down the blacktop to the school.

Then, as we neared the faint turnoff of the dirt road that led past the cemetery and beyond, to the unmarked graves, I saw the strobing blue lights of a Miccosukee County sheriff's car blocking the lane. 'Somebody up there might like us,' muttered Vickery, 'but somebody down here definitely doesn't.'

Angie pulled alongside the cruiser, and Vickery got out to confer with the deputy. He returned a moment later, his cell phone at his ear. 'There's good news and bad news,' he reported as he snapped the phone closed.

'What's the good news?' asked Angie.

'The good news is, Sheriff Judson is on his way out here.'

She made a face. 'That's the *good* news? What the hell is the bad news?'

'The bad news is, I might have to arrest him.'

'Ouch,' said Angie. 'That could be ugly.'

'Maybe I won't have to. Riordan's on his way out here, too.'

The sheriff arrived first, parking his truck behind us with his strobes and his spotlights on us full force, as if we were suspects. He got out and approached the Suburban, his silhouette casting an immense shadow. Vickery drew a deep breath. 'Showtime. Or show*down*, more like. Y'all mind coming with me for moral support? Or to witness my demise? You can tell people I died bravely.' Our doors opened in unison; they closed in unison.

'Morning, Sheriff,' said Vickery. The sheriff made no answer, so Vickery went on. 'We're anxious to get back to our crime-scene search, since you'd like us to complete it today. Any particular reason your deputy is blocking the access road?'

'Doesn't look like you're here to search a crime scene,' said the sheriff. He pointed at the flatbed trailer and the massive machine it carried. 'Looks like you're here to build a damn highway.'

Just then the silver Lexus arrived, and Riordan joined our conclave. He wasted no time with pleasantries. 'What's the problem, Sheriff?'

'Problem is, I say you can have a day to dig up a few

old bones, and you-all want to come in here and start cutting roads. That's not the deal we had.'

'We're not cutting roads, Sheriff.'

'Then why you bringing in the goddamn road-cutting machinery?'

Riordan turned to me. 'Dr Brockton, would you explain why we need the equipment?'

'Of course. Sheriff, the problem is, we've got an area half the size of a football field to search for more graves. We could probe and excavate the whole area by hand, but that would take days, maybe even weeks. Using this road scraper, we can peel back the vegetation and the top layer of soil, so we can see areas underneath where the ground's been disturbed. When we find those, we know where to check for more bones.'

The sheriff stared at me, then at Riordan. Finally he shook his head. 'No.'

Riordan tilted his head slightly. 'What do you mean, "no"?'

'I mean *hell* no. This is my county. I am the law here. Nobody can fire me but the governor, and I have the authority to limit the scope of this crime-scene search. You can bring in all the shovels and fancy-ass PhDs, you want. For the next twelve hours. But get that damn machine out of here.'

Riordan didn't speak for a while; finally he shook his head and, just as the sheriff had done, said, 'No.' He gave another, smaller shake – wistfully, I thought, regretting the clash of wills – then went on. 'Sheriff, I've opened an investigation into these deaths – I have some authority, too – and I've got a warrant authorizing us to locate and excavate any graves on that piece of land, using whatever tools and equipment we deem necessary. I can't fire you, but I can arrest you, and if that road isn't open in sixty seconds, you and your deputy will both be charged with obstruction of justice.' He studied the cruiser that was blocking the way. 'I think it'll be interesting to see what a road grader does to that car when it pushes it into the trees. Not what the machine was designed for, but I suspect it'll do the job.'

Two minutes later, Riordan was ordering the scraper's operator to unload his machine and clear the road. I wasn't sure the nervous-looking equipment operator would actually follow that order, if the prosecutor's push came to the sheriff's shove. Luckily – and surprisingly – the sheriff backed down. The Miccosukee County deputy killed his strobes and crept down the dirt road toward the Bone Yard. Our motley convoy followed: the Avalanche of the pissed-off sheriff, the Lexus of the prosecutor, our Suburban, and, bringing up the rear, the goosenecked lowboy trailer hauling the mammoth machine that I hoped would reveal how many graves – how many dead boys – were hidden in the Bone Yard.

If we'd had more time, the sheriff's mistaken idea – that we'd brought the equipment to cut a road to the site – would have been worth carrying out. The tractor trailer had no trouble negotiating the mile of cracked and weedy blacktop that led to the ruins of the burned school. But progress slowed to a snail's pace after that, when the blacktop gave way to dirt and the dirt to ruts through the woods. The low trailer bottomed out more than once on the uneven surface, and as it crept around bends in the road, scores of saplings bent, tore, and snapped. The mile to the school had taken less than five minutes; the first half mile toward the Bone Yard seemed to take forever. It took nearly an hour to reach the halfway mark – the clearing with the eleven graves marked by metal crosses – and when he learned that the roughest stretch was yet to come, the driver parked the trailer and unloaded the scraper, and the machine lumbered the last half mile under its own steam.

By the time the machine was in position it was nearly 9 A.M., and the rumble of the idling diesel sounded more and more like the ticking of a clock. I'd stuck survey flags in the ground to mark the initial path I wanted it to follow, and Angie had sent the remaining techs scurrying ahead with metal detectors. Their search yielded a small midden of objects, but as evidence, the only crime they seemed to point to was redneck littering: beer cans, bottle caps, Vienna sausage tins. As soon as Angie gave me the all-clear signal, I walked toward the scraper and beckoned it forward. With a roar and a billowing cloud of diesel smoke, my Florida earthmoving experiment began.

The machine I'd used in South Dakota had been called a Tournapull, a clever word that managed to combine the name of the inventor, R. G. LeTourneau, with the suggestion that the scraper – a two-wheeled blade-and-hopper assembly towed by a tractor – was highly maneuverable. Its latter-day Florida counterpart, manufactured by Caterpillar, was *not* a Tournapull; the operator had indignantly informed me that it was an 'open-bowl scraper.' To me, that didn't sound like a macho earthmoving machine; to me, 'open-bowl scraper' sounded like the rubber spatula my mother had used when she was frosting chocolate cakes. But I didn't give a fig what the machine was called, so long as it worked.

Behind the blade of the behemoth was a vast, bellylike hopper, slung so low it nearly dragged the ground. The dirt removed by the blade would be collected continuously in the hopper, which would need to be emptied regularly. As I gave hand signals to guide the operator, the scraper eased forward and the blade eased down, a fraction of an inch at a time. When the depth of the cut reached two inches, I signaled the operator and he locked the blade in position. The machine crept across the ground, ripping up ferns, leaves, sticks, scrub growth, vines, and shallow roots. Just as I'd done a quarter century before in the South Dakota prairie, I walked behind the scraper, this time in a Florida live-oak forest.

The first pass was the slowest, the gnarliest, the most debris-laden. As the machine bulled and tore a path beneath the spreading canopy, a windrow of limbs and shredded brush piled up alongside the cut. When he reached the end of the hundred feet we'd marked off, the operator circled back and shoved the debris farther to the side, to give the machine and us a bit of breathing room and make it easier to monitor the depth of the cut.

The second pass – which bit down another two inches, as would each successive pass – proceeded more smoothly, with less ripping and grumbling. The machine chewed forward and downward, a ponderous, insatiable beast, feeding upon the very earth itself.

By the third pass, the hopper was filling, the topsoil was giving way to clay, and I was giving in to serious worries. What if the technique that had worked so well in South Dakota couldn't simply be transplanted to Florida? What if I'd unintentionally sold everyone a bill of goods? If we failed to find more graves, there would surely be hell to pay. The bill wouldn't come to me, of course – I could simply tuck my tail between my legs and slink back to the safety of Tennessee – but Sheriff Judson would doubtless find a way to wreak vengeance on Vickery, possibly on Riordan, and perhaps even on Angie as well: the three people who embodied the invasion of his county and the challenge to his authority.

There was another possibility, of course. It was possible that no matter what techniques or technologies we harnessed, no matter how much time we invested, we'd never find anything more, because perhaps there were no more graves to be found. Perhaps the dog had already done a thorough job. And shouldn't I be hoping for that, after all: hoping that only three boys were buried here, no more? And yet, though I felt a tingle of shame, I scanned the ground avidly for signs of another burial.

At the end of the third cut, instead of making a U-turn and starting a fourth pass, the operator raised the blade and made for a briar patch at the far end of the site, where we'd decided we'd dump the dirt. There was a slight chance, of course, that we were dumping dirt atop a dozen undiscovered graves, but that was a chance we'd have to take; the dirt had to go *somewhere*, and putting it at the farthest edge of the site seemed a reasonable gamble. When he reached the briar patch, the operator opened a pair of large doors in the machine's belly – like bomb-bay doors in a B-52 – and dropped the load. Then he looped back and resumed where he'd left off.

I was waiting for him. Anxiously waiting. He lowered the blade again, farther, bringing the cut to eight inches, a depth I confirmed by measuring the wall of the trench. As another layer peeled from the ground, the coolness of the underlying earth caused the moisture in the air to condense, giving the clay a moist sheen in the glinting light.

Barely twenty yards after the grader had resumed its course, the blade snagged and yanked at the remnants of a root that had pushed its way down into the clay. But then, as the machine tore the root from the ground, I realized that the soil clinging to the root wasn't pure clay; the clay was mixed with darker, looser topsoil. That same mixture, I saw with mounting excitement, extended well beyond the spot where the root had burrowed in. As I drew close and leaned down, I found myself peering down on an oval patch of disturbed soil, roughly two feet by four feet, Roughly the same dimensions as hundreds of Arikara Indian graves I'd excavated so many years ago in South Dakota. Silently, so as not to raise doubts about my sanity, I raised a triumphant war whoop.

Late in the morning, a Winnebago-like RV lumbered and scraped its way into the site – a mobile command post, Angie informed me. I wondered what Sheriff Judson thought about this latest development. Actually, I had a pretty good idea what the sheriff thought about it, since he chose to boycott the scene. What I didn't know was what cajoling or threatening Riordan had done to get the command post onto the site.

Shortly after noon, a siren whooped from the direction of the command post, followed by a loudspeaker announcement that lunch was available in the tent. *Tent? What tent?* Then I noticed that at some point since the command post's arrival, a big canvas canopy had been raised beside it, and underneath the canvas were tables loaded with food and drink.

I hadn't realized I was hungry, but I ate ravenously

– two smoked-turkey wraps, three bags of potato chips (which helped replenish all the salt I'd sweated out), and half a dozen peanut-butter cookies, washed down with a quart of milk. I consumed all that food, inhaled all that food, in the space of ten minutes, then went out to put teams of forensic techs to work excavating the first three graves.

Angie, as the ranking forensic analyst at the site, was serving as the crime-scene coordinator, but she had delegated the excavations to me, asking me to supervise the teams that would recover the bones from each grave. I assigned three people to each grave: one person to wield the trowel; one to photograph each bone as it was recovered; and one to list, label, and bag the evidence. Fortunately, three of the forensic techs had received basic osteology training – Rodriguez; Raynelle, a pale young brunette who drawled her words as if she'd grown up in Miss'sippi but who pierced her ears and nostrils as if she'd toured with a heavy-metal band; and Thad, an African-American man who said little but seemed to notice everything. The supplies on the FDLE crime-scene truck included Tyvek sheets for collecting hair and fiber evidence, and I spread one beside each of the graves. 'As you recover the bones, lay them out in anatomical order, as best you can,' I said. 'I'll check in periodically and answer whatever questions you've got.'

*

Angie was quick with a tape measure and good with a sketch pad, I'd noticed at the cemetery. But now, confronted by a search scene that was half the size of a football field, she'd gone higher tech. From a nylon bag and a hard-shelled case aboard the crime-scene truck, she unpacked a sturdy aluminum tripod and a black instrument that appeared to be a pint-sized mailbox, with a small LCD screen in one end and what looked like a rifle scope on top. The scope was a laser, and the rig was a laser mapping system, a twenty-first-century version of a surveyor's transit, capable of measuring and charting distances and positions with pinpoint precision. Angie set the tripod at the center of the site, in the small patch of unscraped ground that lay between the graves Jasper had uncovered, and screwed the mapping system to the top. Once she'd powered up the system, she sent Whitney scurrying across the site with the prism, a collapsible measuring rod fitted with optical reflectors at one end. As Whitney paused briefly at various land-marks – the three graves within spitting distance, the live oaks that marked the site's borders, the additional grave uncovered by the scraper – Angie pressed buttons on a keypad, saving the coordinates of each point. Later, the system's software could be used to create a 3-D map of the entire site, including the overall layout, the loca-tions of the graves, even the location and depth of bones or other pieces of evidence as the graves were excavated. The laser system took more time to unpack than a tape measure and a sketch pad, but once it was up and running, the two women worked as a fast, efficient team: Whitney moved efficiently from spot to spot, holding the prism within the laser's line of sight and radioing details to Angie – 'grave two'; 'skull'; 'pelvis'; 'left hand bones'; 'thoracic vertebrae'; and so on. Angie deftly swiveled the laser to track the prism, pressed buttons to capture data points, and added labels from a drop-down menu on the computer screen.

The first grave, being excavated by the young African American named Thad, contained the bones of a prepubescent child, probably no more than five feet tall. As I examined the arm and leg bones, I saw that the ends of the bones – the epiphyses, the knobby structures that formed the bearing surfaces at the ankles, knees, hips, wrists, elbows, and shoulders – had not even begun to fuse to the shafts of the bones. That meant that this boy (I now felt it very likely that he was a boy) was nowhere near finished growing when he was killed. There was no skull in the grave, but there was a mandible, one I felt sure would fit the first skull the dog had brought home.

Rodriguez led the excavation of the second grave, which *did* contain a skull. As if to compensate for possessing a skull, this grave was lacking a femur, and I suspected that the missing bone was Jasper's final find, the one he'd brought home just hours before he and

Pettis were shot. Was the femur still in the possession of Pettis's murderer, kept as a grim souvenir of the killing? Or, more likely, had it been simply tossed off the bridge into the Miccosukee River, along with the GPS tracking collar?

I knelt by the sheet where Rodriguez was laying out the bones. 'I'm thinking white male,' he said, handing me the skull. 'Am I right?' He was. This one looked to be somewhere between the ages of the first two victims – twelve or thirteen, I guessed, from the sutures in the roof of the mouth and the development of the long bones. I had just picked up the pelvis, whose narrow width confirmed that the bones were indeed male, when Rodriguez gave a low whistle. I glanced down into the grave. 'Take a look,' he said. He handed me a thoracic vertebra – it appeared to be the seventh thoracic vertebra, T7, from the middle of the spine – and I noticed two things. First I noticed that the spinous process, the bony fin projecting from the back of the vertebra, had been shattered. Then I saw why: a bullet had blasted through the back of the bone, passed through the spinal canal, and lodged in the body of the vertebra. The boy had been shot in the back. 'Must've been running away,' said Rodriguez. 'Didn't really have a sporting chance, did he?'

The third grave, being excavated by Raynelle, contained big, robust bones. The ends of the long bones were almost fully fused to the shafts, which meant that his growth spurt was ending. From the size of the bones, I guesstimated his stature to be nearly six feet. The bones weren't merely big, they were also heavy, dense – possibly African-American, as Negroid skeletons tend to have higher bone density than Caucasoid skeletons. The skull would give a clearer answer to the question of race, but there was no skull in the grave. Not much of one, anyway; the mandible was there, and the molars – whose biting surfaces were bumpy and complex – were also characteristic of a black boy's.

As Raynelle neared the bottom of the grave, she called me over. 'I've got no clue,' she said, stretching and sliding the word into two blurry syllables –'cluh-OOO' – as she handed me a piece of bone. It was chunky, small enough to close my fingers around, but big enough to make my hand bulge. Roughly conical in shape, it was smooth over most of its surface, but the narrow end of the cone was splintered. 'What is it?'

'It's a mastoid process,' I told her, holding the fragment behind my left ear, 'and I'd bet your next paycheck that it came from the African-American skull that's sitting in the evidence room at FDLE right now.'

'Wait,' she said. 'You're betting *my* next paycheck?' She laughed. 'Not much of a gambler, are you?'

'Not much,' I agreed. 'But actually, I might even be willing to bet my own paycheck about this.' As a matter fact, I might even have been willing to bet my life. The splintered edges of this mastoid process, I knew, would fit the splintered edges of that skull's temporal bone as neatly as the thousandth piece of a jigsaw puzzle fits the first 999 pieces.

What I *didn't* know was what the puzzle, *this* puzzle, was about. I wasn't seeing the picture. Was the whole thing turned upside down – were we seeing only the blank cardboard backing, rather than the pattern that was the point of it? Or was there no particular pattern to the deaths, no discernible meaning to the violence? Maybe there was nothing but the emptiness of gaping eye sockets and the blankness of unbroken clay subsoil.

Except that the clay subsoil here was not unbroken, I reminded myself. The steel blade of the open-bowl scraper was doing its job. With near-surgical precision, it was cutting through decades of darkness and oblivion, bringing the boys of the Bone Yard into the light of day.

Over the course of the day, the scraper cut four swaths, each a hundred feet long, beneath the canopy of live oaks. At the center of the cuts was the cluster of three graves the dog had found for us. Around that cluster of graves, the cuts curved and parted, two and two, like a river parting around an island, like the grain of an oak plank making room for a knot; the lines diverged fluidly and gracefully, then merged again. And as the cuts flowed past the island of graves, more graves surfaced, all within a stone's throw of one another.

Four additional graves in all; four silent war whoops. Like the Indians of the Great Plains, I was counting coup.

*

We did not finish our work at the site by sundown; not by a long shot. In fact, by uncovering the four additional graves with the scraper, we added immeasurably to our work.

When the scraper had revealed the first of the additional graves, I'd hoped that would be enough to override the sundown deadline issued by Sheriff Judson. The sheriff had expressed his hostility by remaining off-site all day, though I had no doubt that he was kept thoroughly apprised of our progress by the deputy he'd posted at the scene. It seemed inconceivable that Judson could object to an extension of the deadline. Just to make sure, though, Riordan left at midafternoon for a five o'clock press conference with his boss, the state attorney for the Second Judicial Circuit. I didn't see the press conference in person, but I did see a live video feed of it, on the large flat-screen monitor inside the mobile command post.

The event was impressive. Actually, it was more than impressive; it was downright astonishing. Standing in a courtroom of the Leon County Courthouse, alongside the state attorney, Chief Deputy State Attorney Clay Riordan, and the FDLE commissioner, was none other than Darryl Judson, the Lord High Sheriff of Miccosukee County. When the state attorney praised the multijurisdictional investigation currently under way in Miccosukee, Bremerton, and Apalachee counties, Sheriff Judson smiled tightly and nodded modestly. I heard a snort from beside me. 'Unbelievable,' Angie said, and I had to agree.

The investigation – the very embodiment of interagency cooperation, according to the state attorney – had found eleven marked graves on the grounds of a former reform school in Apalachee County, and had found seven unmarked graves nearby in Miccosukee County. The state attorney introduced Riordan – whose attention to the case demonstrated the state's unwavering commitment to the investigation – and Riordan spoke briefly. The eleven marked graves, he explained, appeared to be a small cemetery associated with the former North Florida Boys' Reformatory. Familiar images flashed onto the screen: archival photos of the reform school, followed by photos Angie had taken yesterday of the crosses. 'A preliminary investigation indicates that the marked graves contain the remains of individuals who died from illnesses or accidents at the school,' Riordan said, 'including the tragic fire that occurred in 1967. But the seven unmarked graves,' he added – and here the video feed cut to photos taken at the scene no more than an hour or two before – 'appear to contain homicide victims.' An intensive investigation of the graves by FDLE and local authorities was now under way, he said, as was yesterday's slaying of Winston Pettis, a vigilant citizen who had alerted authorities to the existence of the clandestine graves.

Riordan concluded by praising the dedication and exemplary leadership of Sheriff Judson – at this, Angie feigned a retching noise, and several of her colleagues laughed and hooted – and expressing his confidence that the truth *would* be brought to light.

When we'd found the crosses, Vickery had predicted a shit storm. As it turned out, he'd correctly foreseen the form of precipitation . . . but he'd grossly underestimated the magnitude of the tempest. Then again, he'd made his forecast before we found the unmarked graves. The combination of the two finds – the photogenic, enigmatic crosses and the sinister, clandestine burial ground – created the perfect storm. An hour after the press conference, a small squadron of news helicopters appeared above the treetops – three from the direction of Talla-hassee, plus two more from the west, perhaps Panama City or Pensacola. They hovered a few hundred feet off the ground, wheeling and jockeying for position, stirring up dust, anxiety, and anger on the ground. The pushiest of the pilots appeared to be lining up for a landing at one end of the site, until a young agent sprinted from the command post to wave him off. In short order the pilots apparently brokered an agreement among them-selves, for the aircraft began taking turns circling the site. Eventually they backed off, either because they'd gotten enough footage for their newscasts or because the sun was going down or because someone at FDLE got on the radio and threatened the pilots with arrest.

By the time the air force departed, though, infantry reinforcements arrived: reporters from all three of Tallahassee's broadcast television affiliates, plus the local Fox station, plus a reporter and a photographer from the *Democrat*, the Tallahassee daily newspaper. They lined the crime-scene tape at the entrance to the site, their camera lenses straining for a closer look. After shooting everything they could shoot from that vantage point, the cameramen and their accompanying reporters circumnavigated the site to take shots from other angles. Fortunately, after the press conference, Angie had had the foresight to send the recently arrived assistants to tape off the site's entire perimeter, a task that consumed most of a thousand-foot roll of crime-scene tape.

Vickery called FDLE headquarters for guidance on handling the media; headquarters instructed him to be polite, to keep everyone outside the tape, and to refer all questions to the Public Information Office.

As I worked – inspecting the scraper's final pass through undisturbed soil; conferring with Dr Bradford, who served as medical examiner for Miccosukee County as well as Apalachee County; identifying small bones of wrists and ankles – I felt telephoto lenses tracking my movements, zooming in on me, invading the privacy of the graveyard. At one point I looked up and saw the *Democrat* photographer being escorted firmly back to the other side of the tape. But eventually the contingent of cameramen and reporters drifted away by ones and twos.

*

As the sun dropped below the tree line and the work lights switched on, the command-post siren whooped again, summoning us all to an end-of-the-day briefing.

'Okay, first,' said Vickery, 'Winston Pettis. Autopsy report's in; so is the report from Firearms. He was shot with a .45, fired from two, three feet away. The bullet pierced the heart, then hit the spine and mushroomed. Even if we had the weapon, which we don't, Firearms says the bullet's so deformed it'd be tough to match.'

I raised my hand.

'Doc?'

'What about the dog?'

'What about him?'

'Could the bullet that killed the dog be matched?'

Vickery spread his arms wide in a gesture that took in the group of forensic techs and agents. 'See, guys, I *told* you that people from Tennessee aren't all dumb.' He got a good laugh from that. 'We're still waiting on the veterinarian's necropsy. The bullet from the dog won't carry as much weight as the bullet from Pettis, but sure, if we can match it to a weapon, it's good evidence. The tire impressions at the scene are from a set of twenty-two-inch BFGoodrich off-road tires. They might be on an SUV, might be on a pickup. The tires have been rode hard and put away wet, so the vehicle probably has, too. And yeah, that description fits about ninety percent of the trucks in L.A.' He must have seen the puzzled look on my face, because he added, 'You just *thought* you were in north Florida here, Doc. You're actually in L.A. Lower Alabama.' He smiled, then got brisk and businesslike again. 'The GPS collar. Not sure it'll tell us anything, but the dive team is searching the river where we think it got chucked off the bridge. Murky water, bad current, mucky bottom; tough place to search for something small and black. Oh well. If it were easy, they wouldn't be paying us the big bucks, would they?' More laughs, these with a slight edge to them. 'Okay, next: crime scene. Angie, what's the bottom line on the overall site here?'

'The MapStar's working like a champ,' she said, handing out copies of a map that showed the main landmarks of the site – the trees, the boundary, and the seven graves. 'The laser was definitely the way to go. As you can see, we've got a good baseline map. This printout isn't zoomed in enough to show all the details, but we're also starting to map the location of bones within the graves, and we'll keep adding to the map – bones, artifacts, whatever we find – as we continue to excavate.'

'How about we limit vehicle access tomorrow,' Vickery suggested, 'put a checkpoint out at the highway turnoff, so we don't have so many damn cameras and reporters crawling around here tomorrow?'

She nodded. 'Great.'

'Okay, next. Human remains. Doc?'

'First off, FDLE's got terrific forensic techs,' I began. 'I'm hoping to steal 'em all and rope 'em into my graduate program.'

'If I spend five years getting a PhD,' cracked Rodriguez, 'would I get paid as much as you're making for this gig?' There was general laughter at this; it must have been common knowledge that I was working for the heck of it.

'Maybe twice that much,' I joked. 'So far we've got two adolescent males and one preadolescent – the first skull the dog dug up – that's probably male as well. There's skeletal trauma in all three. We'll start excavating the other four graves tomorrow. Be interesting to see what we find once we've got all the remains out and processed.'

'Speaking of processing,' Vickery said. 'The identification lab in Gainesville hired a new director yesterday. Board-certified forensic anthropologist.'

He named the man. 'Oh, I know him,' I said. 'He's good. Almost as good as our Tennessee graduates.' More laughter.

'He called me today,' Vickery continued. 'Not surprisingly, he'd like to hit the ground running on this. He suggested you wrap up the excavations here and send the remains to Gainesville for processing.'

'Have they got enough graduate students to handle it all?'

'He says they do.'

'Sounds like a winner to me. Believe it or not, I do actually have a job in Knoxville.'

'Sure you do,' he cracked.

The crime-scene techs and I spent the next three hours

packaging skeletal material for shipment to the Gainesville lab for processing the next day. It was nearly midnight by the time we reached the Twilight Motor Court. Eighteen hours had passed since I'd closed the ill-fitting door of bungalow number three in the predawn darkness. If someone had told me at the time that I'd look forward to returning to the musty room and crawling beneath the stained bedspread, I'd have laughed. Yet here I was, eager to lean into the rusty, dribbling excuse for a shower, scrub off the day's worth of sweat and dust, and then sink into the dank, lumpy mattress.

I left my grimy clothes on the bathroom floor. The floor was dirty, but at least I could *see* the film of dirt on the linoleum and gauge its depth. The nastiness lurking within the shag carpet, on the other hand, was unfathomed . . . and possibly unfathomable.

I reached behind the slimy shower curtain and twisted on the taps all the way. The pipes groaned and clanged, and a trickle of reddish brown emerged from the showerhead. I let the water run while I brushed my teeth at the sink. By the time I'd finished brushing, the shower was running clear, more or less, and lukewarm.

Half the shower curtain's rings had ripped through the plastic. Carefully, so as not to tear the rest of the curtain loose, I slid the rings along the rod to open the curtain.

The motion of the curtain unleashed an explosion at my feet. I yelled and jumped back just as a four-foot water moccasin – its body as thick as my wrist – thrashed furiously in the tub and then turned and struck at the thin film of plastic between me and him.

I fell back against the sink and then – as the snake reared up, cobralike, and opened its mouth wide – I pulled my legs up onto the counter. 'Stu!' I shouted. 'Stu! Can you hear me? Stu!'

A minute later, I heard a knocking at my door.

'Stu? Help!'

The knob rattled and the door scraped across the carpet. 'Doc? You got a mouse?' I heard a chuckle.

'Stu, have you got your gun?'

'Doc?' The panic in my voice finally registered with him. 'What's wrong? Is somebody else in here?'

'Not unless you count a big cottonmouth,' I said. 'It's here in the bathroom. It's in the tub at the moment, but I'm thinking it could get out pretty easily. Be careful.'

'Okay, I'm coming that way,' he said. 'Exactly where are you?'

'I'm up on top of the sink, where any sane person would be.'

'Don't move. And make damn sure to let me know if that snake starts over the side of that tub.'

'Trust me, Stu, the whole county'll know if that snake starts out of the tub.' Moving slowly, I wrapped myself in a towel.

I could hear his breathing as he approached. 'All right, I'm getting close to the door. He's staying put?'

'Yeah, he's still wiggling around some, but he's still in the tub.'

Stu's head ducked quickly around the door and then withdrew, then reappeared more slowly, and he stepped into the doorway. Just as he did, I heard Angie's voice coming from the doorway of my room. 'Hey, guys?'

'We're in the bathroom,' I called. 'Me and Stu and a huge water moccasin.'

Either the news of the snake or the silhouette of the gun in Stu's hand made a big impression on her, because she exclaimed, 'Oh, *Jesus.*' After a moment, she added, 'Stu, how good a shot are you with that?'

'Well, I keep qualifying every year,' he answered without looking around, 'but they've never thrown a pissed-off snake at me on the firing range.'

'I've got a shotgun,' she said.

'A shotgun? Where? In the Suburban?'

'In my hand.'

'*What?* What are you doing with a shotgun in your hand?'

'Well, right now, I'd say I'm coming to kill a snake with it. Unless you'd rather take the shot with your sidearm.'

'Hey, be my guest.'

'Okay, here I come.' I heard the unmistakable *click-slide-click* of a shell being racked into the chamber of a pump-action shotgun. 'I'm right behind you, Stu. Is your safety on?'

'It is now. Is yours?'

'It is. All right, you want to trade places with me?'

Stu's head disappeared, and an instant later, Angie's took its place. She eased through the doorway, the shotgun angling upward across her chest and left shoulder. Slowly she lowered the barrel toward the tub and snugged the butt of the gun against her right shoulder. I heard the slight scrape of the snake's scales on the bathtub; I heard the deep breaths Angie was taking through flaring nostrils; I heard the metallic click as she released the safety. 'Doc, you might want to cover your ears,' she said. Moving almost imperceptibly, she leaned closer to the tub, close enough to see the snake. '*Damn*,' she said, 'that is one mean-looking snake.'

Maybe it was the vibration of her voice, or maybe it was a slight movement of the barrel; whatever it was, something triggered the snake again, and as I watched in horror, it whipped around and lashed directly at Angie.

I was alive, but I was blind. No, actually, I was *not* blind, I realized as the smoke and my mind began to clear and I saw light streaming through the doorway from the bedroom beyond; I was in darkness because the bathroom lightbulb had shattered when Angie had fired the shotgun.

'Talk to me,' I heard Stu calling. 'Doc? Angie? Are you okay?'

'I'm all right,' I said. 'But I'm not so sure about Angie.'

She was slumped against me, her body rotated from the recoil of the shotgun. 'The snake was going for her when she pulled the trigger.' Suddenly I had a bad thought. 'Stu, watch out. I'm not sure about the snake. It's too dark and smoky in here for me to see.'

'I'm watching out,' he said.

Angie groaned and stirred. 'Wow,' she said. 'Remind me not to do that again.'

Stu appeared in the doorway with a flashlight, whose beam – a solid-looking shaft of light in the smoke – darted back and forth from Angie to me to the wreckage of the bathtub. 'You all right?'

'I guess,' she said. 'Not sure. A place on my right leg hurts. I might be snakebit.'

'Doubtful,' Stu answered. He bent down, and when he straightened up, he was holding a foot-long piece of the snake's tail. It was the only piece of the snake that the shotgun blast hadn't shredded. 'Angie, one; snake, zero.' He played the light slowly over the tub, which had been reduced to fiberglass splinters, then added, 'Bathtub, *minus* one.' He turned and shone the light on the shotgun, which Angie was holding loosely, the barrel pointing at the floor. 'That's a Mossberg 500 tactical, isn't it.' He wasn't asking; he was pronouncing. 'That thing packs a punch.'

Angie nodded. She stared at the shotgun as if she were staring at a ghost. The peppery odor of gun smoke hung heavy in the air; underneath that scent, subtler but unmistakable, was the metallic tang, the rusty taste, of blood. The taste that would have hung in the air at Kate's house.

It was true, what Angie had said at Shell's a few days before. All roads – or at least this road, smelling of blood and brimstone – led to her sister.

It also, I realized, led to my father.

Remember me, remember me, remember me.

CHAPTER 23

I did end up getting a shower; the manager of the Twilight – whose anger at the damage done by the shotgun was tempered by his fear of a cottonmouth lawsuit – grudgingly put me in bungalow number two, which was a dead ringer, stain for stain, for number three. But I did not get the several hours of sleep I'd hoped to get.

Instead, I read the next entry from the diary, which Vickery had handed out at the end of the day. I should have known better than to read it so late at night. Like the television documentary about the lost boys of Sudan – the haunting film that had kept me awake the night I'd first arrived in Tallahassee – the diary was the stuff of nightmares. It *would* have been the stuff of nightmares, that is, if I'd been able to sleep after reading it. Surely the boys of the North Florida Boys' Reformatory and the boys of the Bone Yard had also earned the label 'lost.'

Buck wasn't even over his beating when it happened. He still had scars from the worst of the cuts the strap give him, and he still walked with a limp. But he was getting better.

We were standing up to leave the dining hall after

supper last night, and I was right across the table from him. Cockroach come and stood behind him. Looks like you made a mess at your place, Bucky boy, he said. Look at all those crumbs. And you spilt some gravy on the table. Dont you know thatll ruin the damn finish? Nobody had been talking, but the room got dead quiet now. Im sorry sir, Buck said real fast, I didnt mean to make a mess. Ill clean it up right now. He swept the crumbs into the palm of his left hand, then wiped the gravy with his right hand. Cockroach leaned down and stared at the table, then stared at Buck. Does that look clean to you, Bucky-boy? Look at that stain. Buck licked one of his fingers and went to rub the spot. Goddammit boy, Ill teach you to spit on a dining table, Cockroach said. Please, sir, Ill clean it up real good, spic n span. His voice sounded like somebody had a hand around his throat and was starting to squeeze it. Tell me how you want me to clean it. Cockroach didn't answer, he just kept staring at Buck. He had a mean look in his eyes and a little smile on his face that was scary. Buck started to cry. Do you want me to go get a wet rag and scrub it? Ill put soap on the rag. Ill clean the whole table. Its too late for that, said Cockroach. Please, sir, Buck said. Just let me scrub the table with a clean rag and some soap. Please.

Shut up, said Cockroach. You need a lesson in manners. Buck started to shake, and then I heard a wet, dripping sound. Goddammit, boy, now look what youve done. Youve went and pissed your pants, you little sissy. He looked around the room. The rest of you boys, yall get on back to the dormitory. I went last, and when I looked back, I saw Bucks knees start to buckle, but Cockroach grabbed him by the arm with his one good hand. Dont make me drag you out of here, boy, he said. You stand up straight and you walk, or Ill make you wish you could walk tomorrow. Walk, Buck, I prayed. He did, stumbling along, Cockroach still digging those five fingers of his into Bucks arm.

They didnt head for the shed like I thought they would. Instead he took Buck toward the office, but they didnt go inside. They went around the corner to the back of the building. All the other boys had went inside by now, but I didnt, instead I snuck down toward the office, hiding behind one tree and then another. When I got to the building, I squatted down and looked underneath the floor, through the crawl space. I saw legs, Cockroach and Bucks legs, and a parked car. Then I saw another mans legs step out of the car. I got down on my hands and knees and crawled under the building so I could get close and see what was happening.

I wished I hadnt.

They washed him off with a hose, and then they started talking about doing things, things I knew had happened to some of the other boys. The man with the car said how about if I take him for a little joyride, bring him back later?

I dont care, said Cockroach. Take him wherever you want to. Just get him back before morning.

Come on boy, said the man. Lets go for a ride. He reached down and pulled Buck to his feet. Get in the car.

Wait a minute, said Cockroach. You best put him in the trunk.

No, said Buck. Dont put me in the trunk. Please dont. Cockroach took a step toward him, and then I heard a slap and Buck fell to the ground again. You shut up, faggot. You get in that trunk. And you do whatever this man tells you to do, or youll get a lot worse strapping than what you got before. You hear me? Buck didnt answer, and Cockroachs leg drew back for a kick, but the other man stopped him. He hears you, dont you boy? Dont you? Buck nodded, still crying.

Take him, then, said Cockroach. But boy, remember this. If you say one word about any of this itll be the last thing you ever say. The very last thing.

Then I heard the trunk of the car come open, and the two men lifted Buck off the ground, and I heard the trunk slam shut. The man got into the car and started it up and drove away slowly. Cockroach stood and took a piss in the mud puddle where the hose was still going. I crawled back to the other side of the building and skedaddled back to the dormitory.

It took me a long time to fall asleep. Buck still wasnt back by the time I did. But he was in his bed the next morning when I woke up. There was clean pants at the

foot of his bed for him to put on. But there was blood
on his sheets and blood on the back of his shorts.

I wish I had a gun. I wish I could kill Cockroach.

CHAPTER 24

It was still dark when we left the Twilight at 5:45 A.M. We were waiting at the door of the Waffle Iron at six when the dead bolt snicked open and a waitress let us in. She looked tired, as if she were just finishing a busy shift rather than just starting one. She probably thought the same about me. We snagged half a dozen sausage-and-egg biscuits to go and ate in the car as we took the blacktop out toward the North Florida Boys' Reformatory. The biscuits were hot and flaky, with a golden crust that still retained a bit of crunch. My lap was soon covered with crumbs, but I knew that before long, biscuit crumbs would be the least objectionable contaminants on my clothing.

The buzz of Angie's cell phone woke me during the morning's briefing. Between my lack of sleep and the steady hum of the printer in the command post, I'd barely sat down before nodding off.

Angie stepped outside to take the call. Through the window, I saw her pull out a small notepad and make notes as she cradled the phone between her shoulder and her ear.

Stevenson had dug up an old newspaper account of

the fire at the school, which he handed out. According to the story, the fire began in the school's main building – the structure housing classrooms, administrative offices, and sleeping quarters for the staff – and quickly spread, as embers were carried aloft by the heat and the wind, to the boys' dormitory, the chapel, and the outbuildings. Spared from the flames, by virtue of being upwind, were the school's Negro facilities.

The story named the guard and the nine boys who'd died in the fire – three of whom, Hatfield had told Vickery, were buried in the school's pipe-cross cemetery because no one had claimed their bodies. So the crosses, apparently, marked 'acceptable' deaths, accidents and illnesses for which the school and its staff would probably not be held accountable in any serious way; the Bone Yard, on the other hand, was the closet in which the school's dark skeletons had been carefully hidden.

When Angie stepped back into the command post, she caught Vickery's eye and gave him a look that indicated she'd just heard something interesting. He pointed at her with his cigar. 'What's up?'

'Two things,' she said. 'I just got a call from Steve Hobbs, in Latent Prints. Steve examined the note that was on our windshield last week. The one that said, "Find the Bone Yard." Steve treated the note with ninhydrin and got some prints off the paper.'

I raised my hand like a student in class. 'Let me guess. They were mine.'

'Some of them,' she said. 'Not *all* of them. He ran them through AFIS, the Automated Fingerprint Identification System. And he got a hit. A really interesting hit.'

'Define "interesting,"' said Vickery.

'They matched a guy named Anthony Delozier,' she said. 'White male, age fifty-nine. Been in and out of prison his whole life. Most recently at the Florida State Penitentiary, in Starke, for aggravated armed robbery.'

'So if he's locked away in Starke,' asked Whitney, 'how'd he put the note on your windshield?'

'He was released three months ago.'

'That *is* interesting,' Vickery agreed.

'Here's the most interesting part,' Angie went on. 'Forty-six years ago, at age thirteen, he was sent to the North Florida Boys' Reformatory for truancy.' As she said it, the hairs on the back of my neck prickled.

'Where's he now?' asked Vickery.

'Havana.'

'Cuba?'

'Florida.'

'That's a lot closer. Smaller, too.' Vickery assigned one of the agents to track down Delozier; meanwhile, Angie pulled a stack of pages from the copier and began passing out handouts.

'Flo, in Documents, just sent us the last of the diary,' she went on. 'She thinks it sheds light on the fire that burned down the school in 1967.'

Skeeter, I cant stand it no more, Buck said. He didnt look at me. I just cant stand it no more. Still not looking at me. If I dont get out of here Ill be dead in a month.

It scared me, him talking like that. Partly it scared me because escaping was hard and dangerous. There wasnt a fence around the school, at least not a fence you could see. But sometimes its the fences you cant see thats the hardest to scale. In six months only two boys had tried to get away. One of them come back missing an eye and the other one come back dead. They said he drowned trying to swim across the river, but Id seen that boy swim, and he was part fish. He never drowned. Not unless somebody helped him do it.

But I knew it was true, what Buck said. If he didnt get away he would be dead soon. That was the part that scared me worse, the truth of it. When I went to regular school I saw how teachers picked out some kids as the smart kids and some kids as the dumb kids, and some kids as the good kids and some kids as the bad kids. Once a teacher decided what kind of kid you were, all the other teachers treated you that way from then on. Like you had a big sign on your back saying smart or dumb or good or bad. Same thing in here, only nobodys sign said good or smart. They just said bad or worse or worst. For some reason Bucks sign said worst. I dont know if that meant Buck was the worst or his punishment was worst. Both I guess. No matter what he did hed get singled out and taken down.

Here, I told Buck, take this. I handed him the compass I wore around my neck. You might need it to find your way.

Find my way where, he said. I don't know where to go.

Anywhere but here, I told him. Pick a direction, any direction, and just keep going.

That was yesterday.

When I woke up today, Buck was gone.

I was glad, but I was also scared for him. Hoping he'd make it. Afraid he wouldn't.

I was taking out the infirmary trash today when Cockroach called to me from across the yard. Come on over here, boy, he said, I need you to haul something to the dump.

Will it fit in this trash can, I said. Its only about half full.

Hell no it wont fit in that trash can, he said. Set that down by that tree there, I need you to come do this first.

Yessir, I said, putting down the can. What is it?

Youll see soon enough, he said. Come on.

He started walking toward the beating shed. I had a bad feeling in my stomach, like a buzzards claw was wrapped around it and was squeezing. Mr Cochran, sir, am I in some kind of trouble, I said. He turned and looked at me, his eyes squinting narrow the way they do when hes thinking about getting mad. Not yet, he said, but you are fixing to be if you dont hurry up and do what I say. Yessir, I said. Im coming right now.

I followed him into the shed.

It smelled real bad in there, like puke and sweat and piss and shit and rotten meat all mixed together. It smelled like something had died in there.

With his one hand, he pointed to the iron bed beside the far wall. Get that mattress off that bed, he said. It's a mess. Haul that down to the dump, then come on back up here.

Yessir, I said, and went to get the mattress. It was covered with blood, spatters of blood all over it, and then a big dark spot in the middle, where it looked like a puddle of blood had soaked into the mattress. It was still wet and shiny. I said, what happened, sir? A boy asked me too many damn questions, he said. Now get that out of here before I make you lie down on it and take a strapping.

I grabbed the foot of the mattress by one corner and pulled it off the frame and dragged it across the floor toward the door. Well, shit, said Cockroach. I looked around and saw that the mattress had left a smear of blood on the floor where I had dragged it. There was blood under the middle of the bed, to, where it had soaked clear through the mattress and dripped on the floor. Im sorry, sir, I didnt mean to make a mess, I said. I thought sure Id get a hiding now.

But he let me keep dragging the mattress across the

*floor and on out the door. I had just got down the steps
when he stepped outside. Wait a minute, he said. I held
my breath. That things liable to attract all sorts of
varmints. Buzzards and rats and what-all. Youd best
burn it. You ever burned brush or trash before, boy?
Yessir, I said. You ever used gasoline to do it? Yessir, I
said. Alright. Heres some matches. Theres some gas over
in the tractor shed by the lawn mower. Its in a gallon
glass jug. Use some of that to get it started. Dont use
much, just about a cup of it. Be sure you cap that jug
and set it way off from the mattress before you strike
that match. Strike the match and throw it while its
still flaring. You dont want to be leaning over that
mattress when the gasoline catches fire or youll burn
up. Understand?*

Yessir, I said, Ill be careful.

*I drug the mattress down to the dump, just like I
had the other one. It was heavier than that first one,
because of all the blood that was in it. I laid it on top
of the burn pile and went back to get the gas. The glass
jug was nearly full, and it looked just like apple cider,
so I unscrewed the cap to make sure it was gasoline.
The smell nearly knocked me down when I took a sniff.
The day was hot and I could see the fumes swirling up
out of the neck of the jug and into the air, like smoke
only it was clear. I took the jug down to the dump and
poured gas onto the mattress, trickling it all around
the edges and then pouring more onto the bloodiest*

spots. I didnt pour out but about a cup, on account of Cockroach had warned me not to use much.

Then I screwed the cap on tight and set the jug way over behind a pine tree before taking the box of matches out of my pocket. I could see fumes swirling up from the mattress, making the air shimmer. I lit a match and held it while it flared, then threw it at the mattress. But it went out before it ever got there. I tried another one, and this time I threw it as soon as I drug it across the box. But I was nervous, so I didnt press hard enough, and the match just flew through the air without lighting and plopped onto the mattress and lay there. The third time I pressed harder. I heard the match scraping as I drug it across the sandpaper and flung it away from me, then I heard it sputter as it started to catch. It flared up in midair with a bright flame, and even before it hit the mattress there was a whoosh and a wall of heat hit me in the face and knocked me back. I think maybe it burned my eyebrows and eyelashes some, but I wasnt hurt, just surprised that so much heat could come from so little gasoline.

As the mattress burned, I thought about Buck laying there bleeding to death, and it made me sad. Then I thought about Cockroach beating him, and it made me mad. I wished that Cockroach was the one on the mattress, not Buck. And thats when I got the idea. I thought about it the whole time I watched the mattress burn.

I poked around the edges of the dump and pretty soon I found an empty bottle. Jack Daniels Tennessee Sipping Whiskey. There was a few drops left in the bottom of the bottle, and it was the same color as the gasoline, but it smelled different. Apple cider, gasoline, whiskey. Hard to tell them apart by looking. Easy by smelling.

I wedged the empty whiskey bottle down between some big roots then brought the jug of gas over and started pouring, I had to pour real slow because the mouth of the whiskey bottle was a lot smaller than the mouth of the jug. But I didn't spill much, and pretty soon the bottle was full up to the bottom of the neck. The gallon jug was about half empty now, I hoped Cockroach wouldnt check to see how much Id used. I capped both bottles and headed back from the dump. I started worrying about how I could hide the whiskey bottle. So I took off my t-shirt and held it in my hand so it hung down and hid the bottle. Up close, you could tell I was hiding something, but if somebody just saw me from across the yard Id probly be okay.

Just as I got to the tractor shed, Cockroach yelled at me from across the yard. Hey, boy. I set down the jug and hid the whiskey bottle and my shirt behind a post. Let me see that jug. I held it up for him. Bring it on over here. I walked across the yard with it. Shit fire, boy, did you pour half a gallon of gasoline on that mattress after I told you not to use much?

Nossir, I said. The jug tipped over and some of the gas spilled before I could catch it. Im sorry, sir. I didnt mean to spill any. I didnt use too much, I did just like you said. Just enough to make that mattress burn good.

He looked at me like he was trying to decide whether to believe me. Wheres your shirt, boy? Did you burn that up?

Nossir. It was hot with that fire, so I took it off. I just laid it down over there in the shed. Ill get it when I put this gasoline back where it goes.

He frowned at me. You was best friends with that boy run off last night, wasn't you?

You mean Buck, sir? We got along okay.

You a faggot too, boy? He licked his lips when he said it, and I felt the buzzard claw grab my stomach again.

Nossir, Im not a faggot.

You look like a faggot to me, boy. Maybe we need to find out if your telling me a lie.

Nossir, I said, I wouldnt lie to you, Mr Cochran.

He didnt say anything for a while. Just kept looking at me. Alright, go on now. Its almost dinner time.

Yessir, thank you sir, I said. Ill just put this back and get my shirt and go get cleaned up for dinner.

I took the glass jug back to the shed and set it down beside the lawn mower. Cockroach had walked away, so I picked up the whiskey bottle of gasoline and covered it with my shirt again. Then I walked back to the dorm.

But first I stopped at the chapel to pray. Please god, I prayed, help me kill Cockroach. Then I hid the whiskey bottle behind the radiator.

Does god answer prayers? He never has answered any of mine before.

Put wings to your prayer, the preacher said in chapel last Sunday. What that means, he said, is work to make them come true.

Tonights Saturday night, and that means most of the guards will go into town, but not Cockroach. He stays here on Saturday nights and gets drunk.

I will slip out after dinner tonight and put wings of fire to my prayer.

'Doc?' Stu's voice jolted me back to the present place and time. 'You okay?' I looked around and was surprised to find myself in the command post, and surprised to see that the briefing room was now empty except for Vickery, Angie, and me.

'He calls the guard Mr Cochran,' I said. 'Cockroach is the boys' nickname for Cochran.' I pointed at the newspaper article Stevenson had dug up. 'Look. According to the paper, Cochran was the guard who died in the fire.'

Angie had been out of the room when Vickery had passed out copies of the story; now she snatched the copy from my hands, and her eyes zigzagged down the column of old print until she found it: ' "Also lost in the fire was guard Seth Cochran, age 31, who died a hero's death while attempting to rescue boys from the burning building."'

'Wait a minute,' said Angie. '*Cochran* died trying to save boys' lives? Are we talking about the same Cochran? Cockroach? The sadist who got off on torturing kids? I don't buy it. It doesn't fit.'

I had to agree with her on that. 'But our boy Skeeter, according to this final diary entry, might have set the guards' quarters on fire that night,' I pointed out. 'If that's the case, he put wings to his prayer, and his prayer was answered. He got Cockroach.'

'He got Cockroach, all right,' Vickery agreed. 'But he got nine of his classmates, too.'

'Or maybe he just got eight,' Angie pointed out. 'Maybe Skeeter was one of the nine. We still don't know who he was or what happened to him. Did he run away after he set the fire, or did he get caught in the flames, too? Be good to know who he was and what happened to him.'

Suddenly I had an idea that sent a spike of adrenaline coursing through my system. I'd been puzzled about why so many boys had died in the fire, and the question had continued to tug at the sleeve of my mind even during the frenzied work of excavating the graves in the Bone Yard.

'I need to go back to the school,' I said. 'Can you spare me for an hour or so? And do you still have those old photos that Stevenson showed us? The pictures of the buildings?'

Vickery looked startled. 'I guess I can,' he said. 'And yes, I do. Want to tell me what you're thinking?'

I did, and thirty minutes later, I was kneeling at the edge of what had once been the boys' dormitory, digging into the ground beneath the spot where a fifty-year-old photo showed a pair of wide wooden doors.

A foot down, the tip of my trowel rasped against something hard and metallic, and I began teasing away the dirt to see what I'd hit. A curved piece of rusted steel emerged; as the tip of the trowel flicked lightly along its contours, it revealed a link of heavy chain. I dug beneath the link to expose it fully, and found links on either side of it, and more links connected to those. Then, curling two fingers beneath the exposed links, I lifted. The chain came from the ground like some rusted root I was pulling – a segmented, sinister version of a root – and then it curled back on itself, arching into a loop. At the center of the loop, holding it closed, was a stout, rusted padlock. And on either side of the padlock were stout, wrought-iron handles. Door handles. 'Angie?' She aimed the camera at my face, looking at me through the viewfinder. 'Now we know why so many boys died in the fire.'

Angie had just finished photographing the padlocked chain and the door handles it held together when Vickery's red Jeep Liberty stopped in the circular drive. Angie motioned him over and wordlessly pointed to the chain.

He gave it a cursory glance, then looked up at her quizzically. Before she could answer his unspoken question, though, his gaze shot back down. 'Son of a bitch,' he breathed. 'Those poor boys were locked in. That building burned to the ground with the damn *doors* chained shut.' He flung the cigar away violently. 'God *damn* whoever did this.' His face was crimson and streaming with sweat, and I knew it wasn't just from the Florida sun. 'Hatfield,' he spat. 'If he knew that door was chained – and how could he *not* have known that door was chained? – he's culpable for the deaths of those nine boys.' He took a deep breath. 'So far, Riordan's been reluctant to charge Hatfield for the homicides we've uncovered at the Bone Yard – says we can't prove that the superintendent knew the boys had been murdered, not unless we get some corroborating testimony.'

'The bad-apple theory?' asked Angie. 'The same reasoning that charged enlisted soldiers with torturing Iraqi prisoners at Abu Ghraib but cleared the officers?'

'Yeah, that same reasoning,' he said. 'Maybe this chain will convince Riordan that the whole damn tree was rotten – that Hatfield had to have known and condoned all the bad things going on here.' He paused. 'I wonder if they've ever had a ninety-year-old inmate at Starke.'

'At the risk of raising a sore subject,' I ventured, 'any luck yet finding out how Hatfield got made commissioner of corrections after the fire?'

Vickery made a face. 'Nothing for sure yet,' he said.

'At the moment, my money's on State Senator Jeremiah Judson – the dearly departed father of our friendly neighborhood sheriff. Back in the sixties and seventies, Senator Judson chaired the Criminal Justice Committee, which had oversight over the prison system. He also raised a lot of campaign funding for the governor's reelection bid. Sounds like Hatfield's promotion could've been a case of quid pro quo.'

'What was the quo? Why would a state senator pull strings for a guy who did a bad job of running a reform school?'

He shrugged. 'Maybe Hatfield had some dirt on him. Or maybe Hatfield was bosom buddies with Deputy Darryl Judson, who was just about to run against his boss for the job of sheriff. Whatever smoky backroom deals were cut, they were cut a long damn time ago, and most of the deal makers are dust by now. I'm sending Stevenson over to Dothan to stir the dust now. Maybe something will come slithering out when he does.'

CHAPTER 25

The Bone Yard, grave number six.

I was pedestalling the remains: excavating a deep, moatlike trench around the perimeter of the bones, then working my way in from there, creating a small platform on which I would gradually expose the skeleton, in a ghoulish version of the way Michelangelo freed captive figures from the marble that imprisoned them.

After two hours of digging, I'd defined the skeleton's edges and top surface, and I began digging down to finish revealing the skull, the spine, the rib cage, the legs. The body had been buried on its side, in a tucked position, much like an Arikara Indian warrior. The knees and hips were flexed to fit into the grave's four-foot length, and the arms were folded across the chest.

As I exposed the face, I saw that this boy had not lived in the cedar-shake dormitory, the white-boy dormitory; this boy had lived in the separate, unequal building set apart for blacks. His skull, like the one with the shattered mastoid process, bore the distinctive angled teeth and jaws of a Negroid skull, as well as the broad nasal opening and nasal guttering underneath: evolution's way of allowing Africans to breathe in greater volumes of air – hot, oxygen-poor air – than their Caucasoid cousins in the colder climate of Europe.

Unlike the other African American we'd found, however, this boy's skull didn't show obvious signs of physical trauma. Nor, as I pedestalled the remains, did his other bones. That didn't mean he hadn't died a violent death, of course; he might well have died of soft-tissue injuries – a ruptured spleen, a ruptured kidney, suffocation – whose telltale signs would have long since melted and slipped into the dark, silent earth.

Here and there, shards of rotted cotton – the thickest layers of fabric and stitching – remained draped over the emerging bones: the shredded waistband of the pants; the ragged collar of the shirt; the rolled hems of the trouser legs.

Using a large pair of tweezers, I began plucking the bits of shirt collar from around the cervical vertebrae. The fabric was denser than I'd expected – more bulk, and also more layers – and the weave seemed odd and complicated, with an odd, oblong lump of material on one side of the neck. Then a realization hit me, with such swiftness and force that I recoiled and lost my balance, falling backward against the wall of the grave.

Lying on this earthen altar was a black boy who had a rope knotted around his neck.

Had he taken his own life, I wondered, in a moment of despair? Or had it been taken from him?

I did not have to wonder long. The questions were

answered when I looked closely at the bones of the arms and hands, and found more shreds of rope encircling his wrists.

Word of the find spread quickly across the site, and a spontaneous, solemn gathering took shape around the grave. People looked closely, said almost nothing, spoke only in whispers. Some of the whispers were hushed exchanges between people; others seemed to be prayers, and I saw Rodriguez make the sign of the cross as his lips moved silently. It was curious: every boy we'd found here had been murdered, yet people's reaction to the previous five skeletons had been matter-of-fact – not blasé, exactly, but not particularly surprised or distressed. Now, as I scanned the assembled faces, I saw intense, unmasked emotions: shock, grief, fear, horror, anger.

Vickery motioned Angie and me aside. 'There was a notorious lynching in Marianna, not far from here, back in 1934,' he said quietly. 'A young black man was accused of raping and murdering a white woman. The schedule for the lynching was published in the newspaper ahead of time. He was tortured, castrated, and dragged behind a car before finally being hanged. When the sheriff eventually cut down the body, people protested – not because the man had been lynched, but because the sheriff wouldn't leave the body hanging. When he refused to string it back up, a white mob went on a rampage, beating up hundreds of local black people, including women and kids. It took the National Guard to restore order.' He shook his head sadly. 'You know, it's possible that somebody who witnessed that 1934 lynching – maybe even somebody who participated in it – had a hand in this boy's death. The distant past isn't always as distant as we'd like to believe.'

For some reason – the reference to the atrocities of the past, perhaps, or the similarities between this boy, who'd been lynched decades before, and Martin Lee Anderson, who'd been suffocated in 2006 – I thought back to my lunch with Goldman, the FSU criminology and human rights professor. Over our lunch of oysters, I'd thought it odd and contradictory that Goldman could be so cynical about the justice system and, at the same time, so idealistic – so naive, even – about the possibility of creating a society without prisons. Now I was beginning to share his cynicism, and I wondered whether – and hoped that – I might find my way to at least some of the idealistic antidote to the cynical toxins.

Vickery's phone whooped. He snatched it from his belt and glared at the display, as if the phone itself were guilty of unforgivable irreverence. 'Vickery. What?' His eyes darted rapidly back and forth, as if the words he was hearing were ricocheting wildly. '*What?* . . . When? . . . Oh, hell. Does the M.E. know? . . . Well, call him. Maybe too late, but maybe worth a try . . . Check for video cameras, visitor logs, everything . . . Okay, keep me posted . . . *Damn* it.'

He closed the phone. 'That was Stevenson. I sent him

up to Dothan to put some heat on Hatfield, who fiddled while reform school Rome burned. Take a wild guess what Stevenson was calling to tell me.'

Angie didn't hesitate. 'Hatfield's dead.' Vickery nodded glumly. 'So *Stevenson* interrogated him to death?'

'Didn't get the chance. Hatfield died in his sleep last night, the nursing home director says.'

'How convenient,' she remarked, which I seemed to remember hearing her say once or twice before. 'You suppose he had some help with that? A kink in his oxygen line? A pillow over his face?'

Vickery shrugged. 'We'll see what the M.E. says, if Hatfield hasn't already been pickled – the funeral home picked him up early this morning. Ninety-year-old with emphysema croaks, it doesn't necessarily raise a lot of red flags in a nursing home.' He had a point there. But so did Angie. Winston Pettis had been killed as we were closing in on the Bone Yard; someone had put a venomous snake in my bathtub; and now Hatfield had died as FDLE was starting to close in on him. If the ominous buzz surrounding us were any indication, Angie had gotten her wish: we'd managed to give the bees' nest quite a whack.

She and I packaged up the hanged boy's bones for shipment to Gainesville, along with the other five skel-etons we'd already excavated. Angie asked Stu if she could take them as far as Tallahassee, where she could sign them over to a crime-lab assistant who would drive them the rest of the way. 'I'd really like to sleep in my own bed for a change,' she said. *Me, too*, I thought, but my bed was a lot farther away than Tallahassee. 'I'd like to remind my husband that I still exist, too.' Vickery encouraged her to leave at midafternoon. 'Unless we find something new, I think we're close to winding down here,' he said. 'Go on. Have a nice evening with Ned.'

'Sure thing,' she said. 'I'll sweet-talk him with stories of boys being lynched and burned alive.' She shrugged. 'But seriously, Stu, thanks for the breather. I'll be back by eight for the morning briefing.'

'No rush,' he said. 'Make it eight-fifteen.'

That night I called Miranda on her cell phone – a rare intrusion on her off-duty hours, which I knew were scarcer than they should be. 'Tell me about the three bodies we have hanging from the scaffolds,' I said. 'Are they all still up? Have any of them fallen yet?'

'No. Why are you asking? What's wrong? You sound upset.'

'I think we found a lynching victim today,' I said. 'A black teenager with a rope knotted around his neck.' I heard a gasp on the other end of the line. 'I don't understand it, Miranda. I don't understand how people could do such terrible things to boys. Boys they were supposed to be helping.'

'Of course you don't,' she said. 'I'd worry if you *did* understand it.'

CHAPTER 26

Angie wasn't back by eight, or by eight-fifteen. At eight-thirty, Vickery went ahead with the morning briefing, which was short and to the point. The good news was, FDLE's forensic divers had recovered the GPS collar from the Miccosukee River late the previous day, along with a .45-caliber pistol that the Firearms Section would clean and test-fire, in hopes of matching the bullets from Pettis and Jasper. The bad news was, Anthony Delozier – the reform school 'alumnus' who'd done graduate study at the state prison – had dropped off the radar screen. He'd missed two mandatory meetings with his parole officer, and no one in the rough-edged trailer park where he lived had seen him in the past ten days. Rodriguez raised his hand. 'You think Delozier might have killed Pettis or Hatfield?'

'I don't see him killing Pettis,' Vickery answered. 'What would be his motive? Why would a guy who tells us to find the Bone Yard kill the very person who's helping us find it? Hatfield, though – I can totally see him wanting to take out Hatfield. What's the old saying about revenge? "A dish best served cold"? Delozier had years in Starke to cook it up and let it chill.'

It was nearly nine by the time Angie showed up, and Vickery had checked his watch and dialed her phone at least a dozen times by then.

'Sorry, Stu,' she said. 'I fell asleep without setting the alarm.' She looked exhausted, as if she'd lain awake most of the night before finally nodding off. Or never nodded off at all.

'Is your phone on? I've been trying to call you for half an hour.'

'Sure, it's always on.' She unclipped it from her belt. 'Oh, crap; no, it isn't. I shut it off when Ned and I went to a movie. I totally spaced out. Obviously. I'm really sorry.'

Annoyed, he waved her off, and she motioned to me to walk with her to the one grave we'd not yet excavated. As we walked, she powered up the phone, and once it was on, it gave a chirp. 'Oh, great,' she said when she saw the display. 'A text message from Don Asshole Nicely.' Her finger hesitated, then she pushed a button to call up the message. Her eyes narrowed, and then a hand went up to her mouth. She stared at the screen, as if something astonishing were unfolding there.

'Angie? You okay?'

'Jesus,' she said. 'Read this and tell me what you think it means.'

She handed me the phone. The message read: 'From: Don, May 31, 6:44 A.M. your right I killed Kate and I cant live with it. Im sorry.'

I reread the message. Three times. 'Hard to know,' I said. 'It might mean he's ready to confess. Or it might mean he's suicidal.' I handed the phone back. 'Either way, I think it means you need to call the sheriff.'

She nodded, then scrolled through her phone's contact list and hit a number. '*Dis*-patch,' came a woman's flat voice through the cell-phone speaker.

'Hello, my name's Angela St. Claire. I'm the sister of Kate Nicely, who died from a gunshot wound two weeks ago.'

In the background, I heard squawks and staticky radio transmissions, and the periodic beeps indicating that the call was being recorded. 'How can I help you, ma'am?'

'I just got a text message from Kate's husband, Don Nicely. I think maybe you should send somebody to check on him.'

'Why is that, ma'am?'

'He just text-messaged me to say that he killed Kate and that he can't live with it anymore.'

'Could you repeat that please, ma'am?'

'I just got a text from my dead sister's husband. Don Nicely. He says he killed Kate and he can't live with it anymore.'

'And he sent you this text message just now?'

'Actually, he sent it a couple hours ago, but my phone's been off, so I just now got it. He sent it at . . . hang on just a second . . . at six forty-four this morning.'

The dispatcher was silent for a moment, and I heard radio traffic in the background. 'We'll send someone to check on him. What's that address?'

'The house is at 119 Amherst Drive. If he's not there, you might see if he's shown up at his job. He works at the Walmart out on the bypass.'

'And if we need to reach you, is this the best number?'

'Probably,' said Angie. 'But let me give you my office number, too.' She rattled it off. 'That's the crime lab at the Florida Department of Law Enforcement. '

'I'll send a unit to check on him, ma'am, and we'll contact you as soon as we know anything.'

'Okay, thanks very much,' Angie said. She hung up, then phoned her husband. 'Listen to this,' she said, and told him what had just transpired.

Half an hour later, as she and I were beginning to excavate the seventh and final grave, her phone rang. She glanced at the display and drew a deep breath. 'Angie St. Claire.'

The volume was cranked up high, and I could hear the sheriff's voice clearly, even though her cell wasn't on speakerphone. 'Ms. St. Claire, this is Sheriff Etheridge, up in Cheatham County, Georgia. I'm calling to ask if you could come up and see me today, please.'

'Have you talked to Don? Did he confess?'

'I need to speak with you in person, ma'am.'

'Sheriff, I'm working a big crime scene right now, the

murders at the North Florida Boys' Reformatory. I'll be glad to come up there if there's a good reason, but I'd appreciate knowing what's going on. Has Don Nicely confessed to killing my sister?'

There was a long silence on the other end. Finally the sheriff said, 'Ms. St. Claire, your brother-in-law is dead, and I need a statement from you. How soon could you come in and do that?'

'I'm out in Miccosukee County, Sheriff, about an hour west of Tallahassee. I can probably be there in about ninety minutes.' She hesitated, then asked, 'Can you tell me how he died?'

'No, ma'am. We're not releasing any details until we've done a thorough investigation.'

'Of course. I understand. I'll be at your office in the courthouse as soon as I can.'

She hung up, stared at the phone awhile, and took a series of deep breaths. 'He's dead,' she said. 'The man who murdered my sister is dead. Thank God. There is some semblance of justice in this world after all.' Tears rolled down her cheeks. She shook her head, then looked at me. 'A thorough investigation. Why is it that the locals spent all of sixty seconds on Kate's death, but they're ready to pull out all the stops to investigate that son of a bitch Don's?'

I shrugged. 'He was a man – a white man. That might be part of it.' I hesitated, but decided it would be foolish not to say what was hanging in the air, unspoken between us. 'Might also be that they figure somebody had a pretty good reason to kill him.'

'Somebody sure did,' she said. 'Mainly his own sorry self.' She called up the text message she'd received. 'Look here. He said it himself. "I'm sorry." That's for damn sure. As sorry as they come.'

I shifted my gaze from the screen to her exhausted face. 'Angie? Is there any chance the sheriff might find anything that could implicate you?'

'No,' she said. She shook her head and then I thought I saw a hint of a smile, so brief and slight and enigmatic I instantly doubted whether I'd seen it. 'Not a chance.'

That enigmatic smile scared the hell out of me.

CHAPTER 27

Angie was back at the scene by late afternoon, looking wrung out. Don Nicely had died from a shotgun blast to the head – a blast virtually identical to the one that had killed Kate. The Cheatham County sheriff had questioned Angie for two hours, she said, and would expect her to come back for another interview soon. The sheriff had also questioned her husband, Ned. Ned had confirmed that she'd been with him all night, at the movies and then at home, but the sheriff seemed unconvinced.

She related this to me as she swept a metal detector over a grave – the outermost of the graves we'd discovered. It was the seventh and last of the graves to be excavated; it was also, I suspected, the last of the graves to have been dug, lying as it did on the outermost margin of the Bone Yard.

The skull, which I'd excavated first, was that of another young white male. Judging by the presence of the twelve-year molars and the partial fusion of the sutures in the palate, his age was probably somewhere between twelve and fifteen. Although I couldn't be sure, because of the dirt and remnants of tissue on the bone, I didn't see any skull fractures. The absence of trauma gave me some small hope – foolish, perhaps – that his death had been less brutal than the other boys' deaths appeared to have been.

The bones were slight of stature, and still not fully developed; the ends of the long bones were not yet fused to the shafts, I saw as I began working inward from the margins, so he – like the others – had still been growing at the time of his death. My guess, which I'd be able to confirm or correct when I examined the teeth and bones more closely, was that he'd been in his early teens – older than the prepubescent child whose skull had been Jasper's first find, but certainly younger than the robust lad whose skull had been Jasper's second find.

So: fourteen, perhaps. His hip bones, though, could have come from an arthritic seventy-year-old.

Viewed from the front, human hip bones show more than a passing resemblance to a big, bony pair of ears – the ears of an African bull elephant, to be specific, spread wide as he's about to charge. The top of the hip bone, the iliac crest, looks a bit like the ear's thick upper edge, sculpted in bone. During childhood, the iliac crest is attached to the ear-shaped ilium by carti-lage that eventually ossifies, turns to bone, once the hips have finished growing; during adulthood, the sutures fade, just as the sutures in the skull gradually fill in and disappear over the decades of adult life. In this boy's pelvis, the iliac crest had not yet fully fused, because his growth spurt was just winding down, and the suture was more like a fissure, a valley, than a plain. I'd expected that.

What I hadn't expected, and what I'd never seen before in any adolescent pelvis, was the arthritic appearance of the hips in the region of the iliac crest. Instead of being smooth and graceful, the bone along the suture line – the bone that had most recently been deposited along the growth plate – was thick, uneven, and lumpy, especially on the right side, though somewhat on the left as well.

As I studied the deformity, the realization of what had caused it dawned on me with chilling horror. When soft tissue or bone is damaged, inflammation occurs. Inflammation is painful, but it's crucial to healing, especially in broken bones: blood flows to the site of the break, bringing with it an abundant supply of cells that clot into a thick, collagen-rich splice called a 'healing callus.' Over the course of six or eight weeks, the collagen matrix in the callus fills in with calcium and becomes new bone. In this boy's case, I realized, trauma to the hip bones – trauma at the vulnerable growth plate – caused inflammation, creating a callus that calcified into the thick, lumpy contours I was now seeing. It didn't take a rocket scientist to figure out that the likely cause of the trauma to the hip bones was a five-foot leather strap, slamming again and again into the buttocks and hips of a growing boy. A boy who lived long enough to heal, in a slightly misshapen way, before being killed.

But what had killed him, months after he survived a beating – perhaps even multiple beatings – that had been forceful enough to deform his hip bones? I hoped the grave would contain the answer.

During Angie's absence, Rodriguez had done an initial scan with the metal detector before I'd begun excavating, just as we'd done with the six prior graves. Alerted by the detector's staticky squawk, I'd been watching for metal as I'd troweled down through the shredded plastic and sandy earth, working my way from the edges of the grave inward to the bones. I hadn't gotten far – only as far as the boy's right thigh – when I found a piece of metal embedded in the back of the bone. It was a bullet, lodged in the bone in much the same way as the flint arrowhead I'd once found in an Arikara Indian thigh. But the Arikara warrior had been an adult, a warrior, shot in battle; this was a boy, shot from behind, probably as he ran.

From the legs, I'd worked my way up the pelvis, up the spine, until I reached the third lumbar vertebra, the one centered in the small of the back. That vertebra's spinous process – the knob jutting from the body of the bone, to give muscles a place to attach – was snapped off, and the vertebral foramen – the channel through which the spinal cord ran – was collapsed. Some powerful blow, possibly from the edge of the heavy leather strap, or more likely from something heavier, like a baseball bat or a metal pipe, had shattered the bone and doubtless crushed the spinal cord. The fracture lines here remained sharp, with no signs of healing. This injury, unlike the trauma to the hip bones, had occurred at or around the time of death.

The damage to the spinal cord would almost surely have paralyzed the boy's legs. But would it have killed him? Not directly, though if he'd spiraled down into shock, he could have died within hours or even minutes. That theory seemed plausible, but then, as I continued to probe the grave, I found a small bone that forced a new and terrible realization on me. It was the hyoid – the fragile, U-shaped bone from the front of the throat – and it was snapped, the way a chicken's wishbone would snap if you squeezed its ends together instead of pulling them apart.

I could think of only one sequence of events that fit all the pieces of this skeletal puzzle together: long after the boy's initial beating or beatings – perhaps he still walked with a limp; perhaps, having been damaged already, he was an easy target for continuing abuse – he'd tried to escape. He'd been shot, then beaten again, so brutally that a vertebra shattered, rendering his legs useless. At that point, realizing things had gone much too far, someone had wrapped a strong, pitiless hand around the boy's throat and strangled him.

After I finished excavating the ravaged skeleton, Angie scanned the grave with the metal detector again, and again the instrument squealed angrily in her hands. The signal was strongest in the area where the top of the chest had lain. I dug deeper with the tip of the trowel, watching closely for the glint of metal. As I flicked aside a pea-sized clump of earth, I heard the faint clink of metal on metal, of trowel on artifact. 'Got something,' I called, and Angie came over to crouch beside the grave as I dug deeper. A small hollow took shape beneath a miniature dirt cliff, and tiny avalanches of sandy soil broke free and trickled down. And tumbling down in one of these crumbling little landslides was a disk of blackened metal, two inches across and a half inch thick, its rim rounded and its weight slight enough to hint at hollowness. A seam around its equatorial edge, and a corroded bulge that might once have been a hinge, seemed to corroborate this notion. Might it be a locket, a boy's memento of his mother?

It was not a locket. What it was, I saw as Angie carefully pried it open, was a compass.

We had just found the remains of Buck, I felt sure.

I felt something else, too, something I'd never felt before during an excavation: I felt tears streaming down my face as the story of the boy's death emerged from the ground.

The diary had told us that Buck had died the night he tried to escape. The bones now told us that Buck had died the most painful, brutal death of all the boys we'd found here.

In my mind's eye, I saw Buck checking his compass by the light of the moon, picking a direction, and starting to run. And then I saw him tumble to the ground as a guard's bullet tore into his leg from behind and the guards closed in on him for the kill.

Leading the pack – a rifle still clutched in his one good hand – I imagined Cockroach.

CHAPTER 28

Six days after we'd followed the dog's track across Moccasin Creek and into the fern-carpeted burial ground that was the Bone Yard, a caravan of vehicles, my truck among them, trundled away from the site, and FDLE released the scene. I smiled wearily as I noticed the sun slanting low through the trees to the west. Sheriff Judson had told us to be gone by sundown, and now we were, although a few extra suns had come and gone before Judson had gotten his wish.

As I bumped along the dirt road that led from the Bone Yard, I paused at the pipe-cross cemetery for a final look. My eyes drifted upward from the crosses to the vault of live-oak limbs fringed with resurrection ferns. Were the ferns a cynical commentary on the futility of our efforts to raise these boys from death, or might they be a hopeful portent of progress and justice? Or did it depend on what happened from here out?

I opened my cell phone and called one of the Knoxville numbers in my speed-dial list. 'Osteology; this is Miranda.'

'Miss me yet?'

'Do I know you?'

I was teetering between confusion and indignation

when she laughed, a clear peal of laughter that brought an instant smile to my face. 'Hey, Dr B. Are you ever coming back, or have you jumped the fence for greener pastures?'

'I'm headed for the barn,' I said. 'FDLE just released the scene.'

'So you're done? It's over?'

'Actually, it's really just beginning.' The governor had appointed a blue-ribbon panel to investigate the North Florida Boys' Reformatory, I explained, and the state attorney had empaneled a special grand jury. Leaders of the state senate and house of representatives had announced that they intended to hold hearings when the legislature reconvened in January. Stu Vickery would head an ongoing task force dedicated to identifying the remains of the seven murdered boys and determining whether charges could be brought in any of their deaths. FDLE had established a toll-free citizen tip line, staffed around the clock, to take calls from the school's former students, their relatives, former employees, or anyone else who could shed light on this dark chapter in Florida's history of juvenile 'justice.' Genetic samples from the skeletal remains were being run through the agency's DNA lab, and genetic testing would be offered free of charge to possible relatives. The skeletal material from the seven graves had all been sent to Gainesville for cleaning and study. In short, the complex case could take months or, more likely, years to sort out. By then, most of the school's former employees and many of the boys who'd spent time there would be dead. Former superintendent Hatfield, surely a logical target of prosecution, was dead – the medical examiner had concluded that he'd been strangled, though so far FDLE had no leads in his death – and most of the people who'd worked for him were probably dead or dying, too. 'If anybody's ever charged, I'll have to come back to testify at the trial,' I said. 'Maybe it's too late to bring anyone to account. But at least the wheels of justice are finally starting to turn.'

'Sounds like you put a few dollops of grease on the axles, at least. Good for you.'

'Did you get a chance to water my plants and check my mail?'

'Of course. Three times. Your plants looked like they hadn't been watered in a month. Now they're looking pretty good – and they're asking if you can please just stay in Florida. You got lots of bills and a few checks, or lots of checks and a few bills, but nothing that looked really pressing. Certainly nothing that looked interesting enough to steam open.'

'So nothing hand-addressed from San Francisco? Or Japan?'

'Nothing from Isabella? Not unless she disguised it as a fund-raising letter from the Sierra Club.' She hesitated. 'If she's trying to stay off the FBI's radar, she probably isn't going to be your pen pal, Dr B. Look, I know it's not my business, and I know you hate being in limbo about her – especially the pregnancy thing – but I think you need to assume she's gone, with a capital *G*.'

'How can I do that, Miranda? She's probably pregnant, and the baby's probably mine.'

'I'm just saying,' she said.

During the awkward pause that followed, I put the truck back in gear, left the pipe-cross cemetery behind, and continued down the dirt road toward the ruins of the North Florida Boys' Reformatory. 'So what's going on in Anthropology? Have the culturalists taken over the department while I've been gone? Have *you* taken over the department while I've been gone?'

'Both.' She laughed. 'Actually, things are pretty dead around here. In the boring, figurative sense of the word. We've had two ID cases. One was a homeless guy who made the mistake of passing out on the railroad tracks just before the two A.M. freight train rolled through. The other was a floater in Tellico Lake – you remember that empty fishing boat that ran aground last month with the motor running wide open? That guy finally washed up. Oh, and some woman called in a tizzy yesterday because she'd found human leg bones in her backyard – she watches all the crime shows on TV, so she knows a *lot* about bones – but they were from a deer.'

She was right; it *did* sound quiet up there. I felt relieved, but I also felt let down and expendable. 'Sounds like you've gotten along just fine without me.'

Miranda could read me like a book. 'I lied,' she cheerfully lied. 'We're up to our eyeballs in bodies and bones, the phone is ringing off the wall, and I'm tearing my hair out. For God's sake, hurry home. Please.'

I smiled. 'Aww, y'all *do* need me up there. Okay, then, I'll drive home tonight and see you on campus tomorrow.' I said good-bye to Miranda and stopped again, this time for a last look at the vine-covered chimneys and charred vestiges of the school buildings – the buildings where boys I now felt I knew had lived and suffered and even died.

Angie, Stu, and I had agreed to rendezvous for a parting dinner at the Waffle Iron before I hit the road for Knoxville. On the way to the diner, I detoured to the Twilight to retrieve my meager wardrobe and toiletries. I phoned Angie, who – along with Stu – had headed straight to the diner. 'Y'all go ahead and order for me,' I said. 'I'll be there by the time they get the cat skinned and fried for me.'

As I caught sight of the motel's sagging sign a hundred yards ahead, a truck, painted in the splotchy greens and browns and grays of camouflage, pulled onto the blacktop and accelerated hard in my direction. By the time it passed me, it must have been doing eighty. As it rocketed past, I saw the driver's grizzled, hard-featured face staring at me with venomous eyes. His window was open, his elbow was resting on the door frame, and his short-sleeved shirt was whipping in the wind.

His arm ended at the elbow.

Without stopping to think about what I was doing, I made a sand-slinging U-turn in the parking lot of the Twilight and gave chase. By the time I was well under way, he had a half-mile lead on me, and the gap seemed to be widening. I fumbled for my cell phone and hit redial. It rang four times, then Vickery's voice mail answered. 'Stu, it's Bill Brockton,' I heard myself shouting. 'This probably sounds crazy, but I think I just saw Cockroach. He was tearing away from the Twilight when I got there. I'm following him now, or trying to. Call me back.' I was fumbling with the buttons to end the call so I could try Angie's cell phone instead, when my right wheels drifted off the shoulder and the truck lurched wildly. As I jerked the steering wheel and the truck fishtailed back onto the pavement, the phone flew from my hand and vanished under the passenger seat. In the distance, the truck disappeared around a slight curve, and when the road straightened – just beyond the faded road sign that marked the Miccosukee County line – it was empty clear to the horizon, where the asphalt shimmered and flowed into the darkening sky.

Dumbfounded, I continued hurtling down the road, but suddenly I caught sight of a pair of fresh, heavy skid marks. They ended in a sharp turn to the right, where a small dirt road threaded a gap in the line of pines and scrub growth. I stomped the brake, laying down two skid marks of my own, then slammed the truck into reverse and careened backward to the turnoff. A weathered mailbox clung to a leaning post; the four faded letters that had not peeled off read DSON. Peering down the road in the fading light, I thought I saw fresh tracks on the ground and dust in the air. I turned and followed, slowly now, and when I glimpsed a clearing ahead, I eased the truck to a stop, got out quietly, and continued on foot.

A hundred yards farther down the dirt lane, an unpainted house and a small barn shared a small, blighted yard. I didn't see the camouflage truck I'd been chasing, but I tasted its dust.

The door of the barn was open, and through it I heard the faint sound of crying or whimpering. I crept forward, and the closer I got, the more certain it seemed that someone was in distress or pain inside the barn. I risked a quick peek through the door, but could see nothing in the dim interior. Then I heard a hoarse whisper from inside. 'Help me. Please help me.'

The words sent chills through me, and I slipped through the doorway. Two steps in, as my eyes began to adjust, I froze. Dangling from a beam just ahead of me was a thick leather strap, five feet long and four inches wide, with a wooden handle at one end. The handle dangled from a wrist thong, which was looped over a peg in the beam.

I was just beginning to notice that the strap was swaying gently to and fro – I was just realizing that the sway was worrisome and the plea for help might have been a trick – when I felt myself pitch forward to the dirt floor.

The first thought I had, as I began to come to, was that my head was clamped in a vise, and that somebody had cranked the vise down hard enough to hurt like hell. The second thought I had was that someone had whacked me in the back of the head, and hard.

My third insight was that I was lying facedown on a narrow iron bed, and that I couldn't move my arms or legs. I raised my head, sending a spike of pain shooting through my brain, and saw that my hands were tied to the bed's metal headboard.

'It's been a while since I've used this,' said a voice behind me. 'Hope I haven't lost the touch.' Out of the corner of my eye, I caught sight of the wide, flat strap undulating, and I heard a rasping, slithering sound as the leather snaked across the rough floorboards.

I also caught sight of a human shadow undulating as the right arm swung the strap back and forth. Something about the shadow struck me as odd, and gradually I realized that the shadow of the left arm was incomplete, and that I'd followed the driver of the truck into a trap.

'You're Cockroach.' The strap stopped its slithering, and somehow the quiet was even more sinister than the sound of the leather sliding over the wood. 'Cochran. I thought you were dead. I thought you died in the fire.'

'Whole lotta people thought that,' he said. 'It suited me to let them think that.'

'But if you weren't the guard who was killed, who was it?'

'Nobody. A phantom. "Burned beyond recognition" covers a multitude of sins. There was some shit about to hit the fan even before the fire. So I made a deal with Hatfield. Let the fire burn the slate clean. For the school. For him. For me. You're a professor, right? Bet you read a lot of books, don't you?' I wasn't sure where he was going with this. 'Ever read *Tom Sawyer*?'

'I think so. A long time ago.'

'Remember when Tom gets lost in that cave, hiding from Injun Joe?'

'Vaguely.'

'He finally gets out, and gets back to town, just in time to walk in on his own funeral.'

'I do remember that. But you didn't walk in on your funeral, did you?'

'No, I didn't walk in on it. I walked the other way. By the time they got around to burying my empty coffin up here, I was in west Texas, down around El Paso, where my people come from. Stayed there for forty years, under the radar, till you came along and started pulling skeletons out of the closet.'

'So to keep us from finding the closet, you killed Winston Pettis and his dog?'

'I never killed that man or that dog.'

'I don't believe you. You had the motive.'

'I don't give a shit if you believe me or if you don't believe me. But you're a damn fool if you think I'm the only one with something at stake here.'

'Who else? Look, if you untie me and cooperate with FDLE, I'm sure you can get some sort of deal.'

He spat out a laugh. 'Neither one of us is stupid enough to believe that. We both know there's no way to square this. I'd built a life, I was on the home stretch, but that's gone. You saw to that. And for that, you need to be punished.' The strap began to slither again, tracing faster, rhythmic figure eights on the floor. 'I never beat a grown man before. I'm not sure I'll like it as much as I liked putting the strap to a boy, but I'll give it a try.' He gave the strap a quick swing, and it hit the edge of the mattress with enough force to make the bed shiver. 'What I like about this barn? The hayloft is right about the same height as the ceiling in the shed at school was. So you'll hear the strap when it's coming over the top, just before you feel it. You'll figure out the timing after just a lick or two.'

I was desperate to stall for time. 'One thing I don't understand. Why did the young boys get more beatings than the older boys?'

'Oh, easy. A young boy feels it more. The old ones are harder. Tougher. They don't give you the satisfaction of seein' 'em squirm and hearin' 'em squeal. Besides, if you start 'em in on it nice and young, sometimes you'll find

354

one that takes to it. Gets a taste for the hurt, you know? Likes it. Does things on purpose because he wants to be facedown on that bed feeling that strap come down.' As he said it, something in his voice got huskier, thicker, nastier, and it made me feel sick with disgust.

Before I could answer, I heard him draw a deep breath, and then I saw the strap slither backward, out of my line of sight. The movement was followed by a slight hiss, and then a slapping sound – the slap of leather hitting the rough wooden ceiling at the top of its arc overhead – and a grunt of effort. Suddenly I felt an explosion of heat and pain on the backs of my thighs. Involuntarily I cried out in pain. '*One,*' said Cochran. 'I believe my aim's a little off. Gettin' kinda rusty. If you were a boy, I'd tell you that if you make a sound, or if you move, I'd start counting all over again, from one. But with you, it doesn't make any difference. I'll just keep counting, 'cause I don't have to stop at twenty, or forty, or even a hundred. I can just keep going as long as you're breathing. Maybe longer, if I feel like it.' The strap snaked off me and out of sight, and I thought he was winding up for another blow, but he paused. 'You can bite that pillow if you want to. Or holler if you want to. You can try it both ways. You can try it as many ways as you got the stamina for. Toward the end, I figure you might be whimpering a little bit, and then you'll get pretty quiet for the last of it.'

He took another breath, and this time I heard the

soles of his shoes scraping the floor slightly as he pivoted into the windup. The strap seethed through the air again, slapped the ceiling, and exploded onto my buttocks. This time I'd stiffened up, bracing myself for the blow, but still it made me gasp. 'Two,' he said. 'How's that feeling? You think you might could develop a taste for this, Mister Fancy Forensic Scientist?' The strap slid off me and slithered away; his shoes pivoted, and the leather seethed and slapped and exploded again, this time onto the same spot as the previous blow. It felt as if my flesh were splitting open all the way to the bone. I groaned. 'Three,' he counted. 'You know, after I went to Texas, I didn't get a chance to do this. I thought about trying to get work in a boys' school down there, but they didn't have anyplace as good as what I'd left. And I figured I'd best lie low anyhow.' *Swish*pivot*seethe*slap*explode*. '*Four*. But you know what?' The only answer I could manage was a moan. 'There's a lot of illegals smuggled across the border from Mexico. Sometimes they bring their kids with 'em. *Five*. Sometimes the parents don't survive the trip, for one reason or another.' He paused to breathe and wind up again. '*Six*.' I felt myself on the brink of losing consciousness again. 'So then the smuggler – the "coyote," the smuggler's called – the coyote's got this kid on his hands. So every now and then, I'd get me a boy. The girls, they'd end up somewhere else – in a cage in somebody's basement in El Paso, or in a brothel back across the border in Juarez – but there wasn't as much market for the boys. *Seven*. You'd be surprised how cheap you can buy a little ten-year-old wetback boy.'

Either he miscounted, or I passed out briefly, because 'ten' was the next number I heard him say. It was the last number I heard before unconsciousness – blessed unconsciousness – took me under again.

When I came to once more, I was lying on the floor, my legs and buttocks and back afire, my hands and feet tied. I heard a sound like a dying animal might make – half groan, half whimper – and realized it was coming from me. Then, through the fog and through the pain, I heard the seethe and slap of the leather strap again. 'Stop,' I gasped, flinching and shrinking from the pain as best I could. The strap struck flesh with a loud whack, but this time I did not feel the impact. I heard another groan, but this time the groan came from someone else's mouth.

A pair of feet and legs and the leather strap came into my field of view, and a man I did not recognize squatted down and looked at me. He appeared to be about my own age, maybe a few years older. His face was weathered and bore multiple scars – a thin vertical line down his left cheek, another over his right eye, and one across his chin – and the top of his left ear was missing a ragged crescent of flesh. His neck was as thick as a tree trunk, and his shoulders were beefy. The fingers of both hands – unlike Cochran, he had them both, I noticed, as he squatted with his hands on his knees – were tattooed with letters that spelled out F-U-C-K Y-O-U. His eyes flitted rapidly, never quite settling, as he looked at me. 'Hurts like hell, don't it?'

'Just go ahead and kill me,' I said.

'No,' he said. The corner of his right eye – the one with the scar – twitched slightly. 'That's not what I'm here to do.'

'I don't understand,' I groaned. 'Who are you?'

'I'm not somebody who's got a quarrel with you,' he said. 'I'll cut you loose when I'm done. This here is between me and him. I've got a score to settle, and I'm only up to "five" so far.'

Something was coming together in my mind – something about the man's muscular build and the ragged, amateur tattoos: a prison body, and prison tattoos. 'My God, you're Anthony Delozier, aren't you? You were in Starke until a few months ago.'

'I expect I'll be going back again,' he said, 'soon as I finish up my business here.'

He walked out of my field of vision, and I heard the dreadful sequence of the strap again. '*Six*,' Delozier counted. 'Did you ever think there might come a reckoning?'

In response, I heard what I recognized as a strained, pained version of Cochran's voice whisper, 'Go to hell.'

'*Seven*, you son of a bitch. I hope it takes seven hundred to kill you.' There was another windup, and another blow of the strap. 'How many of us did you beat? *Eight*.

How many lashes? *Nine.* An eye for an eye. *Ten.* And a tooth for a tooth. *Eleven.* I thought you burned to death forty years ago. *Twelve.* I thought I'd put wings to my prayer. Guess I should've put a strap to my prayer instead.'

The phrase cut through the fog of my pain like a knife. 'What did you just say?' My question was punctuated by another blow of the lash on Cochran. I raised my head and said, as loudly as I could, 'Wings of fire. You put wings of fire to your prayer.' The lash stopped. The man's legs walked toward me, and again he squatted. He stared at me as if he'd seen a ghost. 'Jesus,' I said, 'you're Skeeter, aren't you? We found your diary.'

'What are you talking about?' The twitch in his eyes accelerated; it reminded me of a fluorescent light that flickers as it's heading toward burnout.

'We found your diary, Skeeter. It was in a Prince Albert can under a flagstone.'

'I'll be damned.'

'It helped us. *You* helped us. You can *still* help us. Untie me and let's call the police.'

My mind was racing back over the diary's contents. 'Your friend Buck. We found his bones. At least, I think we did. One of the sets of remains we found was wearing a compass around the neck. The compass you gave him to help him escape.'

His face – his iron-hard, lifer's face – twitched and then crumpled, and he put a large, tattooed hand over his eyes and began to sob. His big body shook, and he sat down on the floor, wrapped his arms around his knees, and cried. After what seemed like a long time, the sobs subsided, but still he sat, hunched into himself, his broad back and shoulders rising and falling with deep, ragged breaths.

Underneath the sound of his breathing, I gradually became aware of another sound, and as its volume rose, I knew he heard it, too, because his breathing stopped while he listened. In the distance, a siren was approaching. He raised his head, unfolded himself, and got to his feet, the leather strap still clutched in one hand.

'Skeeter, untie me. Please.' He hesitated, then walked to the bedside and shook out the strap for a windup.

'*FOUR-teen.*' He grunted as he swung the strap at Cochran, putting all his strength into the blow.

'Skeeter, please stop. Let the police take it from here.'

'*FIF-teen.*' Under the rain of intensified blows, Cochran's breaths grew labored now, wheezy. I'd heard such breathing before. It was the beginning of a death rattle.

'Skeeter, we've got a lot of evidence now. We found seven murdered boys. We found the chain around the door handles. We can bring this guy to justice.'

'Justice? What the hell is justice? . . . *SIX-teen.*'

'We can send this guy to prison for the rest of his life,' I said. 'I know it doesn't make up for what he did, but it's the best we can do.' The siren was getting close now.

'It's not the best I can do. *SEVEN-teen.*'

'Did you kill Hatfield?'

'Hatfield? The son of a bitch that ran the place? I like to think I'd've gotten around to it, but I hadn't yet. If somebody beat me to the punch, I'd like to shake his hand. *EIGHT-teen.*'

'Skeeter, if you kill Cochran, you'll never get out of prison.'

'Man, I'm in a place a lot worse than prison. I burned nine boys to death. Didn't mean to. Didn't know the doors were chained. Prison's all I was ever fit for anyhow, thanks to fuckers like this. *NINE-teen.*'

The siren grew deafening, then fell silent. Blue strobe lights pulsed through the open doorway, casting surreal shadows as the strap rose and fell. *'TWEN-ty.'* Outside, a car door opened and closed softly.

I heard slow footsteps, then a low, gravelly voice. 'Seth?' It was Judson's voice. On the bed, Cochran groaned. 'Seth?' Another groan. 'This is Sheriff Judson. Anthony Delozier, if you're in there, come out now with your hands up.'

'All right,' Skeeter answered. 'I'm coming. Don't shoot. Your man Brockton's in here with me. He's all right. But if you shoot, you might hit him.'

'Brockton, can you hear me? You in there?'

'Yes,' I said weakly. 'But I'm tied up. Kinda beat up, too.' Through the fog of pain, I struggled to remember something, but what? *Seth.* Why had the sheriff said Seth? Who was Seth? I knew the name, but didn't know why.

'Delozier, get your ass out here. *Now*. Hands up.'

'Coming.'

I heard a clatter, and saw the handle of the lash bounce and twist as it hit the floor. I breathed a sigh of relief, but my relief was short-lived. Delozier's legs crossed my field of view. He grasped the handle of a tool that was leaning against the wall of the barn, and I saw to my horror that it was an ax. He walked quickly again to the bed where Cochran was tied. In the surreal glow of the blue strobes, I saw the shadow of the ax rise and then descend with a splintering, sickening thud. 'Twenty-one, by God,' Delozier whispered. He turned and walked slowly to the door, the ax hanging from his right hand. 'I'm coming out.'

When Delozier reached the barn door, he stopped. '*You*,' he gasped in the direction of the sheriff. 'I *know* you. It's been forty-five years since you and Cockroach put my friend in the trunk of your car, but I'd know you anywhere, you sodomizing son of a bitch.' He made a low, growling sound – an enraged, animal sound – and ran out of the barn, ran toward the strobing lights. A gun fired – once, twice, in quick succession, and, after a pause, a third time. The third shot was followed by a silence so heavy it seemed solid.

In the silence, I heard the answer to the question I'd asked myself a moment before: Seth was Cochran's first name. The sheriff knew Cochran, and knew him well, I realized; he'd known him well enough to let Cochran select boys for him to molest. The sheriff had known that Cochran didn't die in the fire at the school. And he'd known that Cochran was here; maybe he'd even known that Cochran was luring me into a trap.

And maybe now the sheriff was going to finish what Cochran had started.

'Brockton?' Judson appeared in the doorway. My only hope, I decided, was to pretend I hadn't heard what Delozier had said just before the sheriff shot him.

'Who's there? Sheriff, is that you? I think I blacked out for a minute. Did I just hear a gunshot? What happened? Are you all right?'

There was a pause while the sheriff took in what I'd said, turned it over in his mind, evaluated it, decided what to do. 'He came at me,' Judson said. 'Delozier. He went crazy, said some crazy stuff, and came at me with an ax. I shot him in self-defense.' The sheriff walked slowly toward me. His gun was still in his hand.

'Sheriff, could you untie me?'

He didn't answer. He was standing two feet away, looking down at me, his gun still in his hand.

Suddenly I saw his head turn slightly, listening. I heard it, too: a car careening down the dirt road, then the sound of locked-up wheels sliding to a stop; a door being flung open. Stu Vickery raced into the barn, his weapon drawn. 'Agent Vickery,' said the sheriff slowly. 'Glad you could make it.' During the tense silence that followed, I heard my heart thumping. 'I was just about to untie your man Brockton here, but I'll let you do it instead.'

Should I warn Vickery about the sheriff? *Could* I warn him, without causing the sheriff to start shooting?

Vickery lowered his gun and stepped toward me, stepped between the sheriff and me, and then – just as I was about to shout a warning – spun and aimed his gun at Judson's chest. 'Put down the weapon, Sheriff.'

'Vickery, have you lost your goddamn mind, or are you just bound and determined to ruin your career?'

'Put down the weapon, Sheriff. You're under arrest.'

'The hell you say.' The sheriff's gun began coming up.

'Put it down. *Now.*'

'Under arrest for what? For shooting a murderer in self-defense?'

'No. For *being* a murderer. You're under arrest for the murder of Winston Pettis. We've got evidence that puts you at the scene of his death.'

'You've got shit, Vickery.'

'We've got genetic evidence that puts you at the scene. You really shouldn't chew tobacco, Sheriff. Filthy habit. All that juice. All that spit. All that DNA. One of our crime-scene techs found a nice wad of your spit in Pettis's yard. Perfect match with the wad of spit you left in the ferns the day we found the graves.' Vickery paused. 'That's not all. We found the tracking collar you took off the dog. One of our divers pulled it out of the Miccosukee River. It's got your thumbprint on it, Sheriff. And there was a .45 in the mud beside it.'

Judson's eyes flickered as he took in Vickery's revelations and evaluated his options.

In the darkness outside, I heard a siren racing toward us and, underneath it, another one. Judson heard it, too, and lowered his gun. Suddenly he was an old, weary man.

CHAPTER 29

'I can't tell you how much I appreciate everything you've done for me,' Angie said. She was holding my left elbow and carrying my briefcase as I hobbled toward my truck. Vickery, at my right elbow, had my duffel bag slung over his shoulder. We were crossing the parking deck of Tallahassee Memorial Hospital, where I'd been treated for the lacerations Cochran had inflicted with the strap. 'If not for you,' Angie went on, 'I'd have always had some lingering doubts about Kate. Some fear that maybe she really had shot herself.'

'I was glad to help. I know it doesn't bring your sister back, but I'm glad you feel that some kind of justice has been done.' She nodded. I chose my next words carefully, hedgingly. 'I hope the sheriff up in Mocksville doesn't give you too hard a time.'

'Actually, he called me this morning. Apparently he's decided I'm telling the truth. They found out Don was at his new girlfriend's house drinking until six in the morning' – she rolled her eyes in disgust – 'when they had a big fight and she threw him out. So he would've gotten home, drunk and upset, just before he sent me that text message. And my nosy next-door neighbor, who is *always* spying on us, bless her heart, told the sheriff's investigator that my car and Ned's were both in the driveway from five-thirty, when she got up, until eight, when we left for work. So it looks like I'm no longer a suspect, and they're calling it a suicide.'

'That's good news.' I was relieved not just for Angie's sake, but for the sake of my own peace of mind, the settling of my own questions about whether she'd taken justice into her own hands. 'You think he killed himself because he really did feel guilty about Kate?'

She shrugged. 'You know, this might sound crazy, but really? I think he killed himself because he owed the universe a suicide.' Her eyes brimmed with tears, but her face looked open and peaceful; poignant, but not grief-stricken.

'Well, Doc, we really appreciate all you did for FDLE,' Vickery mumbled through his cigar after a moment. 'You're sure your feelings won't be hurt if we take it from here?'

'My backside's too painful for me to notice anything else hurting,' I said. 'Besides, my globe-trotting colleague in Tampa is back from Africa, and the lab in Gainesville is staffed up again, so you've got plenty of anthropology brainpower in Florida now.' My gait was an odd, stiff-legged waddle, partly because of the painful bruises and lacerations left by the strap, partly because of the layer of gauze the emergency-room doc had applied to my thighs and buttocks.

'You sure it's a good idea to drive back to Knoxville this soon?' asked Angie. 'Why don't you stick around and heal up a few more days? We'll be glad to put you up at the Duval. You've earned it.'

'Naw,' I joked, 'the Twilight's spoiled me for anyplace else. If I can't stay there, I'll just crawl home to my own bed.'

'We'll ship a snake up your way every week or two, if you want,' said Vickery. 'Just to make sure you don't forget us.'

'Hey, thanks.' I laughed. 'So, do y'all think it was Cochran or Judson who put that cottonmouth in my room?'

'My money's on Judson,' Angie said. 'And considering how Pettis and the dog ended up, you're mighty lucky to have gotten off with only a scare. Judson's a bad guy.'

'You think the tobacco juice from Pettis's yard and the prints on the tracking collar are enough to convict him of Pettis's murder?'

'It's a pretty strong case,' Vickery asserted. 'Your testimony will help a lot. We've also got tire impressions from the Pettis place that match the tires from the sheriff's truck.'

'But I thought the tire tracks at Pettis's were from old, worn-out tires. Didn't Judson's truck have newer tires?'

'*Brand*-new tires,' Stu stressed. 'We found the old ones at the county garage this morning. The mechanic will testify that he took 'em off the day Pettis was killed. I think we've got enough to get a conviction. Judson must think so, too – he's looking for a deal, and he's willing to talk. He says Cochran killed Hatfield, because Cochran was afraid Hatfield would tell us he wasn't really dead.'

'How convenient,' said Angie – not for the first time in this case – 'since Cochran's no longer around to deny it.'

'He also says Hatfield and Cochran had half a dozen pals who regularly came and molested boys,' Vickery continued. 'They called it "the chicken-hawk club." One of the members was a high-ranking aide to the governor; one was deputy commissioner of corrections. Conveniently, as you say, both those guys are dead now. But Judson says he's got photos that implicate them.'

'I still find it hard to fathom,' I said. 'The systematic abuse – the torture, no other word for it – heaped on those boys by the very people who were supposed to put them back on the right path.'

'I'm telling you,' Vickery repeated. 'This world's one big crime scene. I hate it that we dragged you into such a messy corner of it.'

'Me, too,' Angie agreed. 'I really thought all you'd be doing was taking a quick look at a skull. Instead, you got backbreaking work, deadly snakes, and a beating that could have killed you – *would* have killed you – if Delozier, aka Skeeter, hadn't shown up. I'm so sorry.'

I thought back over everything that had happened since I'd first stepped off the plane in Tallahassee. I was stunned to realize that only thirteen days had passed.

Despite the pain I felt, and knew I'd continue to feel for days, I found myself smiling. 'Don't be sorry,' I said. 'I'm not. Most interesting two weeks I ever had.'

Vickery studied the end of his cigar, looking hesitant – almost shy, even. 'So here's another possibility, if you'd be interested in extending your Florida vacation by a few more days,' he said. 'Mind you, I understand if you want to get the hell out of Dodge as fast as possible. But I've got a little place down on the Ochlockonee River, right on the bay. It's about the only thing I've been able to hang on to through my divorces, except for my bad habits. Nothing fancy – just a fishing shack, really, which I guess is why I've been able to hang on to it. But the view's pretty, and there's a dock with a ladder, and the salt water'd be good for those welts you've got. There's good mojo at that little place. I don't get down there very often these days, but every time I do, I wonder why the hell I waited so long, you know?'

'I'd better head on home to Knoxville,' I said. 'But thanks for the offer. Can I have a rain check?'

'Anytime.'

CHAPTER 30

Three miles south of a sleepy panhandle crossroads – a place that someone with high hopes or a strong streak of irony had named Panacea – I turned right at a blinking caution light, at the foot of a mile-long bridge across the wide mouth of the Ochlockonee River.

I had waved good-bye and driven away from Stu and Angie with every intention of heading north to Tennessee, but then I'd done a quick mental inventory of the things I needed to get back to, and I'd started to wonder how urgent those things were, really. They were *important* things, sure: I had a job I loved, truly, and a son and daughter-in-law and grandsons I adored; I had colleagues I liked and respected. But they weren't *urgent* things; they'd still be waiting for me a few days from now. Making a quick U-turn in the parking garage of Tallahassee Memorial Hospital, I'd rolled down the window and tooted the horn to catch Stu's attention as he walked toward his car. 'On second thought, Stu,' I said, 'a couple days in a fishing shack on the Ochlock-onee sounds really nice.'

And so it was that I'd headed south instead of north. Thirty miles south of Tallahassee, three miles south of

Panacea, and two miles west of the turnoff at the Ochlock-onee bridge – two miles along the back road to Sopchoppy, a town whose name I found myself repeating out loud, just for the fun of saying it – I turned left onto Surf Road, a sandy dirt lane that led to the shore of the bay, then doglegged to the right, along the water. After a handful of houses and a hundred yards, the road dwindled to a pair of tire tracks, and in another hundred yards the tracks dwindled to furrows of bent grass, and in another fifty the furrows ended in front of a cottage tucked amid the pines, palms, and fern-laden live oaks. The board-and-batten siding was a faded pink, trimmed with turquoise shutters and a rusty tin roof. A screened-in porch stretched across the entire front of the house. Inside the screen, a woven hammock angled invitingly across one corner of the porch. The door at the center of the porch bore a sign that appeared to be a hot dog surfing on breaking waves. WELCOME TO THE SEA SAUSAGE, read a sign over the door.

At the base of the weathered wooden front steps was a broken concrete sidewalk. It stretched toward the water for perhaps twenty feet and then ended, or, rather, seemed to dissolve into the sandy grass, and something about that fading away of pavement and order appealed to me, so I parked there in the transition, between the end of the sidewalk and the start of the dock.

It was late afternoon when I arrived. As I opened the door and climbed from my truck – gingerly, so as not to pull the fresh, fragile scabs from my skin – a wind off the water ruffled my hair, just as it ruffled and sang through the fronds of the palms.

The lawn had been recently mowed; close to the shore, the clipped grass gave way to tall sea oats, their slender stalks widely spaced in the pale gray sand. A fresh line of flotsam from a recent storm surge – pine straw and palm fronds and grass stalks – marked the boundary between lawn and shore, between the cultivated realm and the natural world. Turning back toward the house, I noticed a high-water mark that rose halfway to the window sills: a souvenir of Hurricane Floyd, Vickery had told me. Floyd had flooded the Sea Sausage with knee-high water, but in the arbitrary, offhand way of nature, it had utterly demolished an identical house next door.

The dock looked newer than the house, though the decking was sun-blasted and weathering, and the ends of some of the boards were beginning to curl upward and pull free of the joists. As I stepped onto the dock, I shucked off my shoes, then my socks, and let the soles of my feet settle onto the roughness of the gray, grainy boards. I had scarcely stepped away from my shoes when I saw a pair of small fiddler crabs scuttle over the sides and into the toes.

The far end of the dock widened into a platform ten or twelve feet square, with a broad, sturdy railing all around. Leaning over a corner, leaning into the breeze, I watched the shards of afternoon sun dance across the shimmering, undulant water. The bay's surface was smooth and glossy, but not uniform or even flat: there were gradations of sheen, pools and pockets and whorls. As I studied a long string of whorls, I realized they were spooling downriver toward the bridge and toward the Gulf, against the flow of the incoming tide. I looked closer, and one of the whorls seemed to gather mass, coalesce, and mound itself slightly above the surrounding water. I heard a huffing sound and the mounded whorl receded, and I imagined that I had imagined the sight and sound – fallen prey to some trick of light and tide and tiredness – until it happened again, in two places, then three, and then I glimpsed the soft bulk of mana-tees. I watched them – a herd of six, I decided by counting the subtle eddies they created, these momentous things swirling around me in the current, sensed but not fully seen, just below the surface.

I scanned the neighboring docks and nearby waters; the manatees and I had the entire bay to ourselves. I shucked off my shirt, eased down my pants, and began climbing down the wooden ladder. On the last step, I hesitated – the water looked brown, muddier than I'd have expected from the undeveloped forest and marsh-land bordering the bay – but I decided to trust Vickery's assurance that the salt would be good for my wounds. As my feet and legs descended into the water, I saw that the water was not muddy at all; rather, it was clean but deeply tinted by tannin. It was the rich color of strong tea. Step by step, deeper and deeper, I immersed myself in the briny, bracing, healing water. As I did, my pale and wounded skin took on an orange glow, then a deep coppery hue that rendered me unrecognizable to myself.

As I took a breath and sank beneath the surface in the company of manatees, it looked and felt as if my immersion in these Florida waters, my baptism in the Ochlockonee, was transforming me into someone else, something else. Something wilder and more exotic than I had been before.

I feared that transformation – almost as much as I longed for it.

I stayed beneath the water for what seemed an eternity, then rose toward the coppery light and breached, huffing like a manatee and drinking deep drafts of the briny, bracing, resurrecting air.

AUTHOR'S NOTE:
FACT AND FICTION

Novelist Michael Chabon has described his fiction as occurring in a parallel universe, one that resembles the 'real' universe closely, though not exactly. That description seems fitting for this book. *The Bone Yard* is a novel, a work of fiction . . . but it's fiction that is deeply rooted in the soil of grim realities. Some of those realities have been adapted, expanded, and dramatized here; others appear in these pages without alteration.

The main story here was inspired by events and stories from an actual north Florida reform school, one that – unlike our fictional school – still exists. Opened in 1900 as the Florida State Reform School, the institution has gone by several other names during its history, including the Florida School for Boys, the Florida Industrial School for Boys, and the Arthur G. Dozier School for Boys.

Whatever the name, the school has been plagued by deaths and scandals down through the decades. Just three years after it opened, a state senate committee found boys 'in irons, like common criminals.' In 1911, a special legislative committee investigated reports of severe beatings with a leather strap – beatings that, the legislators were assured, had ceased with the firing of the superintendent who had sanctioned them. In 1914, a fire at the school killed two employees and eight boys. A grand jury investigation of the fire found that the boys' dormitory was locked while three guards and the superintendent visited the nearby town of Marianna 'upon some pleasure bent.'

In 1958, a U.S. Senate committee investigation heard testimony about brutal conditions at Dozier . . . including severe beatings with a heavy leather strap. In 1967, a U.S. Department of Health official called the school a 'monstrosity.' A few months later, Florida's then-governor, Claude Kirk, visited the school and described it as a training ground for a life of crime. Kirk also called the school's conditions 'absolutely deplorable' and said, 'If one of your kids were kept in such circumstances, you'd be up there with rifles.' As late as the 1980s, boys at the school were still being hog-tied, with their arms and legs fastened together beind their backs.

Several years ago, a handful of the school's former students banded together in an informal organization called 'The White House Boys,' named for the small, whitewashed concrete building in which the beatings were administered regularly on Saturdays. Their Web site, www.WhiteHouseBoys.org, shares numerous accounts of beatings and sexual abuse in the White House and in the basementlike 'rape room' under the school's dining hall.

In an unusual and poignant ceremony, Florida's Department of Juvenile Justice officially 'sealed' the White House in October 2008. Former students were invited to speak at the sealing ceremony, and several talked of the abuses they'd suffered within the building's walls. A plaque affixed to the building bears these words: *In memory of the children who passed these doors, we acknowledge their tribulations and offer our hope that they have found some measure of peace. May this building stand as a reminder of the need to remain vigilant in protecting our children as we help them seek a brighter future.*

The White House is one grim emblem of the reform school's troubled past. Another is a small cemetery, tucked away in what was once the 'colored' part of the school's grounds. The cemetery, whose revelation made headlines in 2009, contains thirty-one crosses, made of welded metal pipes. At the request of then-Governor Charlie Crist, the Florida Department of Law Enforcement investigated the cemetery, eventually concluding that the number of crosses corresponded with records identifying thirty-one individuals who had died and been buried at the school (including one student murdered by four others, who feared the boy was about to reveal their plan to escape). FDLE did not excavate or map the cemetery; consequently, there was no attempt to match graves with the number and location of the crosses, or any attempt to confirm the identity of individual human remains. The agency reported to Governor Crist that it found 'no evidence that the school or the staff caused, or contributed to, any of these deaths' and 'no evidence that the school or its staff made any attempts to conceal the deaths of any students at the school.'

And perhaps that is the truth, the whole truth, and nothing but the truth. But accounts by former students – including members of the White House Boys – hint at additional, unmarked graves on the property. And even the FDLE investigation found evidence that another fifty boys had died at the school over the years, but that their remains were unaccounted for.

Several Florida newspapers have kept the school in the headlines during the past half century. The *Miami News* ran scathing articles in 1958 and 1969, including a detailed description of the leather-strap beatings. 'The belt falls between eight and 100 times,' the paper reported, quoting a letter from a former school employee. 'After about the tenth stroke, the seams of the sturdiest blue jeans begin to separate and numerous times the boys' skin is broken to the extent that stitches are required.' The *St. Petersburg Times* carried a long, searing article titled 'Hell's 1400 acres' in 1968. In 2008, the *Miami Herald* broke the story of the White House Boys and shared their accounts of brutal abuse. And in 2009, the *St. Petersburg Times* took another hard look at the school; the paper's two-part series – 'For Their Own Good' (www. tampabay.com/specials/2009/reports/marianna) – became a finalist for the 2010 Pulitzer Prize in local reporting.

Corporal punishment at Florida state institutions was banned more than forty years ago, but another grim reality – the death of fourteen-year-old Martin Lee Anderson, who was suffocated by guards just two hours after he arrived at a 'boot camp' in 2006 – suggests that *banning* physical abuse of juveniles isn't necessarily the same as *ending* physical abuse of juveniles. And if the past is any guide to the future, there's a century of data to suggest that the recurring pattern – the vicious cycle – is this: scandal and bad publicity, followed by expressions of outrage and pledges of reform . . . followed, months or years later, by another round of scandal and outrage.

'Those who don't know history are destined to repeat it,' said British statesman Edmund Burke. He also said, 'All that's necessary for the forces of evil to win in the world is for enough good men to do nothing.' Burke said those things more than two hundred years ago, and 'civilized' societies continue to prove him right. If this book can do anything to raise awareness or vigilance – can do anything to help keep vulnerable boys from being abused by the very people and institutions entrusted with their care – we'll have done good work. 'Light a candle but keep cursing the darkness,' urges an idealistic character in this story. Amen, and pass the matches.

Finally, less grimly, a note on the blurry boundary between anthropological fact and fiction in this story.

At the low-tech end of the spectrum, dowsing or 'witching' – seeking hidden graves with coat hanger wires or forked sticks – remains a technique that is occasionally used, is roundly dismissed by many scientists, but is ardently defended by some advocates. At the high-tech end of the spectrum, ground-penetrating radar likewise has both devoted fans and dubious detractors.

And then there's earthmoving machinery. Half a century ago, as the rising waters of new reservoirs along the Missouri River were on the verge of inundating the sites of long-abandoned Arikara Indian villages, an up-and-coming young physical anthropologist named Bill Bass pioneered the use of road scrapers to uncover graves – thus allowing Bass and his teams of students to find and excavate ten times as many graves in a summer as they'd been able to do when digging only by hand.

Native American remains are no longer considered artifacts for museum collections, so the days of using earthmoving machines to uncover Indian graves with speed and efficiency are over.

Except, perhaps, in the parallel universe of fiction.

ACKNOWLEDGMENTS

As with Dr Brockton, so with us: this book represents our first fictional foray into Florida's Panhandle. Amid the live-oak forests and cottonmouth creeks, we've found a generous and informative group of local informants. First of all, sincere thanks to Michael Peltier, the journalist friend who planted the seed for this novel. Thanks also to Mark Russell and Teddy Tollett for sharing insights about the Dozier School for Boys and about Florida's juvenile justice system.

Florida State University criminologist Dan Maier-Katkin provided valuable perspective on the links between juvenile justice (or injustice) and human rights, as well as a radical and inspiring vision of the better futures we might aspire to offer disadvantaged young people. FSU social-work professors Stephen Tripodi and Eyitayo Onifade shared helpful background information on juvenile-justice problems and potential solutions. FSU law professor Sandy D'Alemberte – a human rights crusader, former legislator, and former FSU president – graciously shared his knowledge of north Florida, past and present, including his contagious appreciation of the Shell Oyster Bar.

Floy Turner – a retired special agent of the Florida Department of Law Enforcement (and a continuing warrior in the battles against child abduction and human trafficking) – generously shared her knowledge of FDLE and local law-enforcement in Florida. Brittany Auclair, an FDLE crime-scene and crime-lab analyst, contributed both technical knowledge and insightful literary suggestions; and forensic guru Amy George – whose father, Paul Norkus, helped bring to the United States the use of superglue-fuming to reveal latent fingerprints – deserves much credit for whatever is accurate and admirable in the portrayal of forensic analyst Angie St. Claire. Additional thanks go to Jonathan Auclair, another friendly and helpful forensic expert; Vince George, a former FDLE chemist; Andy Randall, who opened the first of many important doors; Tony Falsetti, former director of the Human Identification Laboratory at the University of Florida; anthropologist Stefan Schmitt of Physicians for Human Rights; Joe Walsh, at the biohazard-cleanup firm Associated Services; funeral director Susie Mozolic; medical examiner Lisa Flannagan, MD; former prosecutor Pete Antonacci; former public defender Jeff Duvall; artist Stuart Riordan; forensic anthropologist Rick Snow; and – as always – forensic wizard Art Bohanan, whose faith in divining is matched by his expertise in more traditional forensic-science techniques.

Forensic artists Joanna Hughes, in Knoxville, and Joe Mullins, at the National Center for Missing and Exploited

Children – both of whom sportingly agreed to appear in the novel under their own names – were remarkably generous and patient in demonstrating their techniques and their talent for restoring faces to the skulls of the unknown dead.

A bow, a nod, and a pair of commemorative white gloves go to Doris Hamburg, Kitty Nicholson, and Lisa Isbell at the National Archives and Records Administration (NARA), who graciously opened the doors of NARA's paper-conservation laboratory and offered helpful advice on how to save and read a waterlogged old diary. Conservationist kudos also to Andrew Spindler, a knowledgeable antiquary and generous friend, who paved the way for that NARA visit.

This book was written up and down much of the eastern United States. Many thanks to Holly Idelson and Don Simon, in whose Washington, D.C., basement many early chapters were written; to Beth McPherson and Paul Kando, on whose dining-room table in Maine many middle chapters took shape; and to Cindy and Joe Johnson, on whose screened-in porch at the mouth of the Ochlocknee River many late chapters (in every sense of the word 'late'!) were finished.

Our last, lasting, and deepest thanks go to our wondrous wives: Carol Bass, whose life, day in and day out, embodies strength, courage, grace, and humor; and Jane McPherson – Amazing Jane, Beloved Jane – whose many inspiring qualities include unwavering commitment to human

rights and deep compassion for the challenges faced by
the disregarded, disadvantaged, and disenfranchised.

– Bill Bass, Knoxville, Tennessee

– Jon Jefferson, Tallahassee, Florida

THE SKULL

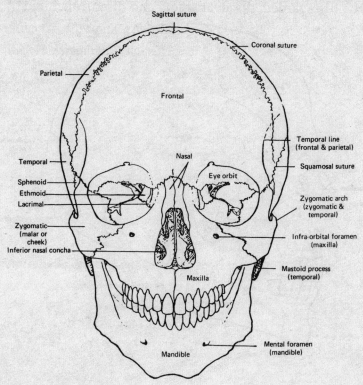

Sagittal suture

Coronal suture

Parietal

Frontal

Temporal line
(frontal & parietal)

Nasal

Temporal

Eye orbit

Squamosal suture

Sphenoid

Ethmoid

Lacrimal

Zygomatic arch
(zygomatic &
temporal)

Zygomatic
(malar or
cheek)

Infra-orbital foramen
(maxilla)

Inferior nasal concha

Mastoid process
(temporal)

Maxilla

Mental foramen
(mandible)

Mandible

BONES OF

PARTS OF

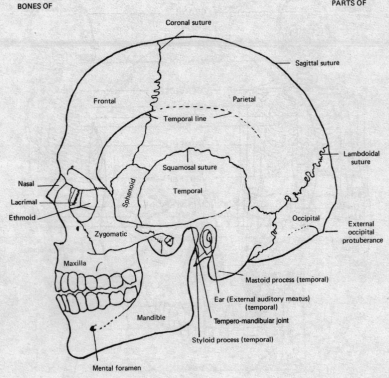

Coronal suture

Sagittal suture

Frontal

Parietal

Temporal line

Lambdoidal
suture

Squamosal suture

Nasal

Sphenoid

Temporal

Lacrimal

Ethmoid

Occipital

External
occipital
protuberance

Zygomatic

Maxilla

Mastoid process (temporal)

Ear (External auditory meatus)
(temporal)

Tempero-mandibular joint

Mandible

Styloid process (temporal)

Mental foramen

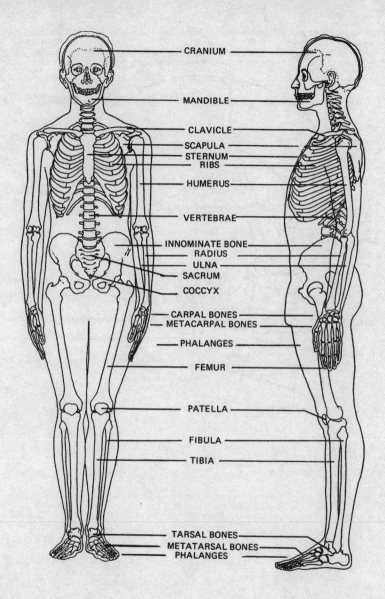

CRANIUM

MANDIBLE

CLAVICLE
SCAPULA
STERNUM
RIBS

HUMERUS

VERTEBRAE

INNOMINATE BONE
RADIUS
ULNA
SACRUM
COCCYX

CARPAL BONES
METACARPAL BONES

PHALANGES

FEMUR

PATELLA

FIBULA

TIBIA

TARSAL BONES
METATARSAL BONES
PHALANGES